THE HARMONETICS INVESTIGATION

THE HARMONETICS INVESTIGATION

GLADYS M. HELDMAN

CROWN PUBLISHERS, INC.
NEW YORK

All characters portrayed in this novel are fictional. The buildings described herein are fantasy. So are most of the potions, lotions and medications, the texts that are cited, the excerpts from the *New York Times,* etc. Any resemblance to actual people or publications or products is purely coincidental.

Printed in the United States of America
Published simultaneously in Canada by
General Publishing Company Limited

Library of Congress Cataloging in Publication Data

Heldman, Gladys.
  The Harmonetics investigation.

  I. Title.
PZ4.H4764Har   [PS3558.E474]   813'.5'4   78-14285
ISBN 0-517-53926-8

Dedication
Juli, Julie M. & Trixie

The author would like to thank Susie Adams, Ron Bookman, Professor Alan Clugston, Ken Collins, Jerry Finger, Larry Freundlich, Sterling Lord, Patrick O'Connor, and above all, Trixie Heldman and Carole Baron.

In Memoriam
Laura Haywood

THE HARMONETICS INVESTIGATION

Excerpt from a television address by Dr. Josiah Minden, President, Harmonetics Society (January 18, 1978)

The nursing home scandals of the last year have demonstrated the insufferable greed of the owners, the cold indifference of the attending doctors and nurses, the incalculable selfishness of relatives who discarded their own parents as useless burdens, and the refusal of the state and federal governments to come to the rescue of the oversedated, underfed, so-called misfits of society—our fathers and mothers. No parent, no matter how frail of body or weak of mind, should be tossed on the scrap heap. Most of our so-called senior citizens can still lead useful lives. We retire them early, put them on Social Security "gifts" that barely sustain life, and when their minds and bodies collapse, we jail them in nursing homes to spend their remaining days victimized by their keepers. I propose to employ the unjustly named "elderly," to take advantage of their talents, and to return to them their independence and their zest for living. The Harmonetics Society creates jobs for their hands and their minds—satisfying and creative work to restore them to the world of the living and to remove them from that dreadful atmosphere of the breathing dead. Of those whose bodies and minds have supposedly been irreparably damaged, we will save hundreds of thousands. None will be considered hopeless or useless. To you who have condemned your own parents to a hell on earth, you who feel your filial obligations are fulfilled by renting them a room in a home for the discarded, you who go to work, to church, to social functions with a happy heart because your sires have been incarcerated for the last, most wonderful years of their lives, give us your victims and let us honor, love, and cherish them. We will return to them their lives, their brotherhood, and their joy in giving as well as receiving. The Harmonetics Society knows no outcasts, and our dedication is to the ethics of dignity, work, and human kindness.

At 8:30 A.M. on October 12, 1982, William Harding, the publisher of *National News* magazine, opened the front door of his five-story house on East 74th Street and walked into the sunshine. He lifted his head and inhaled the cool air. No matter if fine, invisible particles of soot were creeping into his lungs and under his nails and around his collar; it was not the kind of day to fret about impurities. He was enjoying the rare good weather and was disinclined to be critical of the floating chewing gum wrappers, the squashed cigarette butts, the stains of bird droppings and other litter of man and small beast.

East 74th between Lexington and Park was one of the few tree-lined streets in the city. The tough little plane trees, planted several generations before, had been fertilized by hundreds of neighborhood dogs and were surviving nicely in their tight concrete enclosures. The narrow houses, four to six stories tall and abutting against each other, were as solidly embedded in rock as their owners were firmly entrenched in the wealth of Manhattan. These were men and women of substance, either by inheritance or through the system of free enterprise, a way of life that the residents, with the exception of a few dissident children, idealized. Harding's parents had moved from California to New York in 1958, buying a home on East 74th. After the death of his wife, Andrew Harding had lived alone, a widower with an increasing portfolio and a decreasing interest in women, until his death in 1979 at the age of eighty-three. His only surviving son, the founder and owner of *National News*, moved into the empty residence four months later for temporary protection against vandalism. When a buyer eventually made an acceptable offer, Bill Harding no longer wanted to sell.

2

At almost any hour of the day the block on East 74th was peaceful and dignified. No children played on the street. The men left for their offices between the respectable hours of 8:30 and 10:00. Sporadically one of the carefully coiffed women would emerge from her brownstone for a midmorning appointment with her dentist, doctor, or hairdresser. During the remainder of the day an occasional tradesman would make a discreet delivery. The evenings were slightly more lively: visitors came for dinner or residents departed for concerts, theatre openings, banquets honoring Republican party leaders, or charity benefits.

Bill Harding walked to the corner of Park Avenue to catch a cab. He seldom used his car on weekdays. It was garaged two blocks away for a monthly fee of $115; on the days he drove, he could park a few blocks from his office for $6 plus tip. It was easier to take a taxi, read the *New York Times,* and ignore the traffic jams. Arthur Popple, Harding's seventy-six-year-old neighbor, had solved the problem many years ago. The familiar long black limousine arrived at 8:15 each morning and waited until the erect, immaculate senior partner of Blake, Chatterly had finished his morning tea and scones. In the evening the chauffeur, roaring down the block at a screaming fifteen miles an hour, deposited his fragile package in front of his teakwood brownstone door. Harding had no interest in hiring a chauffeur. It would be as effete as hiring a full-time manicurist or barber and as extravagant and corrupting as paying a man for eight hours of work and then using him for only an hour.

Harding had to wait a mere five minutes before flagging a cab. While the driver stepped on the gas, screeched on the brakes, weaved in and out of lanes, honked at the cars ahead of him, and yelled at occasional pedestrians, Harding was buried in the *New York Times.* It was a *Times* policy, originated by Adolph Ochs and continued by his heirs, to avoid human interest stories whenever feasible. Births, crimes, marriages, and deaths were reported on the back pages unless the Queen of England became a grandmother, a member of the Cabinet went to jail, or a President's widow remarried. Jennifer Holiday's probated will had made the front page because the deceased had been rich, social, and eccentric, and because the main beneficiary was a popular new movement. The late Mrs.

Holiday, who had died at the age of seventy-three after outliving three husbands, had left an estate of over $20 million. She had bequeathed $1 million each to her son and daughter, $20,000 apiece to her housekeeper, butler, and cook, $50,000 to Wells College, and the balance to the Harmonetics Society, including her New York City town house and the many treasures therein.

Harding had known Mrs. Holiday casually. He had visited her twice, both times at large soirees where Pinkerton guards protected the objets d'art from the cream of the business world. Jennifer Baker Runson Jennings Holiday (all her husbands were of fine Anglo-Saxon stock) had entertained investment bankers from the right houses, attorneys from the best firms, politicians in high state office, administrators from the leading hospitals, and artists who had already made their name. Many of her guests were seeking sponsorship or contributions. Quite a few of the supplicants had been successful. Mrs. Holiday had annually donated considerable amounts of her income while keeping the capital intact.

When Mrs. Holiday had wished to meet someone she did not know, she would send the potential guest an engraved invitation to a reception honoring the Ambassador to the Court of St. James or the new Director of the Metropolitan Opera or the Secretary of State. Rarely was the recipient unable to accept due to a previous engagement. Bill Harding had received several invitations not because Andrew Harding, his father, had made a fortune from the racetrack but because he, William Harding, had walked away from most of the ill-accumulated wealth, using a mere $800,000 of the less tainted money inherited from his mother to found a publishing empire. Harding had enjoyed the company of the effervescent Jennifer Holiday, who presided at her soirees bedecked in outlandish tiaras and ropes of pearls and surrounded by youthful and middle-aged men and women from the upper walks of life who ardently wished to be added to Mrs. Holiday's coterie. Harding's magazine, *National News*, had run a cover story on Jennifer Holiday and her amusing collection of painters, couturiers, physicians, musicians and ambitious young matrons. In the two years since Harding had seen her, she had become a devotee of the Harmonetics philosophy and had withdrawn

4

from society. Limousines no longer lined up in front of the town house, and the lights in the ballroom had been permanently extinguished.

Harding leaned back against the torn leather seat of the taxi and thought about the late paradoxical Mrs. Holiday. She had undergone the same startling changes as Heyward Broun, he mused. Both, on growing old, had turned to religio-philosophical beliefs that would have been alien to their earlier ways of life. Broun renounced atheism and birth control and became a Catholic; Jennifer gave up her Pierre Cardin frocks, Chanel suits, the divine gold-and-emerald turtles from Tiffany's, the splendid diamond brooches from Cartier's, the chic little scarves by Gucci and instead turned her mind to Harmonetics teleology. She was over seventy when she finally found a purpose to her life. Damn, thought Harding, we should have done another story on her.

Harding's taxi pulled in front of a cruising cab, then jerked to a stop at the corner of 38th and Park. Harding's body was thrown forward, but this was such a customary procedure that he had already braced his back and braked his legs without being aware of it. He paid the driver, rewarding him for the thirty-five blocks of discomfort with a sizable tip.

The avenue was filling up with clerks, executives, secretaries, public relations men, accountants, salesmen, and other white-collar workers of a dozen levels hurrying to their offices to perform their daily functions. They wore their uniforms with pride. Men in business suits that made them appear industrious and successful, their semilong, casual haircuts blown dry that morning to give them a "38th and Park" affluent air. Women in freshly pressed dresses or shirts of assorted colors, their subdued thin gold chains linking them to reliable business establishments, their moisturized, textured faces aglow with Sun Peach and Lip Dew and Violet Honey. And, among the crowd, dark-haired, dark-skinned Bill Harding, large, fortyish, and messy, wearing a sport jacket in a kingdom of business suits, black hair sprouting on his chest where a tie would have been more proper, dark hooded eyes examining the other members of his species who were homing toward their offices. While the men and women of 38th and Park walked purposefully, Harding seemed to lumber aimlessly, his head turning to get a better view of a carefully accoutered young dynamo carrying a leather attaché case, his heavy-lidded eyes examining a paper bag toted by a large-hipped maiden and his peripatetic mind imagining the contents: coffee with cream and two sugared doughnuts, or a sweet roll dripping apricot jam from the center.

Harding crossed Park Avenue and headed east, enjoying the changing scene. Two residential hotels that served as home to some elderly, comfortable widows and as love nests to some middle-aged, uncomfortable men. A convenient restaurant open for breakfast to men who entertained other men on an expense account in the hopes of selling them insurance, printing, investments, or whatever their business paid them to peddle. At Lexington, the quick-service counters and the delis. Shop owners rushing to their cleaning and pressing establishments, their antique shops, their neighborhood groceries. The local residents, elegant, shabby, old-style and mod, a mixture of races and nationalities. And, in the middle of the next block, surrounded by small-windowed brownstones jammed against each other, the mighty, dingy, massive three-brownstone building that was known to its employees and anyone who could decipher the small copper nameplate on the dark recessed door as the headquarters of *National News*, a thick monthly with high advertising rates and a format of carefully researched articles that exposed or glorified what had seemed too unseemly or sacred for other publications. Occasional articles read like wicked Renaissance gossip, but since Harding insisted on accuracy and since he was far more intrigued by financial finagling than by bedroom exploits, *National News* was respected as well as enjoyed by its two million readers.

The magazine was five years old. Harding had started on a small scale: the first issue was 96 pages but the print order was only 30,000. The financial risks were enormous: bank loans for new publications by unknowns were nonexistent and the mortality rate of new publications was 99 percent. Harding had been reasonably confident. From the time he had walked out of his father's baroque thirty-room mansion, located a mile from the Santa Corona racetrack, with a week-old college diploma in his pocket, a savings account passbook worth $27,000 (the accumulation of birthday presents, Christmas gifts, and allowances from loving parents), and four trunks containing his clothes and personal possessions, he had made a living working for magazines.

Harding first conceived the idea of an investigative news magazine in 1977, shortly after Mrs. Andrew Harding had passed on to another and better world where excessive amounts. of gin did not cause migraine. She had left her son, William, her fortune of $800,000, which he felt would carry him through the inevitable early losses of a new publication. He underestimated the amount but was able to keep *National News* afloat by borrowing money from his wicked, unethical father who was delighted to be asked to help. The son disapproved of the source: he righteously insisted on paying 5 percent interest on signed promissory notes. It was another year before Bill Harding forgave his father for his many transgressions, partially because the old man was so pleased with his son's achievements. Andrew never repented but he knew his son well enough to resist the temptation to relate anecdotes about corrupt jockeys, doped horses, venal track officials, and his own misdemeanors at the Santa Corona racetrack, which included arson, bribery, and acts of excessive violence.

Andrew Harding would have enjoyed watching his independent, intransigent son observing the week-day human scene in midtown Manhattan. Everyone was in a hurry except for an occasional retiree and Bill Harding. Bill reached the *National News* office and jumped the outside stairs two at a time. It was one of his few forms of physical exertion. He opened the front door and bellowed, "Hello, hello, hello." It was a signal to members of the staff on the first floor that they had approximately fifteen minutes in which to contact the boss. Once he reached his office in the back, the door would close. It would take a brave staffer to open it.

At the desk in the narrow reception room a woman in tank top, jeans, and an Afro was handling the switchboard with the informality that Harding liked. While one hand worked the board, the other hand extended a sheaf of messages to Harding.

"Hiya," she said as she transferred a call.

"Umph," he replied, patting her hand and flicking through the messages.

In the next room four of the people in the five-desk

rectangular enclosure were waiting for Harding.

"Bill, I've got some good news and some bad news," said Martha Rayburn, a fierce-looking fortyish matron with carbon smudges on her fingers, a coffee stain on her blouse, and ear-length hair that stuck out in four different directions. "Ford came in with a four-page color spread for this issue. The Ad Department was overjoyed but we'll have to cut four editorial pages. These are the stories that can be held," she said, handing him a sheet of paper.

"Did the agency request position?"

"The usual 'up front.'"

"Martha, you don't really want to kill four pages, do you? We'll add an eight-page form instead. That takes care of Ford. The other four pages will be editorial matter. We don't close until Thursday, which gives us enough time to do a pretty good story on Jennifer Holiday. The title could be 'From Socialite to Religious Novitiate.' Here's the theme of the article: For twenty years Jennifer was one of New York's two or three best-known hostesses. Then she hits seventy, joins the Harmonetics Society, and becomes the intimate friend of the leader, Josiah Minden. She changes her life-style and her will. Her son and daughter are practically disinherited: they get a measly $1 million apiece. The bulk of the estate goes to the Harmonetics Society.

"I want you and Roger Silberstein to work on the story together. Roger's a fine detail man. Split the assignment with him down the middle. The butler, housekeeper, and cook each got a bequest. They'll be a good source of information. Ask them whom Jennifer saw in the Harmonetics Society, how friendly she was with Dr. Minden, and how eccentric she became. Her son and daughter live in the city. Find out if they're going to contest the will and who drew up the last testament. Then ask the lawyer about Jennifer's state of mind, her involvement with Harmonetics, when she made out the will, and whether he tried to dissuade her. Who was she seeing the last six months? How sick was she? Were her son and daughter with her when she died?"

"What did you think of her personally, Bill? Was she as charming as they say?"

"I guess so. She wasn't a great wit or a beauty but she had

flair. It probably came from the way she flung her money around. You had to see her sail into Lutèce or Le Cygne like an empress in a brown tweed suit. I've often thought the more millions one has, the better one's posture. She walked like $20 million. She was also highly knowledgeable about her collections. When I visited her, she took me through the front rooms with the aplomb of a curator. She once spent ten minutes giving me the provenance of her incunabula and illuminated manuscripts. When I commented on her Greek artifacts, I got five minutes of mythological anecdotes. The walls were covered with Daumiers, Renoirs, and Manets. If you gave her the smallest encouragement she would tell you how the artist lived and worked and whom he slept with. Martha, the whole damn collection—the Georgian silver, the crystal, the jade, the tapestries—becomes the property of the Harmonetics Society. It's a museum. Five floors of treasures representing fifty years of outbidding museums and other private collectors. Here's a cult dedicated to improving the quality of life and the conditions of humanity. What the hell are they going to do with a Russian dinner service for sixty or the Austrian crown jewels?"

"Should we try to interview Josiah Minden or work up an assessment of the Harmonetics Society?"

"You won't have time. The deadline is Thursday, which gives you and Roger three working days. Harold Gondoler flew in from California last night at my request. He's doing a major piece for us on the Harmonetics Society. It's scheduled for the issue that follows. I've given him a strong research team. He's a good man for this type of investigation because he'll forget any prejudices he may have for or against the Harmonetics Society. He'll be objective. You can be as subjective as you want, Martha, since yours is a study of personality. You'll find you'll be able to provide leads for Harold and vice versa."

"What would you say, Bill, if I asked for thirty days to write the article? Never mind. I already know the answer."

"Everybody asks for extensions. Why? If a writer, particularly one who works for a weekly magazine, doesn't have a time limit, he can fritter away a year on inconsequential research. The Warren Commission spent two years producing thirty volumes that no one will ever read. Congressional committees come up with the answers so long after the fact that no one gives a damn.

9

We're a nation of time-wasters. The dilatory trait has become a national characteristic."

"Help, help!" said Martha, bowing to the inevitable. "I give up. Three days will be more than enough time to get the inside story on Jennifer. What about pictures, Bill?"

"We have a hundred excellent color transparencies in the Jennifer Holiday picture file. They're probably three years old. Some of them are detailed shots of her collection, with plenty of Jennifer herself. The Art Department should be able to locate some recent pictures of Jennifer in a Harmonetics robe."

"Do you want reports on the information as we go along?"

"Yes, feed it through Jerry Marconi. I'm going to have him coordinate the material. Whatever news you get will be passed on by Jerry to Harold and his team, and the data Harold gets will be immediately available to you and Roger."

"Who's on Harold's team?"

"Let's talk about that at the meeting. Harold will be here in thirty minutes and so will the others. You and Roger come to my office then." Harding turned his attention to the other members of the staff who were waiting for approvals, authorizations or answers. Finally, he looked up and called for Jerry.

From a desk in the rear of the room the young man got up, knocking over some papers and bumping his leg in his hurry. He was across the room in eight long strides. He looked twenty-four but he walked like eighteen. His arms swung awkwardly and his shoulders were bent as though in apology for his height. Jerry Marconi wore thick glasses to help him see and a droopy moustache to make him look more mature. When he had been hired the previous year, long, fine hair had covered his neck and a light-brown beard had given him an ascetic appearance. Now his cheeks were clean-shaven. He was nice-looking except for an apologetic chin. He had the studious look of someone working on his doctoral thesis.

When Jerry had first applied for a job at *National News*, his qualifications had been a B.A. from Harvard in Medieval History, a working knowledge of Italian, a year in the Peace Corps, and eighteen months as an aide to one of the administrative assistants to the Mayor of the City of New York. Jerry had regularly received a small monthly stipend but he was not required in return to perform any functions that required ingenuity, speed, or independent thinking. His most interesting assignment was to register a protest with the Publisher of *National News* about a story on City Hall that had been printed seven months earlier. Jerry paid a call in person. He waited in the office for forty-five minutes. When Bill Harding finally appeared, Jerry asked for a job. Harding was in a good mood, having sold a series of twelve four-color full-page ads over lunch. He wasn't sure how a degree in Medieval History would benefit the magazine but he offered Marconi a job in Circulation. Jerry immediately accepted.

Whenever Harding worked late at the office, Jerry was puttering around. He was either cutting galleys for the Layout Department, filing pictures for Art, or answering inquiries from subscribers. One night Harding heard the clatter of the Pitney Bowes machine on the second floor. Who the hell is working now, he wondered. He went upstairs, two at a time, of course, and saw Jerry, sleeves rolled up, running off a promotion mailing.

Harding watched the boy feeding the mailers into the machine. It was mechanical work, a mental killer if you didn't care about the overall purpose. Jerry was treating it like a game: if he could run 425 mailers through in five minutes, he would beat his own previous record. There were two ways of treating the Pitney, the Elliott, the Xerox and other automated office equipment. One could daydream while the hands moved by rote or one could become a mailroom jock, working up one's finger dexterity to become No. 1 on the Elliott. The daydreamer was a drifter whose work was slow, whose attention span was short and who occasionally lost a finger or an arm, depending on the ferocity of the equipment. The racer was competitive although not necessarily athletic.

Jerry stacked the 9000th mailer, then looked up and saw Bill Harding.

"It's 11:00 P.M.," said Harding. "Are you trying for a spot in the Guinness Book of Records?"

"I beat my own record," Jerry said gleefully.

They talked a few minutes. Thereafter publisher and trainee had a number of other late night conversations, few of which lasted more than five minutes. In spite of their mutual hatred of the word, they had established a relationship.

Jerry Marconi had tried to departmentalize his life into Reason and Emotion. He categorized his four years at Harvard as a Rational Experience, his life in the Peace Corps as Emotional, and his eighteen months at City Hall as neither. Working at *National News* was a Discipline. He had learned Applied Thinking at college but he was becoming aware of a new technique, Creative Thinking, through his conversations with Harding and, to a lesser extent because he knew him less well, with Harold Gondoler. He still thought in capital letters: Bill Harding had created a New Investigatory Method in shaping the format of a major story. The Harding Methodology was to pick a specific topic rather than a general one (the structure of Jake Morley's Bakery Union Pension Plan rather than union pension plans in the United States; or the overseas selling methods of Addison Aircraft rather than American corporate bribery of the European political hierarchy). Harding would then select a team of three or more writers, often going outside the staff for one member, and would name a story coordinator who would act as liaison with the researchers. On several occasions the story got so complicated that several more staff members would get involved, as happened in the murder of union boss Earl Childers (Jerry had mentally termed this article "The Case of the Missing Earl") or in the election scandals of Mayor George Braeburn. The bigger the story, the more work and responsibility for the story coordinator. Harding had picked Jerry Marconi to coordinate the material on the Harmonetics Investigation. It was his first Major Assignment. He was making every effort to remain Cool.

Harding walked into his office and Jerry followed. The condition of the furniture and the general messiness and ambience were the embodiment of Harding's philosophy. Hundreds of thousands of dollars were poured into the paper, the printing, and the contents of the magazine but not one unnecessary nickel went into beautifying the headquarters. Harding's wooden desk was old but not antique; any character it had came from cigarette burns, coffee stains, and nicks and scratches. The shelves on one wall were stacked with magazines; the other walls were covered with layouts from major stories in *National News*. Two wicker baskets on the floor were overflowing with manuscripts. The plain wooden chairs looked as though they had been swiped from the clerical department. The coffee table was casual enough to encourage visitors to rest their feet on it. The couch had never been distinguished, and the cracks in the leather added no luster to its appearance. The room was large, well lit, and suitable to Harding's working habits.

"What did you think of Jade Boren's background report on the Harmonetics Society?" Harding asked Jerry.

"I liked it. It read like historical fiction. She has a talent for combining the facts with personality judgments. The few times I met her I thought she was incredibly beautiful but scatterbrained. I've changed my mind: she's beautiful and clever."

"Jade's apparent naïveté fools a lot of people. She's fifty-five masquerading as twenty-eight. There's a mature brain behind those girlish leers. I've put her on Harold Gondoler's team to work on the Harmonetics story."

Jerry's face lit up. "She'll be good. But how is she going to work undercover? Everyone knows she's with *National News*."

"You'll find out when Harold and Jade get here. The third member of the team is an old friend of mine named Henrietta Beale. She's been playing roles all her life; she'll be expert in the part of a Harmonetics convert."

"Does she have writing or research experience?"

"Yes, both. She recently retired from the *Fortune* staff. She was with them for years."

"Then she's over sixty?"

"Yes, by several years. Are you prejudiced against age, Jerry?"

"I never thought about it. I guess I was, but that was this morning."

"You'll have plenty of contact during the next ten days with Henrietta, Harold, and Jade. They have inventive minds but different techniques. Harold is the most knowledgeable, Henrietta the most sophisticated, and Jade the most devious. They should be highly productive. They'll be phoning you at least once a day, probably more often, as they establish contacts or get leads. Keep each of them posted on what the other is doing. Harold may come to the office occasionally to write his reports, but Jade and Henrietta will have to work out of their homes."

"You'll want copies of all their reports?"

"Yes, immediately. We're running another story that's closely affiliated but I'll tell you about that when the others get here."

Henrietta Beale was the first to arrive. She entered the room, glanced at the desk, walls, and floors, and smiled. She walked over to Bill and gave him a kiss. He responded with a hug that lasted more than the requisite two seconds. Her skin smelled faintly of lavender sachet and she felt warm and soft, a slightly overweight woman with green eyes flecked with brown, regular features that had thickened slightly, and a great sense of clothes.

"I hope you're having some evil thoughts about me," said Henrietta, hugging him back. She hadn't flirted with a man in months. Lovely, sloppy Bill Harding with his thick eyebrows and heavy-lidded eyes brought out the best in her.

"You're reading my mind, Henrietta. Would that I were five years younger."

"Or I six months older." They smiled.

Henrietta was sixty-three and he was, she guessed, forty-seven. What a pity, she thought, that the social rules were so stringent. Margaret Mead had described an ideal South Seas community in which boys and girls on reaching puberty were introduced to the gentle art of lovemaking by an experience with an older woman or an older man. Only the American male benefited by this concept: a sixty-five-year-old man could have an affair with a twenty-two-year-old woman, but a sixty-five-year-old woman was "sick" if her lover was in his thirties.

"How is Elliott?" asked Harding perfunctorily. The health of Henrietta's husband was a matter of indifference to him.

"Elliott is active, unquestionably very active," Henrietta replied ambiguously, seating herself.

"I'm glad you'll be with us for the Harmonetics story," said Harding. "What do you think of Jade's preliminary report?"

"It was good," said Henrietta. "Has she worked for you long, Bill?"

"A few months. She used to free-lance. Television scripts and occasional articles for *Sports Illustrated* and *World Tennis*."

"An athlete?"

"Yes, a good tennis player. She walked into *National News* one day with a portfolio of articles and an outline for a story on the Peter Mann Agency. Did you ever hear of Mann?"

"Wasn't he the agent for some of the top athletes?"

"That's the fellow. When Peter first went into business he arranged endorsements and exhibitions for athletes at 15 percent of whatever he brought in. After a few years he expanded: he provided his athletes with legal, accounting, and investment advisory services. He added a service fee for lesser-known clients and billed them for expenses. Some of the overseas investments were in companies that went bankrupt. One golfer who was earning $150,000 a year wound up three years later with zip. A tennis champ named Dowling gave Mann all his prize money and got 30 percent back at the end of the year. One of the Lakers took a $200,000 beating on some property investment in South America.

"We bought Jade's idea. She and Harold Gondoler and a Midwest staffer were assigned to the story. The Midwest staffer was beaten up, some of the athletes in the Mann stable got threatening phone calls from hoodlums, and all the windows in Gondoler's home were broken. I tried to pull Jade off the case. When she refused I hired a bodyguard. Jade had moved out of her apartment and we couldn't find her. Two days later she marched into the office with signed statements from six athletes. I hired her on the spot."

"What happened to Peter Mann?"

"Nothing, considering what we had expected. To date he hasn't been arrested and is conducting business as usual, although he lost most of his clients. He got into a fight one night and had his front teeth knocked out. He never filed a complaint but the guy who did the damage might have been an athlete or . . ."

"Or Harold Gondoler?"

"Or Jade," Harding replied evasively. "She might have cracked him with a forehand crosscourt."

"I hope I'm muscular enough for the job," said Henrietta.

"Here's the Old Champ herself," Harding said, rising to greet the athletic young woman with the straight dark hair who was standing at the door. She had a 1920s figure encased in 1980s clothes: long legs, a willowy body, and small breasts wrapped in a dark green jump suit that seemed to be made of elastic. She had not yet reached thirty; neither time nor the sun had damaged her skin. Harding put his arm around Jade Boren, giving her an affectionate squeeze and a peck on the cheek. He resisted the impulse to kiss her on the lips, perhaps to their mutual disappointment.

Standing behind Jade was Roger Silberstein, the least flashy member of the staff. Harding had to make an effort to look for Roger at a gathering; it was too easy for Silberstein to blend in with the background and become invisible. He was in his thirties or forties, he looked neither traditional nor trendy, and he could have gone to a prep school or a public school. He talked very little but he had a sharp wit with a pen. He continually surprised his co-workers with the depth of his perception, which showed only in his articles. No one disliked him but few sought him out. He lived alone and apparently liked it.

As Harding moved toward Roger, Henrietta walked over to Jade and introduced herself. They talked for a few minutes about the assignment and Jade liked her immediately. Henrietta was an older female version of Bill Harding but much more presentable. Sound, thought Jade, but she doesn't give a shit. She has a flair for clothes. She's bright or she wouldn't be on this assignment. She likes people, particularly me. Bill must have given me a buildup.

"I'm so glad we're going to work together," said Henrietta. "From what Bill tells me, you are an intrepid female. If I had been faced with Peter Mann's method of intimidation, I'm afraid I would have turned into a mold of quivering aspic. There's an Italian adage that represents my philosophy: 'It is better to be a live donkey than a dead doctor.'"

Jade was enchanted by Henrietta's old-fashioned speech.

"I'd rather be a live doctor than a dead donkey," said Jade, waiting for the reply.

"I would rather be a live doctor than a live donkey. If I were dead, it wouldn't matter which I had been."

"Henrietta, you win. In straight sets."

She thinks about death, thought Henrietta, but undoubtedly in the third person singular or plural. One has to hit fifty-five or sixty before it becomes first person singular.

A large man, 6'2" and perhaps 200 pounds, came toward them. His curly black hair was beginning to gray. He had the shoulders and chest of a football player and he walked with the light step of a professional fighter. His carriage and easy manner were attractive; he stood out in the group because, as happened so frequently, he was the only black in a room full of whites. He caught Henrietta's eye, put his fingers to his lips, and silently came up behind Jade. She saw the shadow and turned around.

"You dear, sweet, lovely," said Jade, throwing her arms around his neck and hoisting herself up to kiss him.

"Henrietta, this is Harold Gondoler," she said when she was back on the ground again.

"We're an odd trio," said Harold, who didn't feel it was necessary to specify the obvious differences in age, color and background between the three associates-to-be. He extended his massive hand and shook Henrietta's gently. "Harding has a knack of melding the incongruous into the homogeneous."

"I think we have more in common than is superficially apparent," answered Henrietta.

"We are three individuals whose orientations are miles apart," commented Jade, "and what each of us has said is correct."

"Who are the people talking to Bill?" asked Henrietta.

"Martha Rayburn, Jerry Marconi, and Roger Silberstein. Let me introduce you," said Harold, taking Henrietta's arm and flinging a hand across Jade's shoulder.

Henrietta, the newcomer, put the *National News* staffers at ease. She made Martha feel beautiful, she gave Roger a sense of confidence, and she treated Jerry as though he were a man of her own generation.

"We're all here," said Harding. "I suggest we start."

"Your command is our wish," piped Jade, taking a seat on the couch. The others settled down and Harding, resting on an edge of his desk, began.

"Thirty minutes ago," said Harding when everyone was seated, "I asked Martha and Roger to research a story on the transformation of Jennifer Holiday. It will be completed by Thursday night. It's an introductory story with mass appeal: the Harmonetics Society becomes the beneficiary of $18 million tax free. One week later we will run a story on the Society itself. The first article will concern Jennifer primarily—the prominent social figure turning into a metaphysical recluse: 'From Esthete to Essene in Ten Easy Steps.' The second article, which will be researched by Harold Gondoler, Henrietta Beale, and Jade Boren, will be on the appeal of the Society.

"The first article is a teaser, although it has merit in itself. For the second article we'll need to know more about the Society and its accumulation of property. Our investigation will center on the funds coming in each week and how they are spent; the different echelons of the Harmonetics membership and whether status is determined by contributions; the involvement of such public figures as Lila La Mause, Senator Robert T. Spriggs, Judge Henley Stuart, and Andy Ames; the reason people are willing to turn over their life savings to the Society; and the motivations of Josiah Minden and his lay preachers. The Harmonetics Society owns temples, hospitals, sanatoriums, colleges, hostels for youngsters, cemeteries, hotels, farms, and various other properties. They are even beginning to control a few state legislators. Where is it going? Is Josiah going to run for Mayor or Governor or will a Harmonetics member be the next President of the United States?"

"Excuse me," interrupted Henrietta. "I knew Dorothy Spriggs, the Senator's wife, quite well. She died a year ago and we haven't seen much of the Senator since, but it shouldn't be difficult to reestablish the relationship."

"The Senator is one of the five most powerful men in the movement," said Jade.

"What's your plan of action for our team, Bill?" asked Harold Gondoler.

"Martha and Roger know where they will start and how to proceed because their area of reference is Jennifer Holiday and her will. Harold, your activities are pretty well circumscribed because you're the top investigator for *National News* and everybody knows it. You'll be working in the open, which makes it difficult to find what the Harmonetics Society may not want disclosed. Our best hope for an inside view of the action will come from the two women who join the Harmonetics Society—Jade and Henrietta."

"Jade's on the payroll," said Martha. "How can she possibly work undercover?"

"She was fired two days ago," said Harding.

"Is that believable?"

"With my attitude, yes," answered Jade. "It will confirm my mother's justifiable doubts about my ability. She thinks I'm scatterbrained." Jade looked sideways at Jerry.

"It so happens," said Harding, "that Jade's mother is deeply involved in the Harmonetics movement. She has tried to convert Jade. Mrs. Boren knows the leaders of the Society and would willingly use their influence to persuade her daughter to accept the Harmonetics way of life."

"I'm not going to make it easy for her," said Jade. "The conversion will take all her wiles. Even then she won't be sure I'm a true convert."

"Then why would anyone in the Society trust you?"

"I'll have other reasons for joining," she replied. "Perhaps I'll have a wild affair with one of the leaders."

Jerry wanted to object on grounds other than morality but he couldn't find the words. He hoped Harding would tell her that sex with a Harmonetics member was out of the question.

"Jade," asked Roger, "what Robe does your mother wear?"

"She received her Blue Robe a year ago. She was promoted to the Red Robes four months later. According to my father she's been overgenerous, which may account for the fact that she won her Green Robe well before the year was up. Her ambition naturally is to become a Brown Robe."

"There's sure to be a connection between the awarding of the Brown Robe and the size of one's contributions," said Harding. "The Brown Robes are the financial aristocracy of the Society. The twenty-five White Robes are the notables of the movement. Most but not all of them are rich; all are public figures."

"How many people are in the Brown Robe group?" asked Henrietta.

Jade answered. "There are approximately two million members of the Harmonetics Society. Of that number, 10,000, or one half of one percent, have been presented with the Brown Gown. Only Josiah Minden can award the White Robe. The recipients are the most honored members of the Society. Apparently they don't function as an executive committee or a cabinet. They're simply Dr. Minden's closest friends or, in a few cases, his associates. They're clearly power people.

"Bill," Jade continued, "I'd like to make use of the fact that

I've been fired by *National News*. Since Martha, Roger, and Harold will be working openly, I could prove my goodwill by telling the Harmonetics Society what's going on and whom to watch out for."

"Don't volunteer any information," suggested Harding. "Let it be dragged out of you."

"I'll be a reluctant squealer."

"Henrietta," said Harding, "it's your turn. Please explain your plan of procedure."

"I'll be in the Society before anyone knows it. Since the primary appeal is to older people, I'll find many friends who are already members. Now that I've retired from *Fortune*, I have a great deal of free time. I'm restless. I'm at the age where I need comfort and solace, and I'll find it in Harmonetics. I shall also canvass for jobs at the *New Yorker*, *Atlantic Monthly*, the *Village Voice*, and elsewhere, and when I am turned down, my loneliness will be even more evident."

"What if one of them hires you?" asked Jade.

"Then I shall moonlight," Henrietta replied promptly.

"Investigations can resemble jigsaw puzzles," said Harding. "One of you may pick up what seems like a useless piece of information, but someone is working on another corner of the puzzle and it may be the piece he needs. Jerry is your clearinghouse for information. Keep him posted. We may not have a chance to meet as a group again until the investigation is over. Good luck."

Roger folded his small note pad, placing it and his pen in his breast pocket with the meticulousness of an efficient secretary. Martha brushed the cigarette ashes off her shirt and stood up; the meeting was over and she was ready to move. Henrietta looked at the group approvingly: each was many years her junior but no one had given her the brisk, cool stare that notified you that you were too old to be with it. Harold had similar warm feelings about his confreres: they're my kind of people and they're damned competent. Jade was wondering how her mother would take the news of her conversion. And Jerry Marconi was the happiest in the group; he was on the biggest Assignment of his career and one of his teammates was Jade.

Excerpt from a sermon at the Harmonetics Temple in Los Angeles by Josiah Minden, President, Harmonetics Society (May 1978)

I would like to eliminate from our vocabulary such platitudinous phrases as "old age," "declining years," "permanently incapacitated," "past their prime," and "one foot in the grave." The phrases react like conditioned reflexes, condemning men and women in their sixties and seventies to the status of unwanted, useless survivors. Oliver Wendell Holmes, Pablo Casals, George Bernard Shaw, Grandma Moses, Artur Rubinstein, Bernard Baruch, King Gustav of Sweden, Jack Benny, and many other authors, physicians, painters, judges, entertainers, musicians, and rulers were and are active contributors in their fields in their eighties and nineties. Calendar years do not determine the bounds and limits of one's creativity. One's best years, the ultimate happiness in brotherhood and love, may be in one's mid-sixties or mid-eighties or mid-nineties— much more likely, in fact, than in one's mid-thirties. The healthy skin, the glow of the eyes, the luster of the hair, the straightness of the back, do not automatically disappear on the forty-fifth or sixty-eighth or eighty-first birthday—unless you think they will. Many of the young men and women in the Harmonetics Society have achieved four score or more years of living, but only now are they realizing their full physical and mental potential. They are caring for the spirit by their love of all mankind, they are healing their minds by learning the secrets of Harmonetics, and they are strengthening their bodies with scientific exercises that build muscles and skin tone and re-create and vitalize tissues. Our gowned brothers and sisters are living examples of the psychodynamics of Harmonetics. I defy you to call any of them "aging" or "declining" or "incapacitated."

Jade Boren had a two-room apartment with kitchenette for which she paid $800 a month. The price included the bright sun that shone through the southern exposure, the location in the

East Sixties, the many levels that separated Jade from the ground, and the services of a sixty-seven-year-old doorman whose vigilance was meant to protect the tenants from mugging, robbery, and rape. Jade was lying on a slightly battered ottoman, a cigarette in one hand and the telephone in the other.

"Mom, I'm back from Chicago."

"Oh, Jade, dear. How nice to hear your voice. How was California?"

"Chicago. The weather was terrible."

"What were you doing in Chicago?"

"Working, supposedly. There wasn't much to do. I called Arnie a lot."

"You see him every night in New York. Why do you have to call him long distance?"

"I missed him."

"That's ridiculous, Jade. Your phone bills must be over $400 a month. How can you do that on your salary?"

"I charged the calls to *National News.*"

"And they let you?"

"Not exactly."

"What does that mean, Jade?"

"*National News* and I had a small disagreement."

"You didn't resign!"

"No."

"Then what? Speak up, Jade. Don't make me pump you."

"We agreed to disagree."

"Do you mean to say you were fired?"

"Discharged is a better word. If I'd quit I wouldn't have been able to get Unemployment Insurance."

"You're going on Relief! A child of mine! You simply can't. What would people say?"

"I won't tell them. Besides, it will only be for a few months and then I'll look for another job. I need a vacation. I've been working too hard."

"It sounds just the opposite to me. Before you do anything, I want to have a talk with you. Come for dinner tonight."

"I thought I'd do something with Arnie."

"We are having an early dinner and you can see him afterward. We'll expect you at 6:30, Jade."

"Well, okay, but I'll have to leave early. Arnie's counting on me."

"Has Arnie started to work yet?"

"He does work, Mom."

"I mean real work."

"He's still playing the circuit, if that's what you mean."

Jade could hear her mother sigh.

"When is he going to settle down? He can't play tennis forever."

"When he finds himself," said Jade facetiously.

Her mother sighed again. "Please be prompt, Jade. You know your father dislikes having to wait for his meals. And try not to be argumentative. It does upset him."

"See you at 7:00."

"Six-thirty, Jade."

"Yes, Mom."

Jade hung up, looked at her list, and checked off "Mom." When I turn forty, she thought, Mom will still be issuing reproofs for what she deems are failures in my behavior patterns. If I don't get married, I'll have disappointed her; if I want her approval, I'll have to marry a nice young lawyer or doctor and shape up in the kitchen. Shit! Her idea of the perfect daughter is a virgin who always wears a bra and is never disrespectful. I should scream at her the way Arnie does with his old lady.

There were two other items on Jade's list: "Groceries" and "Clean Apartment." She got up from the ottoman, emptied the ashtrays, picked up clothes, books, and papers and stacked them in piles, hung up the towels in the bathroom, and wiped the sink with a Kleenex. The living room was Spartan: a minimum amount of furniture, uncarpeted wooden floors, neither curtains nor drapes by the big picture window. Jade took her poncho out of the closet, put a pack of cigarettes in her purse, and walked out of the apartment. She pressed the elevator button and waited the customary three minutes. When the self-service elevator arrived, she walked in with a cheery "Hello, everyone." There were mumbled replies. The four passengers stared at the lighted numbers above the elevator door as though this would make the elevator descend more rapidly: 11, 10, 9, 8, 7, 6, 5, 4, 3, 2, and Main. The passengers silently walked down the hall and out the front door, nodding to the doorman and ignoring each other.

"Hello, John," Jade said to the heavyset, surly-looking doorman. "How's everyone in the family?"

"They're all doing fine."

"Did 'Young John' get the job with CBS?"

"Yes. He goes into their computer training program next week."

"Congratulations. How about your daughter? Did she have the baby yet?"

"She's due this week. They're hoping for a girl this time."

John loosened as he talked to Jade, but he did not neglect his work. He kept an eye on the front door to see that no "fresh kids" came in, and he nodded to unseeing, indifferent tenants entering and leaving.

"Where are you off to now, Miss Jade?"

"Marketing. I have to feed the inner woman."

"It's nice having you back again. You were in Chicago a long time."

"It's good to be home. Tell 'Young John' I wish him luck."

Jade walked down the street to the neighborhood grocery. Mr. Panatta, the owner, was standing by the cash register, checking out the customers.

Jade wandered toward the back of the store, picked her selection from the shelves, and then waited behind an impatient woman who was next in line. The woman drummed her fingers on the counter and shook her head negatively while Mr. Panatta rang up the total. Then she flung down a $5 bill, glared and scowled when Mr. Panatta said "Five dollars and *forty-two cents*." She bounced the change at him and stalked out indignantly.

"What a dreadful woman," said Jade.

"She usually ain't so bad. I never seen her like this."

"What a nice man you are. You're always looking for the good side of people," said Jade, not quite truthfully.

Mr. Panatta beamed. "I try to see the best in everyone, rich or poor. It's easy to see it in you. You always got time to talk. You always interested."

"Thank you. How's your wife feeling? Is she any better?"

Jade was ready for Mr. Panatta's customary answer of "She

ain't feeling so hot" or "Last night she had another dizzy spell, then she got these shooting pains in her abdomen."

"She been feeling much better," answered Mr. Panatta. "She don't go to the clinic no more, she just go to the Temple."

"Mr. Panatta, I didn't know she was Jewish."

"No, the Harmonetics Temple, not the Jewish Temple. She go there every day and she looking much better. She feel swell now. You wouldn't know her. She fulla pep and no more sick."

"That's good news. I hear the Harmonetics Society does wonders for many sick people. Is it all free?"

"Yeah, all free."

"But of course you would want to make some sort of contribution to show appreciation."

"Yeah, sure. We make a few contributions, not much. My wife, she give a few hours each day to help."

"They've cured her and that's worth any price. I have a friend named Arnie whose mother's been sick for a couple of years. None of the doctors know what it is but she's been to all kinds of specialists. They've given her every kind of test and they still don't know. Arnie is so worried. You think the Harmonetics Society could help her?"

"Why not? It can't hurt. My wife tell me they very kind people. She sure looking better."

"Will Mrs. Panatta be coming to the store at all this week? I'd like to talk to her and hear her advice."

"Nah, she got no time to go to store. She goes to temple every morning and she get home same time I get home. But she looking good."

"What kind of help does she give, Mr. Panatta? I'm sure whatever she does is deeply appreciated."

"How should I know what she do? She say she pray and she get her treatment and she help in the, I can't say, you call it Dietitianary? It's at the hospital."

"Oh, of course. She works in the Dietetics Department. That's like a scientific kitchen, I guess."

"Yeah, she do kitchen work. But she no mind. She say it help many, many people, and they help her free. She been decorated."

"Decorated? You mean they gave her a medal?"

"No. She get Blue Gown. She wear it allatime now. You have to be pretty special to be Blue Gown."

"I've heard of them. It is special. I'd love to meet her and introduce her to Arnie's mother. Will you ask her?"

"For sure I tell her. She so busy she never at home. But she feel swell. I ask her."

"I'll be back in a few days. Maybe Arnie can bring his mother by to meet your wife."

"You very kind young lady. I ask my wife. You eat good now, you lookin' thin."

"Thank you, Mr. Panatta."

Jade took her grocery bag and walked the few blocks to the bookstore, leaving Mr. Panatta to indifferent, angry, or silent customers. It was a nice day and Jade enjoyed the blue sky and brisk air. She looked at the faces of other pedestrians but they seemed not to see her or anyone else. An elderly, fashionably dressed queen was watering his dog by one of the three trees on the block. He fastidiously turned his eyes away while the dog, a poodle, urinated. A woman in her seventies, wearing a mink cape over a print dress and several heavy charm bracelets on one arm, gazed at her blonde bouffant hairdo and her heavily rouged lips and cheeks in the windowpane of the local cleaning store. A busboy was sweeping the sidewalk outside a Third Avenue singles bar.

Jade stopped at a bookstore and looked in the window at the jackets of the bestsellers. A thick-browed, low-hairlined burly man in his thirties, bare-chested to make him look more macho, was menacing a young, C-cup female in deshabille who was cringing on a bed *(Confessions of a Rapist)*. A black-and-white photograph on a businesslike book jacket showed a row of industrious, classically handsome working men at an automobile assembly line *(Welfare: The Road to Self-Destruction)*. On another cover, standing in juxtaposition, were a fat, sleazy, scowling woman in a formless dress whose hair had been chopped off at the earlobe, and a beauty queen in a bikini, sucking in her gut and throwing out her mammaries *(Health & Weight Loss)*. Three young blacks, looking as though their forefathers had regularly interbred with Anglo-Saxons, were standing waist-deep in a wheat field, staring hopefully at the horizon *(200 Years of Black Poetry and Song)*. In the center of the window were thirty or forty copies of the No. 1 on the Non-Fiction list. A solitary figure was featured on the front cover, a gloriously striking man with deep-set eyes, a few attractive smile lines on an otherwise smooth, tanned skin and a full brown beard. He was wearing an open white shirt and behind him one could see the vast waters of a mighty ocean (*Harmonetics and Humanity: The Path of Peaceful Living* by Dr. Josiah Minden).

Excerpt from *Harmonetics and Humanity* by Josiah D. Minden, President, Harmonetics Society

The purest emotion man possesses is platonic love: it gives all and demands nothing. It is transmitted on two levels—the brain and the heart—and it is an intermingling of the levels. Platonic love is tactile as well as emotional and intellectual: it can be immediately expressed and reciprocated by the touching of hands. In Harmonetics we extend our hands to our brothers and sisters both as a symbol and as a tactile response. Hands touch, hands are laid on shoulders, and the palms of the hands rest softly on the face of the beloved brother or sister. The pulse of the blood is felt and exchanged. It is an intermingling of two hearts and minds; it creates instant emotional response.

Elliott Beale, seated in a soft leather chair in his living room, was doing the *New York Times* Sunday puzzle. Weekdays were like Sundays since his retirement last year, but there was much to keep him busy—corporate board meetings four times a month, two of which took him out of the city, conferences with his investment broker, occasional lunches with former confreres, charity committee meetings, visits to the tailor, the barber, and the bank, and his spare hours devoted to the Museum. He looked immaculate and handsome, his nails groomed, his face cleanly shaven, the faint aroma of an expensive men's cologne emanating from his dignified presence.

The telephone rang and Henrietta Beale rose to answer it.

"I have it," said Elliott, reaching for the receiver.

"Beale here," said Elliott into the speaker. He listened, then his voice lowered slightly, and Henrietta was aware of the nature of the call.

"Rather busy day but—I'm sure I can make time for you. The new Degas arrives at the Museum. . . . Shall we meet there? . . . Other things we can discuss then. . . . Right, in one hour.

"Sorry, dear," said Elliott rising. "Must go to the Museum, y'know."

What if I offered to go with him, thought Henrietta. Poor Elliott, the pathetic Don Juan of the Country Club Set, making assignations with bored ex-beauties in their late fifties, carrying on the travesty of conquests over pushovers. I can afford to be smug, thought Henrietta, because I haven't had a lover in six years.

It was a relief to have him out of the apartment today. Not that he ever was a bother. Elliott always sat so neatly, doing his puzzle, thumbing through a business journal, shuffling papers or talking on the phone.

Henrietta opened the wall cabinet by the window, gave a gentle pull to a hidden switch, and watched the typewriter flow out of its niche on a movable shelf. It would take her a half hour to write letters and mail résumés to the magazines where she was applying for work. That would give her plenty of time to get to her first Temple meeting.

The phone rang.

"Sarah, what a pleasant surprise. . . . Yes, it has been ages. . . . We're both fine. How are you and Edward? . . . How was Florida? Was the weather good? . . . Of course we'd love to see you. Today? Oh, dear, I've been promising myself I'd go to the Harmonetics Temple today. Would you like to go with me? . . . I'm delighted. I'll see you in ten minutes. We can have a cup of tea and taxi to the Temple. . . . A tout à l'heure."

Sarah Robinson rang the doorbell. Henrietta greeted her with the customary hug and kiss.

"You look marvelous," Henrietta lied.

"Do you think so? I feel like hell. Florida was hateful, and with Edward on the wagon and having to be in bed by 8:00 P.M. I was bored stiff. It's been six months since his operation and he's still so lethargic and helpless. I feel like a goddamn nurse's aide. Have you got a drink?"

"Sure, what would you like?"

"Scotch on the rocks. Make it a double. No, change that to a triple."

No wonder Sarah looked so puffy, thought Henrietta. She's got bags under the bags under her eyes, a lump of bloat around her middle, and swollen ankles. If I stuck a pin in her ankles, 80-proof Scotch would run out. Still, it's a rather elegant, chic bloat.

"With all my worries, Henrietta, my face has gone to pot." Sarah took her Scotch and walked over to the big mirror on the wall, examining her skin critically. "John Prowlen did the works three years ago. Damn good job but it didn't last long enough. Now my goddamn jaw is falling into my neck." She stroked her swollen, saggy jowls.

"Have you been doing any exercises?"

"I'm sick of those damn classes at Albert's. I never want to see another leotard again. It's so BORING."

Henrietta tried to think of something that wouldn't bore her friend. During her lifetime, Sarah had tried many novelties. A year ago she had been passionately dedicated to Albert's Exercise Salon, harassing every woman she knew into signing up for five classes a week. Last winter Sarah adopted a "mahvelous" bridge teacher. She persuaded several good friends to take lessons and play bridge with her every afternoon. By March she detested that vile, silly game. During the ceramics phase Sarah wore designer smocks and taxied daily to the Village to her art teacher. The Cordon Bleu Cooking School lasted one month; Ikebana was dropped after one week. Sarah enrolled in a social work course but got the flu. She talked about opening a boutique but she couldn't find the time. Henrietta smiled at her friend sympathetically.

Sarah was a highly self-occupied individual who insisted on changing the conversation anytime it veered toward the intellectual. The only current events that interested her were murder trials, catastrophes (particularly those that occurred in New York or Palm Beach), marriages, divorces, and love affairs.

She couldn't have cared less about business, the European Common Market, or the Panama Canal, and politics were incredibly dull unless she had slept with one of the candidates. Her friendship with Henrietta had lasted over forty-five years. It was solidly based on one of the few totally unselfish gestures that Sarah had ever made.

The girls had been roommates at Vassar. Sarah had arrived from New York by way of Newport, Rhode Island; Henrietta had come from a small town called Albright, twenty miles outside Cleveland. Sarah had played Right Wing on the Saint Bonaventure hockey team, she had been fabulously popular at Miss Van Hover's Friday-night dances, and her parents had piles of money and were enormously attractive. Henrietta's lifestyle was her own secret. Henrietta's mother had stringy hair that was graying badly, bright-red fingernail polish that was frequently chipped, and she wore either too much makeup or none at all. Sarah's mother was a brilliant hostess who gave witty parties. Henrietta's mother was too tired at the end of the day to make dinner, much less to ask anyone over. She spent a good ten hours daily in the Albright Beauty Salon cutting hair, giving permanents, and making her customers younger with henna rinses. When she came home at night her ankles were swollen and her arms ached. Henrietta would run her a hot tub and fix something to eat for the two of them.

While Sarah was scoring on the hockey fields, Henrietta was in the Albright Public Library poring over volumes of prose and poetry. Mr. Renville, the Head Librarian, was her guide. He introduced her to Baudelaire, Mallarmé, Gide, Rimbaud, Proust, Wilde, and Woolf, to books on Nijinsky and the Ballet Russe, the Parthenon and the Roman Forum, costumes in seventeenth-century France and eighteenth-century England, the operas of Wagner and Verdi, the string quartets of Mozart and the clavichords of Bach. Mr. Renville had once invited Henrietta and her mother to join him and a gentleman friend on a Friday evening to listen to a visiting orchestra in Cleveland playing Beethoven's *Eroica*, Mozart's Violin Concerto, and selections from Debussy. Henrietta said her mother was ailing because she was embarrassed about her mother's hair, ankles, and fingernails, not to mention her mother's intellectual failings. Mr. Renville would be so elegant; he had a flair for silk scarves and he owned a marvelous ankle-length Russian-style coat trimmed in black Persian lamb. Henrietta went alone with Mr. Renville and his friend. It was, until that point, the most exciting evening of her life.

Mr. Renville encouraged Henrietta to apply for a scholarship to Vassar. Henrietta was determined to conceal her identity and to become one of the attractive and highly social freshmen. Sarah, her roommate, guessed Henrietta's origins immediately. She never disclosed her findings. She told her friends that Henrietta's family was "simply mah-velous." She lent Henrietta skirts, coats, gloves, and shoes, and would occasionally borrow something from Henrietta to pretend they were sharing equally. She arranged double dates and invited her to her home for the holidays. When Henrietta met Elliott at Sarah's house and fell violently in love, Sarah supported her friend in the only way she knew, telling Elliott all sorts of mad stories about Henrietta's distinguished background.

Elliott was so handsome that Henrietta could hardly breathe when she was around him. He had an air of insouciance that Henrietta mistook for knowledge and a self-possession that Henrietta thought was based on ability. She adored him much more than he cared for her. She would have told any lie to keep him around for a few more months because she realized he would never never marry a nobody like herself. He did fall in love, in his own way, and one night he discussed their impending marriage. Henrietta trembled uncontrollably; now that he wanted her as his wife, she had to tell him the truth. She was not really Henrietta at all; she was the daughter of an Albright hairdresser who couldn't even cut hair fashionably. She couldn't get out the words. She kissed him and pledged her troth repeatedly, deciding the truth could wait another week or two.

Henrietta asked Sarah what she should do. Sarah was still playing games and parried the questions.

"I'm not what you think I am, Sarah," she wept. "I've got to tell you who I *really* am."

Sarah reached out to Henrietta, taking her hands, and spoke heatedly: "I don't give a damn about your background. Neither does Elliott. We love you for you. He and I never discussed what you call 'the real you.' That's because you've got money and social standing confused with quality. Elliott has a good social sense. He knows you haven't got a penny and he couldn't care less about your parents. Let's close the subject. He wants to marry you and that's the end of it."

Henrietta married Elliott, was accepted warmly by his family, and felt her ambitions had been achieved. Mr. Renville, in his black Persian lamb, would have been so proud. Sometimes, when she went to the opera on a Monday night, she would think of Mr. Renville. He would have exclaimed over her jewels and her exquisite Carnegie gown but most of all he would have admired Elliott.

Henrietta's taste for social affairs had diminished in direct proportion with her acceptance in the group. She regretted the lies and evasions of the Vassar days. They had never fooled Sarah or Elliott. She loved them dearly, whatever they did, because they had loved her when she needed their support. Sarah could never be vacuous because her loyalty and affection came when they were needed most. Elliott, the most attractive, enchanting, and desirable man in her Vassar days, had given her marriage and love when he could have had her on any terms.

Here was dear Sarah, forty-five years later, sipping a triple Scotch and looking toward her friend for the answers.

"I'd like to do something, Henrietta, but nothing interests me. I wish I could meet someone new and exciting. No, I don't. I'd scare him off with this frightful face."

"That isn't true at all. You're amusing and charming and well informed. You're also a very good friend," said Henrietta with sincerity.

"Oh, darling, all I do is complain. But it's such a bitch to get old and haggard. The only cheerful part is that it's happening to all my friends. Did you hear Janie Oliver got her eyes done last month by that dreadful quack, Dr. Garnoble, and one eye has already fallen? She looks like the Cyclops after Ulysses gave him a poke."

"Why did she go to Garnoble? He's a butcher!"

"She couldn't get an appointment with John Prowlen for six months. I'm going to call tomorrow to have him take a look at me."

"Sarah, I have an idea. You've always liked Senator Spriggs.

If he's in town I'm going to ask him for dinner. Just six or eight people. I'm sure Edward wouldn't mind your going out for an early evening, and Robbie has always enjoyed your company."

Sarah's face brightened.

"That would be nice. We had a little thing going years ago, and we've been good friends ever since. He was one of the nicest."

"You say that about all your old lovers," said Henrietta, laughing.

"And you listen to all my stories while you've always been faithful to dear old Elliott."

Henrietta smiled.

"If you've finished your drink, let's go to the Temple and find out what Harmonetics is all about. I hear Charlotte is going there regularly."

"Poor Charlotte. She's had nothing but tragedy with those damn kids and that dreadful husband. Did you hear what he did last month? He took that phony Hungarian countess, Irene what's-her-name, to Mexico City and he spent a fortune on her in clothes and jewels. And Charlotte always looks so tacky."

"If we see her at the Temple, let's try to cheer her up. If she's a Brown Gown she can cheer us up."

"The only Brown Gown that could cheer me up," said Sarah contemplatively, "is one made of chiffon and designed by Givenchy."

Excerpt from "Harmonetics Report" by Jade Boren
Sources: The *Wall Street Journal* and Alice Arkley (retired).

The Harmonetics Temple on East 58th had once been the Continental Towers. Robert Weinberger had inherited the property from his father in 1938 and had run it as a successful and elegant hotel for thirty-two years. He sold it shortly after his seventieth birthday to Harris Brothers, operators of a large chain of commercial hotels. The new owners eliminated many of the services for which visitors had paid a premium. The old chef, Francis, and the maître d', Arturo, retired. Dinners in the small, exquisite African Room became more prosaic and less expensive: when a customer ordered filet mignon, the waiter served it with a bottle of ketchup. Robert, the famous doorman at the Continental Towers, left before the first year was over to buy a condominium in Fort Lauderdale. The Continental Towers swimming pool, reserved for guests, was converted into a public health club. The Versailles Ballroom, the scene of the most expensive debutante party of 1964, became a convention selling point of the Harris Brothers Sales Department. In 1975 Bernard Harris, age seventy-six, told the members of his board that the Continental Towers was a turkey, and he suggested they unload it fast. Harris Brothers took a big capital loss (which saved the company $7 million in taxes) and a consortium of three young hotel entrepreneurs, Messrs. Barnes, Larsen, and Manderson, took over ownership in conjunction with four New York City banks.

Messrs. Barnes, Larsen, and Manderson were well connected and successful. They had made a sizable profit in their luxury spa hotels in Palm Beach and Phoenix. Their plans were to refurbish and restore what was now a dilapidated commercial hotel into a palace of Italian antiquities. Barnes and Manderson spent a summer in Rome, Venice, and Florence, and what was Italy's loss became New York's gain. Larsen, meanwhile, supervised the vast overhaul of the lobbies, ballroom, dining rooms, suites, lounges, corridors, and elevators. Plumbers, carpenters, electricians, plasterers, milled through the empty halls with their ladders, paintbrushes, hammers, and saws.

The National Bank & Trust Company shared the enthusiasm of the three young men and extended one of the largest loans in the bank for the purchase and refurbishing of the hotel. The bank was not unduly worried when, a year later, the hotel had not reopened. By mid-1979 it became clear it would not reopen unless city and state property taxes were paid, not to mention the outstanding bills of Pereida Plumbing, AAA Electric Company, and a dozen other creditors. The president of National Bank & Trust, Mr. Harry Case, Sr., spent two hours with the senior bank examiner from the Controller of the Currency's office, at the end of which he promised a resolution of the problem before the next bank examination. Mr. Case spent most of the next two weeks on the phone, searching for a buyer.

He even tried old Bernard Harris. He made appointments to see both the Mayor and the City Comptroller with negative results. The annual meeting of National Bank & Trust was scheduled for December, which put the pressure on Mr. Case to find a solution.

One day, in early November, Mr. Case's secretary buzzed him on the intercom. This is how she remembers it:

"There is a reporter, sir, from the *Wall Street Journal* who wishes to talk to you. His name is . . ."

"I can't talk to him now, Miss Arkley. Tell him I'm tied up for the next few days."

"He says it's about the Continental Towers loan. The *Journal* wants to know . . ."

"Miss Arkley, I have more important things to do than give interviews to everyone who calls."

He snapped off the intercom.

The story in the *Wall Street Journal* came out two days later. Mr. Case stormed into his office that morning and said to his secretary, "Goddamn it, they got all the facts wrong. They're trying to crucify me."

Four days before the annual meeting Case got the call he had been hoping for. It was Senator Spriggs with the news that Josiah Minden might be interested, at the Senator's urging, in taking the Continental Towers off the bank's hands. Case was in no position to negotiate. He told his secretary later: "They had all the high cards. We're just lucky to be out of it alive."

In early 1980 the Harmonetics Society paid the City and the State of New York the back taxes on the hotel, settled up with the creditors, and gave Mr. Case's bank forty cents on the dollar. A few months later the Temple was opened to the public. It was an instant success.

Harold Gondoler owned a modest bungalow on the outskirts of Los Angeles where he and his wife had lived for fifteen years. The Gondoler house, like its neighbors, had three bedrooms and a two-car garage. Harold Gondoler was gone early in the morning and often didn't come home until late at night. Frequently he stayed away three days at a time. Each week Mrs. Gondoler mowed and edged the ten yards of lawn. She also tended the row of dwarf begonias. When the drought came, the grass turned brown and the begonias died. Mrs. Gondoler became fretful and depressed. She stopped making the beds. She would sleep late, sometimes till noon. When she got up she would turn on the television set and fix herself a drink. Sometimes, when Harold came home in the evening, she would be sitting by her television set in her nightgown, stoned out of her head. A year ago Harold had hired a kindly, elderly woman to take care of his wife. When Harold was not traveling, he worked in a small maple study. He traveled as much as he could.

Harold Gondoler hung out at the Ranger Hotel whenever he was in New York. The registered guests included some actors and actresses, widows, retired businessmen, Mid-westerners and Texans who eschewed the large commercial hotels, a smattering of authors, minor executives, and odd-balls. The Ranger's London Pub was crowded at lunchtime with the Regulars, many of whom were writers. It was deserted in the evenings. The hotel was too expensive for the average traveling salesman but not expensive or chic enough for the Jet Set, Smart Set, or Social Set. The food was good and very few rooms were robbed. Only a couple of rooms smelled of pot; angel dust has no odor.

Harold was a Regular. When he was in New York, his hotel room was his office. His expense account was always low; he walked instead of taxiing and he seldom picked up tabs for large groups. Harold was a lonely man, an infrequenter of bars, a solitary diner. He was highly loyal to the woman in his life of the moment, the moments ranging from two years to seven years.

Harold picked up the phone in his hotel room and dialed Harmonetics headquarters. He asked for Dr. Minden and was put on "hold." A high male voice came on the phone.

"Your name, please?"

"Harold Gondoler of *National News*."

"Did you wish information about joining the Society?"

"No, thank you. *National News* is planning a major story on the movement and of course the story wouldn't be complete without some direct quotes from Dr. Minden."

"Just a minute, please."

Harold was put on "hold" again.

"Hartain speaking."

"Dr. Minden, please."

"Just a minute. I'll transfer you."

"Ramba Landry," said a soothing female voice. "May I help you?"

Harold gave his name, his affiliation, and asked for an interview.

"I'm so sorry but Dr. Minden does not give personal interviews. However, if you would like to attend a service at which he will speak?"

"Thank you but I'm primarily interested in the membership and the funding. For example, what percent of the members are under the age of fifty and how many are female?"

"There are approximately two million members of the Society. We don't maintain individual file cards on members. That would make us like the FBI, wouldn't it? Still, if you attend one of the evening services at our Temple, you would get an idea of the representative nature of the membership."

"Then perhaps you could give me some information on the finances of the Society. For starters, how much money is raised in donations each month?"

"Our operations are nationwide, as you know. We assist hundreds of thousands of people, but the money is collected and spent locally."

"Are figures available on the amount of property owned by the Society?"

"That's a very difficult question to answer. It would be like asking the Catholic Church to provide you with a list of all property held in the name of the Church."

"Then could I get a list of major buildings owned by the Society, such as temples, hospitals, spas, clinics, schools, and retreats? Even if the list isn't complete, it would be important to the article to detail some of the Harmonetics facilities."

"There we may be able to help you. The Society produced a magnificent book with large color photographs of the most beautiful Harmonetics temples, hospitals and retreats. You may have heard of it. The title is *Architectural Triumphs in Harmonetics Design* by Franklin Robert Parson. It's one of those enormous coffee-table books that sells for $150. We also have a very nice portfolio and several brochures on the Josiah Minden College in Mississippi as well as some excellent material on the Harmonetics Medical School in Oklahoma."

"By the way, I don't think I know what department you are in. Are you one of Dr. Minden's associates?"

"We all are, in a manner of speaking. My department is called Public Information Services. We answer requests for data as best we can and we provide guided tours of some of the Harmonetics facilities."

"May I take a guided tour?"

"Certainly, Harold. I hope you don't mind if I call you Harold. I would be happy to take you myself tomorrow."

"That's extraordinarily kind of you, Ramba. May I call you Ramba? Shall I meet you at your office at 10:00 A.M.?"

"Would you be able to meet me at 8:00 A.M.? I want to take you to the Morning Service at the Temple. Dr. Minden is speaking and it will be a rich experience."

"I'll be there. What else can I anticipate seeing?"

"We'll visit some of the seminars and workshops at the Temple. Then we'll go to the Uptown Study Hall and we'll visit the Administration Building and the Hospital. I think it will give you a good feel for the depth and breadth of the Society. You may even become a convert."

"You're not a missionary, are you, Ramba?"

"Until tomorrow at 8:00," she said with a laugh.

An hour later Harold made his first investigative foray. He took a subway to 168th Street and Broadway, then walked a half mile to the Harmonetics Hospital. It had been a black-Puerto Rican-poor white city institution called Plaza del Populo, which had opened three years earlier after a nine-month delay, the victim of the city council, a series of strikes, antagonistic patients, immovable bureaucrats, internecine medical warfare, hostile doctors, abused nurses, and an indifferent public. After three months of operation, Plaza del Populo had closed: the patients had complained of critical neglect, the medical chief claimed he was understaffed, the lab technicians walked out because they had not been paid for eleven weeks, and, finally, Con Edison turned off the electricity because its bills had not been paid in more than a year. The magnificent hospital, with its enormous operating amphitheatres, its invaluable collection of kidney, liver, heart, lung, and other organic machines designed to help the sick, the dying, and the believing, its six hundred rooms for patients, its roof gardens, terraces, waiting rooms, emergency halls, nurses' quarters, cafeterias, therapeutic pools, and gymnasiums, remained empty for more than a year. Then, for an undisclosed sum of money, Dr. Minden took over the facility and quickly put it into full-scale activity.

The walk from 168th Street would never be advertised by promoters of the Big Apple image. Harold strode with an eye on the ground to avoid the overflow from the garbage cans, the broken bottles, old beer cans, and refuse seeping out of discarded newspapers. The outside walls of buildings were splattered with chalk or painted graffiti in childish scrawls. The smell emanating from some of the tenements was overpowering. Some, with their boarded-up windows, looked uninhabited until one saw an old woman shuffling in clutching a paper bag. A pre-teen-ager was soliciting pedestrians. The atmosphere was hostile, wary, threatening. There were no friendly smiles; just impassive, appraising looks. Fortunately for Harold, he was big enough and sloppy enough not to invite unpleasant attention. He didn't look rich enough to rob, and his shoulders and height were too powerful to make him an easy victim. Harold had a rough look and, as a black man, he had a visa for this area.

When he was a block from the hospital, the scene changed. The stores were cleaner, a pharmacy was doing a lively business, policemen stood on the corners, and the delinquents, old and young, were invisible. Dr. Minden and/or his staff had transformed the hospital grounds into a combination park and playground.

Harold walked on the private sidewalk with its neat border of box hedges to the main hospital entrance. The gardens were the most carefully tended he had seen in New York, and the reason was clear. Several dozen men and women in Harmonetics gowns were weeding, cutting, snipping, planting, and watering. They worked diligently and steadily, and there was little conversation between them. The two tennis courts on the far right were occupied, one of them with two men in their thirties, wearing $90 warm-up suits, slugging the ball erratically; and the other with four women, all volleying with the wrong grip. Everyone else was going or coming with a purposeful look, nurses in their starched costumes and doctors in their open white shirts, walking briskly. Volunteers in their flowing gowns, even the elderly, were moving at a regular pace toward a specific destination. The only people enjoying their leisure were the tennis players.

Gondoler opened the heavy paneled door of the hospital and entered a large reception hall. The motif was potted plants. There were baskets of rex begonias, philodendrons, tiger aloe, Norfolk Island pines, bird's-nest fern, silver-nerved fittonia, rabbit's-foot fern, tufted fishtail palm, and a dozen varieties of cactus sitting in clusters of pebbles, fine gravel, golden sand, and wood chips. They filled the seven-tiered platform in the center of the hall and they nested in groups against the walls. Even Harold, who didn't know an acacia from an azalea, was overwhelmed. The hall smelled sweet and was extraordinarily quiet. The only sound was the snipping of scissors as two men and one woman in long robes trimmed and watered and dug their fingers into the soil. They moved without sound from plant to plant as though they were in a house of worship.

Gondoler walked across the hall to one of the glass-enclosed partitions that protected the room from unnecessary noise. Behind the partition a woman was clicking rapidly on a typewriter and another was opening a drawer in a filing cabinet. A third woman was talking on a phone. Gondoler could see her lips moving. She finished the call, hung up, switched a button, and said to Gondoler through a speaker in the partition: "May I help you, sir?"

"My mother isn't at all well. I'm anxious to have her see one of the doctors."

"Is she a member of the Harmonetics Society?"

"No, but I'm willing to pay," said Gondoler.

"One of you has to be a member. The hospital is restricted to those who have joined the Society, and this includes doctors and nurses as well as patients."

"How long does it take to join?"

"It takes quite some time to become a full member but anyone who enrolls can be a Probationary."

"Are the Probationaries entitled to hospital treatment?"

"Only if the request is signed by one of the affiliated physicians. Meantime," she said, opening a small window, "here are some papers to fill out in case you or your mother wish to join. Please don't leave any of the lines blank or the application cannot be processed. Be sure to put down the Social Security number, the Medicaid number, the name of her medical insurance company, and the number of the policy."

"Thank you very much. May I look around now?"

"You may go to the Reading Room or the Prayer Room. The patients and staff have privacy, which I am sure you will respect. Only the paneled corridors are open to visitors."

"I'd like to find out more about the hospital. How many patients do you have, how many volunteers, and what is the size of the staff?"

"Sir, I would like to help but we're awfully busy now. If you wish you may visit one of our open rooms. The Reading Room and the Prayer Room are directly to the right of the main door. They are clearly marked."

The woman smiled pleasantly, flicked off the intercom, and closed the small window.

Harold walked down the corridor to the Reading Room. It had the look of a rich private library, with carved bookshelves reaching to the domed ceiling, two subdued Portuguese rugs covering the center of the parqueted floors, and large, comfortable chairs upholstered in soft brown leather placed in groups of two or three. The bookshelves were filled with volumes written by members of the Society along with other suitable works by such authors as Immanuel Kant, David Hume, Benedict Spinoza, Gail Sheehy, Tim Gallway, and Wayne W. Dyer. On a large table, neatly arranged, were the pamphlets, tracts, and newspapers issued by the Harmonetics Society.

More than half of the two dozen chairs were filled with robed men and women chatting in whispers or improving their minds with recommended publications. An ethereal woman of uncertain years was pouring tea out of a silver urn. In this peaceful, harmonious setting was one commercial note: a circular oak table in the middle of the room which served as the repository for cash contributions. There were no coins on the table; this was not a nickel-and-dime operation. There were piles of bills of varying denominations, from $1 to $100, carelessly scattered by the donors. Two men in green robes were casually leaning against a wall. They must be there, thought Gondoler, to protect the approved publications from mutilation, to prevent the elderly, frail readers from rioting and destroying the .

furniture, or to see that the money lay undisturbed.

Harold walked over to the reading table and glanced at the publications. The tracts and brochures varied in thickness and quality of production but all had similar themes: *Health Through Harmonetics* by Dr. Heinrich Fronzhold, *The Fallacies of Aging* by Dr. Josiah Minden, *Companionship and Marriage the Harmonetics Way, Is There Life After Death?* by Dr. Reginald Zinder, *The Road to Achievement and Mental Happiness* by Dr. Josiah Minden, *Physical Fitness: The Development of the Perfect Body, The Harmonetics Road to Mental Strength, Aptitude Testing: The Tests That Will Determine* Your *Career* by Dr. Esme Jennings, and *First Principles of Harmonetics* by Dr. Josiah Minden.

Harold picked up a pamphlet on aptitude tests and sat down to read. He opened it in the middle. Mrs. R, age fifty-three, had four children. All were married. She and her husband had moved to a small city apartment. After a year of city living she became depressed and moody, almost a recluse. She sought help at the Harmonetics Temple and was encouraged to take the aptitude tests. The psychologists discovered she was an extrovert. Additionally she was gifted with pronounced finger orientation. She found fulfillment in the Harmonetics gardens where she could exercise her creativity in the planting of flowers and the tending of shrubs. Miss H, age forty-nine, had had several clerical jobs, all of short duration. On four occasions she had been committed to institutions because of a "black cloud" that hung over her. She visited the Temple and took a battery of tests. To her amazement she discovered she was a highly creative person with great sensitivity. Basically she needed a social organization in which she could play a structured role. She was not, as she had thought, an introvert. She underwent six months of training and was then assigned to the Harmonetics Hospital where she worked with elderly patients. The "black cloud" disappeared. Mr. C, age fifty-seven, had been a factory worker. He suffered from tension and went on periodic binges. He had been arrested six times in the past ten years. His wife had brought him to the Temple and had urged him to take the tests. They revealed a strong but unfulfilled desire to carry out a job through its completion; he was totally unsuited for the assembly line. A Harmonetics psychologist persuaded him to take a three-month course in building maintenance and repair. He stopped drinking. He was assigned to the Harmonetics College in Ohio and became a key man in the Maintenance Department.

Harold heard the rustle of paper money. He closed his pamphlet and looked up. A large blonde woman in a blue robe was fumbling in her purse for a gift to lay on the money table. She hesitated, unable to make up her mind. Harold guessed she would come up with a five. He was wrong. She placed a $10 bill on the table. Then she turned and walked toward the door. One of the green robed guards smiled and spoke to her. She beamed with pleasure and replied animatedly. She returned to the table and added another donation, also a $10 bill. She walked back to the door, her eyes on the guard. He clasped both her hands and pulled her toward him. The donor put her hands on the guard's shoulders, then raised them gently to his face, holding them there for a few seconds. His hands in turn clasped her shoulders and then her face. They stood silently, touching and staring. The woman appeared greatly affected by the ceremony. Harold wondered what the guard would have done had her contribution been $100. She walked out, closing the door softly behind her, and the guard returned to holding up the wall.

A side door opened and a middle-aged woman with light brown hair literally swept in. She was pushing a vacuum cleaner and she zoned in on an electric plug by the door. She was a most unlikely janitor. The thin-boned nose, the high cheekbones, and the narrow mouth denoted the popular Anglo-Saxon look, while the hairdo, the carriage, and the tilt of the eyebrows made her appear more at home in an apartment on Fifth Avenue in the Sixties than a Harmonetics Hospital on the Upper West Side. After plugging in her vacuum she went to work, diligently sweeping the immaculate rugs, begging the pardon of people as she went under their feet. She did the rugs geometrically, up to one end, then back to the other, up again and back again. She stopped at the round oak table, took a small reticule out of a deep pocket in her robe, withdrew two $10 bills and laid them on the table, then returned to her vacuuming. The two men guarding the wall scarcely looked at her. The readers in the room paid no attention. She finished the last corner and returned to the other side to unplug her machine.

Standing in the open door was a doctor wearing the Harmonetics medical garb of a white open-necked shirt with long sleeves and cuffs turned up. Around his neck was his insignia, the stethoscope. He was a rough-looking man, a good twenty years younger than the vacuumer. He watched her pull out the plug and meticulously wrap the long cord around her instrument. As she reached the door, he placed both hands on her shoulders and looked into her eyes. He raised his hands to her cheeks and she took a step forward. Harold was only getting a rear view but he felt her reaction. He had seen it often enough in Third Avenue bars at 2:00 A.M. or at cocktail parties when a lonely woman was touched or stroked by one of the swingers. She was so close that her head almost touched his shoulder. They looked at each other boldly, openly, then the doctor's hands dropped and, a few seconds later, her bony, manicured hands reluctantly fell to her side.

Harold's adrenalin was stimulated by the encounters. They were sudden and direct, like the opening scenes of a hard porn movie. Back to the aptitude tests while he waited for more action. Ten minutes later a blue-robed visitor entered the room. She was stringy, with pursed lips and a look of disapproval in her stern features: laughter or happy children or dancing would be desecration, while solemnity, taciturnity, and lack of enjoyment of the physical world were proper and good. She walked over to the tea table and whispered a few words to the tea pourer, who immediately got up, allowing the newcomer to take her place. The displaced pourer stopped by the money table and put down a $5 bill clandestinely, perhaps in the hopes that no one would notice the small denomination. As she left the room, one of the wall supporters opened the door and she was the recipient of the $5 shoulder and face job, warm but not as fervent as those given earlier.

Harold was getting restless. He replaced the pamphlet, then walked by the money table with his hands deep in his pockets. The door was opened for him by a guard who gave him a friendly smile but no hand clasp.

"Please come back anytime," said the guard with the hint of a lisp.

The Prayer Room was down the hallway. Gondoler opened

the heavy door and entered a candlelit auditorium-temple. The stark, bare floors, the altarlike lectern, the pews, and the flickering light gave the enormous room the aura of a holy place of worship. At the far end of the Prayer Room, behind the lectern, were rows of flowers and shrubs and exquisite plants, resting on tiers, mounting halfway to the ceiling. Emerald Ripple peperomia, butterfly palms, Swedish ivy, purple cyclamens, African violets, sprays of peach blossoms, red gloxinias, polyanthus primroses, and bougainvillea stretched their leaves and branches toward the pale light emanating from the ceiling. The room was filled with their fragrance.

The side walls were decorated with large murals faithfully depicting scenes relevant to the Harmonetic faith. A portrait of the founder of the order, Josiah Minden, in a white shirt open at the throat, fine brown hair falling almost to his shoulders, the silky beard accenting the resemblance to a sixteenth-century Spanish grandee. A painting of Josiah Minden, slim and straight-backed, strolling through the woods, accompanied by seven brown-gowned mature men and women, their backs uncurved by advancing years, their eyes bright, and a look of dedication on their faces. Josiah Minden standing on the marble steps of the Harmonetics Institute addressing a large crowd of robed men and women, his white-robed disciples surrounding him. A portrait of Senator Robert T. Spriggs, 6'4", his hair receding, his smile warm and earnest, addressing the International Harmonetics Congress in San Francisco; a group of white-haired, healthy gowned women working in a garden; blonde, heavyset Minnie Matthews and a Josiah Minden who scarcely looked forty, clasping each other at the second anniversary celebration of the Houston Harmonetics Clinic; a group of doctors and nurses in an operating room looking serious, efficient, and intelligent, surrounded by oxygen tanks and trays of scalpels, ready to ply their instruments on an unconscious patient.

The Prayer Room was in constant flux. Gowned men and women visited for five or ten minutes and left, leaving a donation at the large round oak table by the door. Many worshipers studied the murals as though they were seeing Saint Patrick's Cathedral for the first time. Some prayed or communed. Others nodded their heads in rhythm with the organ music. A few stopped to talk to the guards who were standing ten feet from the large oak table.

Harold felt none of the calmness and serenity that the visitors displayed. His stomach was knotting in frustration. He had spent an hour at the hospital and had learned nothing. He walked out of the Prayer Room through the big hall and out the main door. He crossed the street to the pharmacy he had noticed earlier and walked in. He looked around the counters, noting that toothpaste and razor blades were selling for a nickel more than at the Ranger Hotel. Dental floss was also higher. He went up to the cashier, a handsome black woman in her early twenties, and bought a pack of Marlboros and a box of Tic-Tacs.

"I've just been visiting the hospital," said Harold conversationally. The cashier accepted his money but ignored his remark. *Ex-football player,* she categorized him. *He's throwing me a pass but I won't catch it.*

"Will there be anything else, sir?"

"Yes, I'd like to talk to you." *About Harmonetics or anything else.*

The cashier rang up the sale.

"You're right not to trust strangers," said Harold, giving her his sincere, no-nonsense look. "This is my business card. I work for *National News* and I'm on assignment to do a story on the Harmonetics Society."

"I don't see how I can help," she replied. *If you're doing a story on tits, forget it.*

"I spent a frustrating hour staring at fifty volunteers in different color gowns. I saw one doctor and no patients. While I sat in the Reading Room waiting for the action, I read an interesting treatise on aptitude tests that proves indubitably that fulfillment of one's innate abilities can only come through volunteer work in Harmonetics."

The cashier laughed. *It's not a pickup. I might have misjudged him.*

"These people take themselves very seriously," Harold continued. "They weed the garden and they vacuum the rugs and they make donations. What they don't like to do in their own homes, they do willingly in the Harmonetics Hospital. I saw a Park Avenue lady cleaning a rug that was already spotless.

When she goes home she's sore at the maid if the silver isn't polished."

"They're spacey," said the cashier. *It's OK. He's straight.*

"Do you see many of them in the pharmacy?"

"They're in and out. They buy toothbrushes, hairbrushes, combs—everything but pharmaceuticals. We do a big business in chocolate mints, nail files, and scissors but we're dying in aspirin, nail polish, and cosmetics. The Brown Cats and Blue Cats and Green Cats don't buy perfumes or lipsticks."

"Do you talk to the customers?"

"They're polite and they smile and I'm polite and I smile. I like them and I think they like me. They don't ask me anything and I don't ask them anything. A few seem doped up."

"Drugs?"

"Not that kind. I think they're sedated."

"They look pretty rich?"

"Some do, some don't. It's a mixture."

"Are they generally elderly?"

"Mostly. I don't see many kids. Lately there have been more gowned teen-agers than ever before. When the place first opened it was strictly for older cats."

"Any Afro-Americans?"

"One or two. It's not a black movement."

"How would you classify them?"

"I can't."

"Would you say lonely?"

"They don't seem lonely now. They run in packs. Twos and threes, often four of them. Sometimes they're holding hands."

"Any of them sick?"

"Arthritis, bad legs or backs, trembling of the limbs, hard of hearing, overweight, underweight, the usual. They look reasonably healthy to me. Why not? They're mostly volunteers. If a patient comes in, she's usually with several volunteers."

"You said 'she' for patient."

"There are men, too, but I see more women. I couldn't tell you the percentage."

"Did you ever see a patient arrive involuntarily?"

"There's no way of knowing. The ambulances come into a tunnel inside the hospital. So do most of the taxis and private cars. There's a large garage in the basement. We only see the volunteers and the staff in the front park and playground."

"Have you ever seen anything peculiar or unusual?"

"Yes, once. It's an odd story. One night, as I was closing up, an old woman ran into the pharmacy. She looked really wasted and spaced out. She was crying, 'For God's sake, hide me, protect me.' I thought she was running away from some hoods so I picked up a crowbar and was ready to use it to protect us both. Then two nurses and an orderly dashed in. When the old woman saw them, she screamed, 'Don't let them take me. They're trying to kill me.' One of the nurses cooled her out and offered her her hands while the other nurse and orderly circled around her. The old woman was grabbing my arm. She was trembling. She begged me to let her stay in the store. She kept saying, 'Oh, God, don't let them take me back.' I stood there with the crowbar in my hand; I wasn't about to let anyone touch her. It looked like a shootout. One of the nurses who was acting cool said if I liked she would call the doctor or get a policeman. I told her to do it all. She used the pay phone and said the doctor would be right over. There was a policeman on the corner and she brought him in.

"The old woman was pleading with us for protection. She said she had gone into the hospital unwillingly and she was being held prisoner. The nurses kept her drugged, she couldn't use the phone, and she wasn't allowed any visitors. They wanted her to die. The policeman and I listened, but the more she spoke, the harder it was to believe. The nurses and orderly were standing there cooled out and smooth; how could they be part of some act to kill a little old lady?

"The doctor and an assistant arrived. I'm coming to the bad part. The assistant grabbed the old woman. She was kicking and beating on him. The doctor gave the old lady a shot and the struggles stopped. Some fix it was. I asked the nice nurse the name of the patient. She got as far as 'Mary' when the doctor interrupted. He said, 'Her full name is Mary Margaret Bailey.' I saw the look on the nurse's face. She was wondering why the doctor was lying.

"The next day I went to the hospital to ask about 'Mary Margaret Bailey.' I wasn't sure I had done the right thing but how could I, a lousy cashier, hassle the doctor? The Blue Gown volunteer at the desk said there was no such patient. I said there was: last night Mary Margaret Bailey had run into the pharmacy in the presence of myself and a policeman. It had required three men and two women to subdue her. The Blue Gown talked to a Brown Gown who went into the doctors' offices. Five minutes later I was informed that Mary Margaret Bailey had been discharged that morning. I asked for her address. I was told it was confidential. I got pissed. I said I would go for the heat. The man in the brown gown asked me to wait. He went into the doctors' quarters again. I waited fifteen minutes. The doctor I had seen the night before came out, greasy as slick ribs. He explained 'Mary Margaret Bailey' was not the name of the old woman. Her family didn't want publicity so they'd given her this fake handle. She was suffering from hardening of the arteries. Frequently she was normal but she had spells of hallucination and paranoia. If I wished, the doctor would allow me to meet with the family and, with their approval, I could visit 'Mrs. Bailey.'"

"Did you?"

"Yes. I told the doctor I had no intention of dropping the matter. The more I thought about it, the more I resented the strong-arm fix the doctor had given the old lady. It's a pretty heavy way to end a conversation: shoot the opponent with a needle and you win the argument.

"Two days later I got a call from the hospital. 'Mr. and Mrs. Bailey' would be happy to see me. I closed the pharmacy and rushed over. The 'Baileys' and the doctor were waiting for me. All three were cool as ice and slippery rude: I had forced the Baileys to drop everything and rush to the hospital, the doctor was a very busy man, I was depriving many patients of his presence, and I was acting like I knew more about the patient than her own doctor and her immediate family."

"Did you see the old woman?"

"Yes, but it didn't do much good. I couldn't tell if she was spaced out on drugs or mentally ill. I got to look at her for a few minutes. She didn't respond. She opened her eyes but she didn't recognize me or the doctor or the family. The son and daughter-in-law kissed her and we left. They gave me that 'See all the trouble you have caused?' look."

"Did you ever see her again?"

"No."

"Do you remember the name of the doctor?"

"I never heard it but I'd recognize him."

"When did this happen?"

"About three months ago."

"Do you remember 'Mrs. Bailey's' room number?"

"Not the number but I know the floor and the door. It was the fifth floor, West Wing, Iris Corridor, directly to the right of the Nurse's Station."

"What's the Iris Corridor?"

"They don't name the departments the customary hospital way. There's no Cancer, Tuberculosis, Urology, Orthopedics, etcetera. They call them by flowers and trees."

"I'm coming back officially tomorrow for a guided tour. I'll make a point of looking for your 'Mrs. Bailey.'"

"Thanks. I've never been sure I did the right thing. The old lady may have been senile, but when I look back I know she was being drugged so she would be easier to handle. Harmonetics got a ton of believers because it fought the nursing home bit for the oldies, and now they're doing the same damn thing. What's the difference between that doctor and his connection and some old lady whose kids have shoved her out of sight in a home for the elderly?"

"I don't suppose any more old ladies will come crashing into your store, but if they do, call me. Even if they don't, call me."

She smiled. "And if your wife answers?"

He smiled. "She won't. She lives in California."

Martha Rayburn was scrubbing the carbon off her hands in the *National News* Executive Lounge, which was a euphemism for "Ladies' Room." She noticed the coffee stain on her blouse, dabbed at it ineffectually with a paper towel, creating a wider, wetter blot on the frilly pink ruche. "Damn, damn," she said, giving up. She made a few hopeless stabs at her hair with a pocket comb, then smiled at her image in the mirror and sailed out serenely.

On the street she caught a cab, directing the driver to the Holiday town house in the East Seventies. During the ride she rummaged through her enormous reticule for a note pad and pen, in the course of which search she discovered a large gold bracelet that she thought she had lost a month ago. She popped it on her wrist and felt well groomed.

Martha Rayburn got out of the taxi and paid the fare, adding a dime to the total. Normally the cab driver would have received such a miserable pourboire with an appropriate insult, but Martha's face terrorized him; her wild hair, her matriarchal bosom, her impeccable posture, and the look of benevolence and ferocity in her black eyes reminded him of a frightening experience in the high-school principal's office. He retreated two decades, to a time of life when dominating females overwhelmed insecure fourteen-year-olds.

"Thank you, ma'am," he said, then was so outraged at his own behavior that he poured on the gas and screeched off on whistling tires.

Martha Rayburn rang the Holiday doorbell with authority; no gingerly timid touch of a forefinger but the heavy pressure of a domineering thumb on a passive eyeball. When there was no immediate response, she pressed again. The butler answered the door, opening it enough to see out but not enough to allow access.

"Madam, this house is closed," he said firmly.

"Edwards! Open this door at once!"

He instinctively obeyed the command. By the time his mind took control over emotion, it was too late. Martha Rayburn was in the house, standing legs apart, hair spooking wildly, and coffee-stained ruche trembling indignantly.

"Edwards, I am here to talk to you and to Mrs. Small. It will not be necessary to ask Cook to join us. Please summon Mrs. Small so we can get started."

"Madam," he replied, unsure of his ground, "we do not know you."

"When Mrs. Small joins us I will explain. No need to repeat. Now be quick!"

Edwards hesitated. He had been trained to react to particular tones, and the lady was certainly assertive. Should he flout her? Dare he stand up to her? He looked at her and was beaten down by her eyes and her massive presence.

"Madam, I shall ring for her."

Edwards pulled the tasseled bell cord, his eyes suspiciously watching Rayburn for any sudden movement. She did not look as though she were here to steal the silver but he would be prepared.

A stout woman in a dignified black housekeeper's dress entered the foyer.

"Mrs. Small," said General Rayburn to the Staff Sergeant, "I am here to talk to you and Edwards about the generous bequests you received from Mrs. Holiday. We are delighted to see you both have been provided for, and we intend to uphold your right to these gifts against any attacks in court."

"I'm sure that's very kind of you, Mrs.———?"

"*Ms*. Rayburn. Now where shall we talk? I would be happy to take you both to tea at the Plaza. There is a great deal to discuss and I am pressed for time. Come, now, get your hat or your purse and let's be off."

Martha hustled her charges into the street, summoned a taxi, and whisked them off. Two hours later, at her desk at *National News*, she finished the last of her notes on the Plaza meeting.

The Household of Jennifer Holiday
Sources: Edwards (butler) and Small (housekeeper)

by Martha Rayburn

When we sat down to talk, Edwards was in a panic. He thought Rhonda Mahaffey and Lawrence Runson, Jr. (the offspring of Jennifer's union with Lawrence Runson, Sr.) intended to break the will. For the first ten minutes he continually assured me that Jennifer Holiday was totally sane and the Harmonetics gang were the salt of the earth. I must have told him five times that the bequests to him and Mrs. Small and the cook were as safe as though the money were in the Bank of England (he has great faith in the Queen, the Test Matches, and the Bank of England). It turns out he had no use for the Harmonetics crowd: he despised their shabby gowns and their lack of table manners. He used the word "appalling" to describe the change in Mrs. Holiday's eating habits. No more caviar with blinies, turtle soup, or chocolate mousse. From the time she entered the Harmonetics Temple Jennifer subsisted on cottage cheese, low-cal yogurt, raw beets, raw turnips, skim milk, yeast blended with wheat germ, bananas and orange juice, and other comestibles purchased from the Harmonetics Health Center.

Edwards was indignant about the cancellation of Mrs. Holiday's winter vacations in Palm Beach and summer trips to Newport, Nice, Athens, and, above all, London. Instead she chose to spend two weeks at the Harmonetics Health Spa in Vermont and she several times visited their Body Clinic in Arizona. She was in and out of the New York Harmonetics Hospital four or five times, and each time except the last one she appeared healthier and more vigorous. Edwards said the hospital stays lasted anywhere from two to ten days. However, the last visit was the Big One. She was there for two weeks, at which point she ceased to exist. (The Harmonetics people avoid the word "death"; one "moves onward.")

Mrs. Small was exceedingly talkative. She told me that almost all of Mrs. Holiday's visitors, particularly during her last six months, were from the Harmonetics Temple. They wore brown gowns or white robes or, occasionally, white shirts open at the neck. When they stayed for a meal, they also ate cottage cheese and half-grapefruits. No, they didn't tipple. Mrs. Small thought it was quite vulgar the way they were always touching each other.

"Where did they touch?" I asked.

"Their faces and their shoulders, but the way they did it, it looked dirty."

They both agreed that Mrs. Holiday had been very happy. She was transported when she became a White Robe. Mrs. Small thought this was several months before her death. I asked when she had made out her new will. Neither of them knew. I inquired about the visits from Austin McDowell, Mrs. Holiday's lawyer. Edwards remembered that McDowell had paid only one call in the previous year and he thought this was just about the time Mrs. Holiday was given her White Robe (this date should be checked against Roger's interview with McDowell). Josiah Minden himself presented her with the White Robe in a ceremony at the Temple.

Whenever Minden visited, Jennifer became ecstatic.

The following is from my tape:

SMALL: I'm ashamed to say it but Mrs. Holiday acted like a young girl in love. She fluttered her eyes and wagged her curls like a schoolgirl.

MR: Her curls?

SMALL: Oh, and I forgot to tell you. On the third or fourth visit to the hospital she lost half her hair. Her face looked younger and fresher, but the poor thing only had a few thin strands on her head. She cried so hard it was pitiful.

MR: Didn't this turn her against Harmonetics?

SMALL: It surely did but only for a few days. Then Dr. Minden came and stayed with us for most of a week. He cheered her up something marvelous. She was laughing and happy, and she looked a good ten years younger in her wigs. Dr. Minden told her how lovely she looked, and it was the truth. He was closeted with her for hours at a time. I don't say anything went on but I don't say it didn't.

EDWARDS: Mrs. Small!

SMALL: Now I didn't say a thing, did I?

MR: Were there other visitors she liked as much as Minden?

SMALL: Now there was Dr. Fronzhold, he came often, and Dr. McDonald, who used to be Father Francis Xavier before he left the Church. She enjoyed seeing them. She called Dr. Fronzhold whenever she was ailing, and I must say he came over quick as he could. But for all his being a famous doctor, he never wore a jacket and tie. Imagine that, going around in an open shirt! Crazy people, they were, with their gowns and their touching each other and their raw foods. It's a wonder Cook didn't quit.

MR: Was Mrs. Holiday very sick before her last visit to the hospital?

SMALL: She was feeling well but her face and skin was not so good. In truth, she was beginning to look her age. She used creams and lotions religiously but she couldn't fight the years. Then Dr. Fronzhold came and persuaded her to go back to the hospital.

MR: Did she go voluntarily?

SMALL: Yes, but they had quite a discussion before she agreed. There was arguments back and forth for an hour. Later, when she was packing her bag, she said to me, "Mrs. Small, I hope I've made the right decision."

MR: Did you visit her in the hospital?

SMALL: I did, but each time I had an argument to get into her room. The nurses said she was not supposed to have visitors. I told them I wouldn't leave until I seen her for myself.

MR: How did she look?

SMALL: Oh, very pretty and peaceful. The first time I went she looked as well as ever, but she was so weak and tired she could hardly talk. She said she was glad she had gone and she would be home as soon as she got back her strength. The next time I visited, I had to wait over an hour to get in. The nurses said she was sleeping and I was not to make any noise. I could have set off a bomb and she wouldn't have woken, they'd given her that many drugs. I went back again a few days later and the doctor said she was very sick and couldn't have no visitors. I told him I wouldn't leave without seeing her. I did get in and the doctor was right. She was a dying woman.

MR: Was that the last time you saw her?

SMALL: Yes. She was gone the next day. It's my opinion she should never have . . .

EDWARDS: Mrs. Small!

SMALL: And what have I done now, Mr. Edwards, but tell the plain truth?

I questioned Small as to whether Mrs. Holiday had had a face lift. She said she couldn't be sure she hadn't and she couldn't be sure she had. However, she was positive that Mrs. Holiday had undergone some rejuvenation on each of her hospital stays. Small theorized that the fatal stay was caused by an overdose of rejuvenation.

The idea of excessive rejuvenation as the cause of Mrs. Holiday's death is intriguing. Could the doctors at the Harmonetics Hospital have "frozen" her, as they say is done in some weird Swiss sanatorium? There are several famous Rumanian practitioners who give "youth" injections to extremely wealthy clients. Quite a few aging jet-setters fly in and out of Bucharest for treatment. They check into a clinic for a couple of weeks and they're euphoric, albeit the same age, when they come out. No one knows what the medication is, including the patients, but they're given daily injections of Youth Serum by the Rumanian version of Dr. Feelgood. Whatever it is they take—ground peach pits or chopped monkey glands or simple amphetamine "uppers"—may not make them into teeny-boppers or transform them back a decade, but it gives them a mental lift just because they're told the medicines work.

The FDA doesn't allow untested drugs to be used in the U.S., but American gynecologists regularly shoot menopausal women with estrogen, even though estrogen is cancer-producing. The theory is that it keeps the patients from aging and it gives them a feeling of well-being. You could call that one kind of rejuvenation.

If the Harmonetics Hospital is rejuvenating some of their elderly members, they've certainly kept it a secret. I think we should look into it, specifically with regard to Mrs. Holiday. Please ask Roger to see what he can find out in his interviews.

The following information should be passed on to Harold: Jennifer Holiday's death certificate was signed by Dr. Jean de Moraille. The cause of death, according to de Moraille, was arteriosclerosis.

Excerpt from a speech by Dr. Josiah Minden
at the Astrodome
(November 5, 1981)

For hundreds of centuries leaders of various religious cults have eschewed the material world. Some of these so-called "holy fathers" or "Illustrious Ones" have been adored and canonized because they slept on the bare earth in the wind and the rain, they wore only rags or loin cloths to protect themselves from the cold, their skins were burnt from the sun, and their bodies were emaciated from fasting and dietary restrictions. Millions of men and women admired these holy men for their rejection of every pleasurable aspect of life. But was their admiration justified? The bodies of the Essenes reeked, their breath was foul, their teeth were rotten, and their bodies diseased. Their contribu-

tions to their fellowmen were nil: they did not tend the sick and dying, they did not house the orphan or the homeless and they did not feed the hungry. They were lost in the totally selfish ideal of seeking their own salvation to the utter neglect of mankind. I question whether salvation comes from ignoring the pain and the anguish of others.

The good man need not martyrize himself by starving, freezing, and maltreating his body. The good life does not require rejection of cleanliness and health. Neither does it insist that man be celibate. A healthy, happy person is much more able to succor the friendless and stretch out a hand to the hopeless.

Excessive material goods are harmful only because they become an aim in themselves. There is a golden mean where men and women are well nourished, clean, and healthy, and yet aware of the state of the less fortunate. Man cannot live unto himself like the hermits of old or the pleasure-spoiled, jaded hedonists of today. The sadness in this world comes from dedicating oneself exclusively to pleasures; happiness is born out of an active, creative life, good deeds, thoughts for others, and easing the pain of a friend or a stranger. The ethics of the Harmonetics Society are derived from what makes a man or woman a socially happy being, and so our answers are purposeful work, cleanliness and health, and consideration of our fellowmen.

Henrietta and Sarah got out of their taxi two blocks from the Harmonetics Temple. The log jam of cars made it useless to ride. Gowned Templers were alighting from limousines, cars, and buses while more emerged from the underground. Some were in mufti like Henrietta and Sarah, but the majority were in gowns. Blue was the predominant color but there were quite a few reds, a sprinkling of greens, and an occasional brown. Civilians in the midst of this religious activity felt conspicuous; gowned members were nodding and smiling at each other, making the solitary pedestrian feel isolated and sad.

Henrietta looked for familiar faces in the gowned crowd. Many men and women were her age or older, and some looked to have the same background. The guessing game of where they lived (the Shore, the Island, Brooklyn, East Broadway, Forest Hills, Bronxville, Darien, or Peter Cooper) didn't work as well when they all wore nontailored, ready-made robes. She was theorizing "Park" or "Fifth" at a sixty-year-old face when the woman addressed her:

"Henrietta Beale! Sarah Robinson! How nice to see you."

Sarah stared blankly. Henrietta evoked her warm "You look so familiar but . . ." smile, cocking her head slightly and raising her eyebrows to indicate the connection wasn't made.

"Robinin Judy," said the woman just as a taxi honked, making her words unintelligible. "I worked with you on the Children's Concert Board several years ago."

"Of course, of course," said Henrietta, still trying to place her. Who on earth could "Robinin Judy" be? "And how have you been?"

The green-robed "Robinin Judy" asked Henrietta about Elliott's state of health, whether he was still active with the Museum, how Thomas and Virginia were faring, and if Henrietta was writing as much as ever. Henrietta suddenly remembered. This was Rosalind Schulte! Ernst Schulte, her husband, was that terribly attractive man who had been active for years on the Philharmonic and Metropolitan Opera boards. Rosalind had also been musically oriented. One always saw her at Carnegie Hall or Lincoln Center, and she was generous in her invitations to teas, luncheons, and dinners to meet Leonard Bernstein, Jascha Heifitz, Van Cliburn, and Yehudi Menuhin. Then, perhaps six years ago, their lives fell apart. The *New York Times* printed the story of Ernst's speculations with trust money. He had started by taking small sums from some of the larger trusts. After several years he became less cautious, selling bonds and securities of various old ladies and using the income to install a female opera singer in a suite at the Essex House. He and the singer were arrested at Kennedy Airport on their return from a four-day pleasure trip to Acapulco. Ernst had gone to prison. Everyone felt sorry for "Poor Roz" but nobody ever saw her.

"Rosalind, where are you living these days?"

"I'm at 88th, just off the river."

"In one of those big apartment houses on East End?"

"No, a block away. I live alone so there isn't any need for a big apartment. I hardly spend any time there."

"Are you active in the Harmonetics Society?"

"Yes, it's been marvelous for me. They are wonderful people and their ideals are stimulating and beautiful."

"This will be our first visit to the Temple. Why don't you sit with Sarah and me?" Sarah gave Henrietta a negative nudge.

"Thank you, I'd love to, but I'm presenting a newcomer today so I must sit with her. When we go in I'll introduce you to one of the members who will explain the Society. If you wish, I'll meet you afterward."

"That would be so nice," said Henrietta, ignoring the furious thrusts of Sarah's elbow.

"Look for me by the table marked 'Seminar Lecture Enrollments.' Now hold on to my gown as we walk in or we'll be separated by this mob."

Men and women were streaming through the six large doors of the Temple, formerly known as the Continental Towers. It had undergone its fourth major transformation. The wide entrance hall through which the crowd was moving had been stripped of its baroque chandelier, marble tables, and Chippendale chairs. It was bare, dim, austere, and imposing with its subdued lights and thirty-five-foot ceiling. From here one walked into the Temple itself. It was the width and almost the depth of a city block. The Harmonetics Society had gutted the hotel's boutiques, cafés, bookshops, travel desks, telephone booths, beauty and barber shops, and other small shops. In their place were row after row of wooden pews. The walls, which were three stories high, were paneled in dark oak. At the far end was a large platform with a speaker's table. Several rows of chairs had been placed immediately to the rear of the table, enough to accommodate eighty people.

Men and women were finding their seats according to the color of their robes. The brown gowns were seated in the front rows. Behind them were green-robed worshipers, and further back were the reds and then the blues. The last rows were reserved for visitors. A special area near the aisle in the rear was roped off. It was filling up with pairs of robed and non-robed people of varying ages: a green-robed woman accompanied by a man in a business suit, a blue-robed man escorting a woman in a tailored outfit, a red-robed woman holding the hand of a girl in skirt and blouse.

Mrs. Schulte, acting as cicerone, escorted Henrietta and

Sarah toward a group in blue robes standing near the entry.

"I'm Rosalind Schulte," she said, extending her hand to a small, heavy-featured woman in a blue gown. "My friends are on their first visit. This is Henrietta Beale and Sarah Robinson. Will you take care of them, please? I'm making one of the presentations today."

"I'm happy to make your acquaintance," said Blue Gown in friendly fashion. "Please call me Bertha. We're on a first-name basis here." Then she guided her charges to one of the back rows and took a seat beside them. Most of the seats were already filled.

"The lectures are always interesting but today's should be particularly good because Dr. Fronzhold is speaking. There's Rosalind. She's going into the special section with her nominee. The presentations are made as soon as the lights go down, and it's quite a moving experience. Did you see that man in the brown gown who just walked by? That's State Senator Fritz Hochmann.

"The Temple holds eight thousand people but there are often more, even on weekday mornings. It's going to be jammed today. You can tell because people are already standing by the back walls. They sometimes close the doors fifteen minutes before the services start. You're lucky you came early."

"There seem to be a lot of young people in the blue-gowned rows."

"It's a welcome change from the sixties, isn't it?" said Bertha. "Dr. Minden has been lecturing a lot at the major universities and he always gets a large sympathetic crowd. Columbia and NYU are offering courses this year in Harmonetics. Last summer thousands of students signed up as volunteers. Quite different from the days of student riots and burning of draft cards and holing up in the Village to make homemade bombs. These youngsters are polite and well mannered because Dr. Minden's philosophy is based on respect for people of all ages."

"The boys are still wearing beards and long hair," remarked Sarah critically.

"Dr. Minden and Dr. Fronzhold have beards and long hair, but it gives them a gentle, philosophical look."

"Bertha, are you with the Temple full time?"

"I am now. I had a pretty good job as secretary to one of the partners at Merrill Lynch. It paid well and the work was interesting, but I wasn't getting enough out of life. I used to cry when I came home at night, and there wasn't any reason for tears. I didn't even enjoy my vacations. I was looking for something, maybe happiness, and I didn't know where to find it. Then I came to the Temple just to see what was happening. I heard Dr. Minden speak; suddenly I felt that I could contribute to the happiness of others. I stopped thinking about 'me' and I began to think about the old, the sick, and the desperate. I worked as a part-time volunteer for a few months and then I decided to make the Harmonetics Society my lifework."

"Do they pay you?"

"Yes. It's not as much as I was making at Merrill Lynch but I don't cry anymore. I'm needed in a much more important way. I can't wait to go to bed at night so I can get up early in the morning and come to work. It's exciting to be here. There's an atmosphere of great warmth among the workers, there are no rivalries, and we all try to help each other. For the first couple of months I was assigned to the Health and Body seminars, I am now at the Temple working on Visitor Orientation, and next month I could be sent to the spa or the retreat in Maine or the hospital Uptown."

Henrietta surreptitiously examined Bertha. Her skin glowed healthily and the color was ruddy. Henrietta guessed it was dewy moisturizer. The eyebrows had been done by an expert, there were small signs of oil around the eyes, and the hair glistened and shone like that of a twenty-year-old. The overall effect was non-makeup, and this could only be achieved by a brilliant makeup man. Henrietta was sure Sarah was making the same appraisal.

The lights in the Temple were dimming. Four brilliant spotlights focused on the platform. Dr. Fronzhold stood at the podium, almost a city block away from Henrietta and Sarah. Seated in the chairs closest to him were seven men and three women in white robes. The other seventy seats were empty. The organ music, one of the Bach Brandenburg Concertos, delicately faded off. The Temple was quiet as Dr. Fronzhold's vibrant voice thundered through the speakers and came through thrillingly to the back rows.

"When I trained at Bellevue Hospital thirty years ago to take my residency under Dr. Felix Goldstein, every waking hour was spent in the laboratory and the hospital. I read nothing but medical books and journals and I saw no one but patients and laboratory technicians, doctors and nurses. I had no interests other than my career and the hospital. I was living on three to five hours' sleep a night but I felt no fatigue; the excitement of the work I was doing filled every need.

"Dr. Goldstein was aware of my dedication and was concerned. It was unhealthy, he said, to devote oneself exclusively to work. One evening he insisted on taking me to the theatre. My emotions were a mixture of reluctance and excitement: I was delighted to be invited but I was afraid both of boredom and the possibility of falling asleep in public. My worries were needless. We saw Bernard Shaw's *Saint Joan*. The leading lady was a seventeen-year-old prodigy by the name of Lila La Mause. She opened the world of the theatre for me. Since then I have seldom missed her in any of her Broadway plays and I have seen all of her great movie roles—*Thunder on the Hill, The General's Wife, The Anarchist, Three Sisters,* and her most recent triumph, *The Dowager Queen*.

"Lila La Mause entered the Harmonetics Temple three years ago. She is with us to introduce seventy newcomers to our membership this afternoon. At the three services this morning, 492 newcomers were welcomed, and tonight at our evening services there will be an additional 965. Fellow Harmonetics members, Miss Lila La Mause!"

The applause was frenetic. The worshipers stood to pay tribute and pounded their palms as the white-robed, beautiful Lila La Mause extended both hands to Dr. Fronzhold. The applause continued as her hands reached up to his face and his extended down to hers in the symbolic greeting of Society members. They stood motionless, her head raised toward his, then they moved together, bodies touching, her arms encircling his neck, his entwining around her back. The applause continued until they slowly drew apart.

"Thank you, good friends," said Lila La Mause. "I am honored to have been asked to welcome the new members into the Harmonetics Temple. As I read your names, will the Presenter and the Newcomer please walk down the aisles." She paused climactically, waiting for the coughing and whispering to stop. "Juan Cortez, presented by Maria Felicita Ramon," she said. "Billie Jo Sampson, presented by Maybelle Washington . . . Anna McKenzie, presented by Maureen McKenzie . . . Charlene Farber, presented by Sandra Sakowski."

Lila spoke the names as though these were the characters in a powerful drama and this was the most significant scene. Juan Cortez and Maria Felicita Ramon, Billie Jo Sampson and Maybelle Washington, Anna McKenzie and her daughter Maureen moved out of the roped-off section in the rear and walked hand in hand down the three long aisles. They were followed by other twosomes, some of the newcomers weeping or trembling, many smiling joyfully or nervously. They marched slowly down the aisles and ascended the platform where the white-robed disciples assisted them into their blue robes. They moved in single file to the wooden folding chairs reserved for them while the presenters returned to their seats.

"Today," said Lila, "a small number of our members are moving into a higher rank of responsibility and achievement. They have earned their colors by dedicated work, by newly acquired knowledge, and by compassion. Will the ushers please open the rear portals and will all of you remain seated, please." Another pause, then she called out the names: "Jacqueline Reynolds, Herbert Stalling, Andrew Goodfriend, Mary Mellone . . ."

Two women and three men in brown robes came through the lobby doors and walked down the two far aisles until they reached their allotted places at the far walls nearest the platform. Lila La Mause continued to read in resonant, vibrant tones.

"Slovacek, Conti, Smoot, Goepfert, Krishnan, El Mootaz, Navarro, Knebel, Philpott, Matsuoka . . ."

Sixty men and women in green robes marched in two columns down the side aisles toward the front, taking their positions by the walls immediately behind the five brown-robed men and women. There was a short pause to allow the acolytes time to form a straight line. The doors opened again and several hundred men and women in red robes walked proudly to their allotted posts.

"Rejmaniak, Searle, Contreras, Hobson, Malveaux, Harada, Reilly, San Miguel . . ."

There were whispers from spectators who identified friends or relatives, the spectators sharing in the excitement of knowing an honoree. When the last woman took her post by the wall, the audience applauded with the enthusiasm of those who might soon be so honored themselves.

Dr. Fronzhold returned to the center of the podium to address the gathering. He spoke about the advances in medicine and the number of outstanding doctors affiliated with the Harmonetics Hospital, the Harmonetics Sanatorium, the Harmonetics Health Spa, and the Harmonetics Body Clinic. He warned his audience against self-diagnosis, the risks that came through neglecting annual checkups, the harm done by well-meaning people who fed aspirin or other pain-killers to members of their family or who dosed themselves with sleeping pills, muscle relaxers, inhalants, cough medicines, or home remedies. A layman, he emphasized, cannot accurately diagnose the flu or a stomach upset or indigestion; it could well be the onset of pneumonia, appendicitis, or a coronary. A patient with continued migraine might be suffering from a thrombosis, a blood clot, a tumor, all of which could quickly be spotted and alleviated by the clinics. Prevention, said Dr. Fronzhold, was the strongest asset of the medical profession. Heart attacks could be forestalled by proper diet, tumors could be diagnosed and excised before they became malignant, the amount of exercise a person should take could be determined by a simple series of tests. Anyone who failed to have an annual electrocardiogram, chest X ray, proctoscopy, blood tests, and urinalysis, not to mention skin, ear-nose-and-throat, and eye examinations, was risking ten, twenty, or even forty years of his life.

Dr. Fronzhold told of the loving family that insisted on taking care of their ailing father. They made mistakes in following the prescribed diet, they thought there was no harm in allowing him an occasional drink, and they believed love would compensate for their lack of skill in professional health care. Had they brought their father to the hospital, he would have received the best possible medical attention. The course of the disease would have been followed with scrupulous care by the Harmonetics corps of nurses, lab technicians, and physicians. To leave the ill at home, said Fronzhold, was to issue an early death warrant.

"Occasionally a patient is ready to move onward," said

Fronzhold, his voice ringing through the auditorium. "When this occurs, we have a trained staff who will make the passing an easy transition. Every comfort, physical and spiritual, is given to the sick one. The volunteers who assist in this program have taken a minimum of three seminars under the tutelage of our psychiatrists and nurses. They are taught the ways in which one can bring peace and a calm spirit to those who will soon be entering a new world. This simply cannot be done by a member of the family, no matter how devoted he or she may be. The beloved one who is critically ill requires a type of care beyond the capacities of the layman; this can only be given at our trained centers. However, all of you, I am sure, have many more years of enjoyment and pleasure in this world. We are here to see these years are disease-free and pain-free, and to keep you young in body as well as in spirit.

"We have astounded the medical world by the health, energy, and youthful appearance of members of the Harmonetics Society. Our brothers and sisters who are in their sixties look ten to twenty years younger; those in their seventies and eighties are physically and mentally active and alert; the young people who have joined us will remain young for many, many years. We are grateful to Dr. Josiah Minden who made it possible for my colleagues and me to serve you.

"And now, brothers and sisters, the members seated on the aisle will pass envelopes to all of you. Please write your name on the outside and place your contribution inside. Your gift makes possible the diagnosis and treatment of those of you who could otherwise not afford the health, body, and beauty care of our great hospitals, clinics, and spas. Please be generous. Mark the amount of your gift on the outside of the envelope and print your name legibly. Don't be ashamed if your contribution is not as large as that of your neighbor. Every $5 and $10 we receive will help to relieve the sufferings of others. I repeat: don't feel reluctant to sign your name if your contribution is small. I assure you your gift is welcome.

"Brothers and sisters, I thank you."

The envelopes were passed from Bertha to Henrietta to Sarah and on down the row. Bertha's contribution was $5. Sarah paused, then pulled out two crisp $50 bills. She wrote her address as well as her name on the envelope. Henrietta considered alternatives. Harding might object to the size of her contribution but he wanted action, and this was one way to get it. She took out her checkbook and filled in the amount: $500. On the outside of her envelope she wrote: "My accountant will want to know if this contribution and any others will be tax deductible. Please send such information to me at the address printed on my check."

Sarah and Henrietta thanked Bertha, then moved slowly with the crowd toward the exits. Side doors had been opened, the overhead lights were shining brightly again, and the faint strains of Bach could be heard over the noise of the crowd. They met Rosalind at the Seminar Lecture Enrollments table.

"The seats we had were absolutely dreadful," said Sarah. "Dr. Fronzhold was a tiny little blur. I wouldn't dream of coming back if I had to sit in a back row again."

Rosalind smiled. "If you want to see Dr. Fronzhold close up, you can take one of his medical seminars. They run for three evenings, two hours per session, and the seminar is limited to twenty people."

"Yes, I might sign up for that," said Sarah.

"It's $1,000 a person."

"What! That's an outrage!"

"It's high," explained Rosalind, "but it's Dr. Fronzhold's way of raising money for his research groups. The seminars are almost always filled. Besides, you get fifteen minutes of private conference with him, and I know one woman who says he is positively inspirational. That's Clarissa Kent. I'm sure you know her."

"Clarissa of all people," exclaimed Sarah. "I would think Byron would toss her out of the house for throwing her money away like that."

"Didn't you know, Sarah? Byron Kent was given his White Robe by Dr. Minden two months ago."

"Byron in Harmonetics? That's impossible. He's been wrapped up in copper mines and coal mergers for thirty years. I've had them at my house several times, and although Clarissa is perfectly adorable, Byron is intolerable. He doesn't open his mouth all evening unless someone mentions the Alaska pipeline or Arthur D. Little or the dividends Bethlehem Steel is declaring."

"Byron has been most supportive of Harmonetics for at least two years," said Rosalind. "He is very close with the inner group, and Clarissa is now a Brown Gown."

"How does a woman get to be promoted to a green gown or a brown gown?" asked Henrietta.

"Promotions are based on many factors—understanding the principles of the Society, volunteer work, bringing in new members, attendance at seminars, the number of hours one gives, and one's contributions. The contributions aren't all that important."

"Don't tell me Clarissa didn't 'buy' her Brown Robe," said Sarah spitefully. "I wouldn't say a word against her, but Clarissa has always thrown her money around. She gets whatever she wants, even though Byron screams at her extravagance."

"You wouldn't know Clarissa today," said Rosalind quietly. "She may be a heavy donor but she is also an exceptionally hard worker. She's now on Dr. Fronzhold's personal staff. In fact, if you want to get into one of his seminars, you would have to go through Clarissa. She's devoted to the doctor."

Henrietta knew what Sarah's next retort would be: "I would be devoted to Dr. Fronzhold too if I were married to Byron."

Henrietta inquired about some of the seminars. The prices ranged from $350 to $2,000 (three days, two hours a day, with Dr. Minden, including fifteen minutes of private conference). Henrietta hesitated.

"Rosalind, I want to think about it. I would like to get the literature and see what it's all about. I don't want to enroll in any courses I won't enjoy or that I'm not ready for."

"Of course, take your time. Joining the Society is a major decision and it will affect your whole life-style. You must have attended a week of lectures and you have to take both the Psychological and Aptitude tests to be a probationary Blue Robe. Then, after you have contributed at least one hundred hours of volunteer work, you can be proposed as a member, which means you would receive a permanent Blue Robe. You saw the ceremony today. It involves a lifetime commitment so no one should take it lightly. You can still take seminar courses without joining. We do have people who visit occasionally because they enjoy the Temple and the lectures, but they have not yet elected to join."

"Has anyone joined and then dropped out?"

"I'm sure there must be some but I would think the number is extremely small. That's why the initiation period was made so long. Additionally, a member in good standing must be your counselor, and this member proposes you when it is deemed you are physically and mentally prepared. I would like to offer myself as counselor, Henrietta, but you know Clarissa Kent and of course you have a number of other good friends who are members. I'm sure any one of them would be delighted to sponsor you. Meanwhile, here's my telephone number. Call me if I can be of help, and thank you, Henrietta, for being so gentle. Thank you also, Sarah," said Rosalind with only slightly less warmth.

Henrietta gave her friend a kiss. Sarah followed with a more perfunctory buss.

Excerpt from "Harmonetics Report" by Jade Boren.
Sources: Back issues of the *New York Times, Newsweek* Cover Story on Josiah Minden, Professor Mark John Anderson, Minnie Matthews, and Marilyn McLeod

No one who knew Josiah Minden as a young boy has come forward with much information other than vital statistics. According to his birth certificate, he was born in Chicago sixty years ago; according to those who have seen him, he couldn't be more than forty or, at most, forty-five. Pictures of him as he is today have been shown to fellow pupils at the public schools he attended. *Newsweek* quoted several elderly people as saying, "That kind of looks like him" or "I guess that's Minden but I don't really remember." He didn't leave a clear impression on anyone. No one could say whether he was a good student or a bad one. A couple of old-time school jocks were sure he had not played for any of the teams. The school records of forty-five years ago have disappeared. As far as is known, he has no living relatives. The birth certificate states the mother, Carmina Pinterella Minden, was forty-two years old at the time of

Josiah's birth. His father, Jesse Minden, was thirty-six. There is no record at the FBI of any fingerprints and he has never been investigated.

There is a blank period in Minden's life of approximately twenty-five years. Josiah has said he was a traveling student of comparative religion. He has never gone into detail other than to state that he lived among the Buddhist priests and the gurus in India, he sat at the feet of the lamas in Tibet, and he spent several years in Moslem countries where he studied Mohammedan precepts. When he returned to the United States, he took a variety of odd jobs. He dug ditches, ran a tractor, and worked on an oil rig. He frequently preaches the rewards of manual labor but he has never identified a specific employer nor is there anyone who remembers hiring him.

The first verified employment of Minden goes back eighteen years when he was appointed an Instructor in Religion at the Christian Theology College of Branton. The school, which was a small one (the maximum number of students per semester was less than two hundred), has not been in existence for the last ten years. Minden was appointed Assistant Professor, then Associate Professor, while working for his Ph.D. in Religion. He earned his doctorate fourteen years ago. His thesis, according to Minden, was on "Ecstasy as a Religious Phenomenon."

Twelve years ago Minden was appointed Dean of the School of Comparative Religion at Mount Saint Joseph University in Houston. A great many students and former colleagues remember him. He taught two courses, both of which were heavily attended. He was friendly, good-humored, and often light-hearted. His closest friend was another Professor of Religion, Mark John Anderson. Mark John, as he is called, says Minden seldom talked about himself; in fact, he never discussed his background. Minden occasionally dated but he had no special girl. During the six years that Minden was at Mount Saint Joseph, he was dedicated to physical fitness: he jogged regularly, swam twenty lengths of the pool each day, and played tennis. Mark John regularly jogged with him and irregularly played tennis with him (Minden, he says, was too good).

Seven years ago Minden began lecturing to clubs and groups in Houston. His outside contacts were enlarged and his popularity grew, much of which was due to a rich, cheerful dowager named Minnie Matthews. Minnie had given generously to many civic organizations in Houston, and she sponsored Josiah in a businesslike way: she took full-page ads in the Houston *Post* and the *Chronicle* to publicize his self-help lectures. At first Minnie hired a hall for Minden; when he outgrew the hall, she built him a temple.

Mark John says Josiah was never a religious fanatic: he was interested in the effect of religious beliefs on people. His public lectures were on philosophic ideas (the need for goals, disciplines, and a positive attitude toward one's fellowman), mental health, personality development, and physical fitness.

During the first year of his full-time lecture series, Minden paid $17,000 in income taxes. *Newsweek* got this information from a reliable government source. The second year he incorporated the lecture series into a tax-deductible, nonprofit association called the Harmonetics Society. Minden hired a full-time assistant, Marilyn McLeod, to handle the books. She received a salary of $5,000 a year while Minden's stipend was $18,000. Income to the Society that year was over $700,000, approximately $400,000 of which was earmarked for expenses (mortgage payments on the Temple, travel, TV and newspaper advertising, equipment, etc.). The remaining $300,000 was contributed to medical research and to seven different hospitals. The director of one of the hospitals was Dr. Fronzhold.

The second year Marilyn was given a $1,000 raise, which she thought was more than adequate, considering the fact that she was fifty-eight and had not been employed for the last fourteen years. Additionally, she explained, the Harmonetics Society was an eleemosynary institution. Several dozen volunteers assisted her, a few of whom, she said, were of great help in answering the phones, acknowledging contributions, organizing occasional social affairs, etc.

Minden broadened the scope of the Harmonetics Society that year. He bought fifty acres of beautiful wooded property off Highway 59, some twenty minutes from Houston. This was the site of a large modern clinic surrounded by several hundred inexpensive bungalows. It was dedicated to what Josiah called "the unjustly named 'elderly.'" Dr. Fronzhold was named head of the new facility. Most of the bungalows were sold before the project was completed. The purchasers were the elderly or younger people who were buying cottages for their aging parents. The staff members were of all ages but many were over sixty-five. The majority were volunteers; a few were paid by the hour or the week.

Marilyn is unable to estimate income during the second year. The growth of the Society was so sudden that the financial affairs were put into the hands of accountants who worked directly for Minden. She thinks $5 million came in, most of which went into the Harmonetics Sanatorium in Houston. She believes a small portion went toward the purchase of acreage in Arizona where a new Harmonetics Health Center was to be built. By the third year Minden was spending most of his time in other cities and was in Houston only six or eight weeks.

Marilyn says Dr. Minden is "a wonderful man." She only sees him on special occasions these days, but whenever he is in Houston, he will pick up the phone and call her. He likes to reminisce about the old days. Marilyn gets weepy when she recalls how Minden invited her to sit on the dais when he lectured at the Astrodome. He sent a chauffeur and car to pick her up. He spoke on the origins of the Harmonetics movement and then introduced her to the 45,000 people present. It was the first time she wore the Blue Gown.

Mark John does not see Josiah anymore. He says Minden was always "a nice guy" and he is amazed by his success. He refuses to comment on the Harmonetics Society but says "it probably does a lot of good."

Minnie Matthews is still an active Minden supporter. She is, of course, one of the twenty-five people in the country who were given the White Robe by Josiah. He stays with her on many of his Houston visits and she loves to throw big parties for him. She says:

"He calls me long distance and tells me to send Louise or Barbara to the farmers' market to buy all the fruits and vegetables in sight. Then I ask him when he's coming in and he says, 'Tomorrow.' He loves it when I have my friends over for a big bash, and they love him as much as I do. He's a warm, good man with the right ideas on living."

I have not yet seen Josiah Minden in person and I can only comment on reproductions in the newspapers and magazines and his appearances on the tube. He has either bribed every photographer and TV cameraman in the world or he is an absolutely gorgeous hunk of man.

Excerpt from a seminar lecture
by Dr. Francis X. McDonald
(January 1979)

During the past year the Harmonetics Society has provided free health care for 243,000 people. Another 476,000 have received medical services at partial cost only: in many cases their X rays or hospital stay or surgery were gratis. The average charge at a private hospital would have been $4,690 per person: many underwent four or five operations, some remained hospitalized for two months or more, and quite a few required the services of three or more specialists (diagnosticians, surgeons, anesthetists, therapists, and psychiatrists). In no case was any patient receiving free care given less than the best in treatment. The total amount spent in medical care by the Society was over $2 billion.

In each of the major cities of the United States the Harmonetics Society has sought to establish a Temple, a Health Care Center, and a hospital. In some cases these hospitals are small (sixty or eighty beds only), but the generous contributions of the members—particularly those who wear the Brown Robes— have made it possible to plan for Temples that will give succor to many more brothers and sisters, as well as hospitals large enough to offer preventive health care, physical fitness programs, and psychiatric aid. We consider the mentally ill to be particularly important, and we have made monumental strides in helping these desperate people adapt to society.

Most of you have been unqualifiedly generous in opening your purses to Harmonetics. Some of you would like to give more but you are not certain how it can be done. We have had saintly men and women who have literally opened their vaults and turned over their bank accounts to the Society. Such generosity is rare and such members will have their names inscribed on the rolls in perpetuity. Many of you do not know how much you should give. We have counselors who will help you. They will spend an hour with you, or a day if necessary, to help you arrange a systematic method of giving. You may meet with them as many times as you wish. They are on call when you need them. These counselors are the most respected members of the Temple, many of them being recognized financial experts.

The art of living is the art of giving. The accumulation of needless possessions, the oversatiation of our hungers, the excessive furbelows of clothes and home make us soft of body, sterile of spirit, and weak of mind.

The counselors are here today, and I hope each one of you will work with them on your contributions to Harmonetics.

Telephone Conversation

"Arnie, it's Jade."

"What's happening?"

"Nothing new. I have to go to my mom's for dinner tonight."

"How is she?"

"Don't know. I haven't seen her since I went to Chicago. Did I tell you she's into Harmonetics?"

"Yes."

"Remember two years ago when anyone walking down the street in a gown looked like a freak?"

"Remember ten years ago when anyone carrying a tennis racket looked like a jerk?"

"I walked by the Harmonetics Temple today and it was like the week before Christmas at Bloomingdale's. Have you ever been to the Temple?"

"Me?"

"Why don't we go there sometime to see what it's like?"

"Are you serious?"

"We could take your mother with us. She might enjoy it."

"She'd hate it."

"She doesn't have any friends. She could become a volunteer and it would keep her busy. There are lots of people there who are sickly, and she could exchange symptoms. Why don't you ask her?"

"No, thanks."

"You sound turned off on the Society. Aren't you curious? If you knew someone who was a member, you might feel differently. Aren't any of the circuit players into it?"

"I heard Perkins and Tyler had joined. Perkins went through est a couple of years ago and last year he was wearing an 'I Love Jesus' button. Tyler was reborn at the same time. After he beat Perkins at Wimbledon he said God had guided his racket."

"How about the women players?"

"How the hell would I know what they're doing? I hate women's tennis."

"But you love me."

"I love you, ergo I love women's tennis, and I want my mother to join the Harmonetics Society so she can crap around with the other old broads."

"Arnie, be helpful. Don't any of the players at the Midtown go to the Temple?"

"Yeah, one of your dotty girl friends, Beth Marple."

"You mean Beth is wearing a gown? Then why did she get a Ph.D. in Psychology? Is she out of a job? How could she, of all people, be into Harmonetics?"

"She doesn't wear a gown. She wears the open white shirt, which means she works there. She talked poor old Henry into visiting the Psychiatric Department at the Harmonetics Hospital. I think they locked him up after a couple of visits. She thinks everyone should take aptitude and psychological tests, particularly me."

"She's a bit patronizing toward the little people who don't have their doctorates."

"I thought she was your big buddy."

"We were pretty close in the Juniors. We were once ranked No. 4 nationally in the 18 Doubles."

"Do I have to hear all that crap about what a great player you were?"

"Baby, don't put it in the past tense. Are."

"Why don't you call your nutty friend and ask her to take you to the Harmonetics Temple? Then she can give you some psychological tests and after that you can work up a doubles."

"Very, very funny. Arnie, do you love me?"

"Do I ever ask you if you love me?"

"I do love you."

"Okay, okay. I love you too."

Telephone Conversation

"Beth, this is Jade."

"What a nice surprise. I've been meaning to call you for months. How have you been?"

"I've been traveling some but I'm back. I was in Chicago last month and played almost every day."

"How are you hitting 'em?"

"Not bad. A few in, a few out, but I'm running better."

"Let's see, I usually play Carol Haver on Tuesdays but she's got a bad tennis elbow. I can get a court tomorrow at Midtown at 7:00 A.M. Do you want to play?"

"Seven A.M.!"

"I have to play early because I'm on duty at the hospital at 9:00."

"What hospital?"

"Harmonetics, uptown."

"Now isn't that a coincidence."

"What is?"

"My mom has been bugging me to do some work there. What's it like?"

"Magnificent. It's a thoroughly modern institution, bright and well designed, and some of the best brains in the country have been brought in."

"What do you do there?"

"Lots, which is what makes it so fascinating. I was primarily in psychological testing and aptitude skills but Dr. Jennings, who's the Chief of Psychiatrics, has been letting me do pre- and post-shock treatment tests. Jennings is brilliant. She has one of the best minds in the field."

"Are you a Blue Gown?"

"Jade, you're so naïve. I'm Staff. The Blue Gowns are volunteers."

"My mom would faint if I ever got my Blue."

"Have you visited the Temple yet?"

"Yes, a bunch of times, but I haven't got around to enrolling. I'm not sure it's for me."

"How will you know if you don't try it?"

"I guess you're right."

"Let's play tennis tomorrow morning, then I'll take you with me to the hospital and introduce you to everyone. Then we can enroll you."

"Would I be in the Psychology Department?"

"You're untrained, Jade. The first thing we'll do is give you the aptitude tests. Then we will know where you will be most useful."

"Couldn't I just tell you what I do well?"

"The aptitude tests are extremely accurate. For example, you may think you are an objective person but the tests may show you are highly subjective. Just leave it to us. The aptitudes take two days. You have to pay in advance so be sure to bring $350."

"Three hundred and fifty dollars!"

"It's worth it. You'll learn a great deal about yourself."

"Well, I'm not sure."

"Jade, I'll see you tomorrow at 7:00."

Telephone Conversation

"Mom, I'm going to be a little late."

"Jade, you can't. Get into a cab immediately."

"But I have to . . ."

"Dr. Josiah Minden is coming."

"Yes, Mom."

Jade walked out of the apartment to look for a taxi.

"Let me help you," said the doorman, taking out his whistle and tooting a couple of times down the deserted street.

"Thank you, John. I'm going to my mother's to meet Dr. Josiah Minden."

"Dr. Minden!" said John, then tooted his whistle as loudly as he could.

"Tomorrow's a big day for me too, John. I start work at the Harmonetics Hospital."

"You know Mrs. Randolph in 6E? She's a member. So are Mr. and Mrs. Margolies in 9C. And that quiet little miss on the third floor, Barbara Bittings, she wears her gown all the time. She goes out in the morning at 8:00 and she's not home until 7:00 or 8:00 in the evening. She must be very religious."

"John, there's an empty cab!"

John didn't hear her. "Speak of the devil and here she comes herself. Good evening, Mrs. Randolph."

The tall, thin woman in the green robe smiled and nodded at the doorman.

"Mrs. Randolph, I'm Jade Boren in 18C. I've been wanting to meet you for a long time. I'm a Probationary at the Harmonetics Hospital."

"How very nice to see you," said Mrs. Randolph, extending both hands and beaming at her.

"Thank you," said Jade, extending her hands in return. Mrs. Randolph clasped them, then raised her hands to Jade's cheeks. The cold fingers felt surprisingly gentle but Jade was uncomfortable with the unaccustomed display of familiarity from a stranger. Jade touched the gaunt cheeks and focused on the older woman's smiling eyes. Next, she knew, the stranger's hands would come down on her shoulders. I hope to hell she doesn't hug me, thought Jade, but if she does I'll goddamn hug her back.

"I've got your taxi," yelled John. She could have kissed him. The ceremonial greeting with Mrs. Randolph was aborted before its climax.

The taxi drove off and John opened the lobby door for Mrs. Randolph.

"That's Jade Boren, 18C. She's going to her mother's to meet Dr. Josiah Minden."

Mrs. Randolph turned around to get a last look at the taxi.

Jade arrived at the Berington on 73rd Street and Central Park West fifteen minutes later. This was where she had been raised. Her mother refused to move from the Berington because the rooms were so large, the ceilings so high, and the rent so low. For the same price as they paid for a duplex here, they could only get four small rooms on Fifth. For years Jade had taken the bus to 86th, then transferred to the crosstown so she could get to the Dalton School on East 89th. She was one of the few West Siders who attended Dalton, a school that attracted the children of playwrights, psychiatrists, lawyers, actors, and successful businessmen. After her graduation she went to Radcliffe and thereafter she came home only for occasional holidays. She enjoyed the visits home because she loved the two-story living room with its French reproductions and the enormous terrace that no one ever used, but most of all she adored her large bedroom with the familiar wallpaper, the corny Gainsborough prints, and the bookcases filled with Grimm's, Andersen, the Blue Fairy Tales, *Winnie the Pooh*, The Rover Boys, Algebra I, Latin II, yearbooks, camp songs, and the scrapbook of clippings on Jade's tennis career as a Promising Junior, as collated by her mother.

When she was a block from the Berington Jade could see the crowd. Thirty or forty people were examining the $90,000 Rolls-Royce parked in front of the building. They were peeking in the windows, staring at the chauffeur, and commenting on the beige exterior, the three antennae, and the license plate that bore only the letter **M**. They had all seen a Rolls before but this one had a partition for the chauffeur, the passenger area was paneled in rich cherry wood, and inside one could see the cabinetry, the desk with telephone, and the contour tufted seats. When Jade got out of the cab, the doorman nodded toward the Rolls and said in a stage whisper:

"Dr. Josiah Minden's car. He's in your mother's apartment."

The pedestrians no longer stared at the Rolls. They looked at Jade. People who were raised on the West Side appraised neighbors and strangers openly. They examined the cripple to see if the leg had been amputated at the knee or the upper thigh. They checked out the mink coat Mrs. Schmidt was wearing for color, workmanship, and wear. They noticed the Florida tan of Mr. Goldfarb and the pale countenance of Mrs. Boyle. They would show the same inquisitiveness toward a diamond bracelet in a showcase or a negligee in a department store window. On the East Side one immediately averted one's eyes when the object of the stare caught one in the act. Jade was a native West Sider. She imagined the pleasure she would have given herself and the spectators had she stopped to address them.

She made no speech. Neither did she walk to the elevator like the highly private East Sider shielded from the stares of the proletariat by imaginary blinders. She stared back at the curious who were enjoying their vicarious contact with a person who knew a person who knew a person. They were figures out of her childhood: the overweight grandmother in shapeless clothes who lived at no charge in the maid's room of her son-in-law's apartment; the overdressed, bleached, teased, powdered, and rouged wife of a rich entrepreneur; the skinny, shabby, stooped uncle wearing the fifteen-year-old Brooks Brothers suit generously given to him by his nephew or his brother; the buxom, glittering girl friend of the mousy little guy on Wall Street who was worth $200 million; the retired businessman who had been running to fat for forty years and who had nowhere to go but Schrafft's and the movies; the two pimply fourteen-year-olds who had just spent their $5 allowance on mascara, a hard-porn paperback, and a purse from Woolworth's. They were the people in Technicolor—brassy, flashy, and fleshy, garrulous, argumentative, and rude, dissatisfied and querulous. They could never be described as washed out, bland, and anemic, intolerable to their inferiors and abominably submissive to their superiors, like the majority of the "slightly fashionable" set from the East Side.

As Jade was lofted in the elevator to her mother's floor, the elderly elevator man gave her his brief impressions of Dr. Minden: he was a charming man, he smiled like a regular guy, and he said "Good evening" like he meant "I hope you have a *very* good evening."

Jade stood at her mother's front door. On the elaborate reproduction Chippendale table that had been in the family for thirty years was her mother's newest acquisition, a monstrous Chinese urn that Mrs. Boren called "my fourteenth-century Ming." Jade pressed the familiar doorbell, which was answered by Trudy.

"Liebschen," said Trudy loudly, hugging Jade, "why do you stay away so long? Your mother worries. Look how thin you are."

"You look marvelous," said Jade to Trudy, who was busting out of her uniform.

"Jade, my baby," exclaimed Mrs. Boren dramatically, crossing the hallway to wrap her child in her large arms. Jade's mother was a vibrant woman, statuesque, a mixture of East and West Side. Her manner was flamboyant and her gestures grandiose. As she kissed and petted her daughter, Mrs. Boren tried to disengage Jade from her tweed poncho. "Quick, Trudy, put this away."

Jade was aware of the man immediately. He was standing twenty feet away, watching the scene. She felt panic, exhilaration, dread. This was nonsense. She was behaving like a child, as though this man were the President of the United States or the Prime Minister of England. She felt her face flush and her hands tremble. It must be because Dr. Minden exemplified power. He controlled the minds of two million people. She wanted to postpone the moment when she had to face him so she could get her pulse and breathing under control.

"Mom, you have your Brown Robe. I'm so happy for you."

"It was given to me personally by Dr. Minden tonight."

Mrs. Boren took Jade's hand and guided her toward the man.

How attractive he is, thought Jade. He's smiling as though he'd like to know me better.

"Jade, I'm glad you could make it. Your mother says you are a brilliant writer, a championship tennis player, immensely creative, and outrageously amusing. Is that true?"

He couldn't be sixty. He's got the spark of a man in his thirties. Not a gray hair in that silky beard or that lovely mane.

"Mom never exaggerates. It is the indubitable truth."

Dr. Minden moved close enough to stroke her. He was smiling because she pleased him.

"Let's celebrate our first meeting, Jade, with something special."

"That's a great idea. I'd love a glass of white wine."

"A drink!" said her mother indignantly.

"Roberta, this is a special night," said Minden. "I promise not to tell anyone in the Harmonetics Society if we open a bottle and have a nip."

Minden threw an arm around Mrs. Boren, smiling like a conspirator.

"Trudy," said Mrs. Boren, "I think we have one bottle of wine. Will you open it, please, and bring in some ice if it isn't chilled."

"Good for you, Mom. We can all get bombed," and Jade turned around again to look at Dr. Minden.

"I hear you want to know more about Harmonetics," said Minden.

"I'm getting more interested all the time," said Jade, giving him the look she generally reserved for Arnie.

"And what areas appeal to you most?"

"I'm looking at him."

Minden laughed. "Your mother said you were direct. Did you get this from her?"

"No, I picked up this particular quality when I was eighteen and discovered men."

The tone of the conversation and the exchange of looks were unmistakable, but Mrs. Boren, witness to the contretemps, was oblivious.

"Josiah, I'm delighted you and Jade are getting along so well. I wish I could get you to change your mind and stay for dinner."

"I can't. I must be at a meeting but I would like to stay five minutes more to get to know Jade better."

I'd give you the whole evening, thought Jade. That open white shirt was made for your coloring. Forgive me, Arnie, but this is business.

Minden took Jade's arm and led her to a couch. He sat down next to her, his knee brushing against hers. Trudy gave them their wine glasses and they sipped, staring at each other.

"What do I call you?" Jade asked.

"Josiah." He put down his wine glass and stroked her arm gently, then pressed it and stroked her again.

"That's nice," she said, responding to the gesture. Mom's standing there and doesn't know we're telling each other we want to go to bed.

His hand touched her cheek. To Mrs. Boren, this was the customary Harmonetics greeting. She was pleased that Josiah Minden liked her child and that Jade was responding so warmly.

"I'm a Probationary at the hospital," said Jade. "For the next few days I'll be with Beth Marple in Psychological Testing. Do you ever go there?"

"I've only been there occasionally in the last few months, but now there's a reason to go more often." He was touching her again.

"Hospital duties get more attractive with each sentence," she said, feeling the traveling warmth of his hand on her own.

"My dear Jade, I wish I could stay with you longer." He stood up and offered his hands to her. She rose, her eyes never leaving his face, her hands in his. He touched her arms, her shoulders, and her face. She caressed his arms, then touched his face with her fingers. They moved together. Her cheek was on his and she smelled the faint perfume of his clean, healthy skin. She turned slightly and their lips touched. His arms were around her waist and their bodies pressed together. He was hard, aroused, and muscular. She brushed her lips against his, then dropped her arms and pulled away.

I won't lose my perspective, thought Jade, but I surely won't be assigned to scrubbing floors.

"My husband will be here any minute," said Mrs. Boren. "I wish you would talk to him about Harmonetics. He won't listen to me and he refuses to go to the Temple."

"He needs time. Let's not press him. One of these days he may want to find out more about us and then we can help him. We aren't looking for converts."

Not converts, just conquests, Josiah. You have two million converts and you'd like to see ten million or twenty million. I won't be one of them. I've always been susceptible to charm but I've never been a believer.

"Yes, Dad needs time but I'm sure he'll come around. He's a reasonable man," said Jade supportingly.

"Your father is quite unreasonable when it comes to the Society. Isn't it nice, Josiah, to see Jade involved?"

"And I'll try to get her involved even more," said Dr. Minden, eyeing Jade. "Roberta, I was glad to bring you your gown in person. Thank you for the wine and we'll see you at the Temple."

He put his arms around Roberta Boren, who responded with a motherly squeeze. Then he lifted Jade's chin and kissed her gently on the lips. His mouth brushed her hair and he whispered, "I'll call you, Jade, dear."

When the door closed behind him, Jade turned to her mother.

"What's he like, Mom? Do you know him well?"

"I've heard him lecture many times and I've talked to him personally at the Temple. This is his second visit to the apartment. He's always warm and interested. He wants to know what I'm doing and he's so gentle with his advice."

"How did you earn your Brown Gown, Mom?"

"It's the highest step in the progression toward achieving the Harmonetics spirit."

"In other words if I study and visit the Temple regularly, I could also earn a Brown Gown?"

"You're too young, Jade."

"I thought age didn't matter."

"Maturity does. You're not yet old enough to give what I give."

"You mean financially?"

"I don't like the way you're talking. Don't be flip with me. This is not a fund-raising organization. Anyone who wants to make a donation can do so but it is not a necessity."

"But you do give a lot of money to the Society?"

"That's not for you to know. I don't want to discuss it. I've already heard too much on the subject from your father."

"Does he think you're contributing too much?"

"The subject is closed, Jade."

Jade was quiet. Then her mother reached over and took her hand, squeezing it.

"You're a dear, sweet daughter and you have made me very happy by your interest in Harmonetics. The people at the Temple will stimulate and guide you into proper directions. You need only guidance, Jade, to be fulfilled."

They heard the familiar sound of a key in a lock, then the slam of a door. Mr. Boren came in, saw Jade, and gave her a bear hug. He was not a big man, perhaps 5'7", but he carried himself like 6'2". He looked at his 5'9" wife, then said in exasperation:

"So you went ahead and got your Brown Gown! I thought you said the check you gave last month was to be the last one. May I, as your husband, be permitted to ask you how much you withdrew from our bank account?"

"Not one penny," replied Roberta. "I said I wouldn't touch your money and I haven't."

"You must have given them something. These Harmonetics people are a bunch of gangsters. They've squeezed you, Roberta, for almost two years. I'm positive they wouldn't have given you the Brown Gown just for going to the Temple and nominating new members. You might as well tell me now since I'll find out sooner or later."

"Are my clothes my own?" asked Mrs. Boren defiantly.

"Of course they are."

"And my jewelry?"

"My God, Roberta, did you give them your jewels?"

"I don't need jewelry anymore. I gave up that sort of thing months and months ago. It's useless and pretentious and it's mine to give."

Jade and her father stared at each other.

"Don't look so shocked, Alfred. You refuse to go to the Temple and you don't have any understanding of the principles of the Society. They provide health care and treatments for the needy and their doors are open to everyone. They are the most selfless, saintly people on earth and I am proud to be one of them. My generosity is small compared to what Harmonetics gives."

"The thousands of dollars you have given away, Roberta, have provided the Rolls-Royce that was downstairs for your wonderful, sensitive Dr. Minden. Yes, the doorman told me all about it. I know he was here today."

"Josiah Minden is a splendid, dedicated man, a saint."

"He's a miserable little con man who has three Rolls-Royces, a half-dozen homes, a couple of airplanes, and enough property to make him one of the biggest landlords in the city."

Roberta Boren began to weep. Alfred was helpless. Jade was mute. They all made an effort to control their emotions but the exchange had been too sharp. Mrs. Boren was wounded and Mr. Boren was horrified. Jade wondered how her mother had made the contribution. Had she turned over the diamond bracelet and the pearls to Josiah this evening when he brought her the gown? Or had she brought them to the Temple and then exchanged them for the promise of the Brown Gown and a visit by Minden?

They sat down to an uncomfortable dinner. Everyone was solicitous. "Will you have some more peas, Alfred?" "Mom, may I pass you the bread?" "This fruit salad is delicious, Roberta."

After dinner Jade announced she had a date with Arnie. She

kissed her parents and left. She was depressed for both of them and sick at heart about Josiah's greed. He surely had known of her mother's gift.

<hr>

Excerpt from the Holiday Memorial Service Address by Senator Robert T. Spriggs (October 13, 1982)

We are gathered today to honor the memory of perhaps the most spiritual of our Harmonetics members, Jennifer Holiday. She was a rare being, a great lady who dedicated her last days in this world to providing for the less fortunate.

Jennifer Holiday was a patron of the arts. Her home was filled with the treasures of Germany during the age of Guten-berg, China under the rule of the Ming dynasty, Paris during perhaps its most creative era and ancient Greece in the Mycenaean age. She willed the incomparable artifacts and paintings and manuscripts she had collected to you and me, to all of us who are members of the Harmonetics Society.

I knew Jennifer Holiday well. I knew her when she was a woman of the world, holding large soirees that attracted the fashionable people. I also knew her after she had joined the Society. She became a deeply religious woman, and her religion consisted of love of mankind. I saw her at the Harmonetics Retreat when she rededicated her life to the tenets we all hold so dear.

There are not enough hours to list the many benefactions of Jennifer Holiday. Her daily life exemplified her uplifted spirit. Earthly possessions were no longer meaningful. She strove for the most exalted level of Harmonetics, and she attained it before she moved on to a new world.

Jennifer Holiday was a Probationary Member three years ago. She was in this very Temple when she earned her Blue Gown, and I was her proud presenter. Very shortly she rose to Red, Green, and Brown, to the immense satisfaction of all of us. No woman or man had a better right to these colors. Shortly before she moved on, Dr. Josiah Minden himself gave her the

<hr>

White Robe. She became one of the twenty-five leaders of our movement. Just as she replaced a leader who moved on, so will she be replaced by a new leader who will be granted the White Robe to sustain the exact number at twenty-five. However, her memory will live forever and her name will be engraved in the gold plaques displayed in each Harmonetics Temple in this country.

The boss walked into the *National News* office and shouted his customary greeting. Barbara at the reception desk said, "Hiya, Bill" and Harding replied with an "Umph" and a pat on the hand. He picked up his phone messages and moved to the next room.

Daniel, the Art Director, was waiting for Harding. He had the color transparencies and a four-page layout for the Jennifer Holiday article. The opening page was a full-page bleed color photograph of Mrs. Holiday seated on a divan, a low display table in front of her in which one could see a fourteenth-century Book of the Hours open to a glorious illuminated page with a miniature painting. Directly behind her, on the walls, were a prima ballerina by Degas and a café scene by Monet. Jennifer was dressed in an ivory gown, a mantilla of the same color draped over one straight shoulder. The camera work was detailed: one could make out the lace pattern of the rich garment. Around her neck were the Holiday emeralds. Her hands were folded and rested on her lap. On one finger she wore the 35-carat Holiday diamond.

For the second page of the layout Daniel had selected a two-column picture of Mrs. Holiday in a flowing blue chiffon gown. She was receiving guests in her ballroom. Her impeccable posture and the Renoir on the wall did not detract from the stomacher pearls and the diamond and sapphire tiara. She wore a matching diamond and sapphire bracelet on her wrist. The famous Holiday diamond was visible on the third finger, left hand.

The third page allowed for two columns of copy on the right side and a vertical strip left-hand bleed photograph, also in color. It was a close-up of a display case in the Holiday Library. On the glass-enclosed shelves were a Greek lecythus depicting the marriage of Helen to Menelaus, a small statue of a

Mycenaean bull, several Greek amphorae on which were painted scenes from the war between the Gods and the Giants, a collection of Athenian coins and Mycenaean gold rings, a wine jug showing Antigone with her hair transformed into serpents, an Attic urn on which was represented the birth of Athene, who emerged fully armed from the skull of Zeus, a calyx crater detailing the slaying of the Numean lion by Hercules, a Mycenaean cup decorated with a dance of the priestesses, an Etruscan pendant, plus additional amphorae, craters, cups, urns, platters, and statuettes.

The photograph on the fourth page was centered in the middle of the copy. It was five inches high by two columns in width, leaving a full column of copy on either side. The picture showed Jennifer in a brown gown talking to Dr. Fronzhold in the Harmonetics Temple. She wore no jewelry, her posture was regal, and her eyes looked happy. Dr. Fronzhold's face was stern and serious. The dark beard extended two inches below his chin but thereafter not a hair could be seen in the V of his open-necked white shirt.

"Excellent, Daniel," said Harding. "Were the color separations done at our own lab? Good, good. It's a fine piece of work."

Harding turned to Herb Adams, his Financial Specialist, who was next in line.

"This is the six-page summary of the meeting with Hemingway of Global Publications," said Herb, who, like his boss, wore sports jackets only and eschewed ties. "Hemingway's ready to unload one or more of his magazines. He took a bath with *Cuisine du Monde* and he's hurting much worse than he says. Start-up costs on *Cuisine du Monde* were almost $2 million and he's dying on the newsstands. He claims paid circulation is 80,000 of which probably 10,000 copies were newsstand. The other 70,000 subscribers were the product of a *Cuisine du Monde* contest. The prizes for naming your favorite restaurant and filling out the entry blank were a yacht, a Mercedes, a condominium in Palm Springs, and a trip around the world. The cheaper prizes were a set of copper frying pans, a year's supply of Chloryl Cleanser, steak knives, a small spice cabinet, etcetera."

"Who ran the contest for him?"

"Blair Associates."

"That's bad news for Hemingway. Blair must have nicked him $100,000 minimum for handling the contract. Then he had to pay for the prizes, minus 50 percent; that's an additional $100,000 to $125,000. Blair undoubtedly ran a 'test mailing' for $50,000 to see which lists would be best to use. Then I'd guess he sent out five million pieces to potential contestant-subscribers. The paper, printing, and postage on a five million mailing, third class, was at least ten cents apiece. It had to be more since Blair needed to buy the lists and use a subscription fulfillment house. Blair is big on promotion; I'll guess he spent a minimum of $250,000 on newspaper and TV advertising to publicize the contest. That means Hemingway blew over $1 million to get 70,000 subscribers. The subscribers got the special introductory rates of $4, so it cost Hemingway $10 or more per subscriber."

"Our Advertising Department found out he gave discounts on some of the ads."

"I flicked through the last issue and it looked like a 10 percent ratio of ads to copy. With the lavish way he produced *Cuisine du Monde*—the seventy-pound coated stock inside the hundred-pound coated cover—and with his huge print order to cover sample and newsstand copies, he must have needed 70 percent ads to break even."

"Pretty good guess, Bill. The percentage of ads was 9.6 percent and at least half were discounted."

"What was his print order?"

"A million copies for each of the three issues."

"Then he had to throw 920,000 copies each month in the garbage can. Do you know how many we lose each month, Herb?"

"No, but I'll guess. Five percent?"

"I wish we did that well on the newsstand. We have to eat all the unsold copies. On our best issues we've had sellouts; on the worst we got a 15 percent return from the distributor. Even if we were large enough to distribute ourselves, we could never predict the print order in a particular month because newsstand sales are an unknown variable. Hemingway sold 10,000 copies out of 930,000 distributed; his percentage of returns was 98.9 percent."

"How long can he go on? He says he's planning to change

Cuisine du Monde to a bimonthly to consolidate costs."

"Bullshit. He wants an extra month to unload *Cuisine du Monde*. No one will pick it up. Wait a minute, I'm wrong. One guy will. Herb, see if you can get me Hemingway on the phone. I think we can bail him out. If it works, he'll owe me a helluva favor. Wait, Herb, I've changed my mind. Forget the call to Hemingway. I'm going to help him but he'll never know we did it. I can't tell you about it now, but I promise, if you keep quiet and forget our discussion for thirty days, we'll spend an hour together and you'll know exactly what I tried to do and whether it worked."

"I've blanked it out of my mind."

"Blank it out to your wife or to anyone working on the Global Publications project. One word to anyone in this office and the deal is dead. Herb, I know you'll keep it confidential."

Harding patted him on the back, then waved to Jerry Marconi, who had been waiting fifteen feet away.

"Jerry, come into the office. Herb, I'll read your report later this morning. Thanks."

When Bill and Jerry were in the private office, Harding shut the door.

"I want to talk to Henrietta right away, Jerry, and I want you to hear my end of the conversation."

"I spoke to her this morning, Bill. She gave me her report and I filled her in on what the others are doing. Do you want a rundown first?"

"Okay. Keep it brief."

"Henrietta visited the Temple with Sarah Robinson. Sarah is an old friend who has been into 'causes' all her life. Henrietta says to tell you she made a $500 donation by check for which she would like to be reimbursed. She said she is sorry she couldn't use her American Express card. She estimates eight thousand bodies in the Temple with few contributing less than $5. Perhaps eighty to ninety people were in the $100 category. She thinks she was one of the major donors of the afternoon but she says there were three morning and two afternoon sessions, plus one long one in the evening.

"Henrietta ran into Rosalind Schulte, who is a Green Gown. Her husband, Ernst, is currently living in one of the more social penitentiaries. Rosalind was very friendly. Henrietta thinks

Rosalind was a very lonely woman until she joined the Society. She seems to have made an excellent adjustment and is happy at the Temple. Rosalind mentioned that Clarissa and Byron Kent were leaders in the Harmonetics movement. Byron is a member of the White Robes while Clarissa works as a volunteer directly under Dr. Fronzhold.

"Henrietta says it will cost $350 to take the aptitude tests. She is going to enroll in the Health and Body seminars, which means another $350. She will get samples of the products and has asked me to find a laboratory to analyze them.

"She phoned Senator Spriggs and Sarah Robinson, and both are coming to dinner Friday night. So are Clarissa and Byron Kent. She told Clarissa how much she admired Dr. Fronzhold and how thrilled she was by his lecture yesterday. She said Clarissa was in ecstasy when she mentioned Fronzhold's name. Henrietta thinks they are having an affair. After Clarissa had accepted for herself and Byron, Henrietta asked for suggestions on another couple for the dinner party. Henrietta said she wanted someone 'sympathetic to or active in Harmonetics.' There was a pregnant pause. Then Clarissa came up with the names of Dr. and Mrs. Fronzhold: Henrietta demurred. He would be absolutely perfect for the group but she didn't know him. It would be 'pushy' to ask him. Clarissa thereupon volunteered to invite the Fronzholds on Henrietta's behalf. Since the Senator is coming, Clarissa is sure Fronzhold will be there if he possibly can.

"I briefed Henrietta on the activities of Martha, Harold, and Jade. Henrietta thought Martha's speculations on the causes of Mrs. Holiday's death were perceptive. She also thinks the team should look into the rejuvenation theory. She says she'd be glad to enroll in a rejuvenation seminar if she can put it on her credit card. Jade hit the jackpot. She met Josiah Minden at her mother's apartment and they got along almost too well."

"What do you mean?"

"He was touching and hugging and kissing her in what she called 'White Robe' style. She said they almost had an orgy in front of her mother. It sounded pretty bad."

"Why?"

"Well, she's not that kind. I mean he's a pretty low-class type. He's got the answers for your happiness, provided you sign over your salary to him. Jade says her mother gave him all her jewelry and in turn he gave her the Brown Robe."

Bill saw the grief in Jerry's face. There was no way to protect him from Jade's reports. He changed the subject.

"Jerry, what's Henrietta's number? I want to place the call myself."

Harding dialed and got Henrietta.

"I hear you had a successful and expensive day at the Temple. I'm particularly glad your dinner party is working out because Senator Spriggs may suddenly be in your debt. Here's what I want you to do.

"Lionel Hemingway is the publisher of Global. He's a nice guy, and when he sticks to what he knows he's quite able. He has a chain of movie and detective magazines that sell well on the stands. It's cheap production, a small staff, and low overhead. He's down on 27th Street and he has his own presses in New Jersey. He was making enough money to keep his wife in two homes and to buy mink coats for all his girl friends. He could have lived forever on the profits without working his tail off. Instead he, or maybe his wife or one of his children, decided Global needed a 'class' magazine. He started up a slick publication called *Cuisine du Monde*, which was supposed to knock *Gourmet* the hell out of business. Hemingway's advertising staff can peddle space for athletic supporters, calendar art, muscle-building, and lots of other mail-order catalog items. Neither his Advertising Department nor Hemingway knew how to make a presentation to an agency for a wine or a liquor or an automobile or an airline or an expensive resort. It's a tough sell anyway and an impossibility for the people in Global. Hemingway's magazines were strictly newsstand; he was told he had to have subscriptions as well. He hired a 'Publisher's Consultant,' who undoubtedly told him the chances for success were excellent. Then he shopped around for a classy Editor and a classy Art Director. He didn't know how to supervise this type of publication; he didn't limit the first few issues to metropolitan New York to minimize the risk. He published three issues and he may be out as much as $3 million because of an idiotic nationwide subscription contest. Now the whole company is suffering.

"He would like to get rid of *Cuisine du Monde* but nobody

will touch it. The competition is too good. There's only one group who might pick it up because they have so much money they can afford to waste $500,000. They could probably lose $20 million and not feel it. I'm talking about the group that bought the Continental Towers and Plaza del Populo. In both cases the deal was negotiated by Senator Spriggs.

"If you'll go to Global to see Hemingway, you may be able to do him some good and prove to Senator Spriggs that you can be helpful. Hemingway will grab $500,000 if it's offered. He paid a million bucks for 70,000 subscribers because he went to a contest house that can't produce peanuts unless the magazine is already a winner. Those 70,000 subscribers are a total loss: Hemingway might be able to 'give' the unexpired terms of the subscriptions to another magazine that is trying to build up numbers, but no Circulation Manager would pay for these subscriptions. If Hemingway didn't know it before, he knows it now.

"Spriggs should be interested for many reasons. First, he can change the title to *The Yogurt Road to Happiness* or *Wheat Germ Monthly* or whatever. Second, the Harmonetics Society can peddle the copies to all its members. Dr. Fronzhold can be the Publisher and Josiah himself can write a monthly editorial exhorting the members to eat their way to heaven. Third, they can advertise their own health food stores and their spas, retreats, clinics, hospitals, etc. Fourth, he will be able to sell a limited number of copies on the newsstand. Fifth, if he has a guaranteed sale among members, he may be able to pick up five or ten pages of ads from companies owned by members of the Temple or companies that want to ingratiate themselves with the Harmonetics Society. Sixth, it will be profit-making for Minden and it will get him some new members. Spriggs should go for it.

"Do you have any questions, Henrietta? . . . Yes, there's a good chance you can see Hemingway this morning. Go in person. If you can get in for one minute, you'll have it made. . . . Phone Jerry after you see Hemingway. . . . Good luck, sweetheart."

Harding hung up the phone and turned to Jerry. "There's a report on Global on my desk that I want you to look at. When Henrietta calls back, give her the pertinent information that she can pass on to Spriggs. He's going to fall in love with her when he hears about the deal. Do you have anything else?"

"Everyone phoned in their progress reports and they're typed up for you. Roger's report isn't in yet since he's seeing Mrs. Holiday's lawyer—the one who made out her will—this morning. His name is Austin McDowell and he's a partner at Blake, Chatterly. This afternoon Martha has an appointment with Rhonda Mahaffey, Mrs. Holiday's daughter. Roger is seeing the son, Lawrence Runson, later today. They'll work on their story tonight. Martha says there's enough about Minden and Fronzhold to make a readable article but she's afraid it's too thin. The housekeeper accused the Harmonetics Hospital of 'overkill' in trying to rejuvenate Mrs. Holiday, but so far Martha can't get any leads on the rejuvenation process, if there is such a thing."

"If it exists, Martha will find it."

Excerpt from a Harmonetics seminar
by Emma Neuhauser, Harmonetics Nutritionist
(March 6, 1979)

We are what we eat. The cells in our body are fed by what we put in our mouths. If we eat refined flours, processed cheeses, candy bars, cookies, and cakes, rich sauces and soft drinks, how are we nourishing our organs, muscles, bones, and skin? Further, if we add alcoholic stimulants, caffeine, and nicotine, what does this do to the health of our bodies?

Men and women today are destroying their health by disregarding their diets. Every boy and girl, man and woman, and particularly the more mature people who have passed the age of sixty, should know the foods that are deemed essential to wholesome existence. Basically they are: orange, grapefruit, or tomato juice for Vitamin C; breads made of unrefined flour and special cereals for Vitamin B; carrots, green vegetables, and fresh fruits for Vitamin A; salads combined with special oils for bulk and digestion; nuts, cheese, and eggs for protein, plus yogurt, wheat germ, yeast, and special vitamin and mineral supplements to round out the daily requirements.

Some of these foods may be purchased at any grocery store. Others are scarce, impure, diluted, or inadequately prepared when they are available, and for this reason the Harmonetics Health Food Stores were established. Here you will find the most wholesome of breads, honey that you can substitute for sugar, the best wheat germ, yeast, and yogurt, unsalted nuts, the purest oils, sugarless cookies that give energy, snacks that are healthful, and hundreds of other necessities, delicacies, and taste treats composed solely of wholesome components.

All of you will need some vitamin supplements. Our lectures will explain the role of vitamins, in which foods they are found, and the diseases that ensue if vitamin requirements are ignored. Each one of you will receive, in the course of this seminar, a special diagnosis to enable us to prescribe the particular vitamins you may need. Please don't try to determine your own vitamin requirements; you may do irreparable harm to your body. The determination of each individual's needs will be made by our own highly skilled physicians and nutritionists. We urge you all to come back every six months so that we can check on your progress and add to the vitamin supplements as necessary.

As you all know, this three-day course is $350, which includes four hours of lectures each day as well as a thirty-minute private diagnosis of your personal supplemental vitamin requirements. You will be able to purchase the items in your vitamin package in bottles filled specifically for you; such purchases can be made at the Harmonetics Health Food Store. Your own jars will be ready for you in your personalized Health Food Kit.

Roger Silberstein walked down the black-grimed steps of the Lexington Avenue subway, watching carefully for "live" chewing gum. His descent was slowed by the old man in front of him who was weaving from side to side and singing "Praise Be Je'ez Chris' Our Saverer." The old man was wearing dark, baggy pants, a torn shirt, and an old coat made for a man three sizes larger. The coat had only one of its original buttons. Neither Silberstein nor the other travelers paid any attention to the man other than to avoid personal contact.

Silberstein purchased some tokens and passed through the

turnstile to wait for his train. His eyes gazed unseeing at the big color ads splashed on the tunnel walls that were meant to induce the workingman into sweetening his breath, whitening his teeth, and inhaling smoke with a low tar content. A train pulled into the station and Roger boarded, along with two dozen other passengers. The traffic was light this time of day and one could not only find a seat but could do so comfortably. The subway doors closed and the train buzzed off noisily, jolting the oblivious passengers who were used to its vagaries. Roger cast a quick glance around for degenerates and thugs; there were none. One or two other passengers were dressed as presentably as he. The others wore more casual attire—jeans, sweaters, outfits from ready-to-wear chain stores that serviced the working man and woman. Roger lowered his eyes so he would not meet those of his fellow passengers. He saw scuffed shoes, thick ankles, stockings with runs, and pants that flared too widely or were too tapered. The floor of the train was covered with bits of small refuse—a Kleenex, a copy of the *Daily News*, a torn envelope, an empty matchbook.

Roger had taken the express. He looked up each time the train stopped to check the station: 14th Street, Brooklyn Bridge, and finally Wall Street. He was pleased with the time he had made; he was ten minutes early for his appointment.

He walked up the stairs of the Wall Street station into the fiefdom of the attorneys and investment bankers. The lords of these kingdoms, along with their myriad serfs and knights, worked in long, slim concrete and steel structures that faced each other across narrow streets, casting enormous shadows across the sidewalks. The sun hit the pavements only in the middle of the day. There were no casual pedestrians, no housewives out for a stroll. There were hundreds of lords of the manor, but their female consorts remained in midtown or the suburbs.

This was the Kingdom of the Males. With few exceptions the occupants of the boardrooms, the conference rooms, and the executive suites were of the masculine gender. They had been eating in all-male clubs and all-male company dining rooms for so many years that the occasional intrusion of a female in the areas deemed exclusively theirs was a bit ridiculous, eh, don't y'think? The bigger banks, brokerage houses, and law firms were accepting a few talented young women who, thank heaven, had not been too pushy. Wouldn't want to change the club rules, y'know.

The offices of Blake, Chatterly were on Broadway near Wall. The firm had occupied the same two floors for several generations. Although Blake and Chatterly had been dead for a dozen years, none of the current partners had ever considered moving to newer quarters. The building was old and some of the other tenants were of questionable antecedents, but senior partner Arthur Popple encouraged his associates to take a democratic attitude. Popple himself never failed to greet the old man who sat in the newspaper kiosk on the ground floor or to bid good morning to Max, the elevator starter.

Roger Silberstein ascended to the twenty-first floor where all visitors to Blake, Chatterly were announced. He had put on his one acceptable business suit for his meeting with Austin McDowell, but apparently it (or Roger himself) was deemed deficient in a particular quality that denoted the respectable client. The receptionist asked his name, wrote it down, and waved him to a chair. She then examined her fingernails, typed a few lines of a form, and went back to her nails. Finally, with a sigh, she buzzed Mr. McDowell's office.

"There's a Roger Silberstein to see Mr. McDowell. He claims he has an appointment."

Roger waited for a word from the receptionist. She ignored him. Twenty-five minutes later a secretary appeared from one of the inner offices.

"Mr. er, ah, Silberstein, Mr. McDowell will see you now."

She led him down a paneled wood corridor, past a series of closed doors. One that was open revealed a small law library or perhaps a large partner's office. Another was an equally small conference room. They reached McDowell's office. The secretary knocked, then opened the door.

"You may go in now," she said, averting her eyes.

Austin McDowell was on the telephone. He was a grave young man of forty-two who worked in an office dominated by men in their late sixties. He had the thin pointed nose, lean face, and receding chin characteristic of certain members of the British aristocracy. His shoulders, like theirs, were narrow, his knees as thin and knobby, and the color of his legs was the same untanable white. Every year he and his wife made a pilgrimage to London. While Cissy McDowell invited impoverished duchesses to lunch at Claridge's, Austin McDowell was fitted by bespoke tailors on Bond Street and Saville Row for shooting jackets, country weekend tweeds, and business suits.

McDowell gave Silberstein a quick glance, then went back to his phone conversation.

"I can't play on Saturday morning. We always go over to Cissy's mother's. What about 2:00 P.M.? . . . Did Woolcott say he would play? . . . Then how about getting Sandy for a fourth? . . . How are Buffie and the boys? Oh, I'm glad. . . . Yes, Cissy's fine too. I'm taking her with me to the Coast next month. . . . No, it's a business trip. . . . Why don't we lunch one day next week? Tuesday? . . . If you're going to be downtown we'll eat at my club. The sole amandine is excellent. . . . Hold on, that's fine, let me put that on my calendar. . . . Thanks and same to you. Give my best to Buffie. . . . Yes, I will."

McDowell hung up, shuffled some papers, and looked at Silberstein.

"I understand you are from *National News,*" he said. "I agreed to see you but I'm extremely busy. Shall we keep this short?"

"Certainly. We are doing a tribute in the next issue to the late Jennifer Holiday. The story refers to her as one of the great benefactors of the city. I have a list of the contributions she made over the years to the Philharmonic, the ballet, the Met, Columbia University, Wells College, and many other important institutions. If you would care to take a look, you could tell us if any major gifts were omitted."

Roger handed a sheet of paper to McDowell, who put on his reading glasses.

"Yes, yes, that looks about right."

"And of course we refer to her last and most generous bequest to the Harmonetics Society."

"Yes, yes."

"I thought you could add some comments about the size of the gift."

"No. She made her own decisions. No one in this office ever attempted to guide her."

"But you were her lawyer and you did draw up her will?"

"Yes, yes," said McDowell impatiently. "You already know that."

"Weren't you surprised that almost everything—the money, the collection, and the town house—was left to the Harmonetics Society?"

"I can't comment on that."

"What about any previous wills? Did she intend, before she joined the Society, to leave most of her estate to her children?"

"Mrs. Holiday was a client. I'm afraid I can't add any more to what I've already stated."

"Perhaps you can give me the date when the will was drawn up."

"My secretary can look it up. You can ask her as you leave. And now, if you have no more questions, I really must . . ."

"Please bear with me one more minute. Was Mrs. Holiday, in your opinion, sound of mind when she made out her new will?"

"This is getting a bit ridiculous. I don't know what you are getting at but I find your questions rather impertinent. I must repeat: Mrs. Holiday was my client and I followed her instructions to the letter. Period."

McDowell stood up. Roger tried one more stab for the record:

"Do you feel Mrs. Holiday was unduly influenced by Dr. Minden or Dr. Fronzhold?"

McDowell gave him a frigid look. "I am not about to exchange idle gossip with a reporter. I must ask you now to excuse me."

He pushed a buzzer and his secretary walked in.

"Miss Evans, will you please give Mr.—er—Silberstein the date of the filing of Mrs. Holiday's will?"

McDowell sat down, picked up the phone, and started dialing.

"Thank you for your courtesy," said Roger.

McDowell muttered something that sounded like "Damn you" or, more likely, "Damn Jew."

Martha was much more successful on her appointment. Her destination was 55th Street and the East River, which she reached by Yellow Cab. This was one of the fashionable old sections of the city. On the river side of the street were apartment houses that had been built more than sixty years ago. The rooms were spacious, the ceilings high, and the tenants of white Anglo-Saxon stock. The daughters in the family had gone to Spence, Nightingale, or Brearley and the sons to Choate, Andover, and Lawrenceville. On Sundays most of the families worshiped at Saint Thomas', although one or two attended Saint Patrick's Cathedral. None went to Temple Emanu-El. The residents, many of whom had occupied the same apartments for forty years or more, would not have chosen to live in the apartments across the street. These were the nouveau buildings that had sprung up twenty to thirty years ago on a site that for years had been Rip's Tennis Courts. The rooms were smaller, the ceilings lower, and the tenants an ethnic mixture, many coming from disreputable Eastern European countries. Their conservative neighbors across the street could remember the days when Bill Tilden, Frank Hunter, Helen Jacobs, Billy Talbert, and Sidney Wood had played tennis almost directly under their windows. Still one could not spend one's life regretting the old days, and at least each apartment overlooked the peaceful East River albeit few tenants were reconciled to the bright neon lights advertising Pearl-Wick Hampers.

Martha's concept of warmth had been influenced by her grandmother's home in which were to be found admirable examples of petit-point footstools, tapestried walls, massive Georgian tea sets, Louis XVI armoires, and antimacassars on large Victorian chairs. She felt a pleasant sensation of déjà vu when she entered the apartment house lobby. It looked comfortably worn but not shabby; unquestionably her grandmother would have approved.

The doorman, old and dignified, inquired of Martha whom she wished to see, politely requested her name, then announced her. He personally escorted her to the elevator, rang the bell for the lift, then told the elevator man Ms. Rayburn's destination. Martha accepted the proffered assistance and rode up to the sixteenth floor. She was greeted at the door by Rhonda Mahaffey.

Martha liked her at once. Mrs. Mahaffey might have been homely when she was young because her face was so long; now, in her late forties, she was almost a beauty.

"I was just having some coffee. Will you join me?" Rhonda Mahaffey smiled. That was when Martha noticed how wide the mouth was: all of the front teeth and most of the side ones showed. Yes, she was homely as a child. The smile was much better in an older face. She's a beauty now, Martha thought.

"I would welcome some coffee. I appreciate your seeing me."

"I know you want to talk about my mother," said Rhonda after they were seated. "And I know you want to find out if we're going to contest the will. We're not."

"You could probably break it. At worst you would probably get one-third of the estate. The Harmonetics Society might even offer a settlement."

"Yes, we know. Lawrence's lawyer tried to persuade us to take it to court. If Jon, my husband, had pressed me, I might have agreed. Fortunately he feels the same way I do."

"But all those works of art, the jewels, the millions of dollars, are they so unimportant to you?"

"The art treasures belong in a museum. I loved the jewelry on Mother but I couldn't possibly wear it myself. Mother left me a million, which is quite an extraordinary sum, and Jon makes an excellent living. We aren't wanting for anything," she said with a sweep of her arm to indicate the large living room. It was an exquisite room: old chests and cabinets from seventeenth- and eighteenth-century Europe and several large Orientals that would have fitted just as nicely in her mother's town house.

"I must admit," Rhonda continued, "that there's more to it than what I just told you. I used to be a member of the Harmonetics Society."

"My goodness, that never occurred to me. Whatever made you join in the first place and whatever caused you to leave?"

"I was one of the early proselytes, before the movement got popular. That was about six or seven years ago. I had been divorced for several years and I couldn't pull myself together. The friends I had when Mortimer and I were married seldom called after the divorce. There were so few invitations and I made no effort to ask people over, probably because I was afraid they'd say no. In those days it wasn't as easy to be single or a divorcée. Then I heard about the Temple and I went often because I was lonely. At that time the Temple was down in the

Village in a shabby little building. There were two hundred of us. I thought the people were wonderful, particularly Dr. Minden. When he came to New York and talked to us, we listened to him as we would to a holy man. He wanted to help the old people and he wanted to help us too. I started giving my money—small sums at first. Then I wanted to give every cent I had. I sold some bonds and one day I brought $25,000 in cash to the Temple. All the income from a trust fund my father had left me was going directly to the Society. If I could legally have turned over the trust fund, I would have done so.

"The number of believers increased each month. Sometimes two or three of us would stand on the streets for five or six hours, passing out literature and soliciting money. We knew we could bring happiness to others if we could get them to visit the Temple. We were particularly successful with older people. Finally Dr. Minden bought one of the enormous empty diplomatic mansions on Fifth Avenue. It was five stories and had forty rooms. I was actually going to move in and take care of the house."

"You didn't?"

"No. I got sick, which was the luckiest thing that ever happened. I was at New York Hospital and Jon was one of the doctors. We got friendly, and when I was recuperating he came to see me regularly. I was back in my old apartment and I kept thinking as soon as I was strong enough I would visit the Temple. I postponed the visit. Some of the members started to call me, but I lied and said I was still very ill. I looked forward to seeing Jon each day, and every day I felt happier.

"There was one bad moment a few months later. I had finally recognized I had outgrown my need for the Temple. I was never going back. I couldn't believe I had been such an idiot. Jon and I were engaged, and the Harmonetics Society was a thing of the past. Then I got a phone call from Dr. Minden. When I heard his voice I began to shake. As he talked to me I was weeping. He begged me to go to the Temple and I said I would. I washed my face, grabbed my purse, and got as far as the front door. Then I turned around and went back to my bedroom. It was as though Minden had hypnotized me months ago and I was fighting to regain control of my mind. I must have sat there an hour. Then I heard the doorbell and I panicked. I knew I couldn't let Minden in. If he had had a key, I would either have walked out with him submissively or jumped out the window.

"The bell rang again and again. I was terrified. Then I heard Jon's voice calling my name. I opened the door. I was crying so hard and I was so unnerved that I didn't make too much sense. Jon told me later than I kept saying, 'My God, I thought it was Dr. Minden. Oh, dear God, I thought it was Josiah Minden.' We talked about it later and Jon believes I was hypnotized. Perhaps all of us were."

"How did you feel when your mother joined the Society? Would that have been about a year or so later?"

"Yes, about then. Strangely, I was sympathetic. She had the same compulsions I had had. She believed in the people and she thought they had the answers. I wish I could have seen her more but I was afraid I might meet Dr. Minden or his old associates at her house. There's a dread I can't overcome that he might regain his ascendancy over my mind.

"When I phoned Mother I used to say, 'Are you alone?' When she was, we would talk, sometimes for an hour. If you asked me if she was sane during that last year of her life, I would have to say yes. However, there was one part of her mind she no longer owned.

"It grieved her that I no longer believed. She encouraged me to return to the Temple. She called me a renegade. Every argument she used I had once used to try to make converts.

"I have talked to Lawrence, my brother, about what happened to me and to Mother. I think it gave him a better understanding."

"Rhonda, did your mother ever talk about rejuvenation treatments? Her housekeeper was certain Dr. Fronzhold was treating her with shots or pills that took years off her looks."

"I don't know. I rarely saw Mother after she joined the Society. Not at all during the last year. We spoke on the phone. She never mentioned anything about rejuvenation."

"And you never saw Dr. Minden again?"

"No, never." The answer came in a sharp staccato as though this would dispose of the subject forever.

"What kind of a man is Minden?" asked Martha.

"Josiah?" Rhonda hesitated. The question seemed to make

her uncomfortable. She looked down at her hands and twisted her wedding ring. She's too nice a person, thought Martha, to refuse to answer the question or to tell me to jump in the lake.

"Josiah's a chameleon," said Rhonda softly. "Everyone sees him in a different light. To elderly women he's charming and flippant and flirtatious. He'll tease them and himself; he'll even joke about the philosophy of the Harmonetics Society. He'll be serious with intense young men or sympathetic with someone who's ailing or disabled. In the old days he seemed to have a few minutes for everyone. He's a brilliant speaker but he's also a very good listener."

"What's he like as a human being?" asked Martha. "Does he go to the movies? Does he read popular novels? Is he politically oriented to the left or the right?"

Rhonda paused before answering. "I'd call him a traditionalist and a romantic. I'd guess that he doesn't like modern literature or movies. I'm not really sure."

"Does he like women?" asked Martha.

"He loves them and he hates them," said Rhonda, looking at her hands.

"Does he hate them all?" asked Martha, wondering if she was going too far.

"No. He only despises the women who adore him." Rhonda glanced at her watch, then continued. "It's 5:30, time for a glass of sherry. Won't you join me?"

"That's awfully nice but I feel I've taken up enough of your time. May I call you again if some other questions pop up?"

"Of course you can. Sure you won't change your mind about the sherry?"

"I'd better get back to the office," said Martha. She looked at the friendly woman with the long face and the wide mouth. She was indeed beautiful.

"I'm trying to visualize Rhonda Mahaffey as a believer," Martha said. "If it could happen to you, it might happen to any one of us."

"That's what Jon says," replied Rhonda with a wide smile.

The offices of Runson, Mayberry, Elder, Constable, and Quigley were packed to the walls with desks, ticker tapes, salesmen, secretaries, customers, and delivery boys. The sound level was low but continual, a nonstop ringing of telephones, clatter of typewriters, heels clicking on bare floors, and conversations between salesmen and secretaries or salesmen and clients.

Roger walked over to one of the three receptionists whose desks in the front were separated only by the width of a body.

"Name, please? . . . Who did you wish to see? . . . Yes, Mr. Silberstein, Mr. Runson is expecting you. Take the elevator up one floor to 45 or use the staircase. I'd advise the stairs. The elevator takes forever. His office is in the far left rear. You can't miss it."

Roger used the stairs as did the messengers, the salesmen, and the partners. Men and women were walking up from the forty-third or down from the forty-sixth bearing manila envelopes, file folders, securities, mail sacks, attaché cases, and leaky paper bags. The forty-fifth floor was just as crowded. The voices on the telephone were buying six hundred shares of CBS at 63 or selling nine hundred shares of Shell at 71. Roger caught the words Polaroid, Con Ed, Duke Power, Citicorp, Greyhound; 33⅜, 29¼, 88½, 7⅞; three hundred shares at 42, ten shares at 93¼, fifteen shares at 51.

The president of Runson, Mayberry had a small office at the left rear corner. His thirty partners had equally small cubicles around the periphery of the floor. The aisles between the crowded desks were narrow. In some cases the chairs that customers had pulled up were blocking the traffic.

Runson, Mayberry was a controversial brokerage house. The younger men on Wall Street despised the penny and nickel operations. The older partners in the powerful houses admired Runson's ingenuity and envied his income. A few thought it was shameful that a member of an old family should have transformed the inherited and highly respected small house of Runson Brothers into the Woolworth's of the New York Stock Exchange. Runson had even had the temerity to transport his troops from the traditional Runson Building on Beaver Street to 45th Street in the midtown area.

Runson's door was open. Roger stood in the doorway, introduced himself, and was invited in. Runson stood up politely and gestured to a chair adjacent to his desk. He was a pleasant-looking hyperactive man of forty-five: he talked quickly, his hands were constantly moving, he chain-smoked, and he didn't carry an extra pound on his six-foot frame. Roger felt at ease as soon as he saw him.

"I understand *National News* is doing a story on my mother," said Lawrence Runson. "You fellows are tough but you're accurate. That's why I said I'd see you."

"Thank you. The thrust of the story is going to be your mother's will. Before I start, would you mind if I use a tape recorder?"

"Not at all."

Roger put a cassette on the desk and pressed the button. He much preferred the cassette to the tiny but highly efficient recorder in his lapel.

"Do you plan to contest the will?"

"No. My sister and I would rather have seen the art collection go to the Metropolitan Museum. I dislike the idea of the Harmonetics Society getting $18 million tax free. You know, I'm sure, it has tax-deductible status so the government won't get a dime. Neither Rhonda, my sister, nor I are starving. She has no children and mine are too damn rich already.

"Rhonda and Jon, her husband, and I had a long talk last night. We saw no reason to hide anything about our mother or about Rhonda herself. Rhonda was one of the early members of the Harmonetics Society but she hasn't been back since she met Jon, which was a little over four years ago."

"Was your sister a fringe member?"

"No, she was in very deep. She says she must have given the Society well over $150,000. In return she was permitted to scrub floors, attend lectures, and stand out in the rain soliciting contributions. She went from Blue Robe to Red Robe to Green Robe before she quit."

"What do you think was the reason she joined?"

"She'd made a rotten marriage to a fellow called Mortimer Winston. They were together ten years but the last three years were misery for Rhonda. Sometimes he'd come home at night and sometimes he wouldn't. He'd had several girl friends and at first he was reasonably discreet. Then he stopped giving a damn. Rhonda never made scenes, and Mortimer got ruder and cruder. He could hardly be civil. When Rhonda finally told him to buzz off, we thought she'd be able to work out a new life. It was just the opposite. She gradually stopped seeing everyone. She had always been a bit shy but after the divorce she lost all her confidence. Mortimer had continually put her down and she got to believing she was useless and worthless.

"When she joined the Society, she got back some of her vitality and confidence. Her friends were a bunch of screwballs and dingbats, but at least she was getting out in the world. Whenever she saw me or Hilda, my wife, she would try to convert us. She wanted me to resign as trustee for the estate she had inherited from our father so she could turn all the money over to Dr. Minden.

"Rhonda is very open about this period in her life because she thinks it may help others who get trapped by the cultists. She and Jon talk about the possibility of mass hypnosis at the Harmonetics lectures. I have a different theory. Some people are born followers. They spend their lives running after leaders who will tell them what to do, what to wear, and how to behave. The leader has to provide them with all the answers. No matter how crazy it is, they swallow the dictates and tenets of the cult."

"Was your mother a born follower?"

"No, she wasn't. She was strong-willed and strong-minded most of her life. She lost some of that strength when she developed the fear of getting old. Minden castigated the shunting aside of the elderly; he was their champion. He was a powerful force in attempting to change social attitudes toward older people. Unfortunately, it didn't take him long to start using the elderly for his own benefit."

"Do you think the Harmonetics Society developed rejuvenation drugs to revitalize people like your mother?"

"I do. I have no proof, but my mother had periods of two or three months when she did look ten or fifteen years younger. The liver spots on her hands disappeared and the skin around her arms was firmer. I asked one day what had happened. Her face looked marvelous but it was the hands that surprised me. The heavy blue veins were gone and the skin was clear. She told me it was the result of proper diet and a happy mentality, which was bullshit. Whatever was happening was her secret."

"Were there periods of retrogression after the rejuvenation? I mean did her hands and face turn old again?"

"Definitely. The rejuvenation periods coincided with her

stays in the hospital. She would be there for a week or ten days at a time, if that's any help."

"When she died, were there any suspicious circumstances?"

"Just a feeling that Fronzhold and Minden were quite capable of helping her into the next world. I talked to my own doctor about doing an autopsy but he said it would be unethical and impertinent of him to question either Dr. Jean de Moraille, who signed the death certificate, or Dr. Fronzhold, who was treating her regularly. I asked my doctor if he thought Fronzhold was a capable physician. He said he would make no judgment about a colleague. So the only conclusion I reached was that my doctor was a frightened, silly little ass who wouldn't dare go up against the Harmonetics Hospital."

"A lot of people seem to be afraid."

"That's why Rhonda and I decided to talk to *National News*. After all, what is there to fear?"

Bill Harding poked his head out of the door and called for Jerry.

"Any new reports?"

"Yes, here are the transcripts of Roger's interviews with Austin McDowell, who drew up Jennifer Holiday's will, and with Lawrence Runson, Jennifer's son. If you have a moment, I'd like you to hear the Austin McDowell tape. It's less than a minute."

"Okay, play away."

Jerry put the tape on a recorder, gave Harding the earphones, and pressed the "Forward" button. Harding listened. He heard McDowell's last words.

Harding banged his fist on the desk and said to the recorder, "Damn YOU."

Excerpt from patient files
Harmonetics Hospital (Psychiatric Ward)

Patient's name: *Pedro Morales*   Age: 67
Place of Birth: *San Juan, Puerto Rico*

Classification: *Blue Gown*   Computer number: *M862–974*
Length of stay at Harmonetics Hospital: *8 months, 16 days*
Diagnosis: *acute schizophrenia*   Cure: ☑*Yes* ☐ *No*
Attending physicians: *Jennings, Kohl, Karozomov, Enders, Levinthal*
Summary of treatment: *Patient entered the hospital suffering from severe abdominal pains. Dr. Karozomov ordered routine laboratory tests plus complete set of X rays. Results were negative. Dr. Karozomov assigned patient to Surgery. General exploratory was performed by Dr. Enders, with Dr. Levinthal as anesthetist. Findings were negative. Patient's attitude was uncooperative. Psychiatric tests showed patient was disturbed, irrationally angry, complaining of nonexistent abdominal pains. Patient was kept heavily sedated and restrained. Shock treatments ordered by Dr. Jennings. Patient violent toward attending nurses and physicians. Shock treatments increased. Patient kept under twenty-four-hour restraint and heavy sedation. Pronounced deterioration in attitude of patient. Diagnosis of acute schizophrenia confirmed. Psychosurgery performed by Dr. Kohl with excellent results. Patient calm and peaceful. Patient transferred last week to Permanent Care Ward.*

A Tour of the Harmonetics Facilities
by Harold Gondoler

I had hoped to be able to provide *National News* with some facts and figures. Instead I can only confirm some conclusions that I had formed before I took the tour. The Society is offering hope and a new way of life to disoriented, sad, frantic, bored, and troubled people. Harmonetics seems no worse and no better than other sects (religious or philosophical). The basic premise is to treat those over seventy with dignity and respect, but the Society also puts great stress on health, physical fitness, and beauty. Classes, seminars, and activities keep the members occupied and happy. The people who join are members of the overwhelming majority: they want an explanation of life and they want to be comforted with solutions because they can't face the idea of death. They want friendships that come to them through ritual. They want recognition because they can't stand to be anonymous. They want love. They believe that if they are young and beautiful, people will love them more. They fight death and disease through health foods and a large corps of doctors and nurses. They want authority in the form of lecturers who will interpret and explain, and they want respected leaders whom they can adore. Harmonetics fulfills their needs.

My tour guide was Ramba Landry, a kindly Harmonetics member whose statistics are as follows: age, 55–60; height, 5'5"; weight, 135–140 pounds; texture and color of skin, excellent; color of robe, green; health, outwardly perfect; intelligence, above average; personality, gentle but dull; education, high school or junior college; character, unblemished.

Ramba first took me to the Temple where we arrived just before the doors closed for the first morning service. Dr. Josiah Minden was the lecturer and Andy Ames, star of cinema and television screen, read the names of those being inducted into the Society. The scene was highly emotional as the Nominees and the Presenters walked down the aisles. The standees were packed against the rear walls. We were jammed in the pews body to body.

Although he was unknown for the first fifty years of his life, Josiah Minden is a born leader and a remarkably handsome man. He walked into the Temple after everyone was seated, and he strode down the aisle, accompanied by eight or ten elderly men and women in brown robes. He was wearing his famous open white shirt, and as he walked to the podium he nodded and sometimes smiled to those closest to the aisles. I looked at the faces of those nearest me; they were transported with happiness merely because he was there.

Minden's address seemed extremely meaningful while he was speaking but it was actually a well-delivered membership drive. He talked about friendship among those who believe in the Harmonetics Ethic. He said the bonds between the members were strong, that the family became closer when all were believers, and that Harmonetics had made possible the close relationship between those in their seventies and those in their thirties and forties. He told an anecdote about a woman of eighty-three who was just appointed Assistant Director of the Health Spa. She jogged 120 miles last month and plays three sets of tennis every day. She gets sore as hell when it rains. He talked about an ex-convict who had joined the Society and is now the Cashier at the Harmonetics Retreat in Maine. The former Chairman of the Board of Carbide Chemicals is the Chief Landscape Designer (which Minden explained meant Head Gardener) at the Harmonetics Sanatorium. A housewife in her late seventies is taking seventy Harmonetics missionaries to Calcutta. Minden concluded by urging the members to bring lonely neighbors to the seminars, to ask the sick and the frightened to visit with them at the Temple, and to share their happiness in Harmonetics with those who were less fortunate. He turned the microphone over to Andy Ames who emphasized the importance of regular contributions to aid the helpless. Envelopes were passed among the faithful.

When the service was over we took a tour of the Temple building. Ramba pinned a "Guest Badge" on my jacket; without it I would not have been allowed in the elevators. Blue-gowned aides on each floor checked the badges. Most of the badges limit the bearer to a particular floor. Ramba's badge said "Open."

The first ten floors are used exclusively for aptitude and psychological testing. We spent fifteen minutes on the third floor. In the rooms that were formerly suites, twenty or twenty-five people would be taking the written portion of the aptitude examination. In the smaller rooms, examiners would be giving one-on-one problems to individuals. I popped open several doors to the dismay of Ramba. In one room I saw an eighty-year-old man with palsy doing his best to place pegs in a board. In another room words and pictures were being flashed on a screen while a corpulent fifty-year-old woman tried desperately to write down the description. In a third room a white-haired, blindfolded man had his arms extended and was trying to make his forefingers meet. Ramba said if I opened one more door she would cancel the balance of the tour. She said it was not possible for me to get a copy of the aptitude tests or to see how the tests were scored.

The eleventh to fifteenth floors are used for the Health and Body seminars. Large sections of each of these floors had been converted into gyms equipped with mats, pulleys, exercise bicycles, rowing machines, ropes, bar bells, steam cabinets, saunas, massage tables, and some extraordinary machines that looked expensive and scientific. Ramba permitted me to view a men's exercise class. The average age was sixty, and although some of the older men looked in terrible shape, quite a few were extremely fit and some had the bodies of men thirty years younger. One man in his late sixties was doing flips on a bar.

I got a feeling from brief glimpses (when someone opened or shut a door) that some of the rooms on these floors were beauty salons. I swear I saw a guy getting a dye job. I also spotted a woman pushing a cart filled with jars and bottles that looked suspiciously like cosmetics. I started to ask the woman what the jars contained but Ramba interrupted before I finished my question. I told Ramba she was treating me like a corporate spy for a rival sect.

The Visitors Corps, which is the missionary section of the Society, occupies the sixteenth to twentieth floors. Here people carry the Harmonetics message to those in need of spiritual aid, viz., men serving life sentences in prison, old ladies in nursing homes, college students seeking ultimate reality, travelers using the airports and railway stations, and hapless pedestrians. Ramba told me she had served in the Visitors Corps for a year. The training period is thirty days during which the visitor is indoctrinated in Harmonetics theory. Ramba let me look in on a classroom where twenty-five men and women were learning the fine art of parting people from their worldly possessions.

There is a clear stratification in the Visitors Corps. At the very bottom are the street-corner solicitors who stand at the intersection of Alexander's and Bloomingdale's passing out tracts and asking for donations. They are allowed to pick their own location—Penn Station, Grand Central, Kennedy, La Guardia, subway and bus stops, lines in front of movie houses, office buildings, or whatever. Every cent they collect, said Ramba proudly, goes to the Society. Formerly they were treated quite shabbily: policemen threatened to arrest them or bell captains rudely asked them to vacate hotel lobbies. The Harmonetics Society took several cases to court, and the Visitors now have the legal right to solicit in public areas.

Ramba had been a Visitor at state hospitals and prisons, which is the highest echelon in the Corps. I asked her how effective she was in converting felons. She told me a number of prisoners had become Probationaries (they cannot receive their gowns while still incarcerated) and a few had volunteered for special projects. She would not elaborate on these projects but assured me they were the acme of selflessness.

We went up the elevator again, this time to the twenty-first floor where seminars on diet were being held. Our next stop was the twenty-fifth floor, where men and women, mostly over sixty, were being taught arts and crafts. In one room they were weaving baskets and in another they were carving wood. I told Ramba I was getting restless. I asked if we could skip the floors where members were taught to play the tambourine or transplant ferns into large pots or to boil an egg. She was upset with me: these floors, she said, were the heart of the Harmonetics program. I told her I believed her but I wanted to speak to one of the administrators about the size of the membership, the structure of the administration, and the finances of the Society. She sighed. I was obviously a major disappointment to her.

We took the Down elevator to the Temple floor. Ramba then whisked me by taxi to Administration Headquarters on Fifth Avenue. The building was formerly a diplomatic residence; five years ago it was purchased by the Society and converted into a Temple. The Society had grown so fast that the Temple was converted into office space. The clerks, accountants, and administrators in the building wore robes of assorted colors rather than business suits. The color of the robe, said Ramba, did not indicate their responsibilities even though the Chief of the department happened to be a Brown Gown. Ramba introduced me to Ralph Smedley who was wearing a red robe, and he in turn said he would be pleased to answer my questions. He could only guess the number of members (over two million and growing every day). He was unable to give me any estimate of income. He said no taxes were paid because Harmonetics was both a charitable and a religious institution. He offered the well-known fact that $2 billion was spent by the Society for medical care. He did not have a list of the properties owned by the Harmonetics Society. When I asked how many hospitals the Society owned, he said some of the hospitals were quite small and could almost be classified as clinics. When I rephrased the question to ask about how many hospitals and clinics were owned, he replied that new ones were being established all the time. I asked if I might see the other floors of the Administration Building (so far I had only seen the lobby). He replied that visitors were not permitted in other areas: everyone was terribly busy, the rooms were small and over-crowded, and visitors would create a distraction.

I told Ramba I wasn't getting much material for my article. She said I would have had plenty if I had visited the other floors at the Temple. She suggested we tour the Harmonetics Study Hall, a newly acquired building near Columbia University.

The Study Hall is a large building (seven stories) filled with many small "study" rooms and a few that are auditorium size. It is a proselytizing center for college students. One convert brings in another student who, in turn, is converted and brings in another student. I was astonished at the number of students as well as the number of young professors. The majority were wearing blue gowns.

The Study Hall has a cafeteria in which could be seen many Christlike students in gowns. Ramba and I decided to eat there. I had a choice of several Harmonetics health food platters. I selected cottage cheese with Jell-O and a slice of health food bread, which came with a small packet of honey and a fluted paper thimble of nuts. Ramba took the parsley and watercress salad, a cup of watery vegetable soup, and a dish of yogurt. We ate silently. Around us we could hear voices exclaiming intensely: "It's beautiful" or "It's so real."

In the Study Hall were a Vitamin Shop, where the cash register was ringing merrily; a Health Food Store offering a "Special" on wheat germ; and a Reading Room much like the one I had seen at the hospital.

Our final destination was the Harmonetics Hospital. I can only compare my guided tour here to the reception of a group of Americans at a Russian nuclear plant. I was permitted to see the swimming pool, the therapy rooms, the outdoor gardens, the Reading Room, and the Prayer Room. I cannot tell you why there is such secrecy. The "off limits" areas included the Emergency Room, the Admitting Office, all wards, the operating theatres, and both semiprivate and private rooms. The reason I was given was protection of the patient's right to privacy.

The tour was over and my knowledge of the operations of the Society had not increased dramatically; however, the day was not an entire bust. Ten minutes after I got back to the Ranger Hotel, I got a phone call from Ellie Sue Brown, the cashier at the pharmacy whom I met two days ago when I first visited the hospital.

Ellie Sue told me she frequently walked around the hospital gardens during her lunch hour. She did so today and, as usual, there were no patients in the area. She saw volunteers tending the flower beds and occasional nurses and doctors. She was walking around aimlessly, eating a sandwich and enjoying the sunshine, when a limousine pulled up to let out some visitors. They were pretty far away, she said, but she was sure she recognized them. They were the putative son and daughter of Mary, the patient who had come into the pharmacy and begged for help several months ago. Ellie Sue saw no point in running after the son and daughter. Instead she walked toward the car. The limousine started up the street and slowly came past her. And guess what? That lovely Ellie Sue saw the license plate. It's L56P2219 and the car is a Cadillac.

I checked out the license plates with a buddy at Police Headquarters. The car is registered in the name of Franklin Robert Parson. He lives on East 58th and he is an architect with offices on Park and 47th. I called an old friend, Nell Arden at the *New York Times,* and she got the following information from their morgue:

Franklin Parson's mother died eight years ago and her name was Betty. However, his mother-in-law is still alive and her name is Mary Hamble. She is a widow who maintains an apartment on the East River. There was no answer this evening when I phoned. I'll try again tomorrow. Meantime, if Jade is a volunteer at the Harmonetics Hospital, she may be able to find the files on Mary Hamble. Three months ago Mary was in a private room on the fifth floor of the West Wing, Iris Corridor.

Beth Marple and Jade Boren had been playing tennis since they were twelve. Both had learned the game in cold northern cities before the indoor tennis club boom. Beth was from Chicago. In the late fall and all through the winter she would travel halfway across the city three or four times a week to play on the fast boards of the Broadway Armory. By the time Jade was thirteen, she knew the underground routes of the BMT and the IRT. Twice a week in the winter she tunneled her way to the Heights Casino in Brooklyn. Once a week she took the uptown subway to Nick's or Elwood's. Occasionally she played as a guest at the Seventh Regiment on Park Avenue. In the summer both girls switched from boards, the fastest surface in the game, to clay, the slowest. When they were fourteen they met up on the Summer Circuit at the TVI in Chattanooga, the Southerns in Louisville, and the National Girls' in Cincinnati. They gravitated together because the Californians and Floridians already had their doubles partners. They each did respectably in singles; Beth had match point against Kathy Harter in the National Girls' 18 and Jade took a set off Julie Heldman and had point for 4–1 in the third.

They played in college but without the same dedication. Beth once reached the third round of Wimbledon and the quarters of a Virginia Slims tournament. Jade's best efforts in singles were winning Gstaad and upsetting the No. 1 in France at Forest Hills.

At 5:00 A.M. Jade was awakened by the soft scraping of violins and cellos from WQXR. She switched off her radio alarm and slowly reoriented. Yes, I am in my New York apartment and this is the day I am playing tennis with Beth at 7:00 A.M. Jade was a night person: she had to get up two hours before a practice match and three and a half hours before a tournament match. She struggled out of bed, turned on the coffee pot in the tiny kitchenette, poured herself a glass of ice water to pat on her face, and took it with her into the bathroom. Five minutes later she was sitting on the side of her bed sipping coffee. Arnie was in the middle, sleeping peacefully.

As Jade drank her coffee, she devised imaginary responses to possible psychological and aptitude test questions:

Word Association Test:

"Shock treatment"	"Health"
"Experiment"	"Success"
"Harmonetics"	"Peace"
"Dr. Minden"	"Saint." No, "Leader"
"Dr. Fronzhold"	"Genius"
"Hospital"	"Cure"

"Death"   "Fear"
"Old age"   "Sadness"
"Doctors"   "Selflessness." No, "Dedication"
It would be perfectly proper to demonstrate finger dexterity and memory feats such as language, but one should be low on curiosity, fail on botany (they'll have me working in their goddamn garden), and show relatively poor leadership qualities.

Do you cry often? Yes.

Whom are you closer to, your father or your mother? My mother.

Do you ever feel lonely? Well, yes, I guess so.

Have you ever felt you needed psychiatric help? Uh, I guess we've all felt that way at some time.

Do you like music? Yes, the works: classical, rock and roll, country music.

What TV shows do you watch? Where the hell is my *TV Guide*. Okay, let's see, don't be too obvious. The "Tonight" Show, "All in the Family," "Marcus Welby." No, that's overdoing it. "The New Interns," "live" tennis, "Kojak." That's not right either. I'm overcomplicating the answers. Just the "Tonight" and "Tomorrow" shows.

Jade put on her tennis clothes and packed a small bag.

Do you like people? Yes.

Do you like big parties? No.

How often do you go to a doctor for a checkup? Every few years but I know I should go more often.

Do you like to be alone a lot? No.

Do you believe in psychosurgery? I don't know enough about it.

Jade was walking out the front door when she remembered she had forgotten to say good-bye to Arnie. She ran back to the bedroom and kissed him. He didn't wake up. It was nice when he was there but it was equally pleasant when he slept in his own pad. Their arrangement, she felt, was properly loose.

Once she was in the taxi, Jade switched her thoughts from Arnie and aptitude tests to the forthcoming game with Beth.

The taxi pulled up to the Midtown at 6:45. Beth was just arriving. Jade was hyped up for the game because it was the only way she enjoyed it. Beth was a good practice partner: she tried hard and concentrated well, and there were no quick serves, smart remarks, or close calls.

Both women were 5'7" and 124 pounds but Beth had always seemed more mature because of her padded bras. Today was different. Beth wore an unpadded bra, a V-neck shirt, and a flared skirt; Jade wore no bra, her tank shirt was yanked down tight, and her shorts curved tightly over her butt. Beth was a handsome woman with long blonde hair pulled scalp-tight to reveal the good bones in her forehead, cheeks, and nose. Had she tied her hair in a ponytail, she would have looked like an aging cheerleader. Jade was the epitome of the Italian Madonna: straight dark-brown hair, almost black, large eyes, high cheekbones, and a full mouth. Her looks were not currently in style but they wore well.

The game was enjoyable: both were hitting solidly, anticipating well, and running all out. There wasn't the same tenseness as in tournament competition where you won and moved up to the next round or you lost and were sidelined, but there was satisfaction in good concentration, hard work, and, in particular, making impossible gets. Several times during the match Jade thought: nice player, nice girl, nice sport. When they stopped after their hour was up, Beth suggested a standing weekly 7:00 A.M. date.

"That's awfully early," Jade said, looking soulfully at Beth with her large Madonna eyes. "However, if they accept me in Harmonetics, I'll have to get up early anyway, so why not?"

"I hope you are assigned to the hospital," said Beth, giving Jade a maternal pat on the shoulder.

She's just decided to be my sponsor, thought Jade.

The two players showered, changed, and drove from the club to the hospital in Beth's Volkswagen. Beth was in an expansive mood.

"I've been writing up a case history for Dr. Jennings on one of her patients. The woman had been severely depressed for seven or eight years. She couldn't function normally. She'd been to several psychologists and had been treated with chemotherapy, Thorazine, and several experimental drugs. Nothing worked. She underwent a series of shock treatments. They didn't help either. Dr. Jennings discussed the case with Dr. Kohl, and they agreed to try psychosurgery. The patient had the operation two months ago. I want you to see her now. She's alert, cheerful, rational, and about to be discharged."

"Incredible," said Jade. "I thought psychosurgery was pretty dangerous."

"Absolutely not. The mortality is less than 1 percent."

"But how about the success rate? How many are cured like this patient and how many end up vegetables?"

"The percentage of success is very high. I have only seen a limited number who have undergone the operation, but Dr. Jennings says that of her last sixteen patients where psychosurgery was performed, all showed improvement and several were totally cured. Even if the operation didn't help in a particular case, it still would be worth the risk: the patient can't be much worse off."

"Is the operation used just on specific kinds of mental illness such as depression?"

"No. Dr. Jennings has authorized it for almost every kind of severe mental problem that will not respond to other types of treatment."

"You said you tested patients before and after shock treatment. What's the percentage of success there?"

"It's often a matter of time. The first shock treatment may not work but the third might, or the tenth. Often it takes a large number of treatments. I've seen it where it's brought the patient out of an impenetrable cloud."

"Is it sometimes ineffective after a hundred shocks?"

"Yes, but we have to keep trying. Once we are sure shock won't work, we have the option of psychosurgery."

"Is your department called Psychology or Psychiatry?"

"Neither. Dr. Fronzhold believed it was bad for the mental attitude of a patient to assign him to the cancer ward or the psychiatric ward. Tell a patient he has meningitis and he could die from fear. The wards are named after flowers and shrubs. Our department is Iris. Dangerous patients are in Iris I, those who are unable to take care of themselves are in Iris II, etc."

"So someone in Iris V would be in reasonably good shape?"

"Not necessarily. Iris V is for private patients. Some are violent, some depressed, and some are alcoholics drying out. There are no wards in 'V.'"

"Do you work in all the Iris departments?"

"Theoretically my office is in Iris V but I do most of my work in the other Iris wards."

They were approaching the hospital. Beth turned into the staff parking lot and drove to a slot marked "Iris: Marple." As they got out of the car, Beth said:

"Better take your tennis bag, Jade. I might have to work late, which means I couldn't drive you home."

Jade followed Beth into the building. They walked down a flight of stairs along a service corridor to a door marked "Staff Women's Change Room." It was small, plain, and cramped. There were lockers, low benches, and a laundry bin in the corner. Beth opened a small locker and pulled out a pair of businesslike shoes, which she exchanged for the sandals she was wearing. She took off a bracelet and chain, put them in the locker and closed it. She was already wearing the required open white shirt which, together with her straight, narrow skirt, gave her a look of efficiency.

"Wait a moment, Jade. I'm going to wash my hands," said Beth euphemistically.

Beth walked through the swinging door to the sinks and toilets, leaving Jade alone in the locker room. As soon as the swinging door closed, Jade moved to the laundry bin. It was filled with rumpled gowns, some spotted with blood. Jade grabbed a blue gown, opened her tennis bag, and quickly stuffed it in. Then she sat down· on a bench and stared at the wall.

Beth returned and gave Jade her instructions for the day. She was to go to the Reading Room and wait until someone from Aptitudes came for her. The tests would take six hours with a one-hour break. She would have to return tomorrow for more Aptitudes and the Psychology Test. Beth would talk to Dr. Jennings and would try to get them together either on the break period today or tomorrow. Everything depended on the results of the tests and whether Dr. Jennings could use her.

(Reprinted by permission of the *New York Times*)
March 3, 1979

Dr. Mcdonald Dedicates
Harmonetics Resting Grounds
Former Jesuit Priest Addresses Capacity Congregation at
Opening of New Jersey Cemetery

Pappatana, N.J. *Dr. Francis X. McDonald of the Harmonetics Society gave the dedication address at the opening ceremonies today of the Harmonetics Resting Grounds, the largest cemetery in the New York metropolitan area. The property was purchased a year ago from the Pappatana National Bank, the bank having acquired the acreage when the Pappatana Country Club defaulted on its bonds.*

Dr. McDonald is one of the twenty-five men and women in the Harmonetics Society who wear the White Robe. He is the author of Casuistry in Catholicism *and* The Harmonetics Doctrine. *During his seventeen years as a Jesuit priest, he was known as Father Francis Xavier. He resigned from the Catholic Church in 1974. In his sermon Dr. McDonald spoke about the four doctrines of Harmonetics: the knowledge of self, the work ethic, love of mankind, and dedication to the Harmonetics spirit.*

The Temple of the Harmonetics Resting Grounds has four large Worshiping Halls. The walls, from floor to ceiling, have niches on which rest small urns in multicolor designs of blue, red, green, brown, and white. The design for the urns was commissioned from Roberto Del Bello of Milan. Mr. Del Bello also is responsible for the design of the carved stones with bronze markers that can be seen on the rolling hills of the vast Resting Grounds.

The fifty acres of the Resting Grounds were landscaped by Pericles Maniadis. Mr. Maniadis utilized the many trees and shrubs native to New Jersey to create small meditation groves. He imported large quantities of smooth rocks and pebbles from the Greek islands to form the base and sides of a brook that meanders across four acres and feeds into Lake Pappatana.

The renovation of the old clubhouse and the four small chapels were the work of New York architect Franklin Robert Parson.

One of the pleasures in Elliott Beale's life was his customary morning ritual. He would sit down at the dining-room table and ring the bell. Almost immediately someone would bring him a glass of freshly squeezed orange juice that he would sip slowly while he read the *Times*. After three or four minutes he would ring the bell again. Someone, either the maid or Henrietta, would appear with his bacon and eggs, crisp rye toast, jam, and a small pot of coffee. He would eat slowly, studying the obituaries, the business section, and the editorial pages. When he had finished the paper, he would ring for another hot cup of coffee. Then he would move to his desk, reach for his gold pen, and do the crossword puzzle in ink.

Elliott had just finished his juice when the telephone rang. He buzzed for his eggs but no one appeared. It was the maid's day off, and that blasted female was gabbing on the phone with some silly friend while his eggs hardened. Ten minutes later Henrietta brought his breakfast. Elliott ignored her. He jabbed angrily at his omelet and took the first bite. Ah, quite nice. A delicate cheese flavor with a sprinkling of parsley. The toast was crisp and hot. Elliott, mollified, turned to the obituaries. Although no one he knew had died today, he checked the ages and the causes of death: 83, after a long illness, in a nursing home; 76, heart attack, at Bellevue; 58, after a long illness, Sloan-Kettering Cancer Center; 63, cause of death not given, New York Hospital; 71, after a long illness, Harmonetics Hospital. He was feeling extremely well but it might not be a bad idea to have another checkup. Last week Woodings was telling everyone at the club how well he felt, and two days later he dropped dead.

Elliott dutifully turned to the business section. Atico's earnings had slid 26 percent, Gulf Marketing's had soared to a record $18 million in the second quarter, Parco Minerals had acquired 17 percent of the outstanding shares of Canadian General Copper, the GNP had risen 5.7 percent, Hydro Power Consolidated was seeking $300 million. . . . His head started to nod. The phone was ringing. He pulled himself erect and buzzed for more coffee. He could feel the rising irritation but he sought to control it. Bad for his blood pressure. He waited patiently for thirty seconds, then buzzed again. No response. Elliott folded his paper, got up, and opened the swinging door to the kitchen. Henrietta was standing with her back to him, talking to one of her idiotic friends.

"Jerry, will you give me that name again? Austin McDowell? Yes, I know the law firm well." Henrietta turned around and saw Elliott. She returned to the phone and spoke more rapidly. "I'm so sorry but I'm in the middle of making breakfast. I'll call you later."

Henrietta took a fresh cup, filled it with coffee, and followed Elliott back into the drawing room.

"Who's Austin McDowell?" he asked.

"He's a brilliant attorney with the firm of Blake, Chatterly. I believe he's a partner."

"Blake, Chatterly, well, that's all right. Who's the Jerry you were talking to?"

"He's that nice young man, the son of those charming people we met a few weeks ago at that big garden party. He was so interested in several of the articles I had written for *Fortune,* particularly the one . . ."

Elliott had gone back to his newspaper. Henrietta finished her sentence and unobtrusively left the room. She went into her bedroom, shut the door, and picked up her small telephone directory. Popple, Arthur. Business phone, WHitehall 5-4840.

Henrietta dialed. The operator answered: "Blake, Chatterly, good morning."

"Mr. Arthur Popple, please."

"Mr. Popple is on vacation in Florida. Would you like to speak to his secretary?"

"Yes, please."

There were two sharp buzzes.

"Mr. Popple's office."

"This is Mrs. Elliott Beale. I want to talk to Mr. Popple about changing a codicil in my will. Can you give me his number in Florida, please?"

"Certainly, Mrs. Beale."

Henrietta dialed the Florida number.

"Hello, Arthur? This is Henrietta Beale in New York. How are you? Are you enjoying the sunshine? . . . It's very nice here. We're having a lovely autumn. . . . Elliott is fine, thanks. . . . I'm sorry to bother you on your vacation but I want to make a major change in my will. I've been thinking it over carefully for several months, and now my mind is made up. I want to do it immediately. You know how we women are: once a decision is reached, we want to go ahead full steam. . . . You're going to be in Florida three more weeks! Oh, Arthur, I wish you could come back now. This is so important to me. . . . Well, if you must stay in Palm Beach, is there anyone at your law firm who specializes in wills? I would like to talk to someone today. . . . Martin Bradshaw? No, I don't like that man. He has no patience with women. . . . Yes, I realize we girls are demanding. Is there anyone else, Arthur? . . . Austin McDowell? Is he nice? Will he listen? . . . All right, I'll be here for the next twenty minutes. . . . Maybe I am being unreasonable but I'm going through a deep emotional crisis and I must talk to someone today. . . . Thank you very much, Arthur. I am so sorry to put you through this but I know you understand it's important to me. . . . Yes, I'm feeling fine. Don't worry, and thanks again."

Ten minutes later the phone rang.

"Hello, Mrs. Beale? Just a minute for Austin McDowell."

Mr. McDowell was charming. He would be happy to see Mrs. Beale if she would come to his office tomorrow at 4:00 P.M. He would be able to give her plenty of uninterrupted time. She was not to worry. He would take care of all the changes. Yes, he did have a copy of the old will in his office. He would see her at 4:00 P.M.

Henrietta made a brief call to Jerry at *National News*. Then she picked up her purse and went into the study to say good-bye to Elliott. He had finished the puzzle and was now shuffling through the mail and the business journals on his desk. He nodded absentmindedly.

Henrietta's first stop was Global Publishing, where she was fortunate enough to see Lionel Hemingway. He had four thousand square feet of office space in a loft building on 27th Street. The difference between a loft and regular office space is the difference between a barn and a house. Loft space will rent from $2 to $5 a square foot as opposed to $7 to $25 for offices. Often some or all of the amenities—rugs, curtains, blinds, painted walls, large windows, and partitions—are omitted. Since many companies that rent loft space move heavy equipment in and out on a regular basis, loft buildings offer freight elevator service only.

Henrietta shared the freight elevator with two large muscular men who were pushing a dolly loaded with heavy metal beams. They were arguing with the freight elevator man, an elderly, wizened fellow with a sullen attitude, because he had refused to take them up on his last load. The arguments stopped as soon as Henrietta got on. She heard the shouts begin again after she got off at the third floor.

The third floor was pleasant, as is true of much New York City loft space. Lionel Hemingway provided comfort, cleanliness, and good light for his employees. There were no leather chairs or Orientals and no Frankenthaler murals on the walls, but each of the editors had a good 250 square feet of privacy and the art directors had equivalent space. The secretaries were provided with secondhand desks but they were set far apart to give them a feeling of freedom. Dress was optional. One of the editors had kicked off his shoes, and sweaters, jeans, and open-neck shirts were de rigueur.

Henrietta liked the atmosphere. It was typical of most small magazines and newspapers. This particular publishing empire was unique in that loft space was cheap, which gave the people who worked at Globe the most precious commodity in the city: room to breathe.

Lionel Hemingway was an affable, easy man in his mid-fifties. He had a florid complexion, the result of high blood pressure or excessive amounts of rich foods and liquors. He was thirty pounds too heavy but it was evenly distributed. He had the jovial manner of a popular restaurateur and the reputation for dealing fairly with people. He was pleased to meet Henrietta and even more pleased when he found out she might be able to help him unload *Cuisine du Monde*.

"Henrietta," he said, "I got a bomb. I've lost $2 million and I'll lose a helluva lot more if I can't get rid of it quickly."

She stared at him curiously. "You're certainly open about it and I appreciate your directness. I'll be equally frank. There's a group that might be interested in taking over the entire *Cuisine du Monde* property, which means advertising contracts and subscription lists only."

"You mean they won't keep the current staff?"

"No. It means you'll have the responsibilities for current indebtedness."

"How much will they pay, Henrietta?"

"I don't know. I think $500,000. The magazine has lost four times that in three months, and whoever takes it over would be paying an extraordinary fee to acquire 70,000 subscribers and less than eight pages of advertising."

"I won't argue. I'll take it."

"It's not a deal yet. I'll be talking to Senator Spriggs and I will recommend the property. He will negotiate directly with you."

"Do we pay you, Henrietta?"

"My payment," she replied with a smile, "is the great pleasure I have had in meeting you and seeing your operation."

After Henrietta left Global, she taxied to the Temple. She proceeded directly to Seminar Enrollments and signed herself up for both the Aptitude and Psychological Tests and the Health and Body seminar. She would take the tests the following week but meanwhile she would begin Health and Body immediately. The first class was about to start and would run until noon. During the hour break she could have lunch in one of the Harmonetics Health Restaurants on the three top floors. The seminar would reconvene at 1:00 P.M. and would end promptly at 3:00. Now, if Henrietta would make out a check for $350, she would be given her Health and Body Badge, which would admit her to the eleventh floor. Her class was starting in Room 1146.

In return for her check, Henrietta received a badge which said "11th." She was directed to the bank of elevators. She found Room 1146 and took one of the two empty chairs. She had twenty-three classmates, all female. The youngest was in her thirties and the eldest in her seventies. A few were too thin but the majority were overweight. Only two of the women wore blue gowns; the rest were Probationaries or civilians like Henrietta.

The lecturer, a Green Gown in her forties with a silky,

125

glowing complexion, outlined the subjects that would be discussed: nutrition, vitamins, exercise, skin, and medications.

"Do not," she said, "use your old cosmetics. Doctors in our Harmonetics Laboratories have proved that many of the so-called 'best' skin creams will actually age the fine tissues on your face and will destroy the hormones your skin produces to keep you young. We have oils, lotions, and creams to repair the superficial damage you have already incurred. Massage will make many of the muscles firm again. Our shampoos will bring back the natural luster to your hair.

"This morning both the lecture and the lab will be on the skin. Each of you will be shown how to use the unguents and nutrients that are vital for a healthy, radiant complexion. Since this is a three-day introductory seminar, many of you may wish to enroll in further courses. I am speaking particularly to those in this class who have literally poisoned their skins with cosmetics or starved their organs through poor nutrition. Your minds are young and your capabilities are unlimited but physically you have allowed your bodies to deteriorate. You may check with me later on advanced seminars we recommend.

"If you will follow me to Health Lab I, we will divide you into groups of five. Each group will be assisted by a volunteer. First you will be given a gentle hormone cleanser, which is used twice. This is followed by a clear lotion that freshens and firms the skin. Then come the massage unguents that stimulate the blood, which in turn feeds the skin. Then several Protector creams are rubbed in, each with a circular, brisk motion. We select these creams individually to suit your coloring. Finally, the Elixir Rejuvenation Nutrient is dotted on and blended. That finishes the process. No cosmetics are used. The result is a fresh, young, glowing complexion.

"Now, ladies, shall we start?"

The twenty-four ladies formed a line and marched in twos to Health Lab I. The name belied the interior. It was a brightly lit salon containing five magnificent circular tables of exquisite marble. Around each table were five white and gold antique chairs covered in pale blue satin. A tall pentagonal mirror, the circumference of which was dotted with fragile half-inch bulbs, occupied the center of each table. In front of each chair were a dozen delicate jars and bottles in rose, aquamarine, lemon, frost, pale green, and violet, the ingredients lettered in gold. Several delicate porcelain bowls held small sponges, cotton puffs, and dainty 5-inch towels. To a woman enamored of the cosmetic counters of Bonwit's or Bendel's, entering Health Lab I was like walking into the Prado or the Sistine Chapel. Several of the ladies lifted their eyes to the walls, and the marble tables with their promise of youth and beauty were forgotten.

The photographs on the walls were case histories in color, each a series of four studies of a particular woman. Henrietta examined a series: first, a woman in her mid-sixties, the skin lined, the hair mousy, deep creases and pouches under the eyes, the powder and rouge uncomfortably visible; in the second picture, the hair was soft and glossy, the coloring of the skin was marvelous, and the face glowed but the wrinkles and pouches were still evident; picture No. 3 showed the same woman looking ten or fifteen years younger; in the fourth photograph all lines and pouches had disappeared, just as though the woman had stepped backward into her prime.

The ladies wandered from one row of pictures to the next, the jars and pots ignored. Here was the photograph of a woman moving heavily into her late fifties. Two frames later she was transformed into her young forties, abloom with life. The second picture was always an improvement on the first, but the next two were miraculous. Was it the magic of the plastic surgeon or some potent lotion available only in Health Lab II?

"Attention, ladies," said the lecturer. "Step One always precedes Step Two. Please take one of the chairs and let's begin the Harmonetics Way to Health right now."

For two hours the ladies enjoyed an orgy of sweet-smelling balms. The constant massage brought color to the cheeks. Cotton puffs, towelettes, and sponges were dropped into the throwaway boxes as new jars were opened and old ones closed. Then volunteers mixed the Protector creams which, to Henrietta, seemed to be moisturizers of varied beige and tan and rose colors. The excess was blotted, then a deeper rose was rubbed on the cheekbones and blended in. A cosmetic to replace a cosmetic, thought Henrietta, who relished the experience. Last came the Elixir Rejuvenation Nutrient, which was a heavy oil dotted around the eyes to make them shine and on the lips to make them glisten. The result was light, soft, and shiny, a definite improvement over the pasty foundations and heavy shades of lipstick the ladies had been buying for a decade.

"Our lab is completed for the morning," announced the lecturer. "You may go upstairs to the top three floors for the Health Luncheon, which we recommend, but please return to Room 1146 by 1:00 sharp. This afternoon we will study vitamins and nutrition, which is fundamental in order to proceed to Step Two. By 3:00 P.M., when the seminar is dismissed for the day, your personalized Facial Health Care packages will be ready. You may take them home with you. Tomorrow morning we will start Step One in Treatment of the Hair.

"Ladies, one hour only."

The future Beauty Queens took the elevators upstairs. To some, the last two hours had been a moment in history, equivalent to the first time one slept with one's future husband or the first view of one's newborn child. Laura Hambridge, the seventy-three-year-old woman who was senior citizen of the class, had discarded her lumpy, disgruntled expression and was archly preening like an elderly Scarlett O'Hara. Skinny fiftyish Rita Bloom straightened her stooped shoulders and tossed her limp hair as though she were going to the Senior Prom. Fat Andrea Sellinger, age sixty-two, giggled girlishly. Life had begun again. These ladies feel terrific, thought Henrietta. They need a little pleasure in the monotony of their lives, and if they can afford it and it makes them happy, why begrudge it? It's certainly healthier, she thought, than getting sloshed every day.

After the luncheon of eggplant, orange slices, and crisp spinach leaves, the ladies returned to Room 1146, still euphoric. They were each given a syllabus, which was an exact duplicate of the lecture. Pencils, newly sharpened, were passed out. The pupils were asked to underline the major headings as they were read by the lecturer. All were able to do so successfully.

A ten-minute break came at 2:00 P.M. A tray containing plastic cups and steaming pitchers of bouillon was wheeled in by a woman in a red gown. The ladies could buy a cup for fifty cents. Most did. The two women in blue gowns put a $1 bill down and asked for no change, to the shame of many of the other ladies.

Class resumed. The lecturer spoke about her own life.

"There is no such thing as age. In calendar years I am fifty-eight, in looks I am forty-two, and in health and heart I am twenty-four. I serve the Society because of my deep love for our leaders and my admiration for their thoughts. They are brilliant, wonderful men. They perform miracles. We are given a way of life and the answers to so many of our questions. Peace and harmony is brought to us through our service, just as the leaders serve us."

When the class was over, Henrietta went up to the lecturer and thanked her. The lecturer extended her hands. Henrietta took them. They raised their hands to each other's faces. To Henrietta it was a highly unusual expression of friendship. The implications of touching seemed sexual. It might have been easier with someone who also had never "touched" before.

Henrietta took the Down elevator with four classmates. All had already decided to take the next seminar. Henrietta said she would also enroll. At the Temple door they parted in different directions, some to take the subway, others to taxi, and Henrietta to walk to the nearest telephone booth.

Excerpt from "Harmonetics Report" by Jade Boren
Sources: The *New York Times,* Dr. Peter Weldon, Maria Palenti, Minnie Matthews

Dr. Heinrich Fronzhold was born in 1922 in Yorkville, which is a section of Manhattan. His parents, who had emigrated from Germany, lived on 84th Street and Second Avenue. Fronzhold went to public school, then to Columbia where he had been given a small scholarship. He had few friends in the neighborhood and even fewer at college. He lived in the three-room family apartment, taking the subway uptown every day.

Karl Uberwelt, who owns the Brauhaus in Yorkville, was acquainted with Fronzhold. He refers to him as Fronzie. According to Uberwelt, Fronzie was sickly as a child. He always had colds in winter and he wasn't allowed to play in the snow. He studied very hard and his parents were strict. He went to

Lutheran Church every Sunday but Uberwelt could not say if Fronzie was religious.

Fronzhold was 4F in World War II. He finished at Columbia and went on to medical school. Myron Greenberg, who was in the same class as Fronzhold, found him cold and unfriendly. However, he won't say Fronzhold was anti-Semitic because he was cold and unfriendly to almost everyone, with the notable exception of the professors.

He interned at Bellevue and did his training there in surgery. Dr. Peter Weldon, who is still on the staff there, remembers him as methodical and slow. He said Fronzhold took such a long time removing stones from a gallbladder or excising a section of the intestine that several patients may have made a premature exit. Weldon did not like Fronzhold.

Fronzhold took his residency in Houston and later established his practice there. Dr. Cawley, a noted surgeon, says Fronzhold's technique was acceptable but slow. A surgical nurse at the hospital, Maria Palenti, was the most outspoken critic. (She has asked that her name be withheld.) She accused him of operating on a great many aging people—men and women in their eighties and nineties—who could not survive the trauma. She was particularly angry about an uncomplaining elderly man who came into the hospital for a prostate examination and never came out. In three months, said Maria, Fronzhold sawed and hacked and carved until there was hardly anything left of the poor old guy.

Many patients had wonderful things to say about the good doctor. Minnie Matthews claims he saved her life. She suffered for a number of years from gastric pains and could find no relief until she went to Fronzhold. There is a large clique of loyal Houston patients who attribute their recoveries to him. There is a smaller clique that finds him dominating and rude. Minnie Matthews says some women go to doctors to be pampered and petted; Fronzhold pampers none, insults many, and, according to Minnie, performs miracles.

The friendship between Fronzhold and Josiah Minden began through their mutual friend, Minnie Matthews. Fronzhold went to several of Minden's lectures and Minden in turn took an interest in Fronzhold's work. The doctor grew a beard and began to wear his hair in the Minden style. He also slowed down his own practice of surgery, although he was in great demand, and he spent many more hours on hospital administration. Whereas he had been a solitary man, he started going to the opera and the ballet. He married a rich widow, Ruth Jansen, who was one of Houston's well-known hostesses. She was a great admirer of Dr. Minden and became one of the early members of the Harmonetics Society. Shortly after their marriage, Fronzhold became the director of the newly built Houston Harmonetics Clinic.

Six years ago Dr. Fronzhold established the Harmonetics Medical Research Laboratory off South Main, in the heart of Houston's medical center. A rich Texan, Burgess Croft, donated the land, and Minnie Matthews spearheaded the fund-raising. The lab is small and there are few staffers, maybe eight or ten. It's an animal experimental station and it's equipped with the usual mice, guinea pigs, frogs, dogs and cats, plus a vast number of parakeets, monkeys and baboons. Two years ago a joint suit against the lab was filed by the SPCA and the Anti-Vivisection Society, but the local judge would not issue a restraining order and the case was thrown out by a higher court.

Three years ago a small fifteen-bed Harmonetics Hospital was erected adjacent to the lab. It's primarily for people over fifty and the treatment is free. There's an unsubstantiated rumor that these people are being used for human experimentation. Minnie Matthews says that's a canard (actually the word she used was "bullshit").

Quite a few women are physically attracted to Fronzhold. Minnie says he has the brute charm of an excited stallion. Maria Palenti does not agree. She finds him overbearing and arrogant. She says his thick features (the dominating nose, the fleshy cheeks, and the puffy bags under the eyes) are thoroughly revolting.

Dr. Fronzhold moved to New York several years ago to take over the management of the Harmonetics Hospital. He and his wife have a duplex apartment on Park Avenue and he drives to the hospital each morning in a chauffeured limousine. He is dedicated to the Harmonetics movement. He will not allow a doctor to affiliate with the hospital unless he is a member of the Society.

Martha Rayburn and Roger Silberstein were seated on the torn leather couch in Bill Harding's office. A cigarette hung out of the corner of Martha's mouth. Ashes had fallen on her ruffled white blouse and on the papers in her lap. She noticed them and brushed them onto the floor.

"We're writing up the Jennifer Holiday story, Bill," she said to Harding who was in one of his nervous moods. He was pacing back and forth, checking papers on his desk, fidgeting with the chairs, and thumbing through his phone messages.

"We're both worried about the consequences of one paragraph," said Roger. "We talk about the rejuvenation treatments at the hospital but we don't have any proof. Martha has the unsubstantiated opinions of Mrs. Small, the housekeeper, and I have the observations of Lawrence Runson, Jennifer Holiday's son. Runson's reasonably sure Jennifer underwent a transformation. I believe him."

"Then what's the problem?" asked Harding.

"If Jennifer's face did look younger and if the liver spots and heavy veins in her hands disappeared, how can we prove it was due to an attempt to rejuvenate her? Maybe she was taking drugs for other symptoms and, coincidentally, the liver spots and wrinkles disappeared."

"If the Harmonetics Hospital does offer rejuvenation to the aging, why do they keep it so secret? Particularly if it works?"

"That's the question," said Roger. "*Does* it work? Maybe the cure for old age is worse than the disease. The treatments might be a real killer. That's a damn good reason to keep it quiet."

"Martha, you said you were going to talk to one of your gossip columnist friends about rumors on rejuvenation. Any items about celebrities looking thirty years younger or elderly movie stars making comebacks?"

"Just the usual, Bill. My friend Beverly, who writes 'The Hot Seat' syndicated column, says she's been hearing rejuvenation stories ever since she entered the business. Ten years ago everyone was talking about a mysterious Chinese doctor on an island off the coast of Venezuela who rejuvenated rich ex-beauties and dying industrialists with hormones extracted from unborn calves. Now Beverly says it's a young, handsome South American doctor, the place is Guadalajara and the supposed treatment is a milky substance made of whale sperm. She says she knows for sure that A.G. Fernwood of Fernwood Films spent hundreds of thousands of dollars at an Austrian health clinic. He went there every year and he sent his top stars as soon as they turned fifty. I think it was forty for the women. Beverly says it didn't do a damn bit of good: A.G. got older every year. I asked her if she had heard anything about Jennifer Holiday. She said Jennifer dropped out of sight completely several years ago, which means she stopped going to Studio 54. Beverly offered to provide me with a list of women who have had confirmed tummy tucks or of men who've had hair implants, but she doesn't know anyone who has had a rejuvenation."

"Let's see if Jerry has any more information," said Harding. He opened the office door and bellowed, "Jerry!"

Jerry Marconi, looking as though his pet dog had just been run over, entered the room, doing his best to smile.

"Have Harold, Jade, or Henrietta phoned in any new material?" asked Harding. He wonderd what was bugging the boy.

"Jade just called. She's been talking to her mother. Josiah Minden went to see Mrs. Boren today and returned all her jewels. He told Mrs. Boren she had already been extremely generous and that as long as Mr. Boren was not a believer, the gift of the jewels would only create dissension in the family. Mrs. Boren was crying and Jade, as she told me the story, was almost crying too. The mother thinks Minden is a totally sensitive, wonderful man. Jade says he's not as cruddy as she thought."

"Very clever of Josiah," commented Martha, wisps of ashes dropping on her blouse. "It was done to impress Jade. It will make him look awfully good to her for at least twenty-four hours."

"You think she'll see through him?" asked Jerry.

"She already does," answered Harding. "The Harmonetics article was her idea."

"That's better," said Jerry, smiling for the first time.

"What else?" asked Harding.

"After Mrs. Boren told Jade the story of the jewels, Jade asked her mother if she should tell Minden that *National News* was planning an exposé. She used the word 'exposé' deliberately to stir up her mother. It worked. Mrs. Boren wanted to know why Jade hadn't told her before. Jade said it was a matter of professional ethics. The magazine had paid her salary and she didn't want to be a fink. Mrs. Boren said that was nonsense. Jade got huffy and they had an argument. She's positive her mother will call Minden immediately and that Minden will get in touch with her."

Harding's edginess had disappeared. He was reclining in his chair, his eyes vacantly staring at the dirt spots on the ceiling. "She should have a small recorder, one that will fit in a match box or compact, for her meetings with Minden. We don't want any misquotes. Jerry, will you see Jade gets one?"

"I'll do it tonight. Are there any specific questions she should ask Josiah?"

"She'll know what to do," assured Harding.

"Clever girl," said Martha, spraying ashes.

"Henrietta had a fine time today," continued Jerry. "She had a meeting with Lionel Hemingway at Global Publications and he was overjoyed with the idea of unloading *Cuisine du Monde*. When Henrietta mentioned a possible $500,000, Hemingway almost jumped into her lap. She went to the Temple immediately after for her Health and Body seminar. She said to tell you she had a $350 facial. Tomorrow she has an appointment to see Austin McDowell. He's going to draw up a new will for her, with a nice, fat bequest for the Harmonetics Society. She'll be in touch again after her meeting with McDowell.

"Harold's on the trail of something hot. He hopes to have something positive by tomorrow."

"Everyone's doing a good job," said Harding. "We're getting a better picture of the Society but it's not yet precise. The rejuvenation treatments are still theory. The old woman, Mary, who tried to escape from the hospital, may have been a psychopath. Austin McDowell, who drew up the Holiday will, has done nothing illegal or unethical. The Society has a perfect right to train missionaries, solicit funds, establish hospitals and clinics, and expand its membership. There are plenty of established religions that do exactly the same things. I don't feel we should criticize the Harmonetics Society merely because the movement is new or because it is expanding so rapidly.

"If we accuse the Society of influencing people to turn over all their property to them, then why don't we make the same accusations against a respectable religious sect? Nuns and priests give all their possessions to the Church and all Mormons tithe. Most people admire them for it. Why are we investigating the Harmonetics Society?"

"We suspect the leaders," answered Roger.

"Do we? Which ones? Minden at the Temple, Fronzhold at the hospital, or Spriggs in the government? What have they done that breaks the law? Their motives may well be pure. Roger, you are convinced they are after power and their motives are rotten. Isn't every major executive and every top corporation and every labor union motivated by profit and/or power? Why should we tell our subscribers to distrust the Harmonetics leaders? Why shouldn't we tell them instead that it's a sect that respects and honors the elderly?"

There was an uncomfortable silence.

"I think there's something sinister about the Society," said Martha, "but two million people would disagree with me."

Another silence.

"The Jennifer Holiday story isn't bad," said Roger, "but it would be a lot better if we didn't have to cut the rejuvenation paragraph."

"We can't gamble," said Harding. "You'll have to take it out. However, if you get positive proof of hanky-panky at a high level before tomorrow night, I'll authorize a change. You can insert a box, a bold one with a flashy headline. The copy will read 'Next Week: Corruption in the Harmonetics Society.' It will have the effect of stirring up Minden, Fronzhold, and Spriggs, but as individuals or as a group they could well be innocent. There is certainly no evidence of a criminal conspiracy."

"And there's no chance we'll get the proof by tomorrow," said Martha.

"One chance, but a slim one," replied Harding. "To quote Jerry, 'Harold's on the trail of something hot.'"

New York Harmonetics Temple
A List of Seminars in Continuing Education

Health and Body I   3 sessions, 4 hours per $ 350
day; 15-minute private
consultation

Health and Body II   5 sessions, 4 hours per   500
day; 4 private
consultations

Health and Body III   group exercise classes, 3   600
hours per week, 10-week
course

Nutrition I   3 hours per week, 10-   500
week course

Nutrition II   3 sessions per week, 4   500
hours per day, 10-week
course (classes held in
Dietetics Kitchen at
Harmonetics Hospital)

Introduction to   3 sessions, 2 hours per   1,000
Medicine   session, 15-minute
private consultation.
Lecturer: Dr. Heinrich
Fronzhold

Visitors Corp I   10 sessions, 1 hour each   350

Visitors Corp II   5 sessions, 2 hours each   350

Visitors Corp III   5 sessions, 1 hour each;   500
two 15-minute private
consultations

Harmonetics I   3 hours per week, 10-   500
week course

| Advanced Harmonetics | 3 sessions, 2 hours per session, 15-minute private consultation. Lecturer: Dr. Josiah Minden | 2,000 |

Other Recommended Courses (listed alphabetically)*

Acrylics
Aerobic Exercises I
Aerobic Exercises II
Arts and Crafts I
  Basketry
Arts and Crafts II
  Wood Carving
Arts and Crafts III
  Leatherwork
Ceramics
Dried Flower Arrangements
Dualities
Flowers and Plants I
Flowers and Plants II
Advanced Flowers and Plants
Furniture Repair I
Furniture Repair II
Graphology
Jewelry Design I
  Construction
Jewelry Design II
  Copper Enameling
Machine Shop I

Machine Shop II
Music I
  Tambourine and Drums
Music II
  Guitar
Music III
  Appreciation
Parent Education I
  Child Development
Parent Education II
  Goal Setting
Photography
Pottery
Quilting
Radio and TV Repair
Self-Improvement
Sewing I
Sewing II
Smoking Cessation
Transactional Analysis I
Transactional Analysis II
Advanced Transactional
  Analysis

*10-week courses, 3 hours per week, $500

Harold Gondoler awakened to the ringing of the telephone.

"Good morning, Mr. Gondoler," said the switchboard operator. "It's 7:30."

Harold, a morning person, sprang out of bed. He had formulated a plan of attack the previous night. First he would make sure that the "Mary" who tried to escape from Harmonetics Hospital was Mary Hamble. That should be reasonably easy. Second, he would find out if Mary Hamble was mentally disturbed. There was no point in trying to get into the hospital but he could check with her friends and relatives. If they said she was a dingbat, that would finish off that lead. Third, if Mary Hamble was sane, how did her son-in-law, Franklin Parson, get her committed? Furthermore, how had Parson convinced a doctor to sign the commitment papers?

Harold seldom used a tape recorder. Today he slipped a miniature tape recorder with a telephone pick-up into his pocket.

Harold's first stop was Mary Hamble's apartment house. It was a quiet building on East End Avenue in the eighties with a bored doorman who spent most of the day staring at the tugs and the tourist boats chugging their way around the island. When Harold arrived, the doorman was absorbed in the examination of a slow-moving rusty Greek freighter. Harold pulled out a business card.

"Our office has been trying to reach Mrs. Mary Hamble for several days. Do you know how we can get in touch with her?"

The doorman looked at the card and stared at Harold.

"Nope, don't know where she is," he said and turned away.

"I don't want to waste your time so if you'd accept this."

The doorman was no longer bored. He looked at the $10 bill and hesitated. He wanted the money but he didn't know where Mrs. Hamble was.

"Keep it," said Harold. "Would she be down south this time of year?"

"Nope, she never traveled except in the summer when she'd open her home on Long Island."

"What about her maid?"

"Nope, she's not here and neither is the cook."

"Do you know where I could reach them?"

"Nope."

Harold took out his wallet and examined it. The doorman examined it also.

"Maybe I could call up one of the maids who was friendly with them."

"That would be helpful," said Harold, taking out a $10 bill.

"My name is Ben," said the doorman, pocketing the money. "Wait here and I'll see what I can find out."

Five minutes later Ben returned. "It took a lot of phone calls," he said.

"What did you find out?"

"I must have phoned six different apartments," said Ben stubbornly.

Harold reached for the wallet again.

"Gretchen the cook is staying at this address." Ben handed him a piece of paper. "Can you read my writing? That's her phone number."

"Do you know where the maid is?"

"Nope."

"What's her name?"

Ben paused, then decided to pass the name on at no extra charge.

"Helga."

Gretchen lived in a four-story building a block from Riverside Drive. There was no doorman, no elevator man, and no elevator. The small lobby had a buzzer system by which one gained entry. The paint was peeling off the plaster and the floor was dark with layers of soot and stains embedded in the boards, but there was no litter. Merely a smell of cooking that permeated all the floors.

Harold walked up two flights to Gretchen's apartment. She opened the door immediately with the happy anticipation of the friendly soul who has few visitors. She had a pleasant, round face, red cheeks and looked as though she enjoyed her own cooking: she wore a plain dress, size 18, and rubber stockings for her varicose veins. The full face and padded flesh made it difficult to guess her age. Perhaps mid-fifties, possibly early seventies.

"How's the old building on East End? How's Ben?" she asked.

"Still watching the boats," Harold replied. Gretchen laughed.

"You said on the phone you wanted to ask me some questions about Mrs. Hamble. You better come in. I've got to sit down. My poor old legs can't carry me anymore."

The room was small and dark but clean. A lovely aroma of kuchen wafted toward Harold. Gretchen hospitably offered him a large slice and a cup of coffee. They sat down together at a dark linoleum-covered table. Harold took a bite.

"Delicious," he said and meant it.

"What is it you wish to know?"

"We're trying to locate Mrs. Hamble. Have you any idea where she is?"

"Poor Mrs. Hamble, she had terrible varicose veins, just like me. She was going in the hospital to get them stripped, that must have been three or four months ago. Helga and me, we stayed in the apartment. Then one day Mr. Parson, that's her son-in-law, comes over and tells us he's closing the apartment. He said Mrs. Hamble had complications and she would go out west to recuperate. He was very nice to both of us and he give me six months' salary. He said he'd get in touch with us again when Mrs. Hamble returned to New York. So Helga and me, we put all the slipcovers on the furniture. It's beautiful furniture, covered in beautiful blues and whites. Then we cleaned out the refrigerator and the deep freeze and we left."

"What about Mrs. Hamble's clothes?"

"Mr. Parson said to leave them. He'd take care of it."

"What hospital did she go to?"

"Mr. Parson belonged to the Harmonetics Society and he got her into their hospital."

"Was Mrs. Hamble a member of the Society?"

"No, she didn't believe in that kind of stuff. The Episcopal Church was good enough for her, and for Helga and me too."

"Why do you think she went to that hospital?"

"Her doctor belonged there. He said the rooms was lovely and she would be very comfortable."

"Would you remember the doctor's name?"

"Dr. Jean de Moraille."

"Was he a specialist?"

"No, he took care of Mrs. Hamble whenever she wasn't feeling well. She liked him because he would come over to the house."

"Did you ever hear the name Dr. Fronzhold?"

"I don't think so."

"I'm going to ask a question that may sound crude, but we have to check all possibilities. Did Mrs. Hamble ever sound a bit cracked? I mean were there signs she might be mentally unbalanced?"

"Oh, no. She was as fine in her head as me or Helga."

"Would you know if she had any heart problems or high blood pressure?"

"If she had them Helga and I would have known about it. Helga had bad asthma, and Mrs. Hamble and me, we had problems with our legs."

"Who were her friends? Did she have people over and did she go to other people's homes?"

"Sometimes, not too often. We had company maybe once a month or maybe not. She talked on the phone a lot and she went out maybe once a week. Her special friends were Mrs. Ryder and Mrs. Tompkins, but she didn't see them regular."

"Did they call when she was in the hospital?"

"Yes, they both called several times. That was two or three months ago, before Mr. Parson closed down the apartment."

"What about Mr. and Mrs. Parson? Did Mrs. Hamble see them often?"

"They talked on the phone. She saw them once a week or once in two weeks."

"What's Mrs. Parson like?"

"She's a quiet woman. He does most of the talking. I think maybe she's afraid of Mr. Parson."

"How long have they been married?"

"About two years. Angela, that's Mrs. Parson, had been a widow for nine years."

"Did you and Helga ever try to visit Mrs. Hamble?"

"Yes, we did. We called and were told she couldn't have visitors. They said she was doing fine and we should write her. I called Mr. Parson once and he said not to worry, Mrs. Hamble was having a complete series of tests."

"Did you like Mr. Parson?"

"He was always nice. He didn't talk to us much but he always said hello. Helga thought he was very handsome."

"I'd like to phone Mrs. Hamble's special friends, Mrs. Ryder and Mrs. Tompkins. How would they be listed in the phone book?"

"I don't know. They're both widows like Mrs. Hamble. Mrs.

Ryder lives at 85th and Park and Mrs. Tompkins is at 81st. Here, use the phone book."

Harold found the names and the numbers.

"Go ahead and use my phone," offered Gretchen.

Harold dialed the Ryder number. Mrs. Ryder answered. Harold identified himself and explained briefly that *National News* was trying to locate Mary Hamble.

"I'm glad you called," said Mrs. Ryder. "Missy Tompkins and I have been so worried about Mary. We haven't heard from her in over three months. Missy called Mary's son-in-law several times and he tried to be reassuring but Missy felt from his tone of voice that Mary was much sicker than we thought."

"Let me tell you a story," said Harold, and he related the incident of Mary's capture in the pharmacy. As he talked, he could hear Gretchen mumbling "Gott in Himmel" while on the receiver Mrs. Ryder was saying "My God, that poor woman!"

"I have a plan," said Harold, "and I'd like your help."

"Of course," said Mrs. Ryder. "I'd do anything to help poor Mary. Do you know that she and Missy and I went to Barnard together? We've known each other over fifty years."

"If you are available this morning, I'd like to come by in an hour or maybe an hour and a half. I have one call I want to make first."

"I'll stay home and wait for you."

"If Mrs. Tompkins is also available, she could be helpful too."

"I'll call Missy right now."

"Then I'll see you shortly."

Harold turned to Gretchen who was dabbing at her eyes with an enormous handkerchief.

"Gretchen, it may be a false alarm. Maybe we'll find out that Mrs. Hamble is in California or Arizona and is recovering nicely. If I get any news, I'll be in touch."

"Yes, she might be just fine."

It was an optimistic statement that neither believed.

(Reprinted by permission of the *New York Times*)
May 13, 1982

Judge Henley Stuart to Run for Governor
Well-known New York Jurist to Seek Republican Nomination

Judge Henley Stuart today confirmed rumors that his hat is in the ring for the post of Governor of the State of New York. He is the fifth and probably the strongest of the Republican contenders. He expects to receive the endorsement of the Harmonetics Society and its powerful leader, Dr. Josiah Minden.

Judge Stuart made the announcement of his candidacy at a small luncheon given for him by Senator Robert T. Spriggs. Among those present was Dr. Francis X. McDonald, often called the right-hand man of Harmonetics founder Dr. Minden.

Judge Henley Stuart has risen in the Harmonetics ranks to the top echelon. He received his White Robe from Dr. Minden six months ago. Senator Spriggs is also a member of the elite White Robe group.

The platform of Judge Stuart will be based on rigorous control of the budget, lowering of taxes, cracking down on crime, reduction of the bureaucracy in Albany, and state assistance to the Harmonetics Health and Research program.

Harold Gondoler took the subway to midtown and walked to the offices of *American & International Architecture* on Madison and 53rd. This was a bustling publication block that attracted the better-known slicks and specialties. The location was ideal for the advertising geniuses in the publication world. They could take their customers to La Cote Basque, Four Seasons, La Toque Blanche, or even Le Cygne where one could get a highly satisfactory lunch for as little as $50 a person (including wine). There were also adequate neighborhood coffee shops for managing editors and assistants to the publishers. *AIA* was a solid magazine produced for a limited but influential group of creative people—the architects who designed the airports and art galleries, buildings and bridges, cathedrals, condominiums, country clubs, churches, and cemeteries, not to mention yacht harbors and zoos. The editor, Helen Mandel, frequently lunched at the London Pub in the Ranger Hotel; she and Harold had had a waving and greeting acquaintance for several years. She was in her mid-forties, Gondoler's age.

It was Harold's first visit to the office. Helen, who was never surprised by any visitor, automatically handed him the latest issue and escorted him back to her office. When they were seated, Harold began. He was there to ask for her help in uncovering what might be a criminal action by architect Franklin Parson. He told his story chronologically: Mary Hamble's flight and capture at the pharmacy, Ellie Sue's visit to the Iris Corridor and, later, her recognition of Franklin Parson, his own interviews earlier in the morning with the doorman and Gretchen, and the telephone conversation with Mrs. Ryder.

"I've heard of Parson," said Helen, "but Ezra is our expert. Hold on while I buzz him."

Every magazine that can afford it has an Ezra. He is just out of college and is paid $8,000 a year because of his ability to accumulate, file, and store in his brain the data relevant to his field. Ask him in what issue *AIA* ran the picture of Mr. X and he will reply: "We ran two pictures: June 1953 when he received the Man of the Year Award and February 1972 upon his demise."

"What do you know about Franklin Parson?" Helen asked Ezra.

"Franklin Robert Parson is a New York architect. He has his own firm. He got his first big contract when he was commissioned to design the Harmonetics Resting Grounds Temple in Pappatana, New Jersey. He is the son-in-law of Mary Hamble whose late husband, Harland Hamble, owned the largest construction company in the Northeast."

"Then Mary Hamble is rich?"

"Exceedingly," replied Ezra. "Upon his marriage to Angela, Parson moved his office from the small suburban community of Carsneck, Long Island, to Manhattan. He bought into Donald Alexander's firm. A year ago, when Alexander retired, Parson paid him a lump sum to take over the entire operation."

"Where did he get the money?"

"Everyone says from his mother-in-law, Mrs. Hamble."

"What's his reputation?"

"He's generous with his salaries and has some excellent young architects working for him. He's strictly administrative now. He gets a lot of Harmonetics commissions."

"Don't we have some pictures of him?" asked Helen.

"Yes. Someone sent us a batch of photos when the Harmonetics Resting Grounds were dedicated. I'll get them for you."

Ezra returned with the Harmonetics file from which he took several eight-by-ten glossies. The captions were pasted to the bottom of each picture.

"Dr. Francis X. McDonald (left) shaking hands with Franklin Robert Parson (right), architect, who designed the Harmonetics Resting Grounds Temple." McDonald, wearing a white robe, was a small, slight man with sandy hair. Parson was at least eight inches taller and much broader. He had chiseled, handsome features and hair much darker than the brown robe that covered his massive body.

"Dr. Heinrich Fronzhold (seated, left) looks at the architectural drawings of the four Worshiping Halls. Franklin Robert Parson (seated, right), the architect, is pointing out some of the special features. Standing in the background (left to right) are Dr. Reginald Zinder, Ruth Jansen (Mrs. Heinrich) Fronzhold, New Jersey Governor Ralph Emley, Angela (Mrs. Franklin Robert) Parson (half hidden), and the Mayor of Pappatana, Marco Zugelli."

"Standing on the marble steps of the Harmonetics Resting Grounds Temple in Pappatana, N.J., are the architect, Franklin Robert Parson, and his wife, the lovely Angela Spotswood Parson. The Resting Grounds were dedicated today in a ceremony conducted by Dr. Francis X. McDonald." Parson, wearing a brown gown, was smiling at the camera. Angela Parson, almost as tall as her husband, was also robed in brown. She was looking at him. She had well-cut short hair and nondescript features, possibly because they were expressionless.

"May I borrow one of these pictures?" asked Harold.

"Of course, take whichever you want."

Harold selected the photograph of Mr. and Mrs. Parson. Ezra, his job finished, excused himself.

"Helen, I want a good pretext to see Parson. I need to ask

him some questions that will seem pertinent to the interview. I can only think of one legitimate excuse: I could go as a writer on assignment for your magazine. Let's suppose *AIA* is planning a feature article on the life-styles of five famous architects. You pick out four big names in the field, and the fifth one is Parson. You tell Parson that six or eight pages are to be devoted to each architect. My assignment is to interview him. You can say I'll be asking questions about his background, his family, friends, associates, hobbies, etc. He'll feel highly honored, and if he's in town I'm sure he'll see me today. Will you do it?"

"I'll help provided you tell me what happens."

"I'll tape the interview and get a second transcript made for you. By the way, can I borrow Ezra? He can throw in the architectural questions."

"Ezra is yours. Let's see, four architects for our Lifestyles story. I think we'll use Benson of Atlanta, Schwarzkopf of Phoenix, Martingale in Houston, and Pirelli in Los Angeles. Parson doesn't fit in that group but he'll be the last to know it. I'll call him now, if you want, to tell him he's been selected."

"I'd appreciate it."

"Watch me improvise on your scenario," she said to Harold with a smile.

Helen looked up the number, dialed, and was put straight through to Mr. Parson. She told Parson he was to be one of the five distinguished architects in the Lifestyles. Then she elaborated:

"Mr. Parson, we've asked William Reynolds to do the cover for the issue. He's planning five drawings of Schwarzkopf, Benson, Martingale, Pirelli, and yourself. That means he'll need several good pictures of you, head shots if you have them. Now for the best news. We have completed arrangements with Harold Gondoler to write the five Lifestyles. I'm sure you've read his articles. Remember that fantastic Lifestyle on Henry Kissinger in the *New York Times Magazine* section? My favorite was the Profile he did for *The New Yorker* on Princess Grace. Mr. Gondoler is in my office right now. He's going to be in the city today and he wants to do a preliminary interview with you. He's in a bit of a rush, practically between planes, and he will have to talk to you again, perhaps three or four times. Let me put him on and the two of you can work out the time."

Gondoler, who had never met Kissinger or Princess Grace, got on the phone. Parson, he thought, was trying to keep the exuberance out of his voice. Yes, he could reorganize his schedule to meet with Gondoler at the latter's convenience. Yes, 2:00 P.M. was fine. Gondoler ended the conversation on a warning note:

"By the way, Mr. Parson, Helen selected you as one of the five architects for the *AIA* article, but I explained if I don't get the cooperation I need to do a Lifestyle, she will have to select an alternate architect. I ask a lot of questions because I need a well-rounded picture of my subject. I hope you'll bear with me. Sometimes the interview seems to get off the track, but it's deliberate: it gives me a feel for the person I'm talking to."

Parson gratefully accepted the warning. He assured Mr. Gondoler of his cooperation.

Harold Gondoler arrived at Mrs. Ryder's apartment at 11:30 A.M. Caroline Ryder opened the door. She was a healthy seventy-three-year-old who liked to be (and was often) taken for sixty-three. Her dress, like the apartment, had been with her for many years but, as she said to her friend Missy, if you wait long enough the dress will come back into style.

"I'm Harold Gondoler," he said.

"Oh, how very nice." Mrs. Ryder emphasized the "very." She gave him her warmest smile and extended her hand ("to show me," thought Harold, "that color doesn't make any difference").

He followed Mrs. Ryder into the old-fashioned living room with its faded Oriental rugs, wine-colored velvet drapes, and assorted couches and chairs covered in silks bleached by the sun and in frayed petit point. In one corner stood a mahogany parlor grand piano, a tasseled moiré fabric draped over its back. A dozen silver-framed family pictures of assorted sizes decorated the tops of the coffee tables. In the middle of one wall, facing the dark, draped window, was a fake fireplace, its colored stones reflecting the flickering light of an electric bulb placed under a small electric fan. An old Victrola had been converted into a piece of furniture, perhaps a bar stocked with sherry and port.

Standing by a love seat was Missy Tompkins, her bony legs

sustaining her fragile, bent frame. The skin on her face and arms was heavily wrinkled and hung in loose folds. The outer covering was dying but the eyes were alert, smiling, and a bit wicked.

"Missy," said Mrs. Ryder, beaming at her friend, "this is Mr. Harold Gondoler. And Mr. Gondoler, this is my good, close friend Missy Tompkins. I'm Caroline Ryder."

Mrs. Ryder was being especially nice to colored folks, but that was a lot better than a freeze. Later she would tell her friends she met the loveliest black gentleman and they had such a "nice" conversation. Well, I can tell Bill Harding I met the loveliest white lady.

"I'm glad you could both see me," said Harold. "I've just been with Helen Mandel who edits a magazine on architecture. I'd like to fill you in on what we discussed."

Caroline and Missy listened as Harold related the tortuous Mandel-Gondoler plots. The idea of entrapping Franklin Parson brought a faint glow to Caroline Ryder's pale cheeks. Missy's wrinkled eyes were smiling.

"You came here for a reason, Harold Gondoler," said Missy. "Speak up. Do you want information or some co-conspirators?"

Harold gazed at the tiny, fragile body clad in long, shapeless black.

"Two co-conspirators, of course," he said smiling.

"You've got them!" said Missy triumphantly. "But first let me tell you about Franklin Parson. He's quite a naughty fellow, you know. He latched onto Angela because he knew how rich the Hambles were. Mary literally has millions! She was so happy when Angela finally got married that she couldn't do enough for Franklin. He only had to hint and she made out the check. You might say they had a joint bank account: Mary deposited and Franklin Parson withdrew."

"Franklin seemed like the perfect son-in-law," added Caroline. "He is extremely attractive and he was very attentive to Mary. They would go out to dinner almost every week, and he always let Mary decide the restaurant. Mary liked that little restaurant on 76th, Le Chat Noir. It's not particularly expensive or chic . . ."

"The food is vile," interrupted Missy. "I'll never know why Mary liked it. Franklin much preferred 21 or Elaine's."

"What about Angela?" asked Harold.

"If she cared one way or the other, no one asked her," said Missy, who relished a good gossip. "She was very quiet, almost submissive. She was even quiet when she was married to Danny Spotswood. A nice girl, I suppose, but not very deep, and certainly not a strong personality."

"How did Franklin behave toward Angela?"

Missy and Caroline looked at each other. After a pause Caroline asked, "Would anyone like some coffee?"

"Did Mrs. Hamble tell you something in confidence and do you think it should still be considered confidential under the circumstances?"

Caroline nodded to Missy and Missy nodded back.

"You're an astute man, Mr. Gondoler," said Missy. "Mary swore us to secrecy but she would want us to tell you now. Angela was desperately unhappy. Five months ago she found out Franklin was having an affair with an actress. Franklin was the ideal husband the first year of their marriage. He would bring friends home and he would buy Angela all sorts of presents. They went to California together and to Vail and Hawaii. The next year he was too busy to take her anywhere. He had to 'work late at the office' or 'meet with some clients.' Angela believed him. She told Mary how hard Franklin was working and how she wished she could be of more help.

"One day Angela picked up the phone in the bedroom and heard Franklin on the extension in the living room talking to a woman named Lila. She said it was the most horrifying experience in her life. It wasn't the fact that Franklin had a woman, but he was talking to her in the most explicit terms. To put it bluntly, he was describing how he would make love to Lila that night. Angela said Franklin had never, never talked to her like that. When the conversation was over, Angela couldn't decide what to do. Then Franklin came into the bedroom and said he had to be at a meeting. He told her not to wait up. She didn't say a word. As a matter of fact, she didn't tell Mary for a couple of weeks.

"Mary thought if she spoke to Franklin, it might help. She asked Caroline and me if we felt it would do any good to tell Franklin she knew. Caroline wasn't sure but I was against it. My advice to Mary was common sense: tell Angela to find herself an actor or a truck driver or an old friend of the family and have a good fuck."

Harold stared at the little old lady in the long black dress. Missy sat primly on the love seat, meticulously neat and mousy, waiting for his comment. Her eyes were laughing.

"Missy, I wish I had known you two years ago, when I was a little younger," he said.

"Thank you for the compliment, Harold."

"To get back to Mary, she did talk to Franklin," said Caroline, continuing the story. "Mary was blunt. She said she wasn't unpleasant, just firm. She gave Franklin two alternatives: break up the affair with Lila La Mause and be attentive to Angela, in which case he would continue to get financial support from Mary; or play around, come home late, and forget about asking Mary for help. Franklin was in a bind. He had expanded his office, he and Angela were living in an enormous apartment with three servants, and Franklin was entertaining friends regularly at one of his clubs or at 21.

"Mary felt she might have been too harsh with Franklin. She said if he and Angela were reconciled, she would like to give them a month at a lovely villa in Nice or Florence, whichever they preferred. Franklin had been subdued; except for a feeble denial, he had hardly spoken. When Mary asked what his decision was, he said he would end the affair immediately. As for the offer of the villa, he thought it was most generous and it would be the best thing in the world for Angela. However, he wanted to wait six months to clear up some business matters. Then he hoped Mary would join them. They would become a family again."

"I'd like to give you the timing, Harold," said Missy. "That was five months ago. Franklin became the perfect husband again. Three months ago Mary went to the Harmonetics Hospital and none of us has talked to her since."

The three friends were silent.

"I need a drink," said Missy. "Harold, can I fix you a Bloody Mary?"

"Thank you, yes."

"Missy, please make me one too," said Caroline. "I'm going in the kitchen to put a casserole in the oven and we can all have lunch together."

The Bloody Marys were ready when Caroline returned. Missy slugged hers as though it were soda pop. Harold decided she was thirty, not seventy-three.

"Do either of you know Dr. Jean de Moraille?"

"Just that he was Mary's doctor," said Caroline. "Did you know him, Missy?"

"No."

"Had Mrs. Hamble been going to him long?"

"Forever," said Caroline. "Mary must have met him forty years ago."

"Then he's not a young man?"

"Good heavens, no. He's our age."

"I understand he's a member of the Harmonetics Society."

"Half the people we know have joined. Missy and I aren't joiners."

"I wonder if Angela knows Dr. de Moraille. Have either of you spoken to her lately?"

Missy and Caroline exchanged looks.

"Angela's never been friendly with us, particularly the last six or eight years," said Missy. "When you talk to her, you get a monosyllabic answer. For instance, 'Did you have a nice time in Hawaii, Angela?' 'Yes, thank you.' That's why I called Helga or Gretchen or even Franklin when I wanted to find out about Mary."

"Did Angela love her mother?"

"If I were forty years younger, I'd say yes," answered Missy. "It's difficult to know what Angela feels although she's always polite."

"I might give her a call now," said Caroline hesitantly.

"Go ahead," said Missy, "there's nothing to lose."

Caroline picked up the phone and made the call.

"Hello, may I speak to Mrs. Parson, please. This is Mrs. Ryder. . . . Yes, I'll hold, thank you. . . ." Caroline put her hand over the receiver and said, "The maid is calling her to the phone. She put me on 'hold.'. . ."

Twenty seconds went by; forty seconds; a minute.

"Hello, yes . . . When do you expect her back? . . . You're not sure? . . . Will you tell her that Mrs. Ryder called? . . . No, no message, thank you."

"I'm sorry, Caroline," said Missy. "She's a little beast."

"I'm very sorry too," said Harold awkwardly. "She couldn't be a very nice person."

"Thank you, Harold," said Caroline, and her smile this time was real.

She's forgotten I'm black, thought Harold. If I stay for lunch, I may even forget she's white. Harold smiled back. Caroline suddenly realized how much she liked him.

"I'm going to be with Parson most of the afternoon. Caroline, suppose you call him at 2:15 while I'm still there. Ask him where Mary is and how she's feeling. Of course he may not accept the call. Wait, I have an idea. I'll ask him to let all calls through while I'm with him so I can get the feel of how he handles his affairs."

"Last time I phoned he said Mary was doing very nicely and would soon be going to Arizona."

"Let's see what he says this time when I'm in the office."

"If he didn't know my voice," said Missy, "I would phone and pretend to be a nurse at the Harmonetics Hospital."

"What a thought!" said Harold. "And what would 'the nurse' say?"

"I'd tell him Mary Hamble was not in her room and we were afraid she had left the hospital without permission."

"Missy, you're a genius. Let's see, could there be any repercussions for Mary? She won't have left the room; it's a false alarm. Franklin won't find that out until later. He'll be worried, particularly if I stay another hour. He's hamstrung on his calls as long as I'm there. I can get Barbara at *National News* to be 'the nurse' and make a call. Caroline, I'll ask Barbara to call at 2:15; why don't you call at 2:30?"

"And then let him tell me Mary is doing nicely and on her way to Arizona!"

"There's one more call I'd like to make," said Harold. "Dr. Jean de Moraille."

The ladies waited while Harold phoned. The nurse who answered had disappointing news. Dr. de Moraille had retired from practice several months ago. She did not know where he was living but she thought he might have moved to California or perhaps it was Arizona. He had not been in touch with the office since his retirement. The new doctor who had taken over his practice was not a member of the Harmonetics Society. He had no patients at the Harmonetics Hospital.

A new concept of the duality of nature was presented by Dr. Josiah Minden in his fourth and most famous book entitled *Living with Our Dualities*. The book was the number one best seller in the country for seventy-three weeks and its popularity has only waned slightly in the last six months. Permission to reprint this excerpt from the Minden introduction was given by McKane Stuart Publishing Company.

We recognize the duality of man through the conscious and unconscious selves. Our conscious consists of whatever we can verbalize: names, dates, and facts that we have learned, theories we have been taught, experiences we remember, etc. The unconscious mind hides many of the desires that conflict with our training, many terrors and quite a few experiences we would like to forget. The unconscious mind has as large a memory bank as the conscious: we have all had the experience of temporarily forgetting the name of a friend, but if we allow the unconscious brain to take over, the name frequently returns to the conscious.

The duality of our nature exists in more than just the conscious and unconscious. This book will treat with the most important elements in these dualities. Briefly, we will discuss the following dualities and how we may best reconcile them.

• We enjoy keeping busy but we take great pleasure in extended periods of idleness. The men and women who cease work involuntarily are being deprived of one of the most instinctive traits in human society. If the person willingly relinquishes all forms of daily duties, then either the job has proved unsatisfactory or the delicate balance of mind has become weighted in the other direction. In the case of the former, one must discover more suitable job capacities; in the case of the latter, the balance of the mind has to be restored.

• We consciously believe in a moral code of behavior but we also experience conscious desires to break the code. In daily life

patterns we continuously face opportunities to behave un-
ethically: we believe in law and order but we get in a car and
deliberately break the speed limit; we believe in a rigid code of
sportsmanship in such games as tennis, but at a crucial moment
we fight (or give in to) the desire to call the "in" ball out; we
believe in a business ethic, but if a customer overpays us, we
hesitate to issue a refund; we believe in human equality but the
husband wants his wife to be the maid or the white man won't
let the black man into his club. The moral code has to be
examined and the desires have to be properly channeled to
reconcile the duality that exists.

• **We know certain phobias are irrational but we cannot rid**
ourselves of the phobia. *A man admits air travel is safer than*
taking a bath or riding in a car or even walking down the street,
but he refuses to fly because of unreasoning panic that his plane
will crash. A woman loves horses and rides regularly until one
day she is thrown by a horse that is out of control. She still loves
the horses but fear has overwhelmed her and she is not able to
pat the muzzle of a horse although she consciously knows he will
not bite. The overcoming of such phobias eliminates the
irrational duality.

Briefly, other dualities that can be recognized are:

• **We want to be generous and considerate but we also want to**
amass goods, keep the best for ourselves, and cut out the other
party in competition for a prize.

• **We want responsibility but the opposing self wants no re-**
sponsibilities.

• **We want to dominate and we want to submit.**

• **We want to obey and we want to rebel.**

• **We want to criticize but we do not want to accept criticism.**

• **We want to talk but we do not want to listen.**

At 1:55 P.M. Harold Gondoler handed his business card to
the receptionist. At 1:56 Mr. Parson's private secretary, looking
as though she were ready to go tea dancing, entered the
reception room.

"How nice to see you, Mr. Gondoler. Mr. Parson is looking
forward to meeting you."

Harold followed the wiggling rear of the secretary through
two enormous, well-lit rooms where draftsmen, old and young,

were working at large tables, each with its own space of sixty square feet or more. The aura was space and light.

"You're victims of undercrowding," said Harold.

"Mr. Parson believes creativity is in part a function of working conditions. There are six private offices for the architects," said the secretary, pointing to a row of doors separated by a distance of fifteen feet. "On the other side are six equally large rooms: the library, the conference room, the mail room, the canteen, the stat machines, and a file room. This," she said opening a door, "is Mr. Parson's private office."

They entered an anteroom which by itself could have been the office of the president of a prosperous company. There were two large desks for Parson's secretaries. At one of them sat a young woman who could have entered the Miss New York State Beauty Contest, judging from her features, measurements, high heels, low-cut blouse, gold earrings, bracelets, and Farrah Fawcett haircut. A couch and five chairs were unoccupied. Harold, a two-finger typist, noticed the oversized typewriter whose stand formed a right angle with one of the desks.

"Is this one of the IBM machines?"

"Yes, it's the IBM Memory Typewriter. We paid $6,000 apiece and we have ten of them."

"This looks like a kitchenette," said Harold, poking his head into a narrow room.

The secretary flicked on a light. There were a stove, refrigerator, sink, dishwasher, and kitchen cupboards, as well as a chopping-board table.

"And now the pièce de résistance," she said with a creditable accent, knocking on a door and opening it. "Mr. Parson," she said to the man who sat at a desk sixty feet away, "this is Mr. Gondoler."

It was a room in which one could work, go to bed, have lunch, show a movie, hold a seated dinner, get bombed, or make love. Space was the predominant feature: it was a good twenty feet to the nearest couch; a grouping of chairs and a table were forty feet away; and the large corner windows that extended from floor to ceiling offered an unimpeded view of the other skyscrapers.

As Harold entered the room, Franklin Parson rose and walked toward his visitor. They met at the halfway mark. Parson was as tall and as powerful as Gondoler. He was a strikingly handsome man, with black hair, dark sparkling eyes, and ruddy, healthy skin.

They shook hands and Gondoler asked: "Football?"

"Michigan State. Right guard. And you?"

"UCLA, quarterback."

I've put him at ease, thought Gondoler. He likes me, thought Parson.

"I want to make two requests," said Harold. "First, don't let me interrupt your own routine. If your secretary has letters to sign or if someone on your staff needs to see you, they should come in freely. Don't cut off your telephone calls, either incoming or outgoing. I want to see you, Franklin Parson, operating in your own environment, not talking to me in a vacuum. Second, I'll be asking a lot of questions that may seem irrelevant. I may not use any of them in the Lifestyle. Please answer them fully since it all helps in creating a well-rounded portrait. Will you also tell your secretary while I set up the tape recorder that a young fellow, Ezra Samuels from *AIA*, will be coming here any moment. He'll ask the technical questions."

While Parson stepped out to talk to his secretary, Gondoler plugged in the recorder and set it on the desk. He pushed the "hold" button on Parson's phone, picked up the receiver, and inserted a small receiving wire into a hole in the "ear" section. He fiddled around with his recorder ("Testing, one, two, three, four") until Parson returned.

"Before we start, please give me a brief rundown on these photographs," Gondoler asked, pointing to one of the walls.

"Certainly. I'll begin at the left. This is a picture of the old Pappatana Clubhouse. Here it is after completion: the Harmonetics Resting Grounds Temple. These smaller photographs show the Four Worshiping Halls and the Chapels.

"The next series is one of my favorites. It's a country estate in East Hampton which I finished a few months ago. The main house incorporates a large atrium used for entertaining. More than 150 people can be accommodated comfortably. I sold the client on the concept of smaller cottages for their guests. I kept the main house simplicity itself: the center is the entertainment area, the left wing for the host and hostess, and the equally large right wing contains the kitchen, pantry, and servants' quarters. I put a game room cottage by the tennis court, a screened picnic bungalow in this secluded arbor, a large gazebo on the top of this knoll, and a chapel in this quiet wooded area."

"Whose house is it?"

"Ruth and Heinrich Fronzhold. He's in the city most of the time but she goes to the Island almost every Thursday afternoon. She's a marvelous hostess, and they've both found the house easy to live in.

"The next photographs are aerial views of a new concept in communal living. On the upper left are a series of colonial one- and two-bedroom town houses. The group of Spanish town houses in the lower left surround a small man-made lake. The Mediterranean two-family villas are scattered near a shallow brook in a setting of live oaks and pines. Over on the right are twenty-five six-story apartment houses. In the center is the Temple, which also serves as the center of the community's life. The large building in the rear is the hospital and health clinic."

"Where is this?" asked Harold.

"It's a new development just past Conroe, a little over an hour from Houston."

"That's a pretty long commute to Houston. Where do most of the residents work?"

"They are older people, most of them retired, and work is provided for them in the community itself. It's one of the Harmonetics retreats. There are now ten of them in the United States. People in their seventies and eighties, married or single, can buy an apartment or a town house. Maintenance is rather reasonable. They grow their own vegetables, raise their own chickens to get their own eggs, and they have their own cows and dairy, which they work themselves. Many tend the gardens or work in the machine shops or clean the apartments for those who are unable to do so. There's a large community kitchen which they man, and they make their own pottery which is used for dishes. We have volunteers who lecture at seminars and who help to staff the hospital as nurses' aides or orderlies. There is also a complete staff of physicians and nurses."

"I see. What are these pictures? It looks like a camp in the woods."

"It's the private retreat of Dr. Josiah Minden in the Adirondacks, a wooded 25,000-acre tract with its own lakes and rivers.

The trout fishing is superb. The house itself is rather simple. We used logs from the property, and the wooden beams in the high ceilings are exposed. It gets cold in the winter so there are large fireplaces, some fifteen feet wide, in the main rooms, with smaller ones in the bedrooms. Over here are the tennis courts and back here are the stables."

"What's that bare strip in the corner? Was there a fire?"

"No, that's the private airport so Dr. Minden can get in and out quickly. The hangar is half hidden but you can make it out if you look closely."

"And last of all, what are these sketches?"

"That's what I'm working on right now. It's a beach house. We've already started construction and if the weather holds out, we should be finished in a couple of months."

"Tell me if I'm correct. Is the main salon actually 80 by 40 feet?"

"Yes, the client who commissioned the home likes large uncluttered areas just as I do. We're probably both claustrophobic."

"Your client must be very rich. What does he do?"

"The client is a woman. Lila La Mause."

"Ah, yes, the great actress."

There was a knock at the door. Miss New York State, her bracelets clanging, walked in with Ezra.

"Mr. Parson, this is Mr. Ezra Samuels from *American* . . ." She paused and looked down at the card. "This is Mr. Ezra Samuels from *American & International Architecture*." One more pause. "*American & International Architecture* magazine."

Just then the phone rang.

Excerpt from the Harmonetics Code

A Probationary who has given the required number of hours to the Harmonetics Society takes five vows before receiving the Blue Gown symbolic of full membership. The vows are designed to further both the physical and mental health of the individual and to create a happier society in which to dwell.

The vows consist of positive and negative, acceptance and negation.

Each new member pledges loyalty to every other member and to the Harmonetics Society itself. To join is to dedicate one's life to the principles of Harmonetics.

Each new member pledges to tithe to the Harmonetics Society. This vow is binding. It is meant to protect and provide and find meaningful work for men and women whose calendar years have made them outcasts in society.

Each new member pledges to abstain from cigarettes, alcoholic beverages, and the eating of flesh. The inhaling of smoke into the lungs, the dissipation of alcohol into the bloodstream, and the digestion of rancid, putrid organs and flesh of dead animals are proven abuses to the human body.

Each new member pledges to dedicate no fewer than five hours a week as a volunteer in the services provided by the Harmonetics Society. Members may be assigned to the Temple, the gardens, the seminars, the workshops, the Visitors Corps, the hospital, or any other service recognized by the Society.

Each new member pledges to accept the orders of the Harmonetics Society as symbolized in the colors of the gowns. The progression of the orders is blue, red, green, brown, and white.

These pledges are perpetual and may never be broken.

Jade Boren had finished the last of the afternoon Aptitude Tests. The lady in blue who had monitored the final segment had picked up her papers and left, leaving Jade alone in the small room. More like a coat closet, she thought.

Jade lit a cigarette and stretched out in her chair with her arms reaching into the air and her legs extended like a cat waking up. She blew a puff of smoke toward the ceiling and watched it curl.

"Don't you know smoking is forbidden in the hospital?" said a harsh male voice.

Jade jumped up and turned around. Josiah Minden was standing in the doorway smiling. He was wearing the open white shirt that he had made traditional. He carried his jacket casually, one finger looped through the label and the jacket itself tossed over his shoulder. His neck, Jade noticed, was unlined.

"God, you scared the hell out of me," she said.

"I couldn't stand to see you so happy. Do you always sit in a chair with your legs sprawled out? It's very suggestive, you know."

Jade smiled, ignoring the comment, and handed Josiah the cigarette. He smiled at her, then ground it out.

"Josiah," said Jade nervously, "thanks for returning Mom's jewels. I called her at noon and she told me."

Josiah didn't answer. He was smiling, staring at her.

Jade looked at his marvelous, deep eyes. Josiah slowly lifted his hands and touched her. He stroked her arms, her face, then her throat and breasts. She put her arms around his neck and felt his sweet kisses on her lips and face. She wondered if the door were open or closed but she didn't give a damn. He tasted like sugar. His breath was perfume. Her lips were thickening, her eyes closing, passion was flowing through her tingling fingers, her taut breasts, and in that glorious center of all passions, between her legs. His hands moved down her body, circling her stomach, pressing the small of her back, separating her legs. She was stroking his hard, strong back, her hands moving forward and downward, the tears streaming down her face as she felt his hardness, that beautiful magnificent hardness. He kissed her tears, licked them, and closed his own deep, beautiful eyes. Her blouse was open, his pants unzipped when the door opened.

Dr. Josiah Minden, founder of the Harmonetics Society and its beloved leader, said "Shit!"

The intruder quickly shut the door but the moment was over. Jade buttoned her shirt and Josiah zipped. He stroked her face and kissed her softly. The Madonna eyes expressed her sadness. They both sat down, he holding one hand in the two of his.

"Your mother told me you used to work for *National News*."

Jade was silent.

"Isn't there something you wanted to tell me?" he persisted.

"I don't want to be a fink."

"You'd rather I didn't know?"

Jade leaned over and kissed him. "Mom shouldn't have said anything." Jade wiggled uncomfortably. "I'm sure she already told you that Bill Harding, the Publisher, is planning an exposé. I don't know the line of attack but I found out whom he's assigned to the story. They're his best researchers. One is Harold Gondoler whom he brought in from California. The others are Martha Rayburn and Roger Silberstein." Jade looked miserable.

"I'm writing down the names," said Josiah, "because I've got the most God-awful memory. Now that I've got them on paper, I don't know what the hell I'm going to do about it."

Jade peeked over his shoulder. He had written *"National News 'Exposé' on Harmonetics. To be written by Harold Gondolier, Martha Rayburn, and Roger Silverstein."*

"Very good. You only misspelled two of the names."

"Does it matter?" asked Josiah. He stuffed the paper in his jacket pocket and stood up.

"I've got an appointment with Fronzhold now and I'm due at the Temple immediately after. If you meet me in the garage in fifteen minutes, I'll give you a ride."

Jade got up and followed him to the door.

"You're a hell of an absentminded chick," he said. "Isn't that your tennis case in the corner?"

Transcript Excerpts from the Interview of Franklin Parson by Harold Gondoler

(Telephone conversation between Franklin Parson and Barbara Ewing, switchboard operator at National News.*)*

FP: Parson here.

BE: Mr. Parson, this is Nurse Roberts at the Harmonetics Hospital.

FP: Yes, Miss Roberts. What can I do for you?

BE: I'm sorry to disturb you, but I thought you should be informed immediately.

FP: Go on.

BE: It's about Mrs. Mary Hamble. I believe she's your mother-in-law.

FP: What has happened, Miss Roberts?

BE: I don't know how to tell you but we, uh, we can't locate Mrs. Hamble.

FP: You WHAT!

BE: She isn't in the room or on the corridor. We've looked everywhere.

FP: When did this happen?

BE: One of the nurses went to give her a shot two hours ago. She had simply vanished. We've been searching the building ever since.

FP: Have you told the doctor?

BE: Which doctor?

FP: Dr. Fronzhold, of course.

BE: No, I'll call him immediately. Do you want me to keep you posted?

FP: Absolutely.

BE: Shall I call your wife?

FP: No. There's no reason to worry her needlessly. However, I want to be kept informed of any developments.

BE: Yes, Mr. Parson. I'm very sorry this happened. It's really inexcusable.

FP: Keep me posted, Miss Roberts.

BE: I will. Good-bye.

(*End of telephone transcript*)

HG: What was that about? You sounded worried.

FP: It was, uh, personal.

HG: Would you mind elucidating?

FP: My mother-in-law, Mary Hamble, is quite ill. That was the hospital.

HG: I'm very sorry. Perhaps you want to call your wife?

FP: No, it's not really serious. I wouldn't want to worry her unnecessarily.

HG: If it's not serious, why did they call you?

FP: It's, they, well, they let me know her condition every day.

HG: What is she suffering from?

FP: I'm afraid it's senility. That's why it's so hard on my wife.

HG: Of course. How sad for all of you. I noticed on the phone you said, "You WHAT!"

FP: Did I? I can't remember.

HG: Would you like me to play back the tape?

FP: No, that's not necessary. Let me see. It's coming back to me now. The nurse said she had forgotten to give Mrs. Hamble her shot. Mrs. Hamble was quite disturbed.

HG: Ah, that explains it. Is Dr. Fronzhold Mrs. Hamble's doctor?

FP: He keeps a special eye on her. There isn't much they can do for her now.

HG: How long has Mrs. Hamble been senile?

FP: It's been coming on gradually. My wife and I noticed occasional symptoms six months ago. It got bad, quite bad, three months ago and we had to hospitalize her.

HG: Dr. Fronzhold did the diagnosis?

FP: We had another doctor then, but Dr. Fronzhold concurred.

HG: What about Mrs. Hamble's affairs? I imagine you have to handle them now that she's incapacitated.

FP: Yes. It takes a lot of time but I feel I must do it for my wife's sake.

HG: You have power of attorney then?

FP: It's automatic in such cases.

HG: Didn't you have to appear before a judge to get the power of attorney?

FP: I did.

HG: Then Dr. Fronzhold had to sign a paper certifying that Mrs. Hamble was not competent?

FP: Exactly.

HG: Which judge handled the petition?

FP: I can't remember his name offhand.

HG: Perhaps your secretary could look it up.

FP: No, it will come back to me. Let's see now. Ah, yes, it was Judge Henley Stuart.

HG: He's quite prominent in the Harmonetics Society, isn't he?

FP: Yes, I believe he is. So many people we know these days are members of the Society.

HG: Judge Stuart is one of the White Gowns.

FP: Yes, a highly respected man.

HG: You are also highly respected in your field, Mr. Parson. I'm going to ask Ezra to do the technical questions on your background and architectural achievements. Ezra, will you take over, please?

(Fifteen minutes of the transcript are deleted as unrelated to the investigation.)

(Telephone rings.)

(Telephone conversation between Franklin Parson and Caroline Ryder.)

FP: Parson here.

CR: Mr. Parson, this is Caroline Ryder.

FP: Yes?

CR: I've been so worried about your mother-in-law. We haven't heard any news. Did she go out west?

FP: No, not yet.

CR: How is she feeling?

FP: The situation hasn't changed much.

CR: Last time I called, you said she was feeling much better. Can she have visitors?

FP: Not at this time. I'll let you know when she can.

CR: What exactly is wrong with her?

FP: I have some people here with me now, Mrs. Ryder. Can we talk later?

Gondoler: Please go ahead, Mr. Parson. We're here as observers.

CR: Is it still her varicose veins?

FP: It's a bit more than that.

CR: I am Mary Hamble's oldest friend, Mr. Parson. I think I'm entitled to know. If I don't get a direct answer from you, I'm going to take the matter to some people who will force you to tell the truth. I'm quite angry, Mr. Parson.

FP: I have been holding back on the truth for the sake of my wife. My mother-in-law, I regret to say, is hopelessly senile.

CR: I don't believe it.

FP: I'm very sorry.

CR: Her mind was as sharp as yours: I saw her just before she went into the hospital.

FP: The symptoms appeared shortly after. Regretfully, she got progressively worse.

CR: I would still like to see her.

FP: You will have to call Dr. Fronzhold. He is the only one who can authorize visitors.

CR: I shall do that right now.

FP: Good-bye, Mrs. Ryder. Thank you for calling.

(End of telephone transcript)

HG: A friend?

FP: An old friend of my mother-in-law. She's about the same age, seventy-three. I found it very difficult to tell her the truth about Mary. These older women sometimes get hysterical, you know.

HG: How is your wife bearing up?

FP: Not badly, considering the circumstances.

HG: She's a member of the Harmonetics Society too?

FP: Yes, we're both dedicated members.

HG: I understand you wear the Brown Gown.

FP: Yes. There's something I'd like to tell you, but first I must get your promise to keep it secret until the official announcement on Sunday.

HG: Naturally, Mr. Parson.

FP: I'm counting on your word, Mr. Gondoler, but I thought it might be useful for your Lifestyle story. I am to receive the White Gown from Josiah Minden.

HG: Congratulations. That's quite an honor. This Sunday?

FP: Yes, at the Harmonetics Temple during the 1:00 P.M. service.

HG: If I'm in town I shall certainly be there. There are only twenty-five members of the White Gowns. Whom do you replace?

FP: The late Jennifer Holiday.

(Twelve minutes of the tape are deleted as irrelevant to the investigation.)

(Telephone rings.)

(Telephone conversation between Franklin Parson and Barbara Ewing, switchboard operator at National News.)

FP: Parson here.

BE: Mr. Parson, this is Nurse Roberts again.

FP: Yes. How is everything?

BE: I'm afraid I have no news. We still haven't found Mrs. Hamble. Do you suppose she would have gone to your home?

FP: No, I don't think so.

BE: Have you any suggestions as to where she might have gone?

FP: I don't think I can be of much help in that department.

BE: Perhaps we should notify the police.

FP: Absolutely not.

BE: We generally do so in such cases. The police put out an all-points bulletin, which means everyone would be looking for her.

FP: No. In this case it would not be a good idea.

BE: If she's wandering around the streets in her condition, anything could happen. I'd hate to be responsible.

FP: I'll take the responsibility.

BE: All right, Mr. Parson. I'll call you back later. Good-bye.

(End of telephone transcript)

FP: That was my stockbroker.

HG: What was he asking?

FP: He wanted to make some changes in my portfolio.

HG: Don't they always? Who is your broker?

FP: Er, Boyd Fortune.

HG: And he's with?

FP: Gordon, Pine, Simpson.

HG: And your bank?

FP: National Bank & Trust.

(The balance of the tape has been deleted as unrelated to the investigation.)

Henrietta Beale sat in a leather armchair facing Austin McDowell. Her skin was glowing from her second treatment at the Health and Body Seminar. As Mr. McDowell studied the clauses in her old will, Henrietta checked her personalized Beauty Kit. There were fourteen different containers in her kit, each a different color. A brochure listed each procedure that Henrietta was to follow. She thought of the many pleasant hours her friend Sarah Robinson could spend at her dressing table, dabbing on throat cream with her fingertips, patting on eye lotion with cotton puffs, removing the cleanser, mixing the Protector gels, and, as the climax, opening the last and smallest exquisite little jar and dotting on the Elixir Rejuvenation Nutrient.

"Mrs. Beale, Mrs. Beale."

"I'm so sorry, Mr. McDowell. I was reading my Health and Body I brochure. It's rather complicated. So many procedures. You were saying, Mr. McDowell?"

"To get back to your will, Mrs. Beale, you wish to make certain changes. Would you like to tell me what they are?"

"Humm, I believe when Arthur drew up the will eight years ago, I left everything to Elliott."

"Not exactly, Mrs. Beale. You left the bulk of your estate to your son and daughter but you named your husband as trustee and co-executor. He has the right to use the income from the estate and the capital if necessary for the balance of his life. In this way your children are protected from paying a double inheritance tax."

"I remember now. Yes, Arthur explained it to me."

"You also have six small bequests of $10,000 each. The recipients are the Rehabilitation Center, your three grand-children, Marnie O'Brien . . ."

"Yes, yes, my old housekeeper, she's retired and is living in Belfast."

". . . and Vassar."

"I haven't been back to a reunion in years. Isn't it sad how we lose touch with the past?"

"You're absolutely right."

"Where did you go to college, Mr. McDowell?"

"Princeton, Class of '58, and Harvard Law School. Now, shall we go over the changes? We could start with the six bequests."

"All right. I want to make sure I'm doing the right thing so please advise me. Marnie already receives a small pension from me, and I'm not so sure I like the attitude of the Rehabilitation Center. They only get in touch with me when they need money."

"If you eliminate these bequests, Mrs. Beale, did you plan to substitute others?"

"One other. I think I might also drop Vassar. I gave them some money several years ago."

"I see. How large do you want to make the new bequest and will it be to an individual or a charitable organization?"

"I haven't decided. I mean I haven't decided the amount. I know I want to make it substantial."

"And what group or person would this be?"

"Do you think $100,000 would be too little?"

"If you'll tell me a little more about the recipient, perhaps I can help you work it out."

"Oh, didn't I say? The Harmonetics Society."

"Well, one must admit the Society has high ideals."

"Are you a member, Mr. McDowell?"

"Yes, Cissy and I joined the Society two years ago."

"How lovely. I'm so glad Arthur suggested that I see you. You are simpatico."

"I try as best I can to carry out the instructions of my clients."

"That's the way it should be, Mr. McDowell. I want to leave an important contribution but I also want to be fair to Elliott and the children."

"Why don't we try to analyze the situation in reverse? For example, if you predeceased Mr. Beale, would he have ample means to continue without turning to your estate?"

"Oh my word, yes. He has lots of stocks and all sorts of marvelous properties."

"That's comforting. And your children? Do they have adequate incomes?"

"Adequate. I wouldn't say they are rich but they haven't had to turn to us for financial aid in years."

"Of course you wouldn't want to remove them from your will entirely, but if they are reasonably secure you might state a specific amount which they would receive. Mrs. Beale, would you like to estimate the size of your estate?"

"You mean everything?"

"Yes."

"Elliott and I own some stocks jointly."

"Are there also some in your own name?"

"Yes. Elliott has always been extremely generous, and I have a marvelous investment counselor."

"You could give me the figures on your own stocks and then on the ones you own jointly with Mr. Beale."

"I would say it comes to $800,000. Perhaps $900,000."

"Is that the grand total?"

"No, there's probably another $150,000 that Elliott and I own jointly."

"Do you and Mr. Beale own your apartment?"

"Yes, we do. I believe that's joint too."

"Then let me make several suggestions. I'm looking at my notes because I want to be sure I understand your desires. First, you are considering eliminating three bequests: the Rehabilitation Center, Vassar, and Marnie O'Brien. Second, you have three small bequests to your grandchildren. You might want to double or even triple this amount and leave it directly to your son and daughter. This would give them no less than $30,000 apiece."

"That would be very nice."

"Since the apartment is in your names jointly, you may want your share to go directly to Mr. Beale. This would seem appropriate."

"Of course."

"Now, we come to the bulk of the estate. Was it your intention to leave all or most of it to the Harmonetics Society?"

"What do you think, Mr. McDowell?"

"That's such a personal matter, Mrs. Beale. I really couldn't advise you. Cissy and I feel deeply about the Harmonetics code and the ideals of the leaders, but I always try to compartmentalize my own feelings from those of the client's."

"Do you think I would be foolish to will the estate to the Society?"

"If it's the entire estate, yes. However, you have expressed thoughts about bequeathing a lump sum to each of your children and the apartment to Mr. Beale. No, I wouldn't call that foolish."

"Then if the children each get $30,000 outright, the Society would receive a gift of $900,000 or possibly $1 million. Mr. McDowell, am I doing the right thing?"

"I wish Cissy and I were able to make so generous a contribution. But let me repeat once again: whether you do so or not must be in accordance with your own beliefs. I shall not attempt to sway you in either direction."

"Should I notify the Society about my intentions?"

"I think public notification of your plans would not be wise. However, if you will permit me, I would like to inform Dr. Josiah Minden. I am sure he would treat the matter confidentially but he would want to meet and talk with you. Such a contribution would, naturally, raise you to the higher echelons of the Society."

"Do you mean the White Robes?"

"That would be presumptuous of me to say. Only Dr. Minden has the right to elevate a man or a woman to the White Robes."

"Would it be a possibility?"

"There are few things not within the realm of possibility but we must be patient. Time is eternal and nothing is given to us overnight."

"You phrase your thoughts so beautifully, Mr. McDowell."

"I try to be a realist. I hate to put an end to this conversation but I'm due uptown in thirty minutes. May I have the pleasure of dropping you at your apartment? We can then chat in the car."

"That's so kind of you. By the way, Mr. McDowell, I'm giving a small dinner party this Friday for Senator Spriggs. My old friend Sarah Robinson will be there, and Clarissa and Byron Kent, and perhaps Dr. Fronzhold. Clarissa is asking him. I would love to have you and Mrs. McDowell join us. I realize it's short notice."

"Henrietta, it would be a great pleasure. Cissy and I shall look forward to the evening. Will you excuse me for just a minute, please, while I leave instructions for my secretary?"

After Austin McDowell closed the door, Henrietta reached into her purse and switched off the tape recorder.

Nurses' Regulations
Iris Corridor V

1. Many of the patients on Iris Corridor V have been suffering from a specific form of mental distress for a number of months or years. You may observe short-term periods of rationality in particular patients but do not relax your vigilance: an unexpected display of violence by a patient could be dangerous to yourself and to others.

2. *You are expected to memorize the code number of every patient on the floor. The families of some of the patients have requested complete privacy. Therefore code numbers are essential for identification. If there should be outside calls to the Nurses' Desk for information on the condition of a patient, absolutely no information is to be given unless the caller refers to the code number.*

3. *Every patient on Iris Corridor V is on medication. The instructions of the physician are to be followed to the letter. Do not make your own diagnosis. Any effort to eliminate or reduce the dosage will result in immediate dismissal.*

4. *Patients on Iris Corridor V may neither place phone calls nor receive them without the specific authorization of the physician in charge. There will be no exceptions to this rule.*

5. *Patients may not go into the corridor unescorted. Any nurse seeing an unescorted patient is expected to ring the emergency bell.*

6. *An escort shall consist of no fewer than two nurses (or one nurse and one orderly). The escorts shall walk on either side of the patient, and each escort shall firmly hold the elbow of the patient.*

7. *Any patient who is being taken to shock therapy must be strapped to one of the wheeled emergency tables. No patient, no matter what his or her condition, may be taken by wheelchair.*

8. *Consult with the Head Nurse for the procedures to follow in prepping a patient for psychosurgery.*

9. *Rooms 34 to 46 on Iris Corridor V are occupied by volunteers from the prisons. The doors of each of these rooms must be kept locked at all times. No nurse is to enter any of these rooms unless she is accompanied by two orderlies.*

These rules are made for your protection as well as for the protection of the patient.

It took Harold Gondoler five minutes to get a call through to Harry Case, Sr., President of National Bank & Trust. Gondoler kept his voice even and unhurried. He said he was with *National News* and he would speak to Mr. Case only. The matter involved a depositor who was fraudulently using the funds of a relative. When Mr. Case came on the phone, Gondoler asked to see him.

"I'm part of an investigative team for *National News*. One of your depositors is misusing the funds of a very rich woman. I have a tape recorder with me, and I am sure you will recognize the voice."

"I appreciate your calling," said Mr. Case. "However, I think this matter can be handled just as well by one of our vice-presidents. I'll see that he cooperates with you fully."

"Mr. Case, I want to speak to you because the Harmonetics Society is involved."

"Harmonetics, eh? Mr. Gondoler, come right over. I am looking forward to hearing the disclosures. Shall I expect you in ten minutes? Fine."

National Bank & Trust occupied the first ten floors of a large Park Avenue office building. The first floor faced the street and was enclosed in bulletproof glass. The windows of this floor rose the equivalent of four stories so that depositors on entering could gaze upward without being offended by a ceiling. All small transactions were negotiated on the ground floor: savings accounts were opened, $5,000 loans approved, checks cashed, and Bantru credit cards issued. The escalators in the back carried larger customers to the carpeted second floor where major business matters were discussed in private offices with Mr. Case or one of the eight heavyweight vice-presidents.

Gondoler rode up the escalator where he was greeted by a substantially endowed woman who summoned a courteous young man who guided Gondoler to the inner sanctum. Harry Case, Sr., a dignified solid citizen in a pearl-gray suit, was beaming. Gondoler was the recipient of a smile Mr. Case generally reserved for the president of one of the top ten industrials.

"I've just been talking to Bill Harding," said Case. "He says you're brilliant and reliable."

"I've never disagreed with any of Bill Harding's opinions," replied Harold modestly.

Case chuckled. "Tell me about this miscreant depositor and what is the connection with the Harmonetics Society? I hope you don't mind if I interrupt from time to time so I can get the complete story."

"Not at all," said Gondoler. "Mary Hamble is a rich widow . . ."

"I know her," Case broke in. "She's been one of our important depositors for years."

"Her son-in-law, Franklin Parson, also banks with you. Three months ago, probably with the connivance of Dr. Heinrich Fronzhold, Parson succeeded in luring Mrs. Hamble to the Harmonetics Hospital to receive treatment for her varicose veins."

As Gondoler told the story, Case interrupted frequently. He wanted the names of Mrs. Hamble's friends, the license plate of Parson's car, and the description of the cashier at the pharmacy. He would have preferred to hear the full tapes, including Ezra's architectural questions, rather than an abbreviated version. He sighed when Gondoler pushed the "Fast Forward" button, skipping to the next taped phone conversation.

Gondoler summarized: "Parson has Mary Hamble's power of attorney. I'm guessing he transferred some of her funds to his own account. He may have sold some of her stocks, then used the money to buy stocks in his own name. I'm sure there's something fishy which will show up when the accounts are examined."

Case went to his desk and turned on the intercom: "Please get me the list of deposits and withdrawals and the stats of all checks for the last twelve months on the following accounts: Hamble, Mary, H-A-M-B-L-E, and Parson, Franklin, P-A-R-S-O-N. He may have two or more accounts, one in the company name. Also see if Angela Parson has any accounts with us."

"We have one more method of proof," said Gondoler. "Parson said his stockbroker is Boyd Fortune of Gordon, Pine, Simpson."

"I don't know Fortune but I can put in a call to his boss." Case flicked on the intercom: "Get me Jim Simpson at Gordon, Pine, Simpson."

For the next thirty minutes the information poured in. There were hundreds of checks, deposits, and withdrawals to be scanned; from Jim Simpson came records of sales, transfers, and purchases. Case and Gondoler sorted them to see if a new pattern were apparent in the last three months.

The unusual or unexplained recent transactions were written down. It was slow, laborious work. Harry Case, Sr., had three men from the bank working with him, each on a different pile.

Case himself flicked through every check, then turned the pile over to Gondoler.

"Look at this one," said Case, laughing and waving a check in the air. His three employees were stunned. During those occasions when they had been invited to the President's office, they had never heard him laugh or behave in such an undignified manner. The check in question was for $1,000, signed by Franklin Parson, Trustee, on the Mary Hamble account. The payee was Judge Henley Stuart and it was marked "Campaign Contribution."

Several hours later, five lists had been drawn up. Each showed what had been discovered in the last three months that was not in accord with transactions the previous nine months.

"Franklin Parson made it easy for the District Attorney," said Case. "There are a dozen checks he wrote as Trustee for the Hamble account that will nail him. Take a look at what he's done." Case read aloud from each of the lists, occasionally pausing for emphasis, shaking his head negatively at the criminality or stupidity of his victim. He held up a finger each time he read the name "Judge Henley Stuart." "The four checks to Stuart," he said, "were written within two days of each other."

Mary Hamble Account:
   Checks signed by Franklin Parson, Trustee,
      on Mary Hamble Account:
      $4,000 to Betsy Pickens for Secretarial Duties
      $6,000 to Cash (stationery supplies and postage)
      $5,000 to Franklin Parson for Expenses Incurred
      $2,300 to Mavor Travel Services for Air Travel
      $52,000, $68,000, and $80,000 to Dr. Heinrich Fronzhold
         for Medical Treatments
      $10,000 to Angela Spotswood Parson for Services (Mrs.
         Parson endorsed the check to Cash)
      $1,000 to Judge Henley Stuart for Campaign Contribution
      $90,000, $70,000, and $86,000 to Harmonetics Hospital for
         Medical Treatment
      $18,500 to Marwell Auto for Car
   Deposits to Mary Hamble Account:

174

$182,640 from Gordon, Pine, Simpson from sale of Hamble stocks.

Franklin Parson Account:
Check signed by Franklin Parson deemed unusual:
$1,000 to Judge Henley Stuart for Campaign Contribution
Deposits to Franklin Parson Account deemed unusual:
$18,000 (cash)
$23,000 (cash)
$15,000 (cash)

Parson Associates Architects Account:
Check signed by Franklin Parson deemed unusual:
$1,000 to Judge Henley Stuart for Campaign Contribution
Deposits deemed unusual:
$20,000 (cash)
$32,000 (cash)

Angela Spotswood Parson Account:
Check signed by Angela Parson deemed unusual:
$1,000 to Judge Henley Stuart for Campaign Contribution

Gordon, Pine, Simpson (GPS):
Stocks and bonds, transactions and sales, Mary Hamble
    portfolio, by GPS:
    Gift: $630,000 (assorted stocks) to Harmonetics Society
    Sales (stock): $4,182,640 (after commissions)
        $4 million in tax-exempt purchases
        $182,640 check made out to Mary Hamble Account
Summary of assets in Hamble portfolio:
    Held by GPS: $2,300, bonds
                $19,821,680 stocks (current market value)
    Held by Franklin Parson, Trustee: $7,375,000, bonds

"Mr. Gondoler," said Case, "let me show you what Parson did. It's a common trick among dishonest trustees. Sometimes they get away with it for years, sometimes forever. Parson converted over $4 million in stocks owned by Mary Hamble into tax-exempts. He took possession of the bonds so he could clip the coupons. He also held in his personal possession another $3,375,000 in municipals from the Hamble portfolio. That gave him the income from $7,375,000 in bonds. Their average yield is slightly over 6 percent per annum, tax free. During the first quarter he cashed approximately $110,000 in coupons. Now look at the unexplained cash deposits made: $18,000, $23,000, and $15,000 to his own account and $20,000 and $32,000 to Parson Associates Architects. That's a total of $108,000."·

"Then he'll have to plead guilty, won't he?"

"Not necessarily. He'll claim he borrowed the money and had every intention of paying it back. He'll show IOUs to prove he meant to return it. They always do. Then he'll say he was mistaken in some of the expense checks he authorized and he will offer to reimburse the estate."

"But he won't get away with it?" asked Gondoler.

"He will undoubtedly, but not positively, go to jail. There will be appeals and delays. He may claim illness or temporary insanity. The judge before whom he appears may be a crook. The possibilities are endless. However, in two years he won't have a dime. The lawyers will get everything he's got."

"What about Judge Stuart?"

"He'll make the usual denials: he wasn't aware of the individual contributions, such matters were handled by the bookkeepers and accountants, he is completely innocent, his opponents are out to smear him, and so on. If it turns out the four checks were given to him on or about the date when he granted the power of attorney to Parson, he may be tried and convicted for accepting a bribe. He certainly will never get the Republican nomination for Governor. He could also be disbarred. He'll be wiped out financially after he pays his legal fees."

"Can Dr. Fronzhold be in trouble legally on his fees? He received $200,000 for taking care of Mrs. Hamble. The Harmonetics Hospital got another $246,000."

"You want an honest opinion? Fronzhold and the hospital will get away with it. There won't be a doctor or nurse in the country who will say a word against Fronzhold or the hospital. The AMA will maintain a dignified silence. Even if Mary Hamble testifies against him, Fronzhold will have a dozen witnesses who will swear Mrs. Hamble was off her rocker and Dr. Fronzhold was in constant attendance.

"You've got one weapon against Fronzhold, the hospital, and the Society: you can print the facts. When the public reads the story, Fronzhold will no longer be Sir Galahad in shining white shirt and stethoscope. Josiah Minden will be forced to can him."

"Then we can't touch Minden?"

"Not if he fires Fronzhold. He will return the $630,000 in stocks to the Hamble estate. He will express disappointment in Fronzhold, Stuart, and Parson. He will sever them from the fold and will continue to lead his flock happily ever after.

"We at the bank will freeze the funds in the Parson and Hamble accounts immediately. Jim Simpson will do the same on sales or transferrals. The District Attorney's office will be notified and the story will break tomorrow."

"Mr. Case, I agree the accounts should be frozen without delay. However, if you and Mr. Simpson do a more thorough investigation, you might not be able to present the material to the District Attorney until Monday. It's now Thursday. Hopefully Parson won't make any withdrawals or can be stalled for one day. On Sunday he will receive his White Gown from Dr. Minden. If Minden hears about the investigation, the ceremony will be indefinitely postponed."

"Thank you for your thoughtful suggestion, Mr. Gondoler. We will investigate more thoroughly over the weekend. On Monday the newest addition to the White Robes will be arrested."

Excerpt from an Address Given by Andy Ames at the Harmonetics Temple of Las Vegas (February 24, 1981)

Comedians are not supposed to give serious talks. When we do, people laugh with the opening word because they expect something funny. I don't want to be humorous today. I'm going to tell you a story built of sadness, grief, and misery, a story about a lost soul who experienced degradation and disgrace but who emerged from his suffering as a wiser and more complete human being.

I was an ordinary boy born into an ordinary family in an ordinary Midwestern city, but I had a special gift: I could tell stories and make people laugh. Thanks to the hard work and encouragement of my parents, I had special opportunities to make the most of my gift. I became an entertainer.

To the comedian, there is nothing more beautiful than a live audience. You want them to laugh with you and love you. When you are finished, you want them to cheer you. You will spend endless hours creating and perfecting a small routine. Your happiness is complete if the audience is attentive, happy, and appreciative.

I went from small success to big success to the pinnacle of an actor's career: a television show of my own with millions of people watching each week and television ratings that turned my head. I was rich, and I thought money could buy everything; I was a popular figure, and I thought that meant I was loved. My idea of happiness was a home in Bel Air on a mountaintop, a Rolls-Royce and a foreign sports car, invitations to parties at the homes of famous movie stars, a large swimming pool that I never swam in, and a group of pals who were always available and who thought everything I did was stupendous.

I lived this life for seven years. In those seven years I had three wives and two children. I never saw the kids grow up. I was too busy rehearsing my shows or going to parties or giving parties myself. My mother got sick but I didn't have the time to visit with her. She died in a nursing home; she hadn't seen me in four years. I started to drink heavily. My third wife, a gentle woman, said she would leave me if I didn't sober up. I didn't.

You all know about the car crash. There were three others in the car and I was the driver. I hit a tree. Two of the passengers died. I was drunk.

I lost my television contract. I couldn't get a job. My so-called pals disappeared within a month. In the space of a year I had lost my home, my cars, and my false friends. I was living in a two-room flat, an alcoholic.

One day I was having a sandwich in a coffee shop. I was unshaven and not too clean. I started kidding with the waitress and asked her if she wanted to meet me later. I knew she wouldn't. To my surprise she said she would, provided we first made one stop. She looked so clean and her skin was so fresh and glowing that it seemed impossible she would want to be seen with a freak like me. The first stop was the Harmonetics Temple on Sunset Strip. She held my hand as we walked in and she introduced me to her friends. They were the kindest people I had ever met. She whispered to me that she was playing a part in the ceremony and she asked me to wait for her. She made sure I was seated with her friends. Kathy Warner (that was the name of my waitress-friend) was Presented that day and received her Blue Gown. I saw the tears on her face as she walked down the aisle. I saw her blessed, glorious face as she stood on the podium, and I wept unashamedly. Then I heard Dr. Josiah Minden speak, and his words went deep into my heart.

Dr. Minden talked that day about our dual nature, and the points he made seemed directed to me: we love our parents but we consign them to nursing homes; we approve the laws of the land but we get into our cars and break all the laws of the road; we desire happiness but we think it comes through flashy cars, large mansions, and false friends. Then he spoke about the brotherhood of man, respect and love for people of all ages, and the true happiness that comes with giving.

I was reborn on the day that Kathy Warner took me to the Temple. Two months later, when I received my Blue Gown, I was Presented by Kathy. I found liquor distasteful and luxuries unnecessary. I pledged my tithe, and suddenly I found true happiness.

I was given a chance for a television series last year, and I returned to an audience I thought would despise me. To my amazement they were sympathetic and warm. I have reexperienced "success" but I no longer yearn for the material appurtenances that were once my only goal.

My dear wife, Kathy Warner Ames, and I greet you as our brothers and sisters. You are gracious, beautiful people, for you not only have laughed with me but today you have joined me in weeping.

Thank you.

"What," asked Bill Harding of young Jerry Marconi, "do you think is the appeal of the Harmonetics Society?"

"People are looking for answers. They want to be told how and where to find happiness."

"Is there more to it than the answers?"

"They must renounce smaller happinesses such as tobacco, booze, and meat to gain a greater happiness. Renunciation is a key."

179

"And brotherhood?"

"Of course. They give and receive friendship. It's tactile as well. We so seldom touch strangers. If you touch the hands and face of a stranger, he or she becomes a friend."

"Jerry, Harmonetics has many appeals but you've named some of the important ones."

"What would you add, Bill?"

"A leadership in which to believe, the promise of health and youth . . ."

The ringing of the telephone cut off the balance of Harding's answer.

"Yes?" said Bill. He listened for a minute, then formed his thumb and forefinger into an "O" for Jerry's benefit. He nodded his head as he listened, as though the caller could see him. The only words he spoke were "Good, good" and "Fine, fine." When he hung up Harding said to Jerry:

"We're running the box with the notice of the exposé. Tell Martha and Roger. Don't go yet, Jerry. That was Harold. He's got some good news and he's bringing a tape with him. He'll type his report in the office as soon as he gets here. Get his tape transcribed with plenty of copies, including an extra one for Helen Mandel of *American & International Architecture*. Harold says she went out on a limb for him. Be sure to tell Jade and Henrietta about the material in the tape and Harold's report.

"Don't forget to type Jade's and Henrietta's material as well. You'll be here late, Jerry. Get some dinner sent in for you and Harold. When all the reports are in, call me. I'll be home all evening."

Elliott Beale was sitting in the living room reading the evening paper. He raised his head slightly when the front door opened, then lowered it again to the papers. It was only Henrietta and she was alone.

She came in and said, "Good evening, dear. Did you have a nice day?"

What an idiotic question. How could he have a good day when he didn't have a damn thing to do? He had hoped to have lunch with Bernadette but she said she was under the weather. How can you be under the weather when you are twenty-four years old? At any rate he would see Jeanne tomorrow. Good, sweet, dear Jeanne. He'd behaved appallingly several times, nerves, of course, and Jeanne had seen him through. For a woman of fifty-five she was quite magnificent. For that matter, Henrietta was remarkable: good skin, fine health, just a little overweight.

Elliott glanced up at his wife. "You are looking very handsome tonight, Henrietta."

"That's a very dear thing to say. Can I fix you a drink?"

"I've already had one but another won't hurt. While you're making yourself one, will you freshen mine?"

Henrietta took his glass and walked to the bar at the corner of the room. "I've stopped drinking," she said.

Elliott looked up from the newspapers.

"Good heavens! Are you trying to lose weight?"

"No. I've been to the Harmonetics Temple several times, and their ideas make sense."

"YOU going to the Harmonetics Temple? I think I would be less surprised if you told me Henry Ford had turned Communist."

"It's not a religion, Elliott. It's a way of life. I'm taking some seminars now and I'll be doing some volunteer work after I take my Aptitudes."

"Your Aptitudes! Henrietta, are you joking?"

"I know what I've said in the past, but I'm a different person. The nice thing about life is the ability to change. I'm not working anymore and I do enjoy the services."

"As a young friend of mine would say, 'I think you're putting me on.'"

Henrietta laughed. "I won't try to convert you. You don't have to take me to the Temple. In fact, I promise I won't discuss my new beliefs if you would prefer it."

"I'm fascinated by the change in you. Tell me what it is you believe."

Henrietta pulled up a chair and opened her purse to take out a cigarette. She took out the whole pack and crushed it.

"I've given up cigarettes, alcohol, and meat."

"Meat! I don't believe it."

"You will when you see the dinner tonight. Don't worry, there's a squab for you. I'm having a cold vegetable salad."

"As your main course?" asked Elliott incredulously.

Henrietta laughed again.

"There's a lot about me that's changed, Elliott. It's a change for the better. I'm happier, and I'm thinking more about other people and less about myself."

"You've never been self-centered, Henrietta. You've always been thoughtful about others. I've been the brute in this household."

"That's not true, Elliott. Look how nice you're being now."

"That's just this moment," said Elliott in a self-recriminating mood.

"You can show what a decent person you are tomorrow night at our dinner party."

"Ah, yes. Who's coming?"

"There will be ten of us. Robbie Spriggs . . ."

"I haven't seen the Senator in a long time. That's a nice surprise."

"His dinner partner is Sarah Robinson. Edward is still not well enough for dinner parties so Sarah's coming alone."

"She's a bit silly but amusing enough at a dinner table. That's fine."

"Then there's Clarissa and Byron Kent."

"Good couple. He's a stimulating talker. She's not my type but she's decorative. Who else?"

"Dr. and Mrs. Heinrich Fronzhold. He's the Director of the Harmonetics Hospital. She was Ruth Jansen before their marriage. She's from Houston and she's supposed to be charming. Clarissa asked if she could invite them, and I thought you might enjoy meeting them both."

"The Hospital Director, eh? Well, I suppose he'll be interesting. No harm there."

"The last couple is Cissy and Austin McDowell. He's a partner at Blake, Chatterly."

"That's the chap you were talking to on the phone the other day. Good. A lawyer, a doctor, a businessman, and a Senator. People from all walks of life, you might say."

"I'm leading up to a favor, Elliott. You adore broccoli and hollandaise, don't you?"

"Ummm, yes," he said, smiling at his wife.

"And salade de Cresson?"

"Very good."

"Pommes de terres au gratin?"

"Excellent."

"Broiled whole tomatoes with a sprinkling of parsley?"

"So far it sounds perfect."

"To start with, chilled cream of avocado soup, and to finish, a chocolate soufflé."

"No complaints. What about the main course?"

"That's the favor. All the guests are members of the Temple. They're vegetarians."

"For God's sake, Henrietta!"

Henrietta tried to soothe him: "We'll have some lovely cheeses and I'll have the cook prepare some croissants. It's just the one night, dear."

"I might as well agree amiably since you're going to do it anyway," he said crossly.

"You are an angel. Thank you, dear," she said, kissing him on the cheek.

"All right," he said, somewhat mollified, "but we're damn well going to serve wine."

"Of course you can have wine. The others don't drink but that certainly doesn't mean you can't."

"Henrietta, you've done many different things with your life, some of them pretty outlandish, but I never would have believed you would join the Temple."

Lecture by Professor Samuel B. Parten
College of Harmonetics, Science Department
September 8, 1980

Everyone enrolled in this class has shown, through the Aptitude Tests, that he or she is gifted with both scientific and philosophical talents. This is an intensive course in Biorhythms. Most of you will go on to further study in Advanced Biorhythms and Altering Biorhythm Patterns. If you are given a passing grade in the comprehensive examinations, you will receive the

Harmonetics Qualification Certificate in Biorhythms. This enti-
tles you to be a Senior Chart Analyst.

In this accelerated course we will discuss the three cycles—
physical, intellectual, and emotional—which determine the
patterns of success and failure. These cycles begin at birth. The
physical cycle lasts twenty-three days, the intellectual thirty-
three days, and the emotional twenty-eight days. First we chart
the birth date of the individual as the base of our graph, which
will swing toward a positive and negative pole. For example, the
physical cycle moves toward the positive pole, peaking at the
end of six-plus days. Then the cycle moves down for another six
days, at which point it crosses the base (a trying and dangerous
period). The cycle continues toward the negative pole for six-
plus days, then moves back to the base (another critical period).
The emotional and intellectual cycles can also be charted: they
move toward positive and negative poles, with the dangerous
periods occurring when the cycle crosses the base.

When we chart the three cycles together, we can make
amazing behavior pattern predictions. There are times when all
three cycles are at the top of the positive pole: this is when
achievement and success will be highest. There are also several
days when all three cycles will simultaneously cross the base: no
decisions of importance should be made at that time. During
high peaks one can gamble and win; on the "base" days,
creativity and stability and physical keenness are lost.

In Advanced Biorhythms we will study the charts of great
statesmen, authors, musicians, scientists, athletes, religious
leaders, and others to determine their optimum cycles. We will
predict scientifically the triple critical days of a baseball
pitcher, a premier, a college president, or a corporate execu-
tive.

In our course on Altering Biorhythm Patterns we will go one
step further. We will negate the triple critical days by breaking
the cycle. This is done through the power of specific rocks:
basaltic lava, coal, granite, limestone, shell, coral, and iron.
These "Protectors" must be carried or worn whenever a cycle
nears the base. The simplest method is to wear the seven rocks
in the form of a bracelet, as I am doing. Each rock represents
fourteen years: basaltic lava is the key if the person has not yet
reached his or her fifteenth birthday. My key rock, as you can

*see on my bracelet, is limestone, which occupies the central
position among the seven rocks. The setting is tin, which is the
best transmitter for the "Protectors." I wear the "double iron"
and "single shell" since my birth date is May 13.*

*The scientists who first correlated the biorhythmic patterns
were men well ahead of their time, but lasting glory belongs to
one man only—Felix Axelman—who, through brilliant research
in the Harmonetics Laboratories, was able to devise the
Protector Rock method of breaking the cycles.*

At 10:00 P.M. the only people on the ground floor of the
National News building were Jerry Marconi and Harold Gondoler. On the second floor two neophytes were working on a
seven-hundred-piece mailing to potential advertisers; one could
faintly hear the sound of the Pitney Bowes machine printing the
indicia. Harold was clicking away with two fingers on an electric
typewriter, crossing out typos with a black marking pencil. He
finished his last sentence and pulled out the page.

"I'm done, Jerry. I'll wait for you if you haven't much
longer."

"I'll be another couple of hours. You go ahead."

"Good night. I'll talk to you in the morning."

"Good night."

Harold pulled on his jacket and walked out the front door, the
heavy latch snapping into place as he pulled it shut. It was a
cold night and the street was almost deserted. Three or four
illegally parked cars but no people. A few doors down, the
sounds of country music. Lights on in many of the windows but
the blinds or curtains hiding the inhabitants.

As Harold started walking west, he heard the sudden sounds
of ignition, spark plugs, and accelerator. Some driver in a
hurry. Foot on pedal, wheels spinning. Something wrong. Too
sudden. A car prowling for a specific victim. He, Harold, the
quarry.

Gondoler lunged for the shelter of a small brownstone. He
pushed off with his feet, his arms stretched out, his body almost
parallel to the ground. He was too late. Four bullets penetrated
his body.

Martha Rayburn had spent the evening at the home of a male

friend named Mr. Pastorini with whom she frequently co-habited. At 8:00 A.M. they got up, made arrangements to meet again that night, and left the apartment together, each going in different directions. Martha, as was her custom, had breakfast at the Hotel Claywell Coffee Shop. She ordered her usual: a half grapefruit, rye toast, cream cheese, and a pot of tea. She was eating her grapefruit and reading last week's *Sunday Times Book Review* when someone brushed her elbow. The grapefruit skidded precariously.

"I beg your pardon," said a nervous young woman.

"We're so sorry," said the tall, heavyset man who was with her.

"Is that your napkin? May I get it for you?" asked the woman.

"That's quite all right," said Martha, bending down to retrieve her napkin. "No harm done."

She continued her meal. She had trouble pouring her second cup of tea. Her eyes would not focus on the *Book Review*. She reached for her teacup but her hand would not function. The coffee shop was growing dark. The darkness was enveloping her. Her throat was tightening. She could not breathe.

The nervous young woman rushed up to her: "Don't worry, dear, we are taking you to the hospital." She felt arms encircling her, lifting her, helping her to the door. She gasped for air, struggling to breathe, paralysis overcoming her. Two people opening the taxi door, her own limp legs giving way. A voice saying, "Harmonetics Hospital, please. This is an emergency."

Roger Silberstein was just getting out of the shower when the telephone rang. The caller was Jerry Marconi and the news was bad. Harold Gondoler had been shot. One bullet had struck him in the neck, another busted his shoulder, a third one had lodged in his side, and the fourth had shattered his kneecap. The bullets had been removed last night but the one in the side had been critical. The doctors said Harold might not live.

"Roger, Harold was ambushed. It wasn't an accident. Harding's afraid someone may try to get you and Martha. I can't reach Martha. Her phone doesn't answer. Harding says watch yourself. He thinks you'll be safer out of the city, even out of the country, for the next few weeks."

"It doesn't make sense, Jerry. I only worked on the first story and the only people I interviewed were Austin McDowell and Lawrence Runson. Martha was also on the fringes: she saw the Jennifer Holiday staff and Jennifer's daughter. Why should anyone want to gun us down?"

"Hold on, Roger, Harding wants to speak to you."

"Roger, it's Bill Harding. I'm going to leave a ticket for you at Kennedy. It will be a thirty-day excursion fare to Paris or London or Rome, whichever leaves the earliest. Have you got a valid passport?"

"Yes, I renewed last year."

"Throw some things in a bag and go to the Pan Am ticket counter at Kennedy. Keep in touch and I'll see you in a month."

Roger packed a suitcase per Harding's instructions although he did not believe he was in personal danger. Nobody's out to get me. Martha probably spent the night with Mr. Pimento or whatever his name is. Harold, the poor bastard, was smack in the middle of the investigation. If he hadn't been so brilliant it wouldn't have happened. Now where the hell is my passport. Damn, it's in my vault at the bank. I can take the subway and pick it up in five minutes. I'll bring my bag with me and get a taxi from the bank out to Kennedy. Might as well check out some money at the same time.

Roger walked out of the building carrying his suitcase and his tennis racket. No gunmen were laying for him. At the corner of the block he went down the subway stairs along with a dozen other men and women. He put his token in the slot and walked to the platform. To play it perfectly safe, he stood six feet from the edge of the platform. Next to him on either side were two middle-aged women. Not a gunman in sight.

He heard the faint sound of the train in the distance. Along the platform people were stepping forward. Roger stayed where he was, proud that he was taking every precaution, needless though it was. The train came nearer. The sound became a roar. The two women on either side hit him hard with their shoulders. The suitcase and racket flew out of his hands, sailing into the path of the oncoming train. Roger went sprawling forward. Dimly he heard screams.

Harding was right, he thought with surprise. Then his body hit the tracks.

During her noon break at the hospital, Jade used the pay phone to reach Jerry at *National News*.

"Harding wants to talk to you, Jade. Hold on. I'll be on the extension."

"Jade? Bill Harding. Remember the first meeting we had when we discussed your Harmonetics Report?"

"Yes."

"I asked you and Henrietta to work undercover, but Harold, Roger, and Martha had open assignments. They were to use their *National News* credentials."

"I remember."

"At the meeting you volunteered to 'feed' information to the Society to make your role more believable. I suggested the information be dragged out of you: you were to be duped into giving away meaningless data. Last night you reported to Jerry that Josiah Minden had been allowed to pump you and that you fed him, as per our plan, the names of Harold, Martha, and Roger. Jade, you did your job perfectly. It's what I wanted and what we all thought was right."

"Oh, God, did something go wrong?"

"If I were to do it over again, assuming the limited knowledge we then had of the Harmonetics leaders, I would tell you to do exactly what you did."

"So would I, Jade," added Jerry.

Jade was silent.

"Harold Gondoler was shot last night, a little after 10:00 P.M.," said Harding. "He had just left the *National News* office. He was alone on the street, a car started up, accelerated, and he was hit. Four bullets. He's in the hospital but we're not sure he'll make it. This morning Martha had breakfast at her usual coffee shop. She had a fainting spell. A man and a woman, apparently strangers, put her into a taxi and took her to the Harmonetics Hospital. Early this morning Jerry and I called Roger. We had arranged for him to take a plane to Europe. He was to go directly to the airport. Instead, for some reason we don't yet know, he took the subway. He was pushed onto the tracks and died at once.

"Jade, we warned Roger and it still didn't save his life. We don't know if Martha is alive. I don't feel we have the right to risk any more lives; we are not in the business of investigating murders. Stay away from Minden. Don't get involved in anything that might implicate you."

"Minden must have ordered the murders," said Jade stiffly. "He was the only one who had the three names."

"Everything seems to point to him," said Harding.

"I did it. If I hadn't told Minden, they would be alive."

"No, Jade, you're wrong. It was no more your fault than it was mine. I gave the orders."

Jade hung up. She went to the Ladies' Room, locked herself in a john, and vomited over and over. She was covered in perspiration and her hands were trembling. After twenty minutes she came out, splashed cold water on her face, combed her hair, and returned to the Study Room to take the last hour of her Psychological Tests.

Henrietta took the phone call in the kitchen. It was Jerry Marconi. Roger was dead, Harold was on the critical list, and Martha's condition was unknown but the prognosis was morbid. Henrietta was unusually quiet.

"Who was that?" asked Elliott, coming in the swinging door just as she hung up.

"Just the tailor, dear. My gray suit is ready."

(Reprinted by permission of the *New York Times*)
October 15, 1982

White Robe Ceremony at Harmonetics Temple on Sunday at 1:00 P.M.
Newcomer to White Gowns not yet announced; Josiah Minden to officiate at the proceedings

On Sunday afternoon, at 1:00 P.M., a twenty-fifth member of the White Robes will be enshrined at the Harmonetics Temple. Traditionally, the name is kept secret until the actual moment of the ceremony. Generally other members of the

White Robes are not informed until the proceedings begin.
The Presentation is always made by Dr. Josiah Minden. At
tomorrow's ceremonies, all of the current twenty-four members
of the White Robes will be in attendance. They will be seated on
the podium to welcome the newcomer to their group. Among
those expected to be present are Dr. Francis X. McDonald, who
is often called Dr. Minden's right-hand man; stage and screen
actress Lila La Mause; Dr. Heinrich Fronzhold, Director of the
Harmonetics Hospital; Miss Minnie Matthews of Houston;
Senator Robert T. Spriggs of New York; Byron Kent, Chairman
and Chief Executive Officer of Kentwood Mining; Judge Henley
Stuart, who is the newest member of the White Robes;
distinguished author Dr. Reginald Zinder; Dr. Anton Kohl,
neurological surgeon; and TV star Andy Ames.

A spokesman for the Harmonetics Society has said that, if any
of those wishing to attend the enshrinement are unable to get
seats, special tickets will be given which will entitle the holder to
preferential seating at the late afternoon or evening services.
Dr. Minden and the members of the White Robes will be at all
three Sunday services.

Harding entered the hospital room with the tiptoe solicitude
of the visitor. Janitors, nurses, orderlies, and doctors barged in
breezily; visitors were fearful that the mere sound of shoe
against floor would cause the patient to lapse into coma or
worse. Harding had been informed by the floor nurse that
Gondoler was "resting comfortably," but this term could be
equally applied to a patient who would be released in one or
two days or to one who was destined to depart this world within
the hour.

Harold lay helplessly on the bed. His eyes were open but
glazed, and he seemed to have trouble following Harding as he
approached the bed.

"Are they giving you a lot of sedation, Harold?"

"Yes." The word came out faintly.

"Are you in pain?"

"Not much."

"Doctors give a helluva lot of pain-killers. Shall I find out if
the drugs can be stopped?"

"Yes. Pain's not bad."

"You did a great job on Parson. Your new recruits, Caroline and Missy, were phenomenal discoveries."

"Hire 'em."

"You want me to put them on the payroll?"

"Sure. Save you some money. Won't have to pay 'em Social Security."

Harold smiled for the first time since he was attacked.

"I have the results of your aptitudes," said Beth Marple from behind her desk. "As I would have expected, you have excellent hand-eye coordination. Finger dexterity is high. Memory excellent. Aesthetic sense is poor and you have almost no artistic interests. What I like best, Jade, is your proven ability to follow orders. If you had scored in a low percentile, neither Dr. Jennings nor I would have been able to use you. Would you like to hear where you rate lowest?"

"Yes."

"You would make a very poor schoolteacher, a terrible museum curator, and a lousy gardener."

Jade laughed. Beth frowned.

"Sorry, Beth, I was showing appreciation for your phraseology."

Beth continued. "You are not mechanically oriented nor are you particularly creative. You would make a poor criminal lawyer and an incompetent criminal investigator. I've listed the areas in which you excel: sports reporter, translator, and, oddly enough, lab technician. If you went back to college for graduate study, you would do well in psychology.

"Dr. Jennings would like to see you now. Both she and I are pleased with your results."

Jade followed Beth to the end of Iris Corridor where Esme Jennings, Chief of Psychiatric Services, had her office. A nurse-receptionist told them Dr. Jennings was examining a patient.

"You both can go in. The patient is comatose. Complete disorientation."

Beth entered the private office, followed by Jade. Dr. Esme Jennings, a stocky woman with short-cropped red hair, was standing with her back to the window. It was difficult to see her features and impossible to read her expression. Facing Dr. Jennings was a patient in a wheelchair.

"Nice to meet you at last, Jade," said Jennings cordially.

Then, turning to Beth, she changed her speech to the clipped staccato of the busy physician: "New arrival, Code No. R–651–8L36. Patient lacks all visual and auditory responses. Physical condition good. Pulse and metabolism normal. Heartbeat regular."

Beth and Jade moved toward the window to look at the patient. Jade felt the blood rush to her face and her heart pump with the same terrifying speed as that time two years ago when she had almost run over a young child on a bicycle. She was overwhelmed by an attack of nausea. Strapped into the wheelchair was Martha Rayburn, eyes blank and jaw hanging slackly. The face was expressionless and the head drooped loosely from the neck.

"Jade, are you all right?" asked Beth.

"It's the first time I've seen a mental patient," said Jade. "I'm sorry to be a nuisance but my mouth's gone dry. Could I get a glass of water, please?"

Dr. Jennings gently guided Jade to a chair. She poured her a cup of coffee from a hot thermos. "Sip it, Jade. The coffee is a stimulant."

Jade took the mug, her hands trembling. She felt a terrible burning in her eyes. The pain from holding back the tears was unbearable.

"I'm so very sorry," said Jade. "I'm behaving like an idiot. Now you won't want to use me in the ward."

Dr. Jennings patted her shoulder and spoke kindly. "You'll be fine in a few minutes. You don't have to apologize. Some nurses and interns get the same reaction; it's normal."

Jade looked up, her enormous, sad black eyes seeing the kindness in Dr. Jennings' blue eyes and the warmth in her face.

"Thank you," she said, almost inaudibly.

Jennings turned to Beth. "Work up the usual tests. I won't prescribe therapy until I get your report. Electroencephalogram, spinal tap, blood analysis results, are in patient's folder. Assigned to Room 8, Iris V."

"Do we have a past history?"

"No. Patient was picked up on the street in comatose condition. No purse or identification. Security is checking to find out her background. We'll keep her here only until her relatives are contacted. Should be a matter of a few days."

"Any guesses on the prognosis?" asked Beth.

Dr. Jennings shrugged. "Too early to tell."

"If the relatives aren't found, would you keep her indefinitely?" asked Jade.

"The decision would be made by Administration," said Jennings. "That's Dr. Fronzhold's department. Normally a patient or a relative must be a member of the Society. Are you feeling better, Jade?"

"Yes. You've been extremely kind."

"Jade, you may wear the gray gown of the Hospital Probationary. This gown, as you can see by the badge, entitles you to work on Iris V. Beth, take Jade with you on your rounds. If you're tied up, Jade can work with the nurses. Good idea to let her learn medication. She can start with the charts."

"Esme, Jade has one other qualification that entitles her to work in this department. She's a fine tennis player."

"As good as you, Beth?"

"Almost," said Beth. "Better," said Jade, simultaneously.

Jennings laughed. "Jade, I'm not a very good player but I hate to let the hospital courts go to waste. Keep a set of tennis clothes here. Perhaps we'll have a chance for a game if you don't mind playing a duffer."

"She's quite good, Jade," said Beth.

"Quite good" in tennis lingo meant a C or a B player. "Very good" designated a club champion or runner-up. "She's a real player" denoted someone who had once played the circuit.

"I'd love it," Jade said. That sealed the bond.

Jade pushed the wheelchair down the corridor to Room 8, Iris V. Beth walked in front of her at a brisk medical gait. Jade moved her hand to Martha's limp shoulder. She touched Martha's cheek. She patted the hair that stuck out in four directions. Jade's hands had stopped trembling but the nausea had not left.

Beth stopped at the Nurses' Desk to leave information on R–651–8L36. Then she introduced Jade.

"This is Jade Boren who will be assisting me on the ward. Jade, this is Charlene Calderwood, the Head Nurse. Jackie Volts, Ellen Dixon; Jade Boren. Dr. Jennings wants Jade to learn medication and to write up the charts."

"Will you be able to work weekends? We're always short-handed then," asked the Head Nurse, a thin, sharp-nosed woman with gray-streaked hair.

"Sure. I'll come tomorrow and Sunday, every weekend if you want."

"I'll leave Jade with you now," said Beth. "She's a good worker. She'll catch on quickly."

Jackie Volts and Jade took patient R–651–8L36 to Room 8. Jackie, a strong, stocky nurse in her late thirties, lifted Martha onto the bed. As she hooked up the intravenous, she kept up a steady monologue:

"When they come off the street like this one, they're usually in terrible shape. This patient's different. Look how nice her nails are. Hair's clean too. Can't have been bedridden: the skin's perfect. Something must have hit her suddenly. A shock of some kind, bad news, who knows. The bodies are flabby when they've been in the hospital for a prolonged stay. I wonder why they gave her a private room. When they come off the street, they always put them in one of the wards. Maybe they figure she's got a rich family. If she stays here, Jennings will probably try shock. Sometimes it works but you never know. The patients hate it. Not this one, though. She won't know what's happening. I wish some of the others were as quiet as this one. If we didn't keep them medicated, we'd need ten times the number of nurses. The nurses do all the work, you know. The doctors pop in for five or ten minutes a day, they look at the charts, they look at the patients, and they move on. I'm on a twelve-hour shift today, would you believe it? I'm glad you're here. I'll show you how to fix the medications. We have our own pharmacy on the floor. Most of them get sedatives but a few are on Thorazine and some are on chemotherapy. Four patients are scheduled for shock later this afternoon. You can help me take them to Iris III where the treatments are given. I have to do a prep for psychosurgery. Kohl will operate. It's the second time for the patient. The first time it didn't take. If you've got a weak stomach, don't watch the operation. It will blow your mind."

"Is psychosurgery similar to a lobotomy?" Jade asked.

"Not according to Dr. Kohl. Lobotomies are passé; almost no one does them any more. Psychosurgery got popular five or six years ago, and Kohl uses it when nothing else works."

"Is it often successful?"

Nurse Volts shrugged. "That depends on your definition of success. It's what you might call a permanent tranquilizer."

As she talked, Nurse Volts efficiently went about her tasks. She fixed the intravenous needle in Martha's helpless arm and pulled up the bars on either side of the bed.

"Not that she'll fall out," said Jackie Volts, "but it's regulations. We can leave her now. She's fine. We'll pick up the charts at the Nurses' Desk and fix up the medication trays. Dr. Molen has six patients on this floor and they're all on the same medication. He'll come in on Tuesday and order shock for four of them or maybe all six. We see him once a week. He's got over 180 patients at three different hospitals. You ought to hear him bitch about how he has to go to three hospitals. He's at Harmonetics on Tuesday and the other two on Wednesday and Thursday. Then he takes off for the country on Thursday afternoon and he doesn't come back until Tuesday morning. What a life. He makes maybe $300,000 or $400,000 a year and we do all the work. Jennings and Kohl between them have most of the patients. Dr. Fronzhold has two on this floor. He usually comes in on Fridays, and if anything goes wrong we all get hell. His patients are in Room 16 and Room 23. The fellow in Room 16 is under restraint. He swung at one of the orderlies two days ago, gave him a real bruise. Room 23 is a quiet one but she has to be heavily sedated. If she comes out of it, she's dangerous. Wouldn't know it to look at her.

"We can't give medication to Rooms 34 to 46 unless two orderlies are present. The convicts are in those rooms and, man, are they crazy. Wait till you hear their language. They volunteered to receive psychiatric help and they were remanded here by court order. Now it looks like they're all trying to bust out. Half of them are getting a combination of drugs and shock. The ones on chemotherapy have gone twitchy and refuse to eat. You can't believe the problems we're having with them. The other half are scheduled for psychosurgery next week. They haven't been told so they're more tractable. Frankly, I can't wait until we get rid of them."

Jackie Volts opened the door to Room 1. Jade, behind her, pushed the medication cart. Jackie checked the tray, picked up a small cup and two pills, and handed them to B196–819–422. The patient, a woman in her early twenties with darting eyes, submissively popped the pills in her mouth and swallowed them.

"That was very good, dearie," said Jackie. "Dr. Jennings is so pleased with the progress you are making. Now we want you to get all the rest you can. You need to regain your strength. Perhaps later today you can go for a walk. Wouldn't that be lovely?"

The woman nodded eagerly six or eight times. She was unable to speak. Her eyes darted from Jackie to Jade. She was still nodding when they left the room.

They finished the first twelve rooms, then returned to the Pharmacy to fill the medication and pill cups for the next twelve rooms.

"Jackie, you look exhausted," said Jade. "Why don't you get yourself a cup of tea and I'll fill the medications. You can check me when you come back."

"You're a sweetie," said Jackie. "I'll take a breather and I'll be back in three minutes."

"Take your time," said Jade. "I'll wait."

When Jackie had gone, Jade took the teapot and filled one of the medication cups. It looked a bit light. She squeezed the teabag to make the color darker. She placed the small paper cup in the space on the tray for Room 23. Next she looked for the aspirin. She shook two pills from the aspirin bottle into a one-inch paper saucer and placed the saucer under "Room 23." Then she used the prescribed drugs to fill out the balance of the medication charts.

When Jackie returned, Jade assisted by pushing the cart to Room 14 (there was no Room 13, just as there was no thirteenth floor, at the Harmonetics Hospital). Jade, under Jackie's guidance, administered the doses. As they were leaving Room 18, Jade made a suggestion: "You haven't been off your feet all day. There are no shots to give. Everyone seems quiet. If you want, I'd be happy to finish the medications through Room 25. I'll see you in ten minutes in the Pharmacy."

"You're a doll," said Jackie. "My feet are killing me."

Jade continued the rounds. In Room 19 a tired, elderly man tried to refuse his sedative. I wish I didn't have to give it to you, thought Jade. You may be a victim. Maybe you entered the hospital willingly, believing you would be under the supervision of knowledgeable physicians. You don't want the drugs and I don't know if you need them. Nobody gives a damn about you or you wouldn't be shut up in this small dreadful room. On the other hand, you might be a homicidal maniac. I'm afraid to give you the medication and I'm afraid not to. Please, dear sir, drink this small cup because your chart says you have to.

The old man drank out of the cup. He drank because he was afraid of Jade. If he didn't do what she said, he might be punished. "I'll try to help you," she whispered. "I mean it." He rolled over on his side. He didn't believe her.

At last she entered Room 23. Lying on the bed was a small feeble woman, groggy, eyes unfocused. She bore a reasonable resemblance to the picture Jerry had given her of Mary Hamble.

The woman reached out a passive hand for the medication cup. Jade took the hand and pressed it.

"Mary? Are you Mary Hamble?" Jade said softly. "I'm here to help you. This is tea . . . can you hear me? . . . it's tea in the cup. The pills I'm giving you are aspirin. . . . Mary, I'm your friend. Caroline Ryder and Missy Tompkins want me to help you."

Two big tears rolled down Mary's face. She didn't speak.

"You must pretend you're sedated. I'll be here tomorrow and Sunday. If you pretend, no one will know what we're doing. Mary, can you understand me? Press my hand if you do."

Jade felt the gentle squeeze. The tears were flowing down Jade's face. Roger was dead, Martha was a vegetable, and Harold was dying. But oh, God, Mary was here and alive.

"Sssh. Not a word, Mrs. Hamble. For the sake of Caroline and Missy. I'll be back tomorrow. Take the tea and the aspirin."

Mary gulped her pills and the tea. She smiled, her eyes still unfocused. Jade kissed her wet cheek and whispered in her ear, "For Caroline and Missy."

"God's Avenger" Suspect Admits Killing 11 Teen-agers
Murderer to Undergo Psychiatric Tests by Harmonetics Staff

Monte Devlin, twenty-nine-year-old employee of Mak's Meat Market in Queens, confessed to police yesterday the mutilation and wholesale killing of eleven girls, all under the age of sixteen. Devlin led the police to three different burial grounds in lonely areas where skeletons and identification were found.

Devlin's first victim, according to his confession, was Ruth Alders, age twelve. The incident occurred one year ago. The youngster had rejected Devlin's advances, whereupon Devlin felled her with an ax, raped her, and brutally hacked off her limbs. The girl disappeared. The only clue was a postcard the girl's parents received, inscribed in blood from "God's Avenger." Devlin was able to tell the police what was written on the card, none of which had been released to the papers.

Devlin confessed to ten other crimes. Parents of each of the girls received postcards from "God's Avenger." Each was written, said Devlin in his confession, in the blood of the victim. Again Devlin told police the words on each card, none of which was public knowledge.

Devlin was jailed yesterday. This morning Judge Jensen ordered psychological tests to determine his sanity. A group of seven psychiatrists and psychologists from Harmonetics Hospital will conduct a complete series of tests for thirty days to determine whether Devlin can undergo trial.

"Henrietta, it's Sarah. I've got the most incredible news. Are you busy?"

"I was just going out the door to Health and Body I."

"This won't take a minute. I saw Penny Payton, and she told me Clarissa Kent had a rejuvenation job last year at the Harmonetics Hospital. Penny said Clarissa lost a good twenty years. It was not only her face but her skin and hands. I ran into her four months ago but I thought she'd only had the usual nips and tucks."

"You'll see her tonight, dear. She and Byron are coming."

"I wonder if the rejuvenation is extensive plastic surgery, or what. Penny seems to think it's a series of injections. Fronzhold sounds marvelous, doesn't he? Just like another Ponce de Leon."

"I don't know because I don't know who's had it. What does Penny say?"

"She heard rumors about Lila La Mause but Lila's too young. The only one she's sure about is Clarissa. Did she tell you anything about her rejuvenation?"

"No, we only talked for a few minutes."

"I wonder if Dr. Fronzhold does rejuvenations. I bet he did Clarissa's. Would it be terribly rude if I asked him when I see him this evening?"

"I'm sure it . . ."

"How much do you think he charges? Penny guesses $10,000."

"I haven't the slightest . . ."

"If Penny's right about the price, then the injections must be pure gold. No, that's what they use for arthritis, isn't it? What do you think, Henrietta?"

"I've no idea. How about the intestinal flora of the carp? That was Aldous Huxley's solution in 'After Many a Summer Dies the Swan.'"

"Did it make the heroine young again?" asked Sarah.

"In a way. The Fifth Earl of Gonister and his housekeeper grew younger and younger over a period of centuries, until they were finally transformed into fetal apes."

"That doesn't sound very attractive. Can you believe paying $10,000 for rejuvenation? It's women like Clarissa who drive up the price. She pays anything the doctors ask. By the way, Henrietta, Robbie Spriggs tells me you invited Cissy and Austin McDowell for tonight."

"Yes, he did some legal work for me. I've never met her but . . ."

"She's the most dreadful little woman, a terrible snob. She was in my ceramics class a few years ago. Everyone knew she only went because Mira di Forgazi was there. Cissy was so rude to the ceramics teacher, who was such a dear young thing. We went to the same beauty salon for years. Thomas, who always does my hair, said Cissy complained about everything and was always late. Once she refused to pay for a permanent and several times she had screaming arguments about the way they streaked her hair. Thomas finally refused to do her."

"I hear she's rather attractive."

"Attractive? She's a little horror. If she likes you, and you better hope she doesn't, she'll call you six times a day and ring your doorbell every two hours."

"Well, I . . ."

"I'd love to talk to you longer, Henrietta, but I'm in a terrible rush. I'll see you tonight."

"Lieutenant Michael Corrigan of the Police Department to see you," said the receptionist.

"Send him back, please," said Harding.

In the two years since Harding had last seen Corrigan, the lieutenant had undergone two transformations common to men in their early fifties. He had gained thirty pounds and he had lost all the gray in his hair. Harding noticed that Corrigan now wore his belt under his full stomach. The once-black hair streaked with gray had turned to henna-red.

They exchanged greetings and told each other how well they looked. One of the staffers brought them some coffee. They sat down on the couch and Harding began.

"We've been hit badly, Lieutenant. I assigned six staff members to our story on the Harmonetics Society. One is dead, another was shot, and a third may have suffered permanent brain damage."

"Who's the third? I've seen the report on Gondoler and I've been working on the Silberstein affair."

"Martha Rayburn. This morning she became ill while breakfasting in a coffee shop. An unidentified couple knocked against her table and apparently slipped something into her tea. A minute later she collapsed. The couple rushed to her table, swept up the teacup, and whisked Martha off in a cab. We located her this afternoon in the Psychiatric Ward at the Harmonetics Hospital. She hasn't been identified by hospital officials. She's breathing but apparently her brain is no longer functioning."

The lieutenant asked a number of questions about the three victims—what specific information they had acquired about the Harmonetics Society and who, in the Society, knew they were working on the case. Harding described Franklin Parson's scheme to incapacitate his mother-in-law, the innocuous interviews conducted by Roger and Martha, and Harold Gondoler's entrapment of Parson. He omitted mentioning Henrietta Beale and he failed to tell Corrigan that Jade Boren was a Probationary at the Harmonetics Hospital.

"That's the background," said Harding. "It's obvious our people were attacked by members of the Harmonetics Society and that the attacks were instigated by leaders of the Society. However, we can't identify one specific person."

"I believe we can," said the corpulent detective with the henna hair.

"You've got someone?"

"Not exactly, but there's evidence pointing to two people in the Silberstein case. There were approximately thirty people on the platform when the train pulled into the station. We can eliminate twenty-eight of them because they weren't close enough to Silberstein. That leaves two middle-aged women standing on either side of him. Either one could have pushed him onto the tracks."

"Which one do you think did it?"

"I believe they both shoved the victim at the same moment but I have no proof. No one saw the incident. The two women claim Silberstein fell. One of them gave a pretty good imitation of hysteria. The other says the incident shocked her so much she can hardly remember what happened."

"How old are these women?" asked Harding.

"In their late fifties, and neither is particularly strong."

"It's hard to believe," said Harding. "Why would Josiah Minden or one of his associates ask two middle-aged women to murder a stranger? There's too much risk. Why would the women agree? There's a great deal of difference between joining the Harmonetics Society and killing for one's leader."

"A great deal of difference for most people, Mr. Harding," the detective answered. "I've seen murderesses who looked as kindly as your grandmother. The person who selected these two women (a Harmonetics hatchet man, no doubt) probably did so for two reasons: they are intensely loyal to the Harmonetics Society and they are the last people you would suspect because of their age and sex. As for leaders asking believers to commit crimes for them, that's routine. The founder of Synanon gets a disciple to put a rattlesnake in the mailbox of a lawyer he doesn't like. The head of the Liberal party in England is accused of paying a pilot to murder an ex-male model. A Texas millionaire is indicted for offering $25,000 to an associate to get rid of a judge. A minister in Guyana orders a loyal follower to shoot a U.S. Representative and the members of his party. He then commands the mass suicide of the entire religious community. A doctor and a nurse thereupon inject poison into children or force the liquid down their throats. Shall I go on?"

"I see your point. If the two women did kill Roger, how will you get the proof?"

"I've got a plan. It's a bit far out. It's based on the fact that the two Harmonetics women committed holy murder. They feel saintly now that they have disposed of Silberstein. If they were accused of homicide, they would indignantly deny it. However, if another Harmonetics member, someone close to Josiah Minden, congratulated them, I believe they would happily pose for pictures with the corpse."

"Particularly if there were tangible proof of the leader's approval."

"Such as?"

"The awarding of the White Gown," Harding said.

"That's a good possibility, provided the two women are convinced it's real. Then they'll not only talk, they'll sing operatic arias."

"Lieutenant, we've got some people who'd give a pretty good performance."

"It could be dangerous if they muff their lines. Ordinarily I'd rather use detectives for this sort of job. They're paid to take the risk and they've masqueraded before. This time I'd prefer to use your people. The Police Commissioner, you know, is a Brown Robe. If anyone in my department blows it, the Commissioner could destroy all chances of convicting the murderers."

"Do you have the names and addresses of the two women?"

"I just happen to have come prepared," said the lieutenant, handing Harding a sheet of paper.

Harding smiled. Under that head of red hair a conniving brain was clicking.

"Can your men get into the Harmonetics Hospital to remove Martha Rayburn?" Harding asked.

"Not very easily. We can't walk through the wards or peek in the private rooms. The best we can do is show pictures of Martha Rayburn to doctors, nurses, and anyone else who works in Emergency or in the Psychiatric Section. Once she's identified, we can pull her out."

"And if you don't get a positive identification?"

"We'd have to get a court order. In either case, the hospital authorities would undoubtedly know what we were doing. Since Rayburn is suffering from brain damage, as you say, she's no threat to anyone in the Society. As long as she's comatose, she's physically safe."

Harding looked down at the sheet of paper Corrigan had given him.

"Eileen McDermott and Betty McLaughlin," he said, "Begorra and it's a multinational movement, this Harmonetics Society."

"Forsooth," replied Corrigan.

Jerry Marconi stuck his head in Bill Harding's office.

"Shall I bring them in now?"

Harding nodded.

Jerry held the door open and two women, one who looked like she was in her sixties, the other in her eighties, entered. "Mrs. Ryder, Mrs. Tompkins. Mr. Harding."

"I'm Bill," said Harding. "I feel I know you through Harold. Did Jerry show you Harold's report?"

"Yes," said Mrs. Ryder. "We read the whole thing—the interview with Franklin Parson and all those terrible lies on the phone, and then the way that dreadful Parson embezzled Mary's funds. How is Harold? Is there any news?"

"The doctors think if he gets through tonight, his chances are better."

"We came here," said Missy, "to offer our help."

Harding was silent.

"Harold used us and we were quite efficient," said Caroline.

"We may not be able to run the hundred-yard dash but we're far from senile," added Missy.

Harding smiled. Missy looked like a ten-mile wind would knock her over.

"Ladies, how would you like to hear a tape recording of a conversation I just had with Michael Corrigan of the New York Police Department?"

Without waiting for their answer he turned on the tape.

When it was finished Missy said: "You want us to visit those murderers who pushed Roger onto the subway tracks. We'll do it."

Caroline nodded: "Mr. Harding, you're remarkable. You know Missy and I are both seventy-three, but you trust our judgment and our ability to react. My elevator man doesn't trust me to open the front door. My doctor started treating me like an incompetent child a dozen years ago, so I dismissed him. Missy's sons thoughtfully suggested she hire a paid companion to live with her, the assumption being that the companion would be better equipped to make decisions in an emergency or to handle routine matters. You and Harold Gondoler are the first people in years who haven't questioned our competence."

"In this case your age makes you better qualified," said Harding. "The women who murdered Roger won't doubt your authenticity. They'll have no worries about hidden tape recorders. They won't be guarded because they'll know you couldn't be investigators. On the other hand, they certainly will not confess to murder. I've got a plan but it will take careful rehearsing. We're taking no more chances."

Harding outlined his idea. It was imaginative but workable. "It all depends," emphasized Harding, "on what you say when these women mention names you've never heard of."

"We'll chatter away like dizzy blondes," replied Missy.

"There are conditions that go along with the assignment," said Harding. "First, you'll work on your roles and practice them this afternoon with Jerry and me. Next, I'm going to contact the Rappaport Agency. They will furnish two armed escorts. They'll be with you from the moment you leave the *National News* office until the investigation is over. Missy, I want you to move into Caroline's apartment, or Caroline will move into yours. The Rappaport men will stand guard at the apartment. Additionally, you both will carry transmitters at all times. There will always be a Rappaport man within transmittal distance. Agreed?"

"Agreed."

"Then we'll begin," said Harding. "I'm Betty McLaughlin. I pushed Roger to his death but I'm not telling anyone. You've just rung my doorbell and I've let you in."

"My dear Mrs. McLaughlin, I'm so happy to see you," said Caroline.

At 3:00 P.M. Heinrich Fronzhold arrived on Iris V to check on his patients. He was accompanied by a volunteer in a brown gown who walked several paces behind him. Thin, long-nosed Head Nurse Charlene Calderwood glowed with good will at the doctor. Pretty Ellen Dixon and stocky Jackie Volts, the other two nurses, stopped filling out charts and waited for instructions. In the background Jade Boren stood flat against a wall, attempting to look insignificant.

"Any problems on the floor?" asked Fronzhold gruffly.

"Nothing we haven't been able to handle," replied Nurse Calderwood. "Room 16 was overly disturbed on Wednesday. One of the orderlies suffered lacerations that required stitches but he's back at work today."

"And the patient?"

"He had to be subdued by two orderlies plus Miss Volts and myself. His eye is swollen, mouth cut, nose broken. He's been in restraint since Wednesday."

"Why wasn't I notified immediately? This patient is under my direct supervision." Fronzhold did not have a foreign accent but the tone was reminiscent of that of German U-boat captains in World War II movies.

"We phoned your office the moment the incident occurred. You were on call and we couldn't reach you. We left the message for you . . ."

"Why wasn't I told?" Franzhold reiterated. "Isn't that the fourth time the patient has been violent since we began the Thorazine treatment?"

Nurse Calderwood examined the chart: "Yes, doctor."

"Four disruptions on the floor through the aggressive behavior of one patient. Has the Thorazine in any noticeable way reduced the violent behavior?"

"No, doctor."

"How many shock treatments, Nurse?"

Nurse Calderwood again consulted the chart: "26."

"For the purpose of institutional management and control, we must consider alternative forms of treatment. I'm going to examine the patient now. Phone Dr. Anton Kohl's office. I want Dr. Kohl to have a look at him too."

Fronzhold started to walk toward the Patients' Corridor. He saw Jade and stopped.

"Are you new here?" he asked.

"Yes, doctor. I'm Jade Boren, Volunteer."

"Boren. Yes, I know your mother. Aren't you Dr. Minden's little friend?" Fronzhold asked with a mixture of benevolence and lechery.

"I'm Dr. Minden's great admirer," replied Jade, staring at the harsh, dark, puffy face she had seen so often in photographs.

"Well, my dear," said Fronzhold, patting her shoulder and her arm, "your friend will be visiting Iris V at 6:00 P.M. this evening. I assume you'll want to wait for him. Perhaps he'll give you a ride to midtown again."

Fronzhold, self-assured, put a hand under Jade's chin and stared at her.

"You're keeping Nurse Calderwood waiting," said Jade insolently.

"You're not very polite for a volunteer," Fronzhold replied angrily.

"We volunteers are as polite as the doctors," Jade replied softly.

"Come along," he snapped. "Maybe you'll learn something."

Dr. Fronzhold marched down the corridor, followed by Nurse Charlene Calderwood and Jade Boren. He opened the door to Room 16. It started to close on Nurse Calderwood, who held it open for Jade.

What's got into Fronzhold? thought the nurse. I'm glad I'm not a patient. With the mood he's in, he'd order a lobotomy for me.

Fronzhold stared at the patient who was lying helpless in the bed, legs and arms strapped down. The area around one eye was badly bruised. The nose was in a cast that was taped across the cheeks and forehead. The good eye, which was the only one that could be seen, looked drugged and deranged.

"Well, my good fellow, so you've been acting up again? Attacking orderlies and nurses, eh? We simply can't have that. I'm going to change your treatment to something more drastic, but I can assure you it will be effective. Nurse, check with Surgery and Dr. Kohl. I want to book our friend here for psychosurgery at 4:00 P.M. next Monday."

The patient was attempting to talk but the words would not come out. The good eye rolled back and forth; perspiration appeared on his forehead.

Dr. Fronzhold smiled. "Now don't you worry, old fellow. You'll be as good as new—even better—in a few months. Some of the nerves in your brain are overfiring. The surgery will alter the neurochemical structure."

Fronzhold's mood had improved. He patted Nurse Calderwood on the shoulder and walked out, this time holding the door for her and for Jade.

"I'm going to order some special sedation," said Fronzhold to the nurse. "We don't want any more violence before the operation."

"Yes, doctor."

Fronzhold, followed by his troupe, entered Room 23. The patient lay quietly on the bed. Her lips were moving but no sounds came out.

The doctor pulled up the lids of the eyes, pressed the skin, and took the patient's pulse.

"Mary, can you hear me?" he asked. "Mary, this is Dr. Fronzhold. Do you know who I am?"

No answer.

"Mary, I'm here to help you. Can you understand me?"

No answer.

"She's peaceful enough," said Fronzhold. "Let's continue the treatment for another week. It appears to be highly successful."

At 5:00 P.M. Nurse Calderwood said to Jade: "You've put in a good day. I like your work and you're learning fast. You can go now, and we'll see you tomorrow morning."

"My ride won't be here until after 6:00, so I can work another hour. Would you like me to check the rooms to see if any of the patients need attention?"

"Yes, go ahead, dear. Thank you."

Jade moved in and out of the rooms, cleaning up patients, talking soothingly to those who could not hear her and trying to maintain some inner calm. Iris V was a jail with intimidated, insane prisoners. Doctors could only speculate on the cause of their illnesses: lack of vitamins, a virus, a thwarted love affair, inherited instability. No one knew where the malfunctioning occurred. Nevertheless, patients were treated. The drugs occasionally produced an adverse reaction: memory loss, inability to eat, permanent distortion of the features, twitching, addiction. Iris V offered seclusion, drugs, shock treatment, and, in a few cases, psychosurgery. The psychiatrists and neurosurgeons ordered specific medications or treatment with the same calm assurance of doctors faced with the same dilemmas over the last few thousand years. It was better to do something positive than to do nothing. The screaming of the insane or the permanent melancholy into which a patient retreated required something, anything. One had to take desperate measures just in case some drug or therapy created a response.

Jade entered Room 8. The body of Martha Rayburn lay motionless on the bed. The heart continued to pump blood through the helpless body. The lungs breathed regularly, carrying oxygen to the bloodstream. The open eyes stared vacantly. Jade picked up a limp hand and stroked it. No response. Gently she put the hand back on the bed. She bent down and whispered to the patient: "Martha, it's Jade." The patient did not hear her.

Josiah, you monster, you did this to protect yourself and your rotten Society. God knows how you thought you could get away with it but before you and I are finished, sweet lover, the Count of Monte Cristo will look like a boy scout.

The patient with the broken nose in Room 16 appeared terrorized as Jade walked in. The restraints kept him from moving his body but he rolled his head wildly on his pillow.

Jade went over to the bed and stared at him. He saw there was no hypodermic in her hands. He calmed down, trying to focus on her with his good eye. According to his chart he was violent. Before he had been hospitalized he had almost killed two men. Two days ago he had attacked an orderly.

"What is your name?" asked Jade.

The patient opened his mouth as though to speak. His lips twisted but the best he could manage was a low moan. It sounded like "Rggh."

"Can you understand me?"

"Rrrr."

"Let's try a code. If you can't speak, perhaps you can communicate by letters of the alphabet. Shall we try?"

"Grrragh."

"I'll divide up the alphabet into twenty-six letters. A to F is Group I, G to M is Group II, N to S is Group III, and T through Z is Group IV. Do you understand?"

"Rrrgh."

"It will take forever if we try too much so keep your answer to one word. First we'll do your last name. Is the first letter of your name in Group I?"

"Hrrgh."

"A . . . B . . . C."

"Rggh."

In less than a minute he had communicated his name: C-L-A-Y.

"Mr. Clay, I have another question. Why were you so frightened when I came in the room? Tell me in one word if you can. Is the first letter in Group I?"

Slowly they spelled out his fear: F-R-O-N-Z . . .

"Fronzhold!" Jade interrupted herself. "Is that right?"

"Rrrr."

"What makes you afraid of Dr. Fronzhold? In one word, please. Is the first letter in Group I? Group II? Group III?"

"Rggh."

Another word was spelled out: P-S-Y . . .

"Psychiatry!" Jade said.

Silence.

"Psychology?"

Silence.

"Psychosurgery!"

"Rrrrg."

"I know nothing about you, Mr. Clay, but I'm inclined to sympathize because you're Fronzhold's patient. You don't want psychosurgery; I wouldn't want it either. Let's see if I can do something to help."

She paused, looked at the ceiling contemplatively, stared at the wall, then turned back to the patient.

"I've got it! It's crazy but it will work. Mr. Clay, trust me. You'll be out of here Tuesday afternoon and I'll get your case reviewed by someone else."

A long, painful "Rggh-rggh-rggh."

"Is there something wrong? Of course. Your psychosurgery is scheduled for Monday afternoon. No sweat, Mr. Clay. We'll have you out by Monday noon. I promise."

The patient in Room 23 was sleeping.

"Mrs. Hamble?"

Mary opened her eyes, saw Jade, and smiled weakly.

"We're going to get you out by Monday. I've got a plan. Are you feeling better?"

Mary Hamble nodded.

"Don't give me away and don't give yourself away. Play possum."

"I will," said Mrs. Hamble faintly.

"I'll be back tomorrow morning. Your son-in-law walked into a trap but he doesn't know it. You'll be sitting in the courtroom when he goes to trial. You'll have revenge, Mrs. Hamble."

Jade returned to the Nurses' Desk. From twenty yards down the corridor she saw him talking to the nurses. She felt the adrenalin pouring into her blood, the same excitement as when she walked onto the court to play a big match. Don't blow it. Play it slow and cool.

Josiah Minden turned around. He watched Jade walking toward him, smiling, happy, and bouncy. The serious look on his face disappeared and he smiled back. He moved to meet her.

"Hello, Leader," said Jade impishly. "Dr. Fronzhold said you were coming so I decided to wait for you."

"I'm glad you did. And what did you think of our Hospital Director?"

"He has excellent taste," said Jade, brushing Josiah's arm with her hand. "If I gave him the least encouragement, which I did, he would consent to take me to his bed, which he tried."

"You're outrageous. Should I be jealous of the good Director?"

"He's not my style. He's a bully, so I bullied him back. He got so furious that he ordered psychosurgery for one of the patients. As soon as he gave the order, he felt much better."

They both laughed.

"You're a clever little monster, Jade. Fronzhold scares most women. When he raises his voice and thunders, they start crying. He's terrorized all the nurses, and plenty of patients too."

"And the men?"

"They generally cave in. His bullying works."

"That's because they're afraid he'll fire them. He can't fire me. I'm a volunteer."

They laughed again.

"Did you enjoy your day on Iris V?"

"It was fascinating. I learned a lot. Josiah." Jade hesitated, looking into his beautiful, fine eyes. "I recognized one of the patients. I didn't want to tell Dr. Jennings or the nurses . . ."

"Who was it, Jade?"

He's been testing me. He knew Martha Rayburn had been brought to the hospital. He came here because she's on this floor. He wants to know where I stand.

"It's the woman in Room 8. She works for *National News* and she was assigned to the Harmonetics story. Her name is Martha Rayburn but no one here knows it. She was brought in unidentified. Josiah, I'm positive it's Martha."

"If you're sure, we should notify her family immediately."

"Is that safe? I mean, couldn't it create problems?"

"Of course not. If the poor woman is sick, her family has to be told."

"I thought that . . . well, *National News* might try to, uh . . ."

"So you'd 'kidnap' the woman to protect me?"

"I'd do a lot more than that to protect you," said Jade warmly.

She moved her hand toward his, gently touching his fingers.

"Let's be serious for a minute, Jade. Remember when I wrote down the three names of the *National News* reporters? I left the damn sheet on my desk and some goddamn idiot took it. Whoever took that list may have thought he was doing me a favor. Martha Rayburn has been hospitalized, Silverstein was pushed in front of a subway, and Gondolier was shot. We've got a damn maniac in the Society who thinks he can play God. That's not the worst of it. Whoever he is, he's powerful enough to get Society members to do his dirty work."

"What are you going to do, Josiah?"

"Obviously I must notify the police."

"They'll think it's you. You'll ruin yourself and the Society. There must be another way. Who was in your office in the late afternoon and evening?"

"Several people. I'm discounting my two young assistants. They wouldn't have the nerve to order a killing and no one would kill for them if they gave the order."

"Who else could have taken the paper?"

"Heinrich Fronzhold. I'm positive he wouldn't resort to killing. Francis McDonald. He's a very gentle person; murder isn't his style. The only other possibility is Anton Kohl, and I would vouch for him on the Holy Bible."

"Did you mention the *National News* investigation to any of them?"

"Damn, I told the three of them. We were all in the office together late yesterday afternoon and I explained what you had told me. I assured them an exposé couldn't hurt us because we had nothing to hide."

"Oh, my poor Josiah. You've got to talk to each of the men."

"I know them as well as I know myself. I'd find it much easier to believe it was one of the guards, but how could they interpret a sheet of paper as being potentially harmful to me or the Society?"

"Make them account for their time, Josiah."

"I'll make all four of us account for our time. Any of us, myself included, could be the instigator."

"Not you, my love."

"I'm going to accept your earlier offer of protection. I believe you're the right size and shape to be my bodyguard," Minden said with a smile.

"I'll guard your body anytime, Josiah."

"You'll have your chance tonight. Meet me in the garage in thirty minutes?"

"Yes, my Leader."

Jade went to a pay phone and dialed Jerry. She told him about her conversation with Minden.

"I'm meeting him in fifteen minutes, Jerry."

"Don't do it," Jerry said tensely. "It's too dangerous."

"He didn't order the murders. I'm sure of it. It could have been Fronzhold, McDonald, or Kohl. It wasn't Josiah."

"What makes you so certain?"

"If he had been the one, he wouldn't have wanted to go to the police. You should have heard him, Jerry. He thinks the killer is a maniac who's trying to play God."

"Please, Jade, stay away from him."

"Jerry, I'll talk to you later. I've got to go."

Jade hung up.

Excerpt from an Address Entitled "No Man Is an Island"
by Dr. Josiah Minden
February 13, 1980

This is the story of a visitor from Kansas who came to New York City for one week. The man, Mr. Smith, stayed at a large hotel in midtown Manhattan. Each day he saw a dozen strangers in the elevator, but they did not speak to him nor he to them. He walked in the lobbies where other men and women were walking. He looked at many of them and many looked at him but no words were exchanged. He ate his meals silently in the big restaurants. Others were dining alone, but none of the lonely people made a gesture of friendship to another: it would have been presumptuous or pushy, and such a gesture would have been rebuffed.

For four days Mr. Smith visited New York without engaging in an intimate conversation with one other human being. He took long walks along the beautiful avenues, a solitary pedestrian. He went to the movies and sat next to strangers. He shopped in the department stores but none of the clerks had the time or the interest to ask Mr. Smith about his hometown or his family or why he had come to New York.

On the fifth day Mr. Smith happened to pass by the Harmonetics Temple. He walked in and he was no longer a stranger. A woman who did not know him extended her hands. Mr. Smith reached out and touched her. It was the first real communication he had had since his arrival in the city. He met others, men and women of different ages who were warm and friendly and genuine. He lunched with them, he visited their workshops, and he sat with them in the Temple and listened.

The next two days were the happiest in the life of Mr. Smith. He found out what it meant to hold the hands of a stranger, to place his hands on the arms, shoulders, and face of an unknown person, to look into the eyes of another human being. There were no strangers in the Temple. They were human beings, men and women, who cared for Mr. Smith and who cared for each other.

Mr. Smith discovered another important quality in the life of the Temple. The people who gathered here were neither idlers nor slaves. Many worked with their hands; they took pride in their accomplishments. They enjoyed their leisure hours in the company of each other. Each had the dignity of the individual while working for the happiness of the community.

Mr. Smith has been to New York City many times since but he has never experienced loneliness again. When he sees an unhappy man or woman, he tells them about the Temple. "In joining the Harmonetics Society," he said, "I made two million friends."

Bill Harding walked into the hospital room that evening in a happier frame of mind. The prognosis was good and the doctors, of course, were claiming the credit.

"You're looking better," he said to the patient. "Which of your many admirers sent you the flowers?"

"My girl friends," said Harold. "Missy, Caroline, Henrietta and Jade. They're in love with me."

"You're a changed man. You get well as fast as you conduct an investigation."

"There's pain, but my mind's not as fuzzy. You were here earlier, weren't you?"

"Yes, for a few minutes. You were heavily sedated."

"I'm doped up now."

"But not as much. Your eyes are focussing."

"Who did it, Bill?"

"Who shot you?"

"Yes."

"We don't know who pulled the trigger."

"Who ordered it?"

"Yesterday we were sure it was Minden. Jade, under instructions, told Minden that you, Roger and Martha were on the case. He wrote down the information, spelling out the names. Late that night you were shot and early the next morning two women pushed Roger onto the subway tracks and someone slipped a powerful drug into Martha's breakfast. Roger is dead. Martha was whisked off in a taxi to the Harmonetics Hospital. She's paralyzed. Her brain isn't functioning."

"Oh God!"

"Roger's parents have been notified. We're trying to track down Martha's family. Her closest living relatives are some cousins on the West Coast."

"D'you call my wife?"

"I called your home, Harold. Your wife was under the weather. I spoke to the housekeeper and I told her I'd keep her posted every day. She'll tell your wife tonight or tomorrow."

"No need for her to fly out, Bill."

"I understand."

"Minden wanted to get the three of us."

"We're not so certain any more. This afternoon Jade phoned from the hospital. Minden said the piece of paper with the names was stolen. He wanted to call the police. Jade asked him whom he told and who could have taken the paper. The three people who knew were Dr. Anton Kohl, Dr. Francis McDonald and Dr. Heinrich Fronzhold. It could well be one of them."

"Who do you think?"

"I'm not sure. The person responsible thought he was doing Minden a great favor, which is a bit insane. What does insanity mean these days? According to the lawyers, almost any client who faces conviction is insane. On the surface Anton Kohl is a respectable doctor who makes a healthy living out of neurosurgery. Does the name sound familiar?"

"A divorce case?"

"Yes. The Kohls accused each other of everything except murder. Mrs. Kohl said Anton liked girls under the age of twelve, boys under the age of sixteen, and corpses of indeterminate age. He said she was a kleptomaniac and a schizophrenic. Thereupon she called him a liar and a sadist. Neither wanted the other to have any of their mutual property. The judge lectured the hell out of both of them and gave Mrs. Kohl a hefty alimony settlement."

"How about McDonald?"

"He's Jerry's choice. Francis has the look of a dedicated eunuch. Have you ever seen him? His skin is soft and hairless and his body looks drained of muscle. I met him once and he reminded me of my great-aunt, a saintly lady whose children despised her. I don't know much about his career as a priest, but he's been a major Harmonetics proselytizer for the last few years. He's probably closer to Minden than anyone. When you think of all the crimes committed in the name of religion, it's believable: Father Francis decides to rub out three reporters to save Dr. Minden and the Society.

"The last candidate is 'Honest Heinz' Fronzhold, my particular favorite. It took $200,000 to convince the good doctor that Mary Hamble should be held against her will and drugged senseless. Parson must have told him about the interview with you, including the faked call from the hospital. Once your story came out, it would be the end of his career. He had everything to lose."

"Strange how Harmonetics is so heavy into medicine."

"Perhaps. It's fairly typical of religions. As they grow up, they train their own doctors and build their own hospitals. The Catholics, Methodists, and Baptists, not to mention the Mormons, Jews, and Seventh-Day Adventists, have their own hospitals and sanatoriums. Many have their own medical schools. Oral Roberts, the preacher, became Oral Roberts, the educator. Now he's creating his own medical center in a city that already has too many hospitals." Harding paused and looked at the patient.

"Harold, you're looking tired. Get some rest and I'll see you tomorrow."

Gondoler mumbled a few words that Harding could not hear.

"Sorry, what did you say?" Harding moved closer.

"It was Minden," whispered Harold.

Cissy and Austin McDowell were the first to arrive at the Beale apartment. Austin wore the expected dark blue suit and his feet were shod in black wing-tip Oxfords. His tie was a dressy blue-and-white foulard and his cuff links plain gold. Cissy's face had the soft glow of Harmonetics Health and Body I. The lips glistened with a pink oil; the cheek coloring was delicate and well blended. Henrietta recognized the moisturizer around the eyes: a refill at Health and Body I cost $18, but the laboratory that had analyzed the oil for *National News* appraised it at 14¢. Cissy's long gown was a well-draped, simple maroon. She wore no jewelry.

"My dear Austin . . ." "So kind of you . . ." "How charming you look . . ." "My husband, Elliott . . ." As the words were exchanged, each appraised the garb and style of the other. To the McDowells Elliott looked "old family" and rich. He smelled rich. His clothes were made by the right tailor with an eye for the dignity of Elliott's position. His affability toward his guests and his arrogance of gesture marked him as someone who curried favor only from prime ministers and presidents. Henrietta was more difficult to fathom because she played so many roles: she was "the old girl" to Elliott, a handsome dowager to Cissy, and a foolish old woman to Austin. Elliott judged the McDowells by their clothes: conservative, careful, slightly understated, a desire to appeal to those who could be of benefit to them. Henrietta had already made up her mind about Austin. She felt that Cissy made him a suitable mate.

Elliott took Cissy's elbow and guided her to the bar at the end of the living room. He fixed himself a Scotch and soda and poured Cissy a soft drink.

"What a marvelous room," said Cissy. "I've always adored

antiques. You and Mrs. Beale must have had so much pleasure collecting them."

"We didn't collect them. We inherited them."

"That's even nicer," breathed Cissy warmly. "Then you grew up with these lovely pieces."

"No, Henrietta did. An old Albright, Ohio, family, y'know." Does she or doesn't she? Elliott wondered.

"Ah, what was Mrs. Beale's maiden name?"

"We've been married so long I've forgotten."

Cissy laughed, eager to please. "How long have you been married, Elliott?"

"Too long."

Cissy laughed again. "You're so funny."

"Tell me, Cissy, what do you do with yourself all day? I find now that I don't go down to the office regularly, I have so much free time."

"I try to be up at 8:00 to have breakfast with Austin. Then I make my calls and plan the menus and do all sorts of things. I seem to be busy all the time."

"What do you do for lunch, my dear?"

At the other end of the room, Henrietta was talking to Austin.

"I've decided to go ahead with what you suggested on my will," she said.

"I made no suggestion. I merely tried to express the many ways in which you could take care of your family while still following the directives of your heart."

"You said $30,000 to each of the children and the apartment to Elliott. That's what I'd like to do."

"If those are your wishes, Henrietta, I would be delighted to carry them out."

"You can tell Dr. Minden about the will. That would be nice. However, don't tell Senator Spriggs. He'll go right back to Elliott with the news."

"Your desire for confidentiality will be maintained. I'll have the new will drawn up on Monday. You can come down at your convenience to sign it, and perhaps you will allow me to take you to lunch."

The doorbell rang.

The entrance of Senator Robert T. Spriggs, with Sarah Robinson on his arm, changed the atmosphere. The Senator was hearty, jovial, and good-humored. He was in his sixties, unstooped, balding, and massive. He wore his rather large stomach well, as though he were corseted. He mixed the groups, bringing Sarah and Henrietta, one on each arm, over to the bar. He now had the ear of everyone. He told a hilarious story about the Assistant Secretary of State flying to the wrong country ("I distinctly told the pilot Guadeloupe, so the damn fool lands in Guatemala"). While he was talking Henrietta caught his eye, and as soon as he could he followed her to the other room.

"Well, dear girl, what's the news?"

"You know how I love writing, Robbie, and I'm doing nothing professionally now. One of my editor friends thought there might be an opening at *Cuisine du Monde*, so I paid them a visit this week."

Henrietta told the Senator the story of Lionel Hemingway's unfortunate venture with *Cuisine du Monde*. Global Publishing was the wrong house for a slick magazine. Competing with *Gourmet* was both risky and expensive. However, the format could be changed to make it a nutrition and health magazine under the auspices of the Harmonetics Society. Once the name of the publication was altered, there would be a natural market for readers in the Society itself. There could be feature stories on the hospitals, the clinics, and the spas. The Harmonetics Health Food Stores would distribute some of the copies, while others could be sold on the newsstand. The Society would do much better than Global since the large volunteer force could be used to sell subscriptions.

"How much?" said Robbie.

"I think Hemingway lost $3 million. You could probably pick it up for $800,000."

"It's a good buy if we could get it for $500,000."

"Then why not try it? The worst that Hemingway can say is no. It will be profitable, Robbie."

"You're a dear, Henrietta. Thanks."

"It's a pleasure. I'm very interested in the Society myself."

"In what way, Henrietta?"

"Please don't tell Elliott, but it's the rejuvenation treatment. It sounds silly, and I know Elliott would despise the idea, but the years are becoming a burden and I'd like to recapture my youth."

"Why, Henrietta, I think you look beautiful just as you are."

She smiled. "I wish the mirror could say those words."

"If you want to go through with it, I'll help. When would you want to start?"

"Monday, if you can arrange it."

"I will, if you're really sure."

"I've been thinking about it a long time, Robbie. I'm absolutely sure I want it, whether or not it's dangerous."

"It's not dangerous; the mortality rate is extremely low. Even when the first tests were made three years ago at the Harmonetics Medical Research Lab in Houston, there were seldom any deaths. The main problem is that it doesn't guarantee permanent results. You understand, Henrietta?"

"Yes, I accept that."

"You'll be ravishing, my dear. Your old friends, myself included, will fall in love with you all over again. It's like recapturing one's mid-thirties in both looks and general well-being. But remember, it lasts only a couple of years."

"Thanks for the warning. There must be hundreds of thousands of women like me, willing to take the consequences for another fling at being young."

"Yes, but very few people know what the Hospital is trying to do. The people in our set are just beginning to hear about it. Even so, Fronzhold says if he accepted everyone on the waiting list, he'd be booked solid for the next six months.

"How many men have signed up for it, Robbie?"

"Not nearly as many as the women, but a few people we know. Dinky Alben had it. It was a remarkable transformation. He looked and felt forty and he behaved like twenty. He was the Dinky we knew back in the thirties. He dated the top fashion models, he partied every night, and he even started to play polo again."

"Didn't he die a few months ago?"

"Yes, poor chap. At least he had one good year before passing on."

"The end result is so wildly marvelous that I'd risk total failure, Robbie. It's like drawing a card for paradise or hell. Our friend who drew the Queen of Spades last month was unlucky," said Henrietta, examining her immaculate nails.

"Ah, you mean Rona Dimmock."

Henrietta felt as though she had been punched in the stomach. She kept her eyes down, played with the ring on her left hand, and tried to look cool and insouciant.

"Mmm," she murmured to indicate agreement. Two months ago Rona had told several friends she was going in the hospital for a bit of this-and-that. This could be, and was, interpreted to mean (1) removal of an unspecified growth; (2) an eye job; or (3) a complete lift, including the neck. Most of her friends had favored the two latter choices since Rona looked perfectly healthy and had seemed almost euphoric prior to going in. They later decided it was an incurable disease, perhaps a melanoma, because Rona never left the hospital. The bulletins got progressively worse until, a month later, the sad news of her demise swept the small thirty-block enclave where she and her closest friends lived.

Henrietta could hear the Senator talking about the new equipment the Harmonetics Hospital had purchased . . . four complete body-scanners . . . a hydrotherapy pool in the basement . . . six newly equipped operating rooms . . . Her voice was under control again.

"I don't mean to change the subject, Robbie, but rejuvenation seems to be one of the few areas in which no government agency has interfered. The FAA issues an order and all the DC-10s are grounded. The FCC determines who may own which TV stations and how much advertising they may carry, the DOE has the final say in the oil industry. The EPA decides who is polluting the atmosphere, and so on into every phase of living. Thank God the FDA hasn't told Dr. Fronzhold what he may or may not do."

"There's never been governmental interference in medicine," the Senator replied. "It's left to the AMA, who leave it up to the individual physician to practice in the way he deems best. The only time the government steps in is with drugs such as Laetrile. Otherwise doctors can give heart transplants, they can perform radical mastectomies, colostomies, tonsillectomies . . ." His voice drifted off.

"From my point of view I'm glad Dr. Fronzhold has full freedom of action," said Henrietta.

"That he has, my dear. He's doing a fine job and he's keeping a low profile, which is important when a form of treatment is still not perfected."

That's the understatement of the year, thought Henrietta.

"I'm looking forward to Monday, Robbie. You're a dear friend to arrange it for me."

"I'm glad to be able to return a favor. It's I who am indebted to you," said the Senator with pompous gallantry.

Clarissa and Byron Kent entered the room, she in a plain mauve dress that effectively displayed her figure. Her neck and arms were bare of jewels. Clarissa had been one of the great beauties of the city twenty years ago. Her posture was still magnificent and her stature imposing. Her marriage to Byron, who was six inches shorter, had come after a long courtship. Byron had been infatuated. He had sent roses every day, written passionate letters, and vowed everything he had belonged to his darling Clarissa. That had been fifteen years ago. Clarissa was now fifty-nine and Byron sixty-two. He had regretted his marriage for more than a decade.

Henrietta hid her shock as she embraced her friend. She tried not to look at Clarissa's damaged face. The right eye was puffy and drooping slightly. The corner of one side of the mouth turned down, and around the edge the fine, tiny wrinkles made the lips look swollen. Clarissa's hair covered her right cheek and the folds of a chiffon scarf hid most of her neck. From a distance one might have thought she had been in an accident, perhaps a fire that had touched only one side of the face. Up close it looked as though an evil goddess had cast a spell on Mrs. Kent: one side of her face would be eternally youthful while the other would undergo an accelerated aging process.

"Has Heinrich arrived yet?" asked Clarissa.

"Everyone's here except the Fronzholds," Henrietta answered. "I'm looking forward to meeting them. Tell me, is he as vibrant in person as he is a lecturer?"

"Heinrich is a complex man. His nature is basically gentle and sensitive, but he can be impatient and demanding when he thinks someone is not performing well. He's a martinet at the hospital. I'm sure that's why everything runs so smoothly there."

Clarissa was on her favorite topic. Henrietta nodded encouragingly, looking at her friend, listening to only an occasional phrase and making such automatic comments as "How interesting," "Do go on," and "He sounds absolutely enchanting." Her back was to Senator Spriggs and Byron Kent but her attention was on their private dialogue.

"Damn it, Robbie, we can't take much more of this. We've got to start mining the new fields by the end of the month or we'll be in serious trouble. I'm sick to death of those idiotic ecologists. Where the hell do they think they'll get their fuel if they don't let us mine the coal? They've stopped production in Idaho and Wyoming, and now they're going to bust us in Colorado."

"Byron, we're working as fast as we can," said the Senator soothingly. "The Emergency Coal Bill comes up before the Committee on Thursday. I guarantee it will go through without major revisions. When it gets to the Senate we may have a few problems."

"What will it take?"

"A statement from you—a promise—to restore the environment."

"I'll promise whatever they want and I'll do it. What else?"

"We'll still need a few more votes. I've got an idea who might switch."

"If it's a matter of money . . ."

"That's your problem, Byron, and I don't want to hear about it. I would advise against it. You'll be ruined if you get caught."

"Just give me the names. I'll take care of the rest."

"Madison, Horlogh, Peters, Macy, Ellis."

"Any of them members of the Society?"

"Peters and Ellis. They've only been in a few months."

Kent pulled the Senator a few steps away, and now only a few words drifted to Henrietta. She heard "Minden" and "brown gown." When their exchange was finished, the two men joined Clarissa and Henrietta.

Robbie put his arm around Clarissa's waist: "I ran into one of your old friends in Washington, Clarissa, dear. He still claims you're the love of his life."

Byron Kent, indifferent to his wife, addressed himself to Henrietta:

"I heard through the grapevine that you're interested in the Harmonetics movement."

"I've been interested for a long time, Byron. It's such a soothing philosophy. Sarah and I are taking several of the seminars; they are so well structured and the ideas are presented in a logical progression."

Byron nodded. "It's a philosophy that has helped many people."

"I'm particularly stimulated by Dr. Minden's theme of the 'Duality of Nature': government versus lawlessness, obedience versus rebellion, the self versus the community. It's a subject I would like to study in greater depth."

"You've always been an intellectual, Henrietta."

"That's a great compliment coming from you, Byron."

"My source at Harmonetics tells me you contributed a check in the amount of $500."

"That was my personal check, Byron. I haven't discussed it with Elliott."

"I understand. The contribution is tax deductible, of course. If you plan to make further contributions, the Society has a special office in the Administration Building to advise people in your tax bracket. If you want, I could set up an appointment for you with the top man."

"How very kind of you."

"No problem. Always glad to help a friend."

The doorbell rang.

"That must be Dr. and Mrs. Fronzhold. Byron, I haven't met either of them before. This is such a thrill for me. . . . Mrs. Fronzhold, Dr. Fronzhold, I'm Henrietta Beale. It's so nice of you to come."

"We're so pleased to be here," said Ruth Fronzhold with a friendly smile. She was wearing a fashionable long print dress. Her hair was dressed simply and her face was plain but warm. Her skin glowed healthily with the unguents of Health Lab I. Her only jewelry was a broad bracelet made of tin in which were embedded a variety of irregular pebbles, shells, and pea-sized coal.

"What a marvelous frock and what an unusual bracelet," exclaimed Henrietta.

"Thank you. They are my Biorhythm stones. They alter the pattern of the cycles. I haven't had an emotional, physical, or intellectual crisis since I started wearing it."

"Yes, it has had a stabilizing effect on Ruth," said Heinrich Fronzhold. Henrietta was not sure whether Dr. Fronzhold was mocking his wife or corroborating her testimony.

"I'm emotional and impulsive," said Henrietta to the doctor. "Do you think the Biorhythm bracelet would make me less impetuous?"

"I would have to know you better to say if impetuosity was your problem," replied Fronzhold ambiguously.

"I wish Elliott thought it was a virtue," sighed Henrietta.

"And what are your virtues?" asked Fronzhold, examining Henrietta as though she were a patient.

"I ask nice people to the house for dinner," she said with a smile.

Fronzhold looked around. "I know everyone here except that tall gentleman standing by the bar, who I presume is your husband, and that overweight lady talking to Senator Spriggs."

"Heinrich!" said Ruth Fronzhold reprovingly.

"That nice lady talking to Robbie Spriggs," Fronzhold corrected himself.

"Sarah Robinson," said Henrietta. "She has been a close friend for years. She's a great admirer of yours, Dr. Fronzhold."

"She is, eh? She's looking thinner all the time."

"Heinrich, you're impossible. His patients adore him," Ruth said to Henrietta, "and he positively idolizes his worshipers."

"Here comes the beautiful lady escorted by the Senator," said Fronzhold. "Good evening, Mrs. Robinson, I am Dr. Fronzhold. I was just admiring your figure."

"Were you really?" said Sarah girlishly.

"I number myself among such great connoisseurs of the female body as Praxiteles, Rubens, and Renoir. None of us liked a bag of bones. The proportions, to appeal to our eye, must be enormous for it is only by a woman's girth that one can judge her appetites."

Sarah was unaccustomed to being the butt of a stranger's attack. A retort failed her. Ruth Fronzhold came to her rescue:

"Heinrich accuses me of stabbing him with my bony shoulders and my pointed ribs. If I were ten pounds heavier, he would complain about being engulfed in my flesh. Pay no attention, Sarah. This man is only happy when he is allowed to carp."

The Senator, always uncomfortable when someone was ill at ease, patted Sarah's rump affectionately. "Heinrich Fronzhold," he said, "is a wicked man. He covets my Sarah."

Fronzhold was happy: his victim had momentarily writhed.

"Mrs. Beale," he said, "I don't know your seating arrangements but I hope you have not placed me next to Clarissa Kent. I see her every day. To be placed by her this evening would be demanding more than I am able to give."

"I wouldn't dream of sharing you, now that we have actually met. You are seated on my left. I do not intend to talk to the good Senator, who will be on my right, except for a few short inquiries. Similarly, I have placed a woman on your left whom I hope you will totally ignore. There is so much I want you to tell me."

"Then you have seated Clarissa next to me!"

"Dr. Fronzhold, does it matter?"

"What would you do if I said it does?"

"I would try to cheer you up because rearranging the seating is an impossibility now."

"You are cleverer and bolder than I thought you would be."

"Is that a detriment?"

"Yes, I would prefer you more submissive."

"Like your wife?"

Heinrich laughed. "You *are* clever and observant. Had I been fifteen years older or you fifteen years younger, I might have married you or, perhaps better, had a glorious affair."

"Had you been five years younger than you are today, I might have consented."

"You have a sharp tongue."

"Occasionally. It's the instinct of self-preservation."

"I'm not sure I like you, Henrietta."

"Please try, Heinrich. Otherwise it will be a very long evening."

"You remind me of a rude young woman I met this afternoon. Her name was Jade."

"Did she upset you?"

"In a different way. The hostility is the same."

"The maid has just signaled that dinner is ready. Dr. Fronzhold, will you escort Clarissa? We can resume hostilities once we have been seated."

"I know I am not going to like you at all, Henrietta, but I shall not be bored at dinner."

"Hatred is akin to love, Heinrich," said Henrietta airily.

Telephone Conversation

"Harding here."

"It's Jerry. Do you want Henrietta's report?"

"Go ahead."

"Her dinner party was a sensation. Dr. Fronzhold insulted everyone. Senator Spriggs and Mrs. Fronzhold ran around the room soothing hurt feelings and providing handkerchiefs. Dr. Fronzhold announced that Cissy McDowell would hop into bed with anyone who might propose her husband for membership at Piping Rock, whereupon Cissy started to sob. Her husband, Austin, told her to shut up and stop acting like a baby. Ruth Fronzhold explained that Heinrich's parents had only been members of one club, the Yorkville Bund, and this was his form of rebellion. The Senator then caressed Cissy on various public parts and she stopped sniveling."

"It sounds like a James Agee scenario."

"The next act is by H.G. Wells. Henrietta finally got some facts on rejuvenation. Clarissa did have the treatments but the transformation was only temporary. Henrietta says Clarissa's face is quite horrifying. She has to go back to the hospital for repairs. Senator Spriggs told her Donald Alben (she calls him 'Dinky'), former President of Amalgamated Fruit, had a successful rejuvenation which lasted one year, after which he died. She found out her friend, Rona Dimmock, had the treatment. Mrs. Dimmock died last month. Senator Spriggs has arranged for Henrietta to undergo rejuvenation at the Harmonetics Hospital. She's to start on Monday. Spriggs was doing it as a reciprocal favor: he hopes to make a deal with Global to buy *Cuisine du Monde.*"

"Hold it, Jerry. What's this about Henrietta and rejuvenation?"

"She'll show up at the hospital but she won't go through with it. She says there are a dozen ways she can back out, such as being overdrawn at the bank. But her friend Sarah still wants rejuvenation, even after seeing what happened to Clarissa."

"It's a strange twist that a cult which came to prominence by defending and protecting the aged now promises them youth at any price. What else did Henrietta have?"

"She eavesdropped on a conversation that may be important. Byron Kent and Spriggs discussed who, among the Senators, might switch their votes on the Emergency Coal Bill. Two of the senators who are now opposed, Peters and Ellis, have recently joined the Harmonetics Society. Henrietta thinks they may both receive the Brown Gown as an incentive for voting 'Yes.' These promotions would be in violation of the established Harmonetics regulations governing the echelons, but Henrietta says they would be merit raises."

"That's very interesting. Senators Peters and Ellis, eh? I think this can be another good lead, Jerry. Call me when you get the other reports."

"Righto."

(Reprinted by permission of the *New York Times*)
June 12, 1980

Harmonetics Visitors Corps
Establishes Temple
in Japan

Tokyo, June 11. When the Dai Nippon Harmonetics Kyokai opened its doors today, over 5,000 Japanese men and women attended the six services, which were held both in Japanese and English. The occasion marked the culmination of a nine-month drive by the Harmonetics Visitors Corps to establish the Society in Tokyo.

Last August ninety-four members of the Visitors Corps sailed from San Francisco to Tokyo on the Harmonetics Good Will ship. The delegation was headed by Dr. Emil Wooster, a distinguished physician who joined the Society three years ago and now wears the Brown Robe. Dr. Wooster personally picked each of the missionaries: twenty were under the age of twenty-

two, twenty over the age of sixty-five, and the remainder a mixture of all ages. Dr. Wooster said each man and woman had a minimum of six months' experience in the Visitors Corps.

At the services today, 145 Japanese were presented with the Blue Robe. Among the prominent citizens were Masao Yamamoto, Director of the City National Bank; Tadao Nakamura, member of the Diet; and Yoshio Sawamatsu, President of Kuki Fishing Industries.

Officiating in each of the six services were Dr. Wooster, who gave the lecture in English, and Dr. Makoto Miki, who spoke in Japanese. Dr. Miki, a Professor of Religion, has been given the Brown Robe.

Seminars in Health, Nutrition, Biorhythms, and the Harmonetics Philosophy have already begun. Dr. Wooster stated he was delighted with the size of the enrollment and with the contributions that have come in from so many of the Japanese converts. A clinic at the Temple is now accepting outpatients only, but Dr. Wooster expressed the hope that the Nippon Harmonetics Byōin would soon be open for both surgical patients and the terminally ill.

At 6:15 P.M. Jade went to the Staff Women's Changing Room to pick up her tennis bag. The room was empty. She walked to the laundry bin, selected a blue gown, folded it and placed it at the bottom of her bag. Jade looked in the mirror and hummed a popular tune as she combed her hair. Then she picked up her bag and went to the garage.

The Rolls-Royce was standing in the slot marked "Dr. Josiah Minden." It was next to the slot marked "Dr. Heinrich Fronzhold." William, Dr. Minden's chauffeur, was wiping some imaginary spots off the fender. He saw Jade, opened the rear door, and helped her in.

"He's not here yet," said William. "Would you like to watch the television?" He turned on one of the news channels.

"Thank you," said Jade, her eyes on the large screen. The newscaster was staring back at her.

"Police said there was no evidence of foul play. Roger Silberstein fell to the subway tracks as the express was pulling into the station. He was killed immediately. Lieutenant Corrigan of the New York City Police says Mr. Silberstein may have suffered a heart attack, which could have caused him to topple over. . . . Psychiatrists who have been examining God's Avenger suspect Monte Devlin have submitted a temporary report, signed by Chief Psychiatrist Dr. Esme Jennings and Chief Neurologist Dr. Anton Kohl, both of the Harmonetics Hospital. Devlin, they say, showed symptoms of derangement in two of the tests but, the doctors reported, it is not yet possible to state unequivocally that Devlin could not recognize the difference between right and wrong. Further tests will be necessary to reach a conclusion. . . . There was a flurry of trading on the New York Stock Exchange today. The Dow Jones was up three points . . ."

Jade switched channels. Four eleven-year-olds, speaking in baby talk, were lauding the nutritional value of Momma Lucotti's Home-Baked Cookies. Jade flicked the switch. An animated mouse was throwing a cream puff at a mean-looking animated cat. . . . Another channel . . . Jade stared. Looking back at her from the screen were the beautiful eyes of Josiah Minden.

"The Harmonetics Society is not, per se, involved in politics, nor do we endorse political candidates. However, I have known Judge Henley Stuart in many capacities and have worked with him closely on the Board of the Harmonetics Hospital. I am speaking personally, not as leader of the Harmonetics movement, when I state that Judge Stuart is a qualified, competent, and able man who will make an outstanding governor . . ."

The rear door of the Rolls-Royce opened and Josiah himself climbed in. He smiled, put his arm around her, and turned to the screen.

"Look how cute you are," said Jade, pointing to the TV.

He leaned over and kissed her on the edge of her mouth. She moved her head so their lips met. With her lips still on his, she said: "I adore you." Then she turned back to the screen.

She heard both of Josiah's voices. One told her the admirable qualities of the judge while the other commented on her physical attributes. She listened to the sincere voice of Dr. Minden urging the voters to elect Henley Stuart, and she felt the exciting hands of Josiah caressing her body and stirring her passions.

The Rolls-Royce was gliding through the streets, weaving

smoothly between pedestrians and lesser cars, its motor softly purring. In the back seat the two passengers were holding each other, hidden from view by the curtained windows, oblivious to traffic.

"You are the most sensuous man I have ever known," said Jade, telling the truth.

"Should I believe you? You're such a little liar, Jade." He smiled but the remark was barbed. He then picked up her hand and kissed each finger. He turned her hand over and kissed the palm. Then he took her head in his hands and kissed her lips and her eyes.

"We're here, sir," said the chauffeur's voice in the speaker.

The Rolls-Royce swung along the circular path of the ramp to the basement of the garage and stopped in front of a knobless door. Josiah and Jade got out. Josiah pulled a key from his pocket and inserted it in the door. Jade heard the sound of an elevator descending.

"It's my private elevator. It goes only to the penthouse," said Josiah.

The door opened. Jade and Josiah walked in, followed by the chauffeur. Josiah took out another key, put it in a lock on the wall, and the elevator began to rise. No one spoke. Jade put her hand on the carved tulipwood paneling. It was the barest and most elaborate elevator she had ever seen. Not a stick of furniture, no buttons to push, no emergency box, no floor indicators. Just an intricate carved box made of tulipwood. They rode in silence, the presence of the chauffeur inhibiting conversation.

The elevator reached the top floor. Josiah turned the key and the door swung open. They entered a small paneled hallway in which stood two chairs bare of upholstery. The chauffeur sat down in one chair to wait while Minden, with another key, opened the apartment door.

"I wouldn't have imagined a room like this," said Jade, looking around her. "It's a temple."

The floors were uncarpeted and the large room was sparsely furnished. Torches in massive iron stands and candles in alcoves on the wall provided the lighting. There were eight chairs with upright wood backs, several carved coffers with cushions on top, a heavy table resting on trestles, two plain benches, and a number of backless stools. Against one wall was a twelve-foot carving of a smiling seated Buddha. On the other side of the room was a raised altar. Directly behind it stood a life-size Jesus carved of wood, painted in dim, fading colors, old nails affixing his hands and feet to the crucifix. In front of the representation was an unadorned table on which rested two unlighted candelabra.

"It's perfect," said Jade, examining one of the torches, "but where are the whips and chains?"

"I've thought of installing a rack, a thumbscrew, and perhaps a torture wheel. If I do, I'll invite you to test them out. I imagine you'd like that."

"I'd scream with pleasure."

"I'm sure you would. The Spanish Inquisitors were particularly ingenious in eliciting agonized shrieks from young women."

"How strange to see a Buddha and a Christ in the same room," said Jade, changing the subject. "Are you a religious man, Josiah?"

"Deeply religious. God is my way of life."

"I keep forgetting you are a minister."

"I'm not. I have a doctorate in religion. I'm a religious-philosophical leader with no church affiliation."

"And this apartment expresses your beliefs?"

"You're astute, Jade. It represents some of the things that please me, which is not quite the same thing."

Jade walked up to the twelve-foot statue that had been carved by Oriental hands more than 1,600 years earlier.

"Why did you put Buddha and Christ in the same room? Are you a Christian?"

"They are two of the many representations of God. I'm a Christian and a Buddhist."

"And a Mohammedan?"

"Yes."

"What a room! It reminds me of one of those old châteaus in the Loire. No carpet and no curtains, heavy wooden shutters. I know what's so unusual: the ceilings are twice as high as mine. Josiah, was this originally two apartments?"

He nodded.

Jade walked toward the oaken table and put her hand on it.

"So many of the objects seem to have come from monasteries. There's so little of the twentieth century here."

"I like the old world. I like to sit on an oak bench hewn from a very old tree. I hate to sink into soft couches or plush chairs. I like the thick unpolished woods of twelfth-century France."

"My rooms are full of me, my family and friends—photographs, yearbooks, scrapbooks, trophies, diplomas, replicas of memorable occasions. I even have a Sportsmanship Award Certificate in one of the drawers. A cigarette company gave it to me when I was fourteen for losing in the semifinals of the National Girls' Championships and never once yelling 'Shit.'"

Minden stared at Jade. He did not comment.

"You look so intense," said Jade. "What nefarious plot have you worked out for this evening?"

"Nothing more evil than taking your coat. Here, let me help you." He stroked her arms as he helped her off with her poncho. He draped it carelessly across an old wooden chest near the entry hall. Then he hung his own jacket over a wooden peg in the wall.

"Where are your mementos, Josiah?" asked Jade, looking at the bare walls.

"I've kept nothing from my youth."

"That's easy to understand. You could hardly haul a steamer trunk around when you were walking through India. But you must have a picture of your parents somewhere. What were they like?"

He seemed not to hear. He picked up a taper from the oaken table, lit it with a wooden match, and held it to each of the candles in the two candelabra. When he was finished, Jade again attempted a conversation.

"What was your early childhood like? Were you happy when you were a little boy?" Jade asked.

"I suppose my life was the same as any other child born in a family of small means."

"That doesn't tell me much. I read a lot, played a lot of sports, and I had no time for boys until I was twelve. When did you discover women, Josiah?"

"Do you mean when did I discover what women were really like?"

"What are they really like?"

"I believe in self-discovery, Jade. You tell me what is the essence of woman."

"Women are the equal of men in abilities but they've been conditioned differently."

"I see women from the male point of view. They may be the products of conditioning, as you suggest, but the net result is female aggression. There is constant tendering of sexual favors, which often become grotesque. The woman visualizes herself as Cleopatra, an irresistible temptress. To the man who sees endless bodies proffered for reasons of lust or pecuniary gain, woman is a parasite, offering the questionable delight of her vagina in return for perpetual support."

"If what you say is right, women would be the aggressors in sex. It's usually the opposite: the woman won't get the promotion in the corporation or the bit part in the movie unless she goes to bed with the guy."

"That's not true in the Harmonetics Society. No woman has earned her Brown Robe through sex. It's the woman rather than the man who is generally seeking sexual favors."

"In your case it's undoubtedly true. It's the price you pay for being the beloved leader."

"It's time to see the other rooms," Minden said, taking Jade's elbow. She felt the strong pressure of his fingers and looked up to smile at him. He smiled back but only with his mouth. The corners of his eyes were expressionless.

"Are you angry, Josiah? Am I intruding on your thoughts?"

His smile disappeared. "I'm tired of questions."

"Sorry. I'll keep my big mouth shut from now on, unless you offer to feed me."

They entered the dining room-refectory: a long, heavy table of plain oak beams that could seat thirty, massive chairs with wooden backs, and a dark tapestry covering an entire wall. The table and chairs were very old.

"I love the simplicity, Josiah," said Jade in a stilted voice. "One would never tire of it."

Minden did not answer. He stared at the tapestry, which portrayed a young doe in a forest pursued by a horned Pan with cloven feet. The gloom and anger in his face had disappeared; his lips and eyes were smiling faintly. He squeezed Jade's hand.

"It's amusing, don't you think?"

Jade nodded.

"You don't like it, Jade. Why not?"

"It's a bit frightening."

"What's frightening about a pastoral scene?"

"The doe's eyes are terrified. Pan's face is cruel. It's the lust of a male pursuing a helpless victim. He'll mount her as roughly as he can because he wants to hurt her."

"You're right. He will probably rake her flanks with his hooves. The buck often injures the doe to stimulate himself to a greater performance. The infliction won't be mortal. However, this is only surmise. I like the tapestry because one can make many different interpretations, depending on one's mood. I view it this evening as Pan and a female deer having a friendly romp in a bosky dell."

He squeezed Jade's limp hand, then guided her to the far door.

They moved through a short corridor to the pantry, whose chilled shelves were stacked with fresh onions, peppers, tomatoes, celery, melons, berries, cherries, and other foods in and out of season; and through the kitchen equipped with an old-fashioned icebox, a wood-burning stove, two ancient tubs for washing dishes, heavy iron pots and pans, wooden dishes and bowls.

"It's smashing," said Jade, peering into a wooden tub. "It would fulfill the dreams of any tenth-century housewife."

"I love the past because it makes the present more meaningful. In this room the food I eat has been prepared in a simple, almost primitive manner. I get a certain pleasure in having food cooked in a wood-burning stove that once served a tenth-century baron. I love vegetables boiled in iron pots that are seven hundred years old."

"Couldn't you get the same pleasure with a deep-freeze and a Cuisinart?"

Minden continued as though she had not spoken. "A thousand years ago every man and woman had a task to perform for which he was honored or beaten, depending on the skill of the performance. The cooks who belonged to the lords or the women who were married to the peasants had identical jobs: to prepare a proper meal for the master. The reward for a job well done was a word of praise, a copper coin, or perhaps a kiss. If the work was careless, the mede was a bundle of thin faggots laid heavily on the sinner's bare back."

"Do you approve?"

"I don't sit in judgment. I merely draw conclusions. Almost always the work was skillful, even artistic."

"If I had lived in those days, I would have been a lord and I would not have raised my arm to my cook."

"You're speaking nonsense. You don't understand the mentality of power. Your ability to sympathize with the emotions of the peasant is due to your identification with them."

"I'm no peasant, Josiah. I'm certainly no cook."

"You're no ruler, Jade."

"Why are we arguing about lords and their serfs? It's 1982. The lords and the serfs have been dead for centuries."

"Their bodies may be dead but the past never leaves us. Come, I'll show you the next room."

He ushered her into the library, a room of deep browns, shelves lined with old volumes of religion and philosophy in many languages, the only furniture a bare working table and two Spartan chairs. Jade walked up to one of the walls: sixteenth- and seventeenth-century volumes, bound in leather, the title and author's name barely legible. A Latin commentary on the Scriptures. A Book of the Hours in German.

"May I touch them?"

"Yes. Be careful as you handle them."

Jade pulled out a tall, thin volume and laid it on the library table. She opened it cautiously, supporting the front cover with her left hand. It was in Latin.

"What's it about? Can you read it?"

"It's Aurelius Augustinus, *De Civitate Dei*. Yes, I can read it. I studied medieval Latin for three years when I lived in Rome."

"When were you in Rome?"

"You're asking questions again."

"If you prefer, I'll talk about me rather than you. I haven't read a religious book since I was in college. Most of the books I read are histories, plays, short stories, or novels. Three-quarters of them are paperbacks. They're all over my apartment. Some are in bookshelves. The rest are in closets, on bureaus, coffee tables, on the floor, in the bathroom, on the stove, and on top of the refrigerator."

"I often read histories and occasionally I reread an old novel," said Josiah. "They're in the apartment downstairs. This is my retreat."

"Of course, that explains it," said Jade. "These rooms are your private museum, not your living quarters. It's a brilliant collection, Josiah. Your taste is remarkable, highly individual."

"You think you understand me now?" asked Minden. "I'll bet you change your mind in the next twenty minutes."

"Will what I find out make me glad?"

Minden laughed. "That depends on you, Jade. What a very funny notion. Remind me to ask you later."

He put one hand on her shoulder. His touch was rough.

"Josiah, you're hurting me."

"Am I, my dear? How careless of me." He relaxed the pressure.

"Am I going to find some strange mysticism in you, Josiah? Has it something to do with your religious beliefs?"

"Perhaps."

"What religion were you taught when you were young?"

He didn't answer.

"Were your parents Methodists, Unitarians, Catholics?"

"Jade," he said angrily, "why do you insist on talking about origins? I don't like to talk about mine and I couldn't care less about yours. One's early background is often the least important factor in one's life. My origins were commonplace. I lived in an ordinary apartment, I went to a church a few blocks away, and I attended the local public school. None of it left an impression because it was uninspiring. When I traveled to China, India, Tibet, when I was out on my own acquiring knowledge and ideas that were important to me, when I was working with my own hands, when I studied for my theological degrees, that's when I acquired a background. Can you understand that?"

Jade nodded.

"You're nodding but you don't understand. American culture idealizes the origins of the great man. Who cares if the great man's mother was a cook or a waitress, a whore or a salesclerk? Does it matter if his father worked on the railroad or in the stockyards or was a drunken bum? The ordinary school, in existence for almost a century, produced only one distinguished graduate in eighty years. Five million—maybe ten million—

children had the same background, but they were all failures. The origin doesn't make the genius or the poet or the great leader; he creates himself."

"That's a valid point."

"It destroys what you were taught, doesn't it? I wonder how many ideas of yours will no longer be valid when the evening is over. But I've been philosophical enough. It's time to see my garden."

"I'm in the mood for flowers," said Jade, carrying *De Civitate Dei* back to its shelf. "It's hard to be depressed in a roomful of roses."

"There aren't any roses in my garden. I collect South American mutants, what you might call biological freaks. Up these stairs, my dear. We're going to the roof."

His hand was on her shoulder, guiding her. Through the hall, up to the top of the staircase. As Jade opened the door to the hothouse, a blast of hot air hit her. The heavy scent was overpowering, nauseating. Inside the enormous room thick tropical vines with giant leaves sucked their strength from large pots and spread their long tendrils across the glass walls. Monster plants that had been nurtured in the jungle sprouted from huge tubs, their deformed limbs touching each other. The heat rose in wet waves from the raised wooden boards under their feet.

"Where did they come from, Josiah? Did you find them in your travels? What part of the world?"

"In the Amazon. I lived there for six months with a small Indian tribe. There were forty men, eighteen women, and a dozen children. They had an extraordinary religion based on these flowers. Do you know how they punished sinners?"

Jade stared at Minden. He picked up a twig and tapped the outside petal of one of the jungle flowers. The petals opened and the flower turned into a gaping deep green and purple maw. Heavy yellow droplets fell, staining the deep-veined leaves beneath.

"The hand of the sinner is held on the flower. The yellow sap acts like a corrosive acid. It eats through the skin and enters the bloodstream. Death comes after two or three extremely painful hours. I saw a woman of the tribe offered to the Goddess of the Purple Flower, their name for the plant. The ceremony was performed in the presence of all the tribe members. The victim screamed for three hours before she died."

"That would make anyone against the death penalty," said Jade. "I'm not intrinsically against the eradication of evil people. It's the process by which one kills them that's so horrible. Your flower is a particularly terrible example."

"You only relate to the people you know in Manhattan, and most of these people live in a twenty-block area. If you'd been born in the jungle and your brothers and sisters were members of this tribe, you would worship Toth, the Goddess of Thunder, and Milth, the God of the Sun, and Reth, the Goddess of the Purple Flower. The thick vine over there, Jade, the one that looks like huge coils of sticky green rope, that's Toth. She's strangling the lesser plants just below her. She feeds off them; they'll all be dead within a week. When the rains are particularly severe and the members of the tribe are starving because their food is rotting on the ground, they sacrifice a girl child selected by lottery to the Goddess of Thunder. The child's arms and legs are tied and she . . ."

"Can we talk about something else? The idea of a physical attack is nauseating. I can't stand to hear about the aggressor or the victim."

"You say that today. You could change your mind in a week."

"Never."

Minden laughed. He appeared to be in a much happier mood.

"Can we go downstairs now, Josiah?"

"I was about to suggest it."

They returned to the library, then down a narrow hallway, a cul-de-sac with a doorway at the end.

"I've saved the best room for the last, Jade. You might be better off if you leave without seeing it."

"Then I won't see it."

"I'm afraid, my dear, it's too late to say no," he said with great good humor.

His arm swept around her waist, squeezing her too tightly. He lifted her off the ground and opened the door of the room.

"Put me down, Josiah." The arm around her waist was cutting into her muscles. The fingers were digging into her flesh.

"Am I hurting you, poor Jade?" He set her on the ground,

looking at her like a cat playing with a dying lizard.

"I'm feeling strange, almost sick," Jade said weakly. "I'm sorry, Josiah. I think I better go home."

"In a few minutes. Not yet. I want you to see the room first. Enchanting, isn't it? I call it my Greek Museum of Exquisite Pleasures. Look around you, my dear."

A room shielded from the sun but with the look of a garden. A fountain in the center of the room: a statue of Priapus clutching himself with both hands, his head thrown back with laughter. No chairs, couches, or bed; instead, on a floor covered with rushes and tatami were cushions grouped in clashing, brilliant colors. In the corner a mad sculptor had created a lascivious Aphrodite dominating a passive, almost frightened Adonis. Green and yellow and scarlet cushions were strewn in front of the carvings. In another area the sculptor had molded a violent Zeus, King of the Gods, straddling an insane, terrified Leda; purple, black, and blood-red cushions were heaped in front of the fornicators. A third corner: the boy Hyacinthus struggling to escape from the Sun God Apollo; orange, crimson, and brilliant yellow cushions were tossed carelessly near the two writhing bodies.

"This is the expression of the cult of the Gods. To them, love is violence," said Minden.

"No, no. Love is tenderness. Josiah, I must leave . . ."

"Not until I change your philosophy. Do you know what you remind me of, Jade? The frightened doe in the tapestry. Your eyes are so large and sad."

"Josiah, please don't . . ."

"I can feel the pulse in your throat. Your heart is beating so violently, my dear."

Minden, one hand on Jade's throat, bent back her head and kissed her. His teeth bit her lip and she tasted the blood. His hand struck her cheek, her breast, her shoulder. She screamed. He grabbed her hair and pulled her to the floor. His hands and fists pummeled her body. She heard the silken shriek of her shirt ripping. His fingernails raked her body. She tried to fight back. A blow to her stomach and her body sagged. She lay there passively, dry-eyed, as he jammed his penis inside her. Finally his hatred subsided. He had committed sex without passion.

He stood up, his shirt stained with her blood. His eyes were glazed. In his hand was a stone heavy enough to crush her head.

"I love you, Josiah," she whispered, fighting to save her life and trying not to look at his hand. "You're right, love is violence."

"You can go now," he said wearily. The urge to kill had disappeared.

She struggled to her feet. "I want to see you again," she said softly.

"We'll see." He turned away indifferently.

Jade stumbled out of the room. She remembered her purse was lying on the floor near a pile of cushions. No way to go back for it. I may need some money, she thought. Josiah's jacket. Perhaps a few dollars there. She put her hand in the jacket pocket. She felt the slip of paper and knew what it was before she pulled it out. The list had never been left on his desk. Only he knew what was written on it: the names of Roger Silberstein, Martha Rayburn, and Harold Gondoler. Dully, she put the list back where she had found it.

An impassive William drove Jade to her apartment. She sat in the back seat shivering, her arms and body covered by her poncho.

"I need a piece of paper and a pencil, William," she said in a controlled voice.

He handed her a pad and pencil through the open partition. Slowly she wrote her note:

Darling: I left my purse in the Museum of Exquisite Pleasures. Will you bring it to me tomorrow morning? I'll be at the hospital by 8:00 A.M. I'm going to have a hit on the tennis courts with Beth Marple and Dr. Jennings. Why don't you be our fourth?

All my love—

Jade

She folded the note and handed it to William.

"Please give this to Dr. Minden tonight." It was late. Hopefully he would have time to read it.

"I will," said William, pulling the car up to her apartment house.

"Don't let me off in front. Stop by the garage," she asked. She would go to her rooms by the back elevator to avoid running into anyone she knew. She was not in the mood for conversation. She got out of the car.

"Don't forget your tennis bag," said William.

Jade picked up her bag and walked into the garage without responding.

She reached her apartment, opened the unlocked door and entered. She put down her bag and began to cry.

Caroline got out of the taxi first, then lent a hand to Missy who did not see well in the dark. The Rappaport Agency car, which was just behind them, pulled up to the curb and one of the men got out. Caroline and Missy entered the old apartment house. There was an outer and an inner door. On the wall between the doors were the names of the tenants. "She's 4G," said Caroline pressing the buzzer.

"Yes?" asked a voice from the intercom.

"This is Caroline Ryder from the Harmonetics Society. I've been sent by the Temple to bring you a gift."

"Come up," said the voice. A buzzer sounded by the inner door. The Rappaport man opened it for Missy and Caroline, then followed them in. The two women used the rickety self-service elevator; the man climbed the stairs.

The door of 4G was open. A woman of fifty-five, medium height, greeted them with a smile. She wasn't tall but she looked strong enough to move a piano and gentle enough to cradle a grandchild.

"I'm Betty McLaughlin."

"My dear Mrs. McLaughlin, I'm so happy to see you. I'm Caroline Ryder and this is my friend Missy Tompkins."

"Please come in."

The living room was genteel shabby. The floor was spotless but there were bald patches on the thin rug that covered an eight-by-six-foot area in the center. Two small coffee tables shone with wax but the overstuffed chairs next to them were shredding on the arms and the skirt. A throw rug covered the torn couch. At one end two white cats were curled up together, sleeping.

"Caroline, will you look at those adorable cats," said Missy.

"How do they stay so immaculate? I've never seen cats so white," said Caroline.

"What are their names?" asked Missy.

"Snow Drop and White Queen."

"Isn't that clever. They must bring you a great deal of pleasure, Mrs. McLaughlin."

"They do. They keep each other company in the day, and at night they curl up in bed with me."

"Are they afraid of strangers?"

"No, you can pat them if you wish."

Missy and Caroline stroked the cats. One of them woke up, yawned, and stretched out its arms, digging its nails into the side of the couch.

"When you have cats you can't worry about minor rips in the furniture," said Mrs. McLaughlin.

"Absolutely," Missy agreed.

"Please sit down," said Mrs. McLaughlin. "Will you have some coffee?"

"Don't go to any trouble for us."

"No trouble at all. I have a pot and I'll just rewarm it."

In a few minutes they were good friends. They had admired Mrs. McLaughlin's immaculate kitchen, praised her housekeeping, and cooed over her cats.

"Mrs. McLaughlin, we've been members of the Harmonetics Society for almost three years. Missy serves as one of Dr. Minden's personal aides. He is so grateful to you and Mrs. McDermott."

"I'm not sure what you're talking about," said Mrs. McLaughlin. Her voice had changed; there was a hint of hostility and menace.

Missy, smiling and nodding, continued: "Let us speak only in generalities. Dr. Minden would not appreciate specific references to favors. He wishes to acknowledge your help. He asked me to tell you that your unselfish and courageous act will not be forgotten. He also entrusted me with an envelope to be delivered to you in person."

Missy fumbled in her large reticule. Mrs. McLaughlin slowly rose from her chair and walked stiffly toward Missy. Her smile had disappeared and the look on her face was decidedly unfriendly. Missy seemed unaware of the change in the atmosphere.

"I can never find anything in this damn fool purse," she said with a sigh. She pulled out her eyeglass case, a datebook, some pens and pencils, a paperback novel, her change purse, and her credit cards. "Ah, here it is," she said triumphantly, holding up an envelope. She handed it to Mrs. McLaughlin with the graciousness of the Queen bestowing the Order of the Garter on a deserving courtier.

Betty McLaughlin suspiciously examined the outside. In the upper left corner was the familiar Harmonetics indicia. The name "Betty McLaughlin" was written on the front in a large bold hand. Mrs. McLaughlin tore the flap and pulled out the letter. She went over to the lamp by the couch and read slowly.

To: Betty McLaughlin
From: Harmonetics Headquarters
Your dedication to the principles of the Harmonetics Society is unquestioned. You have passed a test that took resolution and loyalty. On the first Sunday of the next month, at the 11:00 A.M. services at the Harmonetics Temple, I hope to present you with the White Robe.

We are honored to have a woman of your indomitable character in the movement.

Very truly yours,
Josiah Minden

The signature was Dr. Minden's. Betty McLaughlin sat down on the couch and read the letter again and again. She brushed off the occasional tears with her hand.

"We rejoice with you," said Caroline Ryder, patting Mrs. McLaughlin's shoulder.

"Josiah Minden, by declaration, is expanding the White Robe Society to twenty-eight from the original twenty-five. All three of you will receive your White Robes individually. You are to be the first honoree. One month later the White Robe will be presented to, uh, to, uh . . ."

"Eileen McDermott," said Caroline.

"Yes, to Eileen McDermott. Four weeks later there will be a third presentation. We need not mention the name now, Mrs.

McLaughlin, but we all know to whom I refer. The three of you saved the Society. A wicked, unscrupulous man has been eradicated."

"I don't know what to say," said Mrs. McLaughlin. "I never expected . . . I wouldn't have dreamed . . ."

"Yes, dear, we understand," said Missy. "Six months ago, as Dr. Minden's surrogate, I personally informed Judge Henley Stuart that he had been selected to the White Robes. He stood motionless, the tears streaming down his face. When he regained his composure, he said, 'But I've done nothing, I'm not worthy.' It's a natural reaction. Believe me, Mrs. McLaughlin, you have earned your Robe."

"There could have been a problem," said Caroline elliptically, "but it was resolved when a certain person indicated he was satisfied, if you know what I mean."

"I'm not sure I understand," said Betty McLaughlin.

"He closed the matter permanently, which means the questions are over."

"I'm still not clear," said Betty.

"Caroline, we're alone. Speak up," Missy commanded. "Mrs. McLaughlin is certainly not going to betray us."

"Of course not," Mrs. McLaughlin confirmed.

"I thought my meaning was clear," said Caroline. "I was trying to tell you that the White Robe presentation would have been postponed if the police had persisted in their investigation. Lieutenant Corrigan has stated that Mr. Silberstein fell to the subway tracks. The autopsy results will prove that Silberstein had a heart attack."

Mrs. McLaughlin looked nervous.

"My dear Betty," said Missy, "now that we've stated the so-called crime, we are accessories to the fact. The case is closed. Although we haven't seen, uh, we haven't seen, uh . . ."

"Eileen McDermott," Caroline filled in.

"Yes, Eileen McDermott and, uh, and, uh, uh . . ."

"Collins Graybill," said Mrs. McLaughlin.

"Yes, yes, Graybill," said Missy.

"But to be perfectly safe," Caroline interrupted, "Dr. Minden has asked that you do not communicate with each other for at least a month. You are not to discuss your White Robes or our visit or the case itself."

"A phone could be tapped," said Missy. "A detective who wanted publicity or who hated the Harmonetics Society would jump if there were one false move. Be careful!"

"I certainly will."

"Dr. Minden will be in touch with you through us in three weeks. In the meantime, not a word to anyone."

"I won't say anything."

"Congratulations, Betty. We are so proud of you!"

Missy extended her hands to Betty. Slowly, with great ceremony, the two women performed the Harmonetics rite of touching. Caroline then approached with extended palms. In silence and with dignity each woman touched the hands, shoulders, and face of the other.

"You are a saintly woman, Betty McLaughlin," said Caroline.

Excerpt from a Lecture at the Harmonetics Temple
by Josiah Minden
March 4, 1981

Many people have asked me if I am a religious man. I reply that God is my life. "Which God?" ask the Buddhists. "Do you believe in Jesus Christ?" ask the Christians. God comes to man in many forms. All the forms are true. I study all bibles and I believe in all His incarnations.

People have also asked me why I do not lecture on religion. It is because all religions are good. Each man or woman can go to his or her own church or temple. The Harmonetics Society picks no one religion above another. Harmonetics encompasses all religions and recognizes God in all His forms. Catholics, Methodists, Buddhists, Mormons, Jews, and Mohammedans are welcome in the Society.

What about atheists? I am asked. There is no such thing as an atheist. When a man says "I do not believe in God," he has mentioned God. One cannot sensibly discuss something that does not exist; therefore, to have an intelligent discussion, one must accept the existence of God. To deny His existence is nonsense.

I have, many times in my life, been able to communicate with God. So have countless others throughout the ages. He chooses not just one man or woman but many. Accept God in any form which He may take, and He will come to you, too.

Each of our Harmonetics Temples has a Prayer Room. It is a simple communion room. It is always filled with flowers and it is open to men and women of all races and creeds. We have no fixed doctrine: you may worship Him according to your own tenets.

I have been asked if man has a soul. If we possessed no souls, our lives would be empty. There would be no reality. We could have no true ethics. A man born without a soul could kill and feel no remorse. The goodness in our souls gives us our humanity and our respect for human life.

Bill Harding reached the *National News* building just before midnight on Friday. Jerry Marconi, Lieutenant Corrigan, and one of the Rappaport Agency men were waiting for him. Corrigan was listening to the end of the Betty McLaughlin tapes.

"Excellent job," said the Lieutenant. "If you'll give me a copy of the tape, we'll get warrants for the arrest of Betty McLaughlin, Eileen McDermott, and Collins Graybill."

"Keep this one. We've got triplicates. Missy and Caroline each had a recorder, and they were also carrying transmitters."

"If you want to be at the station house when they're questioned, we'd be happy to have you sit in. I'm grateful."

"Thanks, Lieutenant, I will. What's the procedure?"

"We question Eileen McDermott. We tell her Betty McLaughlin has talked. Then we question Betty. We tell her Eileen has talked. That gives us Collins. He's faced with the confession of the two women."

"You're sure the women will confess?"

"I'm positive."

The phone rang at Jerry's desk and he rushed to answer it. Henrietta, Missy and Caroline had already reported in. This had to be Jade.

"Hello?" he said happily.

Harding watched him. The boy idolized Jade; his phone conversations with her were the high point of each day.

Harding saw the smile disappear from Jerry's face. He took a handkerchief out of his pocket and wiped his dry mouth and wet eyes. He used the handkerchief to hide his face from anyone in the room who might be looking.

"Thanks for everything, Lieutenant," said Harding, walking Corrigan to the door. "I'll wait for your call."

"It might be tonight. We want to make the arrests quickly."

"I'll be ready, Lieutenant."

Harding closed the front door and walked back toward Jerry's desk. He took a seat ten feet away and waited. The boy was in agony. His voice was calm but his eyes were shut and his body bent as though he had just been punched in the gut.

"I'll call you back in a few minutes, Jade. Take it easy, dear heart. Bill is here and we'll do what you ask. Chin up, old girl." Jerry placed the receiver back on the hook. He turned to Harding, trying to keep himself under control.

"Damn bastard raped her," he said in a tight voice.

"Minden?"

Jerry nodded. He wanted to speak but the words wouldn't come out.

"Did he beat her up?"

Jerry nodded again.

"Badly?"

Jerry pounded the desk angrily and nodded again.

"Is she in her apartment?"

"Yes."

"Jerry, how does she want us to help?"

It was a question Jerry was forced to answer. He got himself under control. "I asked if she wanted a doctor. She said no, then she changed her mind. She wants to see Dr. Jon Mahaffey. He's the fellow who married Jennifer Holiday's daughter Rhonda. Rhonda had her own terrifying experience with Minden when she broke away from the Society, and Jade thinks Mahaffey will be sympathetic."

"Where did the attack take place?"

"Minden's apartment. Before she left Jade found the list of names—Harold, Roger, and Martha—in Minden's jacket. He had never lost it. She's angry, not hysterical. She sounded so hard, Bill. She plans to finish the job. She's sure Minden won't try to kill her because he's convinced she loves him. I questioned that conclusion. She asked me if I'd ever known a wife-beater: they knock their wives senseless, then come home the next day as though nothing had happened. The man who socks his wife or girl friend never doubts that she'll be loyal and loving the next day or the next week. I said there was a great deal of difference between a wife-beater and a rapist. She believes he didn't look on his act as rape; he merely exercised his droit de seigneur—forcibly."

"I'm taking her off the investigation, Jerry."

"Please don't. She was afraid you'd say that. I'm begging you for her."

"She'll want some terrible revenge. She's not the type to take a physical beating and a rape without striking back."

"Jade says she has a foolproof plan to get Mary Hamble out of the hospital."

"I can't risk any more lives. We'll have to think of another way to get Mrs. Hamble out. We'll get a warrant."

"As soon as you get a warrant, Minden and Fronzhold will know. That will be the end of Mary Hamble and we'll never be able to touch Fronzhold."

Harding's expression was fierce. Jerry momentarily thought the anger was directed at him. He watched as the distracted Harding opened a desk drawer, pulled out a bottle of Scotch, and two paper cups.

"A drink, Jerry?" he asked, uncorking the bottle.

"Sure. A small one."

Harding absentmindedly poured Scotch up to the top of each cup. He pushed one toward Jerry. He fiddled with his own.

"If I let Jade go ahead with her crazy ideas, I may be doing it to satisfy my own hatred of Minden and Fronzhold." He looked at the cup, picked it up, and took a deep swig. "Whichever way I decide, I'll be risking lives. I'm going to let Jade go ahead with her plan but I know her better than you, Jerry. She'd have Minden put on the rack and hanged and quartered without blinking an eye. And you, Jerry, you're loony enough to help her."

"I'm going over to see Jade. I'll call Dr. Mahaffey to see if I can pick him up on my way." At the door Jerry hesitated. "Are you okay, Bill?"

"Yes, but whatever you do, don't tell me Jade's plan. I'm sure if I hear it, I'll veto it."

Jade looked battered but unbowed. She had a glass of wine in one hand and a cigarette in the other. Both eyes were puffy but it was from the beating, not the tears.

"Why are we sitting around?" asked Arnie. "Why don't we call the police and have Minden arrested?" Arnie's face was hard and his voice angry. He reached over for Jade's glass, took a sip of wine, and returned it to her.

"Minden can't be touched," said Jerry. "If the police arrested him, he'd get ten guys to swear they were with him tonight."

"Then Minden will get away with it?"

"He won't," said Jade. "I have a plan."

"I'd like to be part of it," said Jerry promptly.

"You can count on me too," said Dr. Jon Mahaffey. He was a sandy-haired, congenial-looking man, as tall as Jerry and as strong as Arnie but a good fifteen years older than either.

The two men turned to Arnie.

"Shit, I guess I'm in it too," he said, "provided I don't have to kill anyone."

Jade changed the subject. "Will I be okay tomorrow, Doc?"

"You'll be stiff and fairly uncomfortable."

"I have an early morning tennis game and I'm going to be at the hospital all day. Can you give me a pain-killer?"

"Butazolidin. It will keep down the swelling and make you feel better. Wear your dark glasses. You have a small bruise on your cheek but the glasses will hide it. The lip will look a bit puffy. You can cover up the rest with long sleeves and a scarf. I don't think you'll want to play tennis."

"I have to. I'm playing doubles with Josiah."

"You dumb broad!" shouted Arnie. "Why the hell do you want to do that?"

"It's part of my plan," said Jade calmly. "Josiah must have perfect confidence in me."

"She's right," agreed Jerry. "If Minden isn't sure of Jade's loyalty, he'll stop her access to the hospital."

"I've got to have free access to Iris V," said Jade. "We go into action on Monday at the Harmonetics Hospital. I swiped a couple of blue gowns for Caroline and Missy. They'll surely want to help. Jerry, you'll wear the open white shirt of a doctor. So will you, Doc. Arnie, you'll drive the car."

"Jesus, it sounds like a kidnapping," said Arnie.
"It is, in a way," said Jade. She then proceeded to tell them her scheme.

Police Record: Collins Graybill

Date of birth: May 9, 1934   *Place of Birth:* Baltimore, Md.
Birthmarks: none   *Race:* white
Height: 6'2"   *Weight:* 215 lbs.   *Father's profession:* truck driver
Father's name: John Graybill   *Mother's profession (if any):* none
Mother's name: Carla Mason   *Jobs held:* truck driver, dish washer,
Education: 9th grade   gas station attendant

Arrests (list offenses and convictions):
   4 arrests on charges of petty theft as a juvenile; 2 convictions;
      served 6 months in Juvenile Reformatory
   1 arrest, armed robbery; no conviction
   2 arrests, car theft; sentenced 4–6 years; served one year
   5 arrests, rape; no convictions
   1 arrest, attempted murder; no conviction
   1 arrest, grand larceny; sentenced 8–12 years; released on
      parole after 3 years
Current status: on parole
   Probation Officer's Report: Collins Graybill has been
working in the Reading Room of the Harmonetics Hospital
for the last nine months. He seems to have a sincere belief
in the principles of the Harmonetics Society. He no longer
associates with people who have a criminal record. His
friends are men and women in the Society. The hospital
reports that Graybill is doing his job well and is a trusted
member of the staff. He is cooperative with his Parole
Officer and has expressed repentance for his misdeeds in
the past. He shows no bitterness and has stated that he
feels he has learned his lesson.

Eileen McDermott, age fifty-two, was seated in a small office
in the police station. Five men were in the room, four of them
police officers and one the owner and publisher of *National
News*. Mrs. McDermott had been told of her rights and warned
that any statements she made could be used against her.

"Mrs. McDermott, you know that Betty McLaughlin made a complete confession?"

"I don't believe it."

"She stated that you pushed Roger Silberstein to his death. Is that true?"

"No."

"She further stated that Collins Graybill asked you to commit murder to save the Harmonetics Society."

"I never heard of a Collins Graybill."

"She says you knew Graybill."

"That's not true."

"Mrs. McDermott, are you a member of the Harmonetics Society?"

"I am."

"How long have you been a member?"

"Almost two years."

"You do volunteer work?"

"Yes."

"How often?"

"Half a day, sometimes a full day, three or four days a week."

"What kind of volunteer work?"

"I'm at the hospital."

"What do you do there? Will you tell us some of your duties?"

"I wrap bandages. Sometimes I fill prescriptions."

"Do you do anything else?"

"I've helped in the Dietetics Department."

"Have you ever worked in the Prayer Room?"

"A few times."

"What kind of work have you done there?"

"I helped with the flowers but that was just a couple of times."

"Did you do any clerical work?"

"No."

"Did you assist the nurses?"

"Like I said, when I wrapped bandages and filled the prescription cups."

"Have you ever worked in the Reading Room?"

"I guess maybe a few times."

"What sort of work did you perform in the Reading Room?"

"I poured tea."

"Would you say you poured tea once a week or more often?"

"Once a week."

"Then you probably were in the Reading Room maybe fifty or seventy-five times?"

"No, just a few times."

"Mrs. McDermott, you just said you poured tea at least once a week."

"Did I? Well, maybe I was in the Reading Room a little more often."

"Perhaps fifty or seventy-five times?"

"If you say so."

"Would you say so?"

"I guess I would."

"Fifty or seventy-five times?"

"Yes."

"How long have you been doing volunteer work at the Harmonetics Hospital?"

"Didn't I answer that before?"

"Please answer again, Mrs. McDermott."

"About a year at the hospital."

"And once a week you poured tea in the Reading Room?"

"I did many other things, too, like the bandages."

"Yes, Mrs. McDermott. But you poured tea once a week in the Reading Room?"

"Yes."

"Did you know a man by the name of Collins Graybill?"

"I told you I never heard of him."

"He worked in the Reading Room, too. You saw him once a week for a year."

"I don't know the names of everyone who works at the hospital."

"You talked to Collins Graybill many times, perhaps fifty or seventy-five times."

"That isn't true."

"You never spoke to him?"

"Perhaps once or twice."

"In the fifty or seventy-five times you saw him, you only spoke to him twice?"

"That's what I said."

"Collins Graybill was hired as a guard in that room. He was

on duty every day. Do you mean to say that in the course of a year you only spoke to him twice?"

"We had no long conversations is what I'm saying."

"But you said hello to him when you entered or left the room?"

"Only when I left the room."

"Collins Graybill has a record of fourteen arrests."

"I don't believe you."

"He was arrested five times for rape."

"You're lying."

"He has one arrest for armed robbery, two arrests for car theft, and he was arrested for attempted murder."

(Silence)

"Mrs. McDermott, you did not know that Collins Graybill had a criminal record?"

"I didn't."

"Would you like to see his dossier?"

(Silence)

"Did you know he served three years for grand larceny and he is now on parole?"

(Silence)

"Mrs. McDermott, Betty McLaughlin states that you and she waited by Roger Silberstein's apartment on the morning of his murder, that you followed him into the subway station, and that you pushed Mr. Silberstein to his death."

(Silence)

"There were two witnesses to the murder. Both of them will verify that Mr. Silberstein was pushed onto the tracks. However, because of where they were standing, they could only see one woman push the victim. Betty McLaughlin states you were the woman."

"She's a liar."

"Then she did the pushing?"

"Yes."

"How can you be sure?"

"I saw her."

"Where were you standing when you saw her push Mr. Silberstein?"

"Right next to her."

"Did you push Mr. Silberstein?"

"No."

"Collins Graybill asked you to get rid of him but you refused?"

"Yes."

"You told him you wouldn't kill Roger Silberstein?"

"That's right."

"Then why were you in the subway station standing next to him?"

(Silence)

"Perhaps you had agreed to do it because you were afraid of Graybill but you changed your mind?"

(Silence)

"Did Graybill tell you that Silberstein was trying to ruin the Harmonetics Society?"

(Silence)

"You did believe him when he told you that, didn't you, Mrs. McDermott?"

"I believed him."

"You didn't know that Graybill had a criminal record?"

"No."

"If you had known, you never would have agreed. You only agreed because you thought Graybill was a good man and you wanted to protect the Society. Isn't that right?"

"Yes."

"Did Graybill tell you that Silberstein was going to hurt Josiah Minden?"

"No."

"What did Graybill tell you, Mrs. McDermott?"

"He said Silberstein was going to destroy the hospital."

"How was he going to destroy it?"

"Silberstein was writing a story about the hospital officials being crooks. He'd forged some papers and people would believe him. When the story came out, the hospital would have to close. The staff would be dismissed and the patients would have to leave. I believed him."

"Of course you did, Mrs. McDermott."

"I thought I was saving the hospital."

"Then what you did was understandable. Graybill was using you."

"Yes. I believed every word he told me."

"Graybill must have been very convincing."

"He was. If you had heard him, you'd have believed him, too."

"We're going to type up what you told us, Mrs. McDermott. Then we want you to read it very carefully to be sure it's just what you wanted to say. You can change any part you want. If it's the truth, then you can sign it. Mrs. McDermott, you've had a very trying experience. I'm sure you must be exhausted. May I get you a cup of tea?"

On Saturday morning Jerry Marconi paid a call on Dr. and Mrs. Jon Mahaffey. Rhonda Mahaffey, the daughter of the late Jennifer Holiday, was as Martha had described: a mouth too wide and a face too long for beauty, framed in silky blonde-brown hair. Five years ago she had stood on street corners, passing out Harmonetics brochures. Three years ago she had withdrawn from the Society, one of the few known defectors from the hard core of devotees. Thirty months ago Josiah Minden had phoned her; she had almost yielded to what she called his hypnotic domination of her mind.

Jerry sat down in the living room with the Mahaffeys.

"Please tell my wife what has happened in the last forty-eight hours," said Jon.

"Mrs. Mahaffey, you probably read about the death of Roger Silberstein in the papers last night. He was pushed in front of a subway by two women. Roger was working on a story about your mother. He had interviewed two people: your mother's lawyer and your brother. Less than twelve hours before Roger's death, another *National News* reporter, Harold Gondoler, was shot four times. He was doing an exposé for *National News* on the Harmonetics Society. The woman who interviewed you, Martha Rayburn, is now lying in a bed in the Psychiatric Ward of the Harmonetics Hospital. She is comatose: her eyes are open but she doesn't hear and can't speak. There has probably been permanent brain damage."

Rhonda Mahaffey's eyes were glazed. "Why Martha Rayburn? What had she done?"

"She'd done nothing. The only interviews she had were with your mother's housekeeper and butler and with yourself. Only one person knew that Roger, Martha, and Harold Gondoler were assigned to do a story on the Society: Josiah Minden."

"Why are you telling me this?" asked Rhonda. She looked pale, almost ill.

"The story isn't finished. Last night Josiah Minden took a woman to his apartment. He has a penthouse that's a con-glomeration of medieval Europe, Victorian England, and bac-chanalian Greece, mixed with Middle East and Asian religions. The Greek room is where he makes love. This is where he beat up the woman and raped her."

"I don't want to hear it! Oh, God, make him stop!" Rhonda screamed.

"It's all right, honey," said Jon.

"Have you always known?" she asked with an agonized look. He didn't answer. He stroked her hair.

"He was like a priest to us, Jon," she said, twisting her hands in her lap. "We'd go to the services and he'd talk about our problems. At the end of an hour I'd feel so much more sure of myself. He'd say, 'You are your most severe critic,' and the old banality would be a new truth in the Harmonetics philosophy. Jon, we worshiped him.

"I fell deeply in love with Josiah, but I thought it was a pure love because it was unselfish. I wasn't the only one. There was nothing I wouldn't do for him—wash or sew his shirts, raise funds for his Temple, cook, or scrub floors. It was self-abnegation to obtain fulfillment in his achievements. I was nothing; he was everything. I went to his rooms with him willingly. He made love to me, and I ended up in the hospital. Jon, I pretended that night had never happened. I thought he beat me because I was unworthy; it was the only way he could tolerate me."

"I always knew, Rhonda."

"Last night he beat a woman and raped her. He beat and raped me but I felt the guilt because I had desired him. He was God's instrument. I couldn't bear to think that he was evil."

"Do you know now, sweetheart?"

"Yes. I'm no longer afraid of him. He has no hold on me. I'm only sorry he'll never have to pay for the murders and beatings and the destruction of the minds of so many people."

"He'll pay, Rhonda. He won't go to jail and he won't be

killed, but he'll pay. We're going to make him pay, Rhonda, and so is the woman he beat up last night."

Telephone Conversation

"Hello, Mr. Hemingway. This is Henrietta Beale. I'm sorry to disturb you at your home but I want to talk to you about *Cuisine du Monde.*"

"You're not disturbing me in the least."

"I spoke to Senator Spriggs last night. He's interested in the magazine."

"That's marvelous. At what price?"

"Probably $500,000."

"Henrietta, you're an angel. If I can ever do a favor for you . . ."

"Lionel, when you talk to Senator Spriggs, you might indicate you've received a million-dollar stock offer from Ruggles Publications and that the contract will be signed on Tuesday. Ruggles stock is selling at eighteen times earnings, which should make you a little nervous. Therefore if the Senator will pay $500,000 in cash on Monday before 3:00 P.M., his group will receive 100 percent ownership of *Cuisine du Monde.*"

"That's fine, Henrietta, but the lawyers will take at least three weeks to draw up the contracts."

"Then you won't have a deal. I don't believe the Senator will be interested in making any purchase for his group by Monday evening."

"What group? Why would they change their minds by 6:00 P.M.?"

Silence.

"Henrietta, are you still there?"

"Yes. I was thinking. You've bought small publications in the past. Dig up the old contracts. Pay your lawyers an extra $5,000 to work over the weekend."

"Suppose the Senator doesn't call me?"

"I think he will. Stay near your phone, Lionel."

"Thanks, I will."

"Robbie? It's Henrietta. I'm sorry to call you so early on a Saturday morning."

"Not at all, my dear. I had a perfectly splendid time last night. You looked as charming and as young as ever, and I thoroughly enjoyed your guests."

"Ah, Robbie, I wish I had your knack of making everyone feel beautiful, young, and witty. But to get to the point, I'm calling because I have some interesting information. I just got off the phone with Julius Bender, the Editor of *Women's Week*. That's a Ruggles publication, you know. Julius tells me Ruggles has made an offer for *Cuisine du Monde*."

"Has *Cuisine du Monde* accepted?"

"I'm afraid they have, Robbie. The contract is to be signed Tuesday morning. It's a shame. A publication of this sort would have fitted in so nicely with the ideals of the Harmonetics Society."

"You're right, as usual. What's Ruggles paying?"

"A million, I think, but it's all in stock, no cash. That's not my idea of a good deal at all. However, that's Mr. Hemingway's problem. I would personally prefer $700,000 in cash to a million in Ruggles stock in spite of the capital gains tax."

"Why did Hemingway agree to take stock?"

"I guess he had no choice. There wasn't anyone around making a cash offer. Still, when I spoke to him, he gave every indication he'd sell tomorrow for cash. It was probably wishful thinking on his part."

"That must mean the Ruggles deal isn't firm."

"I'm not sure, Robbie. Hemingway told me one thing and Julius Bender another."

"You don't by any chance have Hemingway's number?"

"I just might. Let me see if I can find his card, if I haven't thrown it away. Ah, here it is. The number is 750–6622."

Excerpt from a Lecture on Psychic Awareness
by Dr. Reginald Zinder at the Harmonetics College,
Science Department
November 21, 1980

For the last three years a group of noted scientists in our laboratories has been testing the sense of psychic awareness. This sixth sense is possessed by very few people. Many claim the ability to feel psychic phenomena; some do to a small extent, and some have extraordinary perceptions. No one, we have found out, has a perfect psychic sense.

We analyzed fourteen people who had special awareness gifts. All fourteen came from different backgrounds and almost all had different methods of approach. Some used psychic playing cards to read the past or the present. Others were able to make predictions through special astrology charts. We had one palm reader and one who was able to feel the unknown by examining tea leaves. Let me give you an example of one psychic consultant who we all agreed had an extrasensory perception. I shall call him Mr. X.

One member in our group had lost his dog the previous day. He asked Mr. X where the dog could be found. For perhaps twenty seconds Mr. X remained silent. Then he spoke:

"I see a tan, no, perhaps a brown dog. Your dog is brown. He is, I feel it now, he is medium, yes, medium size. He has been gone for one day. You need not worry. Your dog is not lost. When you go home this evening, he will be there waiting for you."

The prediction was 98 percent accurate. The dog came home that night rather than in the evening. However, Mr. X himself states that psychic waves can be disturbed by someone deliberately fighting the flow. He prefers to hold five or six séances, as he calls them, to get a better interpretation of the depth and speed of the psychic waves. He describes them poetically: they rise higher and are white-capped when the moon is full, then they ebb and grow calm, lapping the sands of the outer brain. Readings made over a thirty-day period are therefore more accurate.

The scientists in our group rated the fourteen gifted people according to their success and failures in given problems. Only three of them scored less than 50 percent; the other eleven were much higher, with Mr. X reaching 82 percent accuracy when allowed six readings. Because of his high scores, I would like to tell you some of the predictions he made with regard to the Harmonetics Society:

• In the space of two years Dr. Josiah Minden will be recognized as the greatest intellectual philosopher of the twentieth century.

• Membership in the Harmonetics Society will reach five million by 1984.

• During the next thirty days three members of the White Robes will be singled out for special recognition by the American public.

• More than fifty new Temples will be built in major cities throughout the world in the coming year.

• The Harmonetics Society will grow steadily over the years, but its zenith will not be reached until the year 2000. At that time the Society will have established its own schools and will employ, in its various enterprises, more than ten million people.

At 6:00 A.M. Jade woke up to the military strains of a Chopin polonaise. She turned over to switch off the radio and felt a sharp pain in her left arm and shoulder. Slowly she sat up. There was a dull ache in her breast; much worse was the throbbing in her abdomen, where one of Josiah's punches had landed. She gingerly put her feet on the floor. There were several discolorations on her arms and legs; her thighs and stomach were a mottled black and purple. Last night she had scarcely felt the pain; the shock of the attack had blocked off sensation in the sensitive nerve endings. This morning the shock was gone and the agony was almost unbearable.

She gasped as she tried to stand up. She sat on the bed again, trying to breathe evenly. If she could relax . . . She reached for the pills Mahaffey had left for her. She gobbled three and waited for the pain to ease. If she stayed in bed, the plan would fail. She had to get up, wash, dress, and be downstairs by 7:30. There was time. The pills would do their work. Think of something pleasant.

She smelled the odor of bacon coming from the kitchen. She could hear the faint sound of the electric orange juice squeezer, the bang of the refrigerator door, a male voice swearing. She smiled, relaxed, and waited.

Arnie, wearing his boxer shorts, walked in with a tray on which sat a paper napkin and a glass of orange juice. He hadn't yet shaved. His light brown hair curled around his massive head and strong neck. A big man, not really handsome but with great skin and coloring, and nice teeth. Not as big as Harold, she thought, and she felt a sudden twinge of sadness.

"You okay, Jade?"

"Not bad. How do I look?"

"You remind me of my Aunt Shirley."

"She must be young and gorgeous."

"Not exactly. She's been dead for four years."

"Very funny. You've been cooking bacon?"

"Yep. I burned it a little. It tastes better that way."

He sat down gently on the bed and stroked her hair. It wasn't like him at all. He was the least demonstrative man she knew.

"You okay, Arnie?"

"Yes, sure. Your plan is crazy, you know. You've got to give it up."

"I can't."

"Do you want to spend the next forty years of your life in jail?"

"I'm going ahead."

"I could get a couple of guys to beat up on Minden."

"Arnie, no one can get near him unless they're a personal friend."

"Minden's got two million guys on his side. Your plan calls for six of us, and two of them are old broads in their seventies."

"I'm going to brush my teeth now," she replied. "I'll kiss you when I finish."

"Shit, how can I get so lucky?" he groaned.

In the bathroom Jade examined her face. The swelling around her eyes had gone down. There was a deep blue bruise on her left cheekbone but her large sunglasses would hide most of it. The anger toward Josiah flowed through her. She felt the blood rushing to her face. Her heart was pumping too fast. She was breathing painfully, gasping for air. The bathroom cabinet, asthma spray, quick . . . She inhaled deeply, slowly. Relax . . . She sat on the edge of the tub. She was drenched with sweat but she was breathing normally. It was the first seizure in several years.

Jade turned on the shower and let the hot steam pour over her aching body. The pain-killers were beginning to work. She soaped her arms and hummed softly. Now she could peacefully examine the alternatives. She could go to the police, accuse Minden, and perhaps (but not likely) have him brought to trial. He would hire a lawyer from Baker & Fitz or Blake, Chatterly and they would appear before Judge Putz or Judge Stuart. Her own attorney, because of course there would be coun-tercharges, would ask a fee of, say, $150,000 to $300,000, and she would see herself defamed, insulted, and humiliated because, at the age of twenty-eight, she was not a virgin. The trial might even be televised (Parental Guidance, of course) because the outcome was acceptable to current American beliefs. The alternative was much nicer. The hell with Judge Putz and Lawyer McDowell. The victim would not be punished, contrary to the American code. The solution could never be shown on the tube. Thank goodness Bill Harding was not trying to stop her.

She patted herself dry with a large towel. She felt a pleasant lethargy from the heat. I'll wear a turtleneck shirt under my warm-up suit, she decided, and my bruises will be hidden.

When she came out of the bathroom and into the kitchen, Arnie was in the process of making scrambled eggs. She could smell the burned butter. He poured the beaten eggs into a pan that was far too hot. As they hit the pan, there was a crack and a hiss.

She couldn't resist. "Arnie, what are those brown spots on the eggs?"

He turned toward her angrily. Then he looked at the poor, bruised face, the sad eyes, and the battered arms.

"I burned the eggs," he said. He wished that the mores of the times permitted him to weep.

Excerpt from a Lecture Given by Dr. Anton Kohl, Head of Neurosurgery, Harmonetics Hospital April 3, 1982

One hundred years ago people believed that mental patients were possessed of the devil. They were locked up in "madhouses" and given up as hopeless. Fifty years ago Dr. Sigmund Freud published his original thoughts on the conscious and unconscious mind. He explained fixations, hysterical paralysis, and mental disturbances in terms of memories that the patient wished to blot out. The new approach to mental illness was psychoanalysis. Twenty-five years ago psychiatrists realized that the majority, perhaps 95 percent, of people designated as insane could not be cured by psychoanalysis. Instead they turned to drugs to alleviate the anguish and perhaps cure the illnesses of those who were no longer mentally competent. The phenothiazines have been particularly good although there are minor side effects that resemble the symptoms of Parkinson's disease.

Since then many new treatments have evolved, and I am going to talk to you about three of them. The first is electric shock, which has been extraordinarily successful when used on specific patients. Sometimes we see improvement after three treatments only; occasionally we use it repeatedly, perhaps fifty or a hundred times, before the benefits appear. In some instances there is no positive reaction, and here we turn our thoughts to other methods such as surgery.

Before I recommend brain surgery I insist that all other treatments such as drugs and shock be tried. If there is no improvement, we have two alternatives. One is lobotomy, which we use far less than in the old days. A patient whose violence is uncontrollable can be calmed immeasurably by the prefrontal lobotomy. Some of these patients can even become useful citizens. However, even when the cure is not complete, the part of the brain that triggered violent reactions is blocked, and the patient is no longer troubled.

In most cases I favor psychosurgery. The technique is more precise and refined than in lobotomies. We alter the neu-

rochemical structure of the brain, which means we change the electrical impulses of the synapses. The treatment has been extremely effective for patients suffering from depression, schizophrenia, epilepsy, imaginary pain, and suicidal or homicidal impulses. A patient who must be continually restrained because of his or her aggressive behavior can be relieved of such symptoms by surgery.

Psychosurgery has its detractors, I am sorry to say. These are people who will not take the time to obtain a full case history of a patient. We take the desperately ill and we try to restore them to a fuller life; 90 percent of my psychosurgical cases have been pronounced cured. How, then, can a critic state that such surgery is "massive mutilation"? How can an unknowledgeable person compare the delicacy of such brain surgery in curing mental illness with "throwing a wrench into an automobile engine to fix a faulty car"?

Psychosurgery is no longer experimental. It is a necessary method of curing particular patients. The experiences I have had in this field entitle me, I believe, to give a more educated commentary on the benefits of this procedure than can a layman or an idle critic. The work we are doing at the Harmonetics Hospital has been lauded by psychosurgeons all over the world. Patients are being sent to us from every major city in the United States. Our hospital has become a mecca for those who are helpless and hopeless. We will not turn them away.

Clarissa Kent had asked Henrietta if she could see her on Saturday. Henrietta suggested that she come for a leisurely breakfast. Elliott had a previous engagement at the museum, which would give them plenty of time to talk by themselves.

Henrietta had sliced some fresh fruit and had baked two ramekins. Clarissa, holding her head so that the better side of her face showed, praised the cheese and the eggs and apologized for eating so little.

"I'm a little under the weather, Henrietta. I'm going to the hospital for treatments on Monday. I'm sure I'll be fine in four or five days."

"Of course you will," said Henrietta. "I'm going myself. I've decided, after long consideration, to have the rejuvenation treatments. Robbie Spriggs has arranged for me to start on Monday also."

"How wonderful, Henrietta! You won't believe what the treatments will do. You'll feel and look like a new woman."

"I don't care if it only lasts for a few months or if I have to go back for further treatments. It'll be worth it to look twenty years younger."

"Rejuvenation makes you feel good too. My muscles got back their old tone and my hair actually turned brown again. I know I look absolutely shocking now, but in four days Heinrich will have me as good as new."

"It's a miracle, isn't it?"

"Yes. You see old women walking into the hospital and they walk out like young girls. They're so happy: it's as though they were awakened from the living dead."

"I can't help but admire those doctors, Clarissa. The brilliance, the imagination, to create youth out of age, to know which hormones to use and how much to inject."

"It's not an injection, Henrietta. It's transplants."

"I hope it isn't painful."

"Hardly at all. It's minor surgery, the gynecological type, plus two small incisions into the lymph glands. I shouldn't be telling you this. They'll put you under, and when you wake up you'll feel marvelous. Within four days the transplants have done their work. Sometimes the patient can leave on the second or third day. You won't have to go back for another transplant for a year."

"I'd be willing to go back every three weeks as long as the transplants work."

"They do. Some last longer than others. As you noticed, one side of me is just perfect. Heinrich will do the other side and I'll be fine again immediately."

"I imagine when the transplants do deteriorate, they go quickly. But what's the difference if one can have a replacement?"

"You've hit it exactly, Henrietta. I've never regretted doing it. I shouldn't say 'never.' During the deterioration the aging process gets worse, as you can see. It's very rapid when it happens. I looked fine a week ago. I hate myself now; I can't bear looking in the mirror. However, Heinrich insists that I go to work and he made me go to your party last night. I'm not sorry I went, but I was so embarrassed with the way I looked."

"Clarissa, dear." Henrietta put her hand on her friend's hand in sympathy.

"Sometimes I'm frightened, Henrietta. I saw Myra Stricklane at the hospital last week. She's had four transplants. Unfortunately she's one of the few who have had dreadful problems. Heinrich warned her but she wanted to go ahead. The last transplant didn't take at all. They redid it the next day but it was useless. Oh, Henrietta, she's an old, old woman now, and she's dying."

"But Myra looked better than any of us!"

"Heinrich says her body is now rejecting all transplants. He's tried everything. He's so worried about her."

"I guess a certain percent will reject transplants. Since he warned Myra, he certainly can't be held liable. She's the one who insisted and she knew the risks."

"Exactly. Every patient who goes in for rejuvenation is told it's an experimental process. The doctors won't touch a patient who doesn't sign a full release. There are literally hundreds of thousands of women, and a lot of men too, who would be willing to take the gamble."

"Clarissa, there's something I forgot to ask Robbie. How much does it cost?"

"It's expensive: $10,000 for the first series of transplants and $6,000 for each repeat treatment. A patient has to put up a $50,000 bond since the doctors refuse to handle anyone who cannot afford the 'repeats.' The money we pay goes to research so that techniques and transplants can be improved."

"Tell me a bit about Heinrich Fronzhold. I know he's a superb physician, but he's so, well, domineering. Don't you resent his manner?"

"You must understand him. He's the quintessential doctor . . ."

"Ah, of course."

"Doctors like Heinrich haven't the time to develop bedside manners. He knows so much more than we do. If he tried to explain everything to us, he wouldn't find the necessary hours for his medical work."

"Still, Clarissa, it would be more pleasant if Heinrich had a little sensitivity."

"He can be very kind and understanding. Naturally, with all the pressures he has, there are difficult moments. We, as women, must accept the moods of the dedicated physician as part of the price we pay. Heinrich works ceaselessly to find the answers to the aging process. Believe me, he is an extraordinary physician and I am proud to be able to assist him in any way I can."

"Do other women see him as you do? One would think his manner of speech and—forgive me—his occasional display of arrogance would antagonize many patients. After all, they're paying him; why should they pay for insults?"

"Fortunately, Henrietta, most women see him as I do. They come to him for help, not for compliments and chitchat."

Henrietta resisted a sigh. "No doubt you're right, Clarissa. If you truly believe in the wisdom of the physician, you won't be ruffled by such trivialities as lack of courtesy."

"You phrase your thoughts strangely, Henrietta, but I'm glad we're in agreement."

"And now, dear friend," said Henrietta, terminating the controversy, "another cup of tea?"

At 7:30 A.M. Jade was standing outside her apartment house waiting for Beth to pick her up. She was wearing a hot-pink warm-up suit and tennis shoes and she was carrying a tennis case. She put the case down and stroked a few imaginary forehands. The shoulder and elbow felt fine. Then she crouched in the ready position, bouncing on her toes, her knees flexed. She was stiff and sore but the pills were working. If Josiah showed up, there should be no problem playing "customer doubles." Then, still crouched, she tried pushing off to her left and pushing off to her right. It hurt like hell.

The block was empty except for two pedestrians. A large woman, wearing a size 18 housedress over a size 20 body, her red hair in rollers, was impatiently waiting for her equally fat Pomeranian to cease sniffing in the gutter and get down to business. She glanced at Jade crouching, hopping, and swinging, then glared at her dog.

"Fifi," she notified the animal, "I'll give you exactly two more minutes. Do you hear me?" She had already forgotten Jade.

A ten-year-old boy was standing by the curb, holding on to one end of a leash while a German shepherd puppy pranced and strained at the other end. The boy, reading a comic book entitled *Marlo, Master of the Planet Mars*, refused to respond to the tug on his arm. Marlo's enemy, the sadistic Professor Carlos, had hidden a time bomb on Marlo's spaceship and it was set to go off in three minutes. Would Marlo find it in time? If not, the explosion would trigger a nuclear reaction that would poison the atmosphere of Mars. Meanwhile the German shepherd puppy, who had spotted the Pomeranian, was leaping with anticipated pleasure and woofing loudly.

Beth's car drove up and Jade jumped in. She rolled down the window as they passed the Pomeranian and yelled, "You've got one more minute, Fifi."

"You amaze me, Jade," said Beth. "Talking to dogs! I saw you warming up on the street, stroking balls that weren't there. Don't you feel conspicuous?"

"Why should I? Did you see what those dogs were doing?"

"Be serious, Jade. Don't you care at all about appearances?"

"Of course, but we have different ideas about appearances."

Jade had dual feelings about her friend. Beth was a fine athlete and a great competitor. Off the court Jade found her a fuzzy thinker, a pedantic lecturer, a conformist, and a pseudo-intellectual. Beth had dual feelings about Jade. She was an intelligent tennis player who never made excuses when she was beaten. But Jade said or did things for their shock value. She was a semihippy, a semiradical, a nonconformist, and a pseudo-intellectual.

"I think I've got a fourth for our game today, Beth."

Her friend was almost inured to Jade's habit of flitting from one subject to the next. She would have preferred to remain on the same topic in order to get in all her arguments, but she was also curious.

"Who's the fourth?"

"I'm not sure he'll show up. He probably will, particularly since he knows you're playing."

"Who?"

"He's probably a low B, but he's so cute it doesn't really matter."

"Jade!" said Beth irritably.

"Okay, okay. Our fourth is Josiah."

The car swerved.

"Dr. Minden!" she said reverentially. She had heard from Esme and the nurses on the floor that Dr. Minden had visited Iris V. Everyone suspected that Jade was the reason.

"Can he actually play, Beth?"

"I wouldn't think so," Beth replied, "but I'm sure he's better than some."

Once they were on the subject of tennis, they were both happier. Whenever they discussed politics, ethics, art master-pieces, human rights, or psychology, one of them tended to dominate and the other to needle.

"Who should play with whom?" asked Jade.

"You take Dr. Minden and I'll play with Esme, unless you'd rather do it the other way."

"No, that's fine."

They were the first to reach the hospital courts. It was a good day for tennis. The sun was out, it was 55 degrees, and there was no wind. Beth opened a can of balls and they started to warm up.

"Don't make me run," said Jade. "I pulled a muscle yesterday and I don't want to make it worse."

"Just stick out your racket and I'll hit it," Beth replied.

Esme Jennings, coming from the Main Building, stopped a minute to watch them hit and was petrified. They both stood on the baseline and traded groundstrokes. Pow Pow. One of them came to net while the other stepped back. Bang Bang. They were cracking balls off either side effortlessly. One lobbed and the other smashed. Crunch Crunch. Neither missed. Esme had been on the same court with Beth several times, but Beth had hit so gently then. If she got on the court with the two of them, she would make a fool of herself. She decided to watch from a distance.

Beth spotted her. "Esme, join us. We'll warm you up slowly and you'll do fine."

"Oh, no. You two are much too good."

"I promise you it will be okay. Give it a try."

Esme Jennings nervously walked onto the court. She, too, was wearing a warm-up suit, but she was conscious that it was too baggy, the material was too shiny, and the figure inside was too bulgy.

"Hit with Jade, Esme, and I'll watch."

It was as Beth promised. Esme hit a few wild ones, but when the ball sailed toward the back fence Jade volleyed it right back to Esme's forehand. She mis-hit off the tip of her racket but Jade, anticipating, glided to the side fence and returned it. Every ball was coming to Esme with the same depth and pace, and she was gradually finding a rhythm.

Josiah Minden got out of his car and walked to the court. Jade was smooth as silk, graceful, accurate. Poor Esme. She saw Minden, and her cramped forehand got even more cramped. She hit the next ball so late that it almost hit Beth, who was standing by the net post.

"That's the first one you missed," Beth comforted her. "Don't worry, you'll play well. Oh, hello, Dr. Minden. I'm so glad you're going to be playing with us."

Minden, who was wearing a blue warm-up suit, placed his three rackets on the bench. He said something polite to Beth, then turned to look at Jade again. She was at her athletic best. The beautiful body was made for the tight hot-pink pants. Her face glowed from the exercise and her dark hair shone in the sun. The large sunglasses hid her sorrowful eyes, giving her the look of a contestant in the Indianapolis 500. This was her milieu.

Jade deliberately caught the next ball with her racket: she pulled back with her arm at the moment of impact, then broke the arm inward. The ball died. It was a trick that fewer than twenty women in the world could do at will. She walked up to Minden smiling, not stopping until she got within a few inches of his body. It was an outrageous come-on. He responded as though they were alone, putting his hands on her waist and moving them upward until the thumbs just touched her breasts.

"You're looking very well," said Minden. "I thought you might be exhausted after last night."

"I can take it," she replied, "and I can, on request, dish it out. Would you be interested?"

"I'd like to hear more about it," said Minden. He put one hand casually on her shoulder, then dropped it slowly down her arm. He was extraordinarily gentle.

"How shall we do this?" Beth interrupted. She could hear the conversation and felt like an eavesdropper. "Shall I play with Esme and you play with Dr. Minden?"

"We'll kill you," Jade teased. "You'll be lucky to get points."

"It's a good thing you've got on a track suit," Beth retorted. "I'm going to run you all over the court."

"Please don't overpower me with your backhand," Jade needled. "When I see that underspin backhand slowly lofting up when I'm at net, I am transfixed with terror."

Beth laughed. "Up or down?" she asked, spinning her racket.

"Up," said Minden.

"It's up," said Beth.

"I'll serve first," said Minden.

Jade and Beth avoided looking at each other. The weak macho man playing with the strong woman invariably assumed the traditional masculine role, refusing to acknowledge that his serve was not as good as his partner's.

Jade warmed up with Esme and Minden with Beth. If Minden had hit with Esme, he would have tried to kill her. Jade, who was wandering through the warm-up, hit every ball so Esme would have more confidence. She could see Josiah out of the corner of her eye. He was, as she had expected, overhitting.

After five minutes Beth said, "Shall we try some serves?" They practiced their serves crosscourt, Jade and Beth serving at three-quarter pace and Minden serving at a hundred million miles an hour. Esme, who had several extraneous wiggles and a pat-ball serve, was terrorized by Minden's cannonball.

"I'll never be able to return it," she whispered to Beth.

"All those serves are long," Beth reassured her. "And if you miss, think how good he will feel."

Esme relaxed.

Play began. It was the type of match that Jade and Beth had played many times before. One partner was cringing in fear, the other unaware of the quantity of his errors. In the course of the first four games Esme apologized to her partner nine times. ("I'm sorry." "Oh, I'm such a spastic." "I didn't mean to lob short.") Beth regularly consoled and encouraged her. She knew this was the way she would feel if she were in a doubles with Dick Stockton against Vitas Gerulaitis and Betty Stove. Jade's partner was angry with himself ("I'm only angry with myself," he told Jade several times) because he could not drill a ball through Beth, because she returned his big serve as though it were a powder puff, because he served doubles, and because he repeatedly found he could not half-volley Beth's sidespin forehands to the baseline. "Almost" or "Just missed by an inch," said Jade in an effort to bolster his flagging ego.

There were the usual bad calls. At tournament level, almost no one called the ball wrong, particularly in a social doubles. Lesser players were not so fastidious.

A ball landed on Esme's baseline and she called "Out!"

"Esme, for heaven's sake!" said Minden.

"I think it caught the line, Esme," Beth said, "but it came so fast it was hard to see. Your point," she called to Minden.

"It was in by two inches," said Minden coldly.

Esme was desolated. "Oh, dear, I'm so sorry," she apologized. "I better not call any more balls."

"Of course you can call them," said Beth. "We all make mistakes. Please correct *me* if I make a bad call."

A few minutes later Minden called a line ball out. Beth and Jade went about their business as though the call were correct.

Minden served to Esme. His first serve was a fault. His second serve was also a fault but Esme, fearful of cheating, played the ball. Minden returned it as though the ball were still in play. Beth caught it, stopping the point.

"Double-fault," she said briskly, turning her back and walking to the baseline.

Minden stared at Beth's rear. After all, Esme had returned the ball.

"Tough luck, Josiah. Just out," Jade said to her partner.

Thereafter Minden got more competitive. Jade had been hitting the ball as nicely as she could to Esme, giving her a chance to get a good swing at it. When Jade was about to serve to Esme at 15–40, Minden said:

"We need this point, Jade."

He's telling me to throw in a big one at helpless Esme so we'll win by 6–1. Okay, I'll give her a big spinner wide to the forehand. Esme whiffed it.

"We've got to get this point, too, Jade."

Now I have to play like it's the final of Wimbledon. I hope Beth understands. She does. Two more points and the set is over. Sorry again, Esme. Here's a big one to your backhand, Beth.

Jade served at set point, came in against Beth, and punched a backhand winner between the opponents. Set, 6–1.

"Another?" asked Beth. "We want revenge."

"Sure," said Jade. "This is great. How about you, Josiah?"

They played one more set. Beth and Jade were hitting from memory, going through the motions without having to concentrate. From the point of view of their partners, there were many good exchanges. Esme was getting grooved on the forehand and she made, for her, some spectacular returns. Josiah Minden also played better. He got into some good crosscourt exchanges with Beth and he put away several volleys and overheads. At 5–2 Jade decided to show off. Her blood was flowing from the exercise and she was no longer conscious of any pain. She lobbed Beth, came to net as Beth ran back, then drop-volleyed Beth's overhead for a winner. Beth smiled in amazement and even Jade was surprised at herself. On the next point Minden hit a short ball to Beth's forehand. Beth took aim. At the same time Jade moved. She moved too soon. Beth whipped one as hard as she could right at her opponent. Jade stuck her racket behind her back and made a crazy volley. Jade Boren and Josiah Minden had won, 6–1, 6–2.

They shook hands.

"You did beautifully, Esme," Beth said to her partner.

"Oh, I was awful," said Esme apologetically.

"Josiah, I didn't realize how well you could play," said Jade. "You got better and better."

"Thanks. I really did enjoy it," said Minden. "You are a marvelous player and it was a pleasure being on the same court with you."

The match was over and Josiah Minden's adrenalin had ceased to flow. He was once again the charming leader of the Harmonetics Society.

Document to Be Signed by All Patients Who Have Requested Rejuvenation Therapy

I have been warned by my doctor that the rejuvenation therapy is still experimental. I have been informed that the operation will involve two animal transplants, one to the anterior pituitary lobe and another to the uterine cavity. I am aware that similar operations have been performed on other human beings and that the results have not always been successful.

I have been told that no patient to date has succumbed on the operating table. However, 3 percent of the patients have rejected the transplants in the postoperative phase and 9 percent had similar reactions within sixty days after surgery.

I recognize the fact that these transplants are not as yet permanent and that patients undergoing the treatment have often required two or more transplants in the two years following surgery.

I have not been persuaded to undergo rejuvenation therapy by my doctor or by any doctor or nurse connected with the Harmonetics Hospital. I have been asked to consider my decision carefully and to recognize certain risks that could result in my premature demise. I do not consider the doctors, nurses, or hospital involved to be responsible for any illness or surcease of body functions that may ensue as a consequence of my decision.

I herewith present my check in the amount of $10,000 to cover the cost of the transplants and hospitalization. I also attach my bond in the amount of $50,000 to cover the costs of follow-up rejuvenation treatment.

By signing this document, I release the surgeons, anesthetists, nurses, hospital, and the Harmonetics Society from any obligation, financial or otherwise, to me or my family.

(full name)

(date)

It was the third time in twenty-eight hours that Bill Harding had visited Harold Gondoler. He did so from a mixture of responsibility, friendship, and guilt; he hated hospitals. It was obvious to Harding that Gondoler was in pain.

"Shall I ask the nurse to get you something?" he said.

"No, it's bearable. At least my brain is clear."

"I won't stay long."

"I want to hear what's happening. It'll get my mind off my miseries."

Harding related the entrapment of Betty McLaughlin by Caroline and Missy. Harold was enchanted.

"Betty McLaughlin and Eileen McDermott were arrested last night," Harding concluded, "and they got Collins Graybill early this morning."

"Have you hired Missy and Caroline?"

"I sent them a check of $1,000 each for their services."

"Get a picture of them, Bill."

"You're right. Sipping tea in Caroline's apartment. No, Missy cracking open a bottle of vodka."

"How's our friend Jade doing?"

Harding found it difficult to tell the story. There were long pauses. Again the feeling of guilt. The score was one dead, one with damaged brain, one hospitalized, and one raped. After the first three incidents he should have called a halt to the investigation.

"My fault for not canceling the article," he told Gondoler.

"That's the way Minden wanted you to feel."

"I could have turned everything over to the police."

"You couldn't. You wouldn't have gotten Roger's killers. The live witness, Mary Hamble, would be dead. You had no choice, Bill."

A nurse entered the room. "You'll have to go now," she said to Harding severely.

Gondoler was normally a gentle man. "Get out of here!" he roared.

The nurse retreated. Another abusive patient. The hell with him. If she could have banged the door, she would have done so.

Gondoler's outburst had exhausted him. He lay motionless, stretched out, trying to stay conscious as the waves of pain traveled from his side to his brain and back again.

"Jade went back to the hospital this morning," said Harding. He deliberately repeated himself. "Jade went back to see Minden. She's cooked up a scheme to ruin him."

The pain subsided. Gondoler was functioning again.

"Jade was certain that an affectionate note would soothe Josiah, make him confident. Harold, I think she's right."

Gondoler felt the pain ebbing. The stabbing, jarring shocks had diminished to a dull throbbing.

"Josiah Minden went too far this time. He's raped and beaten up members of his adoring coterie before and gotten away with it. He won't this time."

"I wonder if Minden was always this way," said Harold. "My guess is it came with the worship of the faithful. Hundreds of thousands of women who hold him in reverence. Perhaps the boredom of it all, the ease with which he could take them to bed."

"And the power. The Leader is subject to no laws."

"He's the Tiberius or Caligula of twentieth-century America."

Harding stood up. "I'm glad to see you're better. Is there anything I can bring you when I come back tomorrow?"

"A water pistol. I'll fire on the next doctor or nurse who comes in without knocking."

Excerpt from a Speech Given by Byron Kent to the San Diego Chamber of Commerce September 20, 1982

Gentlemen, it is a great pleasure and honor to be with you today. I have been officially designated by Dr. Josiah Minden to act as his spokesman in explaining his plans for a new Harmonetics Temple in your area. It will surely be the Taj Mahal of the Western world.

I am going to show you slides of the projected Temple. I would like you to note the unusual facets of the plan. The first slide shows the large parking areas with space for more than

15,000 cars. This next slide is an overall view of the Temple itself. The conformation is that of a stadium. The seats rise upward to a level equivalent to five stories. On the main floor are enclosed pews with six seats each. These pews will be reserved for members who wear the Brown Robe. One entire section on the ground floor, as you can see, is partitioned for Novitiates and their Presenters.

You may wonder whether those sitting in the rear of the fourth and fifth levels will be able to see the ceremonies and make out the participants. Please notice that directly under the domed roof is the largest television screen ever conceived. The fifth level viewer will therefore be able to see not only the distinguished lecturers but any White Robe members on the dais as well as all the Novitiates and Presenters. This latter group will be stimulated to participate since each time a man or woman appears on the platform, his or her face will clearly be seen by the 45,000 worshipers that the Temple will accommodate. In each of us is hidden a desire for recognition; the new Harmonetics Temple will fulfill that desire by allowing Novitiates and Presenters, as well as those promoted from Blue Robe to Red, Green, and Brown, their proper place on the stage.

What will the new Harmonetics Temple do for your city? It will bring in a constant stream of visitors, it will induce many men and women in their sixties, seventies, and eighties to find a permanent home in the area, it will bring prosperity to hundreds of merchants, bankers, and real-estate agents, to hotels, shops, and areas of entertainment. San Diego will become the boom town of America.

With me today is G. Philip Goodley, Chairman of the Board of Sanco Fidelity. He will give you the details on the Harmonetics Temple bonds, which will be offered to members of your community. The issue is $450 million, the interest rate is 11 percent, and the Harmonetics Society itself will guarantee the bonds. I can assure you there is no financial risk.

The tennis foursome was breaking up. Dr. Josiah Minden thanked his partner once again and shook hands with his two opponents. Jade said, "I'll catch up with you in a minute," to Beth and Esme. She then followed Minden as he briskly walked to the waiting limousine.

"What are you doing tomorrow, Josiah? You want to hit some?"

"Sorry, I've got a White Robe ceremony at the Temple. We've got meetings all morning and pictures and interviews in the afternoon."

"You want to take me out for dinner?"

Minden laughed. "I'm busy."

"I'm pretty busy myself," answered Jade. "Matter of fact, I'm booked every night next week. I'll see you."

She started to walk away.

"Just a minute," he said.

Jade stopped, then pivoted slowly, smiling.

"I'll meet you Monday evening," he told her.

"For fun and/or games?"

He didn't answer. Instead he gently removed her big sunglasses. He looked at the purple blotch high on her cheekbone. His lips brushed softly against the bruise.

Jade, smiling, slowly let her tongue slide across her lips. She moistened her finger and moved it around her mouth. Then she lifted her finger to his mouth and pressed just enough to raise the lip slightly. Then she turned around and walked to the hospital.

As soon as Jade reached the main building, she rushed to the hospital intercom and dialed Nurses' Station, Iris V. Nurse Jackie Volts answered.

"It's Jade. I'll be there in twenty minutes."

"Thank God," said Nurse Volts. "I'm exhausted. We had a problem this morning in Room 39."

"I'm so sorry. You want me to fix up the medicine trays when I get there?"

"They're already fixed." Jade's heart sank. "I haven't taken them to the rooms yet," Nurse Volts added.

"You poor thing," said Jade, commiserating. "I'll try to get there in fifteen minutes. I'd be happy to help with the trays if you wish."

"Good girl. If I'm not at the Nurses' Station when you get here, I'll be in the lounge having a cup of coffee."

Jade showered and changed. She put her gray Probationary gown over her clothes. The white turtleneck sweater showed.

Jade shrugged. Who cared? No one was going to fire her. On her way upstairs she stopped by a fruit juice machine and bought a can of Health-O Root Beer. She stuffed it in her purse.

Nurse Volts was not at her station in Iris V. Jade went directly to the clean white room where the drugs were kept. The medicine trays were on a long metal table. The drugs were laid out neatly according to room number. Room 1, a hypodermic. Room 2, a small paper cup filled with a pale liquid. Jade looked for Room 23, Mary Hamble's scrubbed, sunny prison. A paper cup containing a light brown medicine and another small cup with two pills. Jade carried the liquid cup to the sink and poured it down the drain. She opened her purse and pulled out the root beer. It was too dark. She spilled out some and mixed a quarter-cup of root beer with enough water to give it the proper color. She examined the finished blend with the pleased smile of the skilled apothecary. She rummaged in her purse again, this time for Bufferin. She substituted two for the pills in Mary's cup.

Jade hummed happily as she searched for the medicines listed for Room 16. Perhaps she had been destined to be a druggist. There was a hypodermic needle and two pills of a different shape than aspirin. Room 16, Mr. Clay, was scheduled for psychosurgery on Monday by Dr. Heinrich Fronzhold. C-L-A-Y was afraid of F-R-O-N-Z because of P-S-Y. Jade picked up the hypodermic, wrapped it in a towelette, and placed it carefully in the bottom of her purse.

"Hm-hm-hm-hm," she sang softly, opening the thin, flat drawers of a medicine cabinet. Cotton pads, no. Tongue depressors, wrong. Hypodermic needles! She removed one from the drawer, changed her mind, and grabbed a handful. There were dozens lying row upon row; a few more or less would never be noticed.

The hypodermics would have to be filled.

"Hm-hm-hm-hm," she hummed.

The large bottle dangling from the half-assed coat rack with the long rubber tube and a needle at the end. Intravenous feeding undoubtedly. Yes, Room 8, destined for poor, helpless Martha. Don't think about her now. Can't afford to get weepy. Fill the six hypodermics with the liquid in the bottle. Wrap the needles carefully. Place them in the purse.

Someone will notice that half the contents of the bottle was gone. A small, sharp knife. A thin, almost imperceptible nick on the rubber tube. The liquid drips onto the floor. More liquid needed. Fill a cup with water, then let it spill directly under the bottle. Perfect.

"Hm-hm-hm." Remove the pills from Room 16's cup. An adequate substitute is needed. The Butazolidin pills that Jon Mahaffey gave me are close enough. Out go the old and in go the new. "Hm-hm-hm."

Jade headed for the Nurses' Lounge. Jackie Volts, a pillow behind her back and her shoes off, was seated in a comfortable stuffed chair, her feet propped up on a smaller one. She was asleep. Jade poured half a cup of coffee, spoke the nurse's name gently, and extended the cup to her.

"Oh!" said Jackie, opening her eyes. "I'm beat. Help me with the medicine trays, will you? Some of the patients get hypodermics in the morning, and sometimes it takes two of us to give the shot."

She stuffed her swollen feet into her shoes, then downed the coffee. Together they walked into the Drug Room.

"Damn it to hell!" said Nurse Volts.

"What's the matter?"

"The intravenous tube leaked. What a mess."

"I'll get a rag and clean it. Tell me where to get another bottle and tube, and I'll patch it up."

"It's quicker to do it myself," Jackie Volts said grumpily.

Jade silently cleaned the floor.

"I haven't had any real sleep in a week," said Jackie. "This is no life. They told me there wasn't much work on this floor. Like hell there isn't."

"Why don't you go back to an eight-hour shift?"

"I need the money. I've been saving up for four years. Another couple of years to go."

"What will you do with the money?"

"I'm going to buy a luxury condominium on the water in Fort Lauderdale. I'll work, of course, but I'll take the night shift so I can lie on the beach all day. You meet all kinds of nice people."

Jade imagined stocky Nurse Volts with her thick waist and thick ankles lying in a pile of sand amid thousands of equally bare bodies, waiting for Prince Charming.

"Where do you live now, Jackie?"

"I have a lousy two-room apartment in the Bronx. It's one of those twenty-five-story buildings, they all look the same. If someone blindfolded me and turned me around, and if all the street names and numbers were gone, I'd never be able to find where I live. You ever been to Fort Lauderdale, Jade?"

"Yes, a couple of times."

"Is it as beautiful as the pictures?"

"It's very beautiful," said Jade, not wishing to spoil Jackie's illusions. Block after block of twenty-five-story apartment houses, all identical. Swimming pools filled with urinating children, beach chairs lined up in rows, separated from each other by inches.

"Where did you stay when you were there, Jade?"

"With some friends. I was playing a tournament."

"Did they have a luxury condominium?"

"Yes, they did. It was on the water, like yours." No point in mentioning the noise from the neighboring apartments, kids screaming early in the morning, a hi-fi blaring at 3:00 A.M., the sound of dishes crashing against walls.

"I bet you hated to leave, Jade."

"It was hard saying good-bye."

"Christ, it's 9:30 and I haven't given the patients their sedation yet. I'll get hell if Calderwood sees me. We better get hopping."

Jade pushed the cart with the tray, dutifully following Nurse Volts.

"I'm way behind schedule," Nurse Volts grumbled.

"I'll help."

"Do you know how to clean up a patient and change a bed?"

"I'm sure I can."

"Well, okay, I'll give you a few. They'll be sedated but you still have to be careful. The orderlies handle the violent ones."

"When will the orderlies be here?"

"They are here. They're with Nurse Calderwood in the rear corridor. They only stay till noon, you know."

"If you need them in the afternoon, can you get them?"

"Not unless you phone for one. Then they're sent from another floor."

They entered Room 1.

"Good morning, little lady. How are you today?" asked Nurse Volts.

The young woman, just in her twenties, nodded her head vigorously and darted her eyes back and forth between Jade and Jackie.

"She's been with us for several months," the nurse explained to Jade. "She's perfectly harmless but we haven't been able to get her to speak. Can't send her back to the world like this. Dr. Jennings tried shock but there were no results to speak of. Today we're starting a new treatment."

Nurse Volts picked up the hypodermic. The patient drew up her knees and waved her arms frantically.

"Jade, grab her arms."

"Do we have to do this?"

"Jade, did you hear what I said?" Nurse Volts exclaimed angrily.

Jade held the patient's arms and Nurse Volts leaned heavily against the girl's body to keep her from thrashing. She gave the shot quickly.

Jade was sweating. Obey orders, she told herself. One word of complaint from Nurse Volts and I'll be out of Iris V for good.

"I'm sorry," Jade apologized. "That was stupid of me. I'm here to help and learn, not to argue."

"That's all right," said the nurse.

"What did you give her?"

"Thorazine. We get a reasonably good reaction with long-term use of the drug, but there are side effects. The trade-off, says Dr. Jennings, is insanity versus distortion of the facial muscles."

"Which do the patients prefer?"

"No one knows. They don't complain afterward. They're much more tractable and rational. They can communicate."

"How about the relatives?"

"That's the problem. The relatives don't like them either way."

They walked into Room 2. The old man cowered but accepted the pills and the medicine.

Nurse Volts spent a little more time in Room 5—about three more minutes than the norm. The patient was addressed as Marianne. She looked in her late sixties. Her head had been shaved for surgery and the hair had not grown back. The long scar across the top of the pate was visible. The skin looked the same on both sides but there was a deep declivity on one side of the head, which indicated the area that the surgeon had removed.

Marianne received two pills, which she peacefully accepted.

"She's our best patient," said Nurse Volts proudly. "Marianne had surgery for cancer of the brain and the surgeon is sure all the malignancy was removed. She's just fine now, aren't you, Marianne?"

"Fine, I'm fine. I feel so much better," said the patient, slowly enunciating each word.

"She can almost eat by herself. There's been pronounced tremor of the hands and feet since the operation, but with a little assistance Marianne can do almost anything. Can't you, dear?"

"I—do—try, nurse." The words were slurred.

"The pill may be working. You rest, now, Marianne, hear?"

"Yes—I—hear."

"Jade, she'll probably sleep for the next few hours. You can help her eat and bathe later."

"Has she a mental problem?"

"No. The brain is not as keen as before the operation but she's not unbalanced. She's forty-three—yes, I know she looks older—but she now has the mentality of a five- or seven-year-old. She's friendly and gentle but she lost her hand and foot coordination and she's rather helpless."

"Why is she here?"

"The relatives. I guess they don't know what to do with her."

"Did they try to talk her out of the operation?"

"No, they convinced her it was necessary."

"Ah, the doctor felt she had to have the cancer removed?"

"Yes. Dr. Anton Kohl operated. It was a remarkable surgical feat."

The next few rooms were routine: medication and/or a shot.

"Do you give the medication every day?" asked Jade.

"No, Ellen Dixon and I share on weekdays. She's off today and I'm off tomorrow. Charlene Calderwood comes on at eight every morning and usually stays until eight in the evening. By that time the two night nurses are on duty. They have it pretty easy since we do medication, cleanup, and meals. Charlene is a nice woman, very dedicated. The only two things in life that mean anything to her are her work and her grandchild. Ellen is a good worker but she's flighty. She goes from one boyfriend to the next. Right now she's crazy about some fellow named Jason. According to her, he's a Greek god and as brilliant as he's good-looking. She says she'll marry him as soon as he gets a job."

They were coming out of Room 14 when they heard the sharp ring of the phone at the Nurses' Station.

"Damn it," said Nurse Volts. "Stay here. I'll get it."

As Jackie Volts walked to the Nurses' Station, Jade took a chance and ran into Room 16. The occupant, Mr. Clay, was resting, which was the only sensible thing to do since he was in restraint.

"Wake up, Mr. Clay," Jade said.

He opened his good eye.

"In a few minutes we'll be in your room with your medication. I've switched the hypodermics. Do you understand me? You'll be getting a plain intravenous-feeding injection. I've also switched the pills. I put two of my Butazolidins in your cup."

Was Mr. Clay smiling? Jade wasn't sure. She got back to the corridor before Nurse Volts had finished with the phone call.

The fourteen-year-old girl in the next room looked thin and ill. There were deep circles under her eyes and she had lost all her hair. When she saw Nurse Volts and the hypodermic, she sighed.

"There won't be many more shots now," said the nurse. "You're getting better each day."

"I feel sick," said the girl sadly.

"Two months ago you didn't know me. You couldn't talk. You're practically well now, honey.

"She was in bad shape when they brought her in," said Nurse Volts to Jade. "She's been getting chemotherapy. She's constantly nauseated but there's a good chance of recovery."

"Shall I help her clean up when we're through?"

"Yes, she's harmless. Change the linen too, will you?"

"Glad to."

They walked in Room 16. Mr. Clay was looking at the nurse with his good eye. He ignored Jade.

"I hope you won't give us any problems today," said Nurse Volts. "Are you going to take your pills?"

The patient opened his mouth.

"Well, I'll be damned," said the nurse. She popped the pills in his mouth as though he were about to bite her fingers. Then, as carefully as she could, she raised his head and helped him drink a cup of water.

"That's the first time he's been cooperative since he's been here," said the nurse. "The pills we give him each day affect the vocal chords. If he didn't take them, he'd be screaming at the top of his lungs. He's dangerous, Jade. The orderlies have been handling him and he's been giving them a terrible time. As you can see, they gave him a bad time too. This shot will render him harmless. In an hour he won't be able to move his arms or legs."

The patient passively allowed Nurse Volts to give him the shot.

"I can't believe it," she exclaimed. "He killed two men, you know. That's why they put him here. You can come back in an hour, Jade, and take off his restraints."

"He actually killed two men? Don't you think we should leave the restraints on a little longer?" Jade asked nervously.

"I promise you, Jade, the drug is 100 percent effective. He will be able to hear and, if his brain weren't so addled, he would be able to think, but he won't be able to lift a finger."

"Whom did he kill?"

"I don't know. He wasn't remanded by court order. He was committed by Dr. Fronzhold at the request of the patient's family. Dr. Fronzhold said he was too ill to be prosecuted."

During their visit to the next few rooms, Jade was subdued. Christ, she thought, I wonder if I've blown it. Supposing Mr. Clay is a homicidal maniac. If I'm lucky he'll simply scream his head off. I shouldn't have switched the pills. Once the restraints come off, we'll all be dead. I won't think about it. Fronzhold committed Mary Hamble and Mr. Clay. Clay could be as sane as Mrs. Hamble. I hope.

They entered Room 23. Mary Hamble's eyes were closed and her fists, near her face, were clenched tightly.

"Mary, open your eyes," said Nurse Volts.

Mary stirred and opened her eyes. They looked fuzzy, unfocused.

"Now take your medicine like a good girl."

The patient obediently opened her mouth, accepted the pills, and drank the root beer.

"Shall I clean up this patient?" asked Jade.

"Why not? The sedation we're giving her is quite heavy. She won't be a problem. I've got one more shot where I may need your help. Then I'll give you a list of rooms where you can change the bed linen and bathe the patient."

Five minutes later Jade was back in Room 23. The patient was lying perfectly still.

"Mrs. Hamble," Jade whispered, "it's me, Jade."

Mary Hamble opened her eyes. "I loved the root beer," she said with a smile.

"I'm sorry I had to water it. In two days you'll be drinking one of Missy Tompkins' Bloody Marys."

"Not if I can help it," said Mary.

"Let's practice walking," said Jade. "You've got today, Sunday, and half of Monday before you walk out of here."

An hour later Jade was working up her courage to go back to Room 16. Death, she thought, comes to all of us. Quite true, but we don't all get strangled. Perhaps I could "forget" to undo the restraints.

As she was hesitating, she saw Beth walk into the Nurses' Station. Might as well see how Beth is doing. I can always check on Mr. Clay later.

"I hear you've been helping Nurse Volts," said Beth. "Are you enjoying the work?"

"Very much," Jade replied. She's using the tone of a physician talking to the dumb little nurse's aide. How can you be so nice on the court and such a shit professionally?

"It's difficult when you have so little training," said Beth.

"Nurse Volts is terribly overworked. I'm glad to do whatever I can. Thank God for the two Blue Gowns. They're starting on Iris V on Monday, you know."

"What on earth are you talking about, Jade?" Beth said irritably. "No one's allowed on Iris V, not even relatives of patients. The only reason you're here is because Esme and I pulled some strings."

"Sorry, I thought Josiah told you," said Jade.

"Told me what?"

"That he assigned two Blue Gowns to work here, starting Monday."

"Yes, of course, I quite forgot," said Beth, who was hearing the news for the first time. She turned her back on Jade and addressed Nurse Calderwood.

"Nurse, Dr. Jennings and I will be checking on the patients in Rooms 34 on. I assume they have all been medicated?"

"Yes, all finished. Good news about the Blue Gowns. What time will they be here on Monday?"

"Jade," asked Beth, "what time did Dr. Minden say the Blue Gowns were coming?"

"Noon."

"That's right, at noon."

Four hours had elapsed since Mr. Clay had received his shot. No screams as yet from Room 16. Jade cautiously opened the door.

"Mr. Clay," she whispered, waiting for the outburst.

"I'm awake," he said in a low voice.

She took a few steps toward the bed. The swelling in the left eye had gone down. It was still puffy but he could see with two eyes.

"You're looking fine. I'm glad you're able to speak," Jade said timorously. Would the wild, maniacal shrieks begin now?

"The double dose of Butazolidin was doubly effective," said the patient.

"Mr. Clay, whom did you kill?" God, I really blew it. Here come the screams.

"No one," he said in the same low voice.

"What's your full name?"

"Steven Clay. I'm a doctor."

I'm Napoleon. He's a doctor.

"Where did you practice, Dr. Clay?"

"My office is on 84th, just off Fifth. My associate is Godfrey Waterhouse."

Jade was undecided. Her patient seemed to read her mind.

"My leg is broken. How far could I get if I hopped on one leg?"

Your arms aren't broken. You're strong enough to sock an orderly.

"I have to go now, Dr. Clay."

She moved toward the door, hesitated, and came back.

"I guess I'll remove the restraints."

He said nothing. His face did not reassure her: the lip was torn, a large bandage covered what looked to be a broken nose, and the bad eye was still a mess.

She took off the jacket that had kept him immobilized. There were bruises on his chest and arms, undoubtedly from the encounter with the orderlies.

Jade heard the sound of the door and turned around. Nurse Volts came in the room and walked up to the bed. She examined the patient. One eye was closed and the other rolled frantically.

"Didn't I tell you?" said the nurse to Jade. "The shot is a drastic measure—we don't use it very often—but it will prevent him from harming himself or others. If you don't want to bathe him, an orderly can do it tomorrow."

"I'll do it. I don't mind," Jade answered.

"Rrgh, hrrgh," said the patient.

Telephone Conversation

"Effie? Will you get me Herbert Rowley at the *New York Times's* Washington bureau? Thanks, I'll hold . . . Hello, Herbert? It's Bill Harding at *National News*."

"Bill, old chap, what can I do for you?"

"A few questions, Herbert. First, when does the Senate Subcommittee on the Emergency Coal Bill meet?"

"Monday afternoon at 2:00 P.M."

"Second question. Will the Committee approve the bill?"

"No. The vote will be 7 to 5 against."

"Supposing I told you it would be 7 to 5 for?"

"Bill, I can count the votes."

"I have reason to believe that Byron Kent, President of Kentwood Mining, approached Senators Peters and Ellis to promise them the Brown Robe of the order of the Harmonetics Society in return for their vote."

"What proof, Bill?"

"A conversation overheard at a dinner party."

"That's not exactly proof."

"Not in a court of law but it happens to be a fact. What kind of guys are Peters and Ellis?"

"Not bad but not great. Rather decent on the whole."

"Then perhaps you might want to do them a favor. Tell them several members of the press know that Byron Kent tried to buy their vote with the promise of a brown robe. Herbert, it doesn't matter which way they vote because whatever happens they will never be promoted in the Harmonetics Society. Therefore they should vote as their conscience directs them."

"I don't know if I can do that, Bill. How can I truthfully state they'll never receive the Brown Gown?"

"It's the truth, Herbert. On Monday night they'll know it's the truth and so will you. They'll be grateful to you forever. You'll have a major story as a result. I'm predicting they'll admit Kent's bribery attempt on Tuesday, and they'll be thanking heaven and you for saving them."

"You've never faked me before, Bill."

"And I'm not faking you now."

"I believe you, Bill. I'll tell them."

Jerry Marconi carefully stuck his hand into the brown paper bag so he would not spill the coffee. He spread the contents on his desk. Plastic knife and fork, light coffee in cardboard, a kosher dill pickle wrapped in wax paper, thin slices of roast beef on rye, a small container of fresh fruit, an equally small container of sliced cucumbers, and two paper napkins wet with coffee.

The phone rang.

"This is Caroline Ryder. Is that you, Jerry?"

"Yes, Mrs. Ryder. Thanks for calling back. There's been a small change in plan. The limousine will come by for you and Mrs. Tompkins at 11:30 on Monday instead of 11:00. The driver is from the Rappaport Agency."

"Will it be Palmer, the same one we had before?"

"Yes, it's Palmer. He'll put two blue gowns in the back seat, one for you and one for Missy Tompkins."

"I imagine you'll want us to bring large reticules in case we have to carry transmitters again."

"Reticules, ah, yes. For the transmitters, right. Did you get a chance to look at the photos I sent you of Jade? Will you be able to recognize her?"

"Of course. They reminded Missy and me of Merle Oberon as a young girl, although of course Jade's eyes are much larger. Almost like deep pools, we thought."

"Deep pools. What a lovely, descriptive phrase. Yes, her eyes are like deep pools."

"Jerry, have you heard from Jade today?"

"Not yet . . . Hold on, there's the other phone. . . . Hello?"

"Jerry, it's Jade."

"Honey, are you okay?"

"Sure. I've only got a minute; I'm at the pay phone in the Nurses' Lounge. Will you put a check on a doctor by the name of Steven Clay, C-L-A-Y? He has an office on 84th and Fifth and says his associate's name is Godfrey Waterhouse. That's the Mr. Clay I told you about yesterday."

"Okay. Anything special you want to know?"

"Yes. What does he look like, exact age, birthmarks, etc. When was he last seen? Was he hot-tempered or violent and did he ever kill anyone? Is he married and does his wife know where he is? What's become of him? That's it, Jerry."

"Caroline Ryder's on the other phone. Any messages for her and Missy?"

"Yeah. Mary Hamble is going to walk out of the hospital, even if she has to crawl out. She's very weak; she almost fainted when she tried to stand today. The third blue robe will be used for Mary."

"Anything else?"

"Josiah and I beat Beth and Esme 6-1, 6-2."

"You're not seeing him again?"

"Not till D-Day. He's sure of me, Jerry."

"Take care, honey. Good-bye."

Click.

"Mrs. Ryder, it's Jerry again. That was Jade. She wanted me to give you the following message: there will be a third blue gown in the limousine. Put it in your what-do-you-call-it, your reticule. It's for Mary."

"Will we speak to you again?"

"I'll call on Monday at 10:00 A.M. to confirm."

"Missy says she sends you her love."

"Thank you, Caroline, and tell Missy I love her too."

Jerry put down the receiver and picked it up again. He dialed.

"Rhonda, this is Jerry Marconi. Is Jon there?"

"Yes, Jerry. Hold on."

"Jerry? Jon Mahaffey. What can I do for you?"

"I just spoke to Jade. She's fine. She wants to get a description and background on a psychiatric patient of Fronzhold. It's the same guy she told us about last night. He claims he's a doctor, Steven Clay, with a practice on 84th and Fifth. Associate's name is Waterhouse, Godfrey."

"Steven Clay. That's not a familiar name. I don't think I've met him. Let me check around."

"I'll be at the office, Jon."

"I'll call you back as quickly as I can."

The phone rang again.

"Jerry? It's me, Jade. One more thing. Please try to get me some placebos that are the same size as the Butazolidin Jon Mahaffey gave me. Okay?"

"Okay. Who are they for?"

"Steven Clay. Talk to you later."

Jerry dialed again.

"Rappaport Agency? This is Jerry Marconi, *National News*. We ordered a driver for a limousine Monday morning to pick up Mrs. Tompkins. Will you see if it's possible to get Palmer to chauffeur?"

"This is Palmer. I'd be happy to drive."

"Thanks. Missy and Caroline requested you. We'd like you to stop off at *National News* first to pick up some materials."

"I'll be by at 10:30 on Monday. See you then."

Jerry hung up, then tried Jon Mahaffey. The line was busy. He tried again. On the fourth try Mahaffey picked up the phone.

"Jon, Jade needs some placebos."

"What kind, pill or liquid? They also come in forty different colors."

"The same size and color as the Butazolidin."

"That's a cinch. I just spoke to a friend who has an old picture of Steven Clay from medical school. I'm picking it up now. He says he heard Clay had died. I'll bring the picture and the placebos to your office in fifteen minutes. Meanwhile I got Godfrey Waterhouse's private number. Give him a call and ask away. If a woman answers, don't call her Mrs. Waterhouse. It's not an answering service; it's his girl friend."

"What's the number?"

"751–2533."

Jerry dialed the number Jon Mahaffey had given him.

"Hello, may I speak to Dr. Waterhouse, please?"

"Who's calling?" asked a female voice.

Jerry hesitated. "My name is Walter Furlong. I just got in from Brazil and I'm trying to get in touch with Steven Clay. Do you know where I can find him?"

There was an equally long hesitation at the other end of the phone.

"Just a minute, please."

A male voice came on the phone. "I'm Dr. Waterhouse. Can I help you?"

"Yes, I'm trying to reach Dr. Steven Clay. This is Walter Furlong."

"I'm sorry to give you the sad news, Mr. Furlong. Dr. Clay died in an automobile crash several months ago."

"Good heavens! Where did this happen?"

"On one of the parkways in New York. How did you get this number?"

"From Dr. Parkorsler," said Jerry, slurring the name. "I'm sorry to have troubled you, Dr. Warrhorse," said Jerry, slurring again.

"No trouble. Good-bye, sir."

Jerry looked up the number of the *New York Times*. He dialed and asked for Nell Arden.

"Nell? This is Jerry Marconi at *National News*. I'm a friend of Harold Gondoler."

"How is Harold? I called the hospital yesterday and they said he was doing as well as could be expected."

"He's much better."

"Can he have visitors?"

"Absolutely none. Bill Harding goes anyway."

"What can I do for you, Jerry?"

"I need two pieces of information. Both are related to the case Harold was working on so it's hush-hush. A fellow by the name of Dr. Steven Clay was killed in an automobile accident a few months ago. We need all the details. He had an associate in his practice. Dr. Godfrey Waterhouse. Is there any way to find out if Waterhouse is a member of the Harmonetics Society?"

"On the first question, Jerry, I'll dig up what we have in the morgue on Clay. As for Waterhouse, it's almost hopeless if there's no file on him. You'd have to go through every article every day on the Harmonetics Society, and even then he might never be mentioned. Anyway, I'll call you back with whatever I find. Are you at your office?"

"Yes, I'll be here all afternoon."

Jerry's intercom buzzed.

"Jon Mahaffey to see you, Jerry."

"Send him back, will you?"

Jerry thought of straightening his desk but it was hopeless. The untouched sandwich, the kosher dill pickle, and the salads could wait. He dumped the cold coffee down the sink.

Dr. Mahaffey had brought along a small head shot of Steven Clay and the bottle of pills that Jade had requested.

"Tell Jade not to take the whole bottle at one sitting," Mahaffey said. "Otherwise she'll get sugar poisoning."

Jerry laughed.

"I came in person, Jerry, because I had to talk to you about Jade's scheme. She can't go ahead with it. It's dangerous and illegal. Her friend Arnie was right: she could get twenty years in jail, and so could you and I."

"I'm getting second thoughts myself," said Jerry. "However, if we can't convince her to drop the plan, I know she'll go it alone. I can't let her do that; I'd have to help her."

"There's another way out. I'll willingly be part of the rescue squad. There's nothing criminal involved. We go to the hospital as scheduled but we leave when the rescue is achieved."

"Will Jade accept that?" asked Jerry doubtfully.

"I'm sure she will."

"Do we tell her ahead of time?"

"No, when we get there. Without our help, she can't possibly take Minden on alone. I wouldn't mind giving him a sock on the jaw but I'm against a 'permanent solution.'"

"I'm with you. Maybe Jade will see it our way later."

The phone rang.

"It's Nell Arden. I've got some of the information you wanted."

"Great, Nell, go ahead," said Jerry. He motioned Mahaffey not to leave.

"Steven Clay, age forty-six, specialist in internal medicine, was killed when his car hit a guardrail on Riverside Drive. The accident occurred at approximately 3:00 A.M. on July 14. Clay was driving and there were no other passengers. The gasoline tank exploded and the car was demolished. Clay was burned beyond recognition."

"Who identified the body?"

"His partner, Godfrey Waterhouse. Identification was made on the basis of a ring he was wearing and an examination of the bones. Clay had chipped the right ulna several years back, and Waterhouse said this was positive proof. It was Clay's car."

"Was there an inquest?"

"The coroner said Clay either had a stroke or a seizure or he was intoxicated. The accident did not occur at a curve and the car must have been going well over the speed limit."

"Did Waterhouse have any hypothesis as to Clay's accident?"

"Yes, he said Clay had had a slight heart attack the previous year. He warned Clay to slow down on his activities. He thought it might have been his heart. That closed the case."

"Anything else on Waterhouse?"

"Not a thing."

"Thanks, Nell. You've been extraordinarily helpful."

Jerry stood up, then walked four paces back and forth behind his desk, unaware that he was imitating a Harding mannerism. He relayed the information Nell had given him.

"Let me try one call, Jon, before you go," he said, thumbing through the telephone directory.

"Here it is, Harmonetics Hospital."

He dialed.

"Hello, can you connect me with Dr. Godfrey Waterhouse, please?"

"Just a minute, sir. I'll switch you to Lilac III."
A twenty-second wait.
"Lilac III, Nurses' Station."
"Dr. Godfrey Waterhouse, please."
"Sorry, sir. Dr. Waterhouse won't be in until Monday afternoon. Would you care to leave a message or may someone else help you?"
"No, thank you. I'll call back Monday."

Final Psychiatric Evaluation (Summary)

Patient: *Monte Devlin*
Physicians: *Dr. Anton Kohl*
           Dr. Esme Jennings
This is a brief summary of a 436-page report prepared by the Psychiatric Staff of the Harmonetics Hospital

Patient's name: *Monte Devlin*   Age: 29   Education: *8th grade*

Crime: *Murder and rape (11 victims, all under the age of 13)*

Environmental evaluation: *Raised in a broken home. The father deserted the mother when the patient was two years old. Thereafter the mother had four or more common-law husbands and gave birth to three more children (two boys and one girl).*

Physical condition: *Excellent, with the following exceptions: dental work needed to correct impacted wisdom teeth; calcium deposit on the shoulder which should be surgically removed.*

Mental evaluation: *Patient believes he is "God's Avenger." Acute schizophrenia diagnosed and confirmed. Patient's abnormality is expressed in the following ways:*

1. Hostility to the doctors
2. Refusal to answer questions
3. Verbal abuse of hospital staff
4. Displays of physical violence when medication is given

Conclusions: *Monte Devlin is unable to go on trial at this time. The Harmonetics staff have determined that Devlin should be given psychiatric help for no less than one year, after*

---

which another evaluation will be made. Hospital staff request the Court's permission to perform such surgery as deemed necessary. This would specifically include the extraction of the impacted wisdom teeth, removal of the calcium deposit from the shoulder, a possible tonsillectomy, and psychosurgery to rectify overfiring neurons.

Sarah Robinson and Henrietta Beale had been alerted by Senator Spriggs to get to the Harmonetics Temple on Sunday forty-five minutes before curtain time. They arrived with an hour to spare. The police had cordoned off the four blocks around the Temple. Buses, taxis, and automobiles were being rerouted. A mounted policeman directed Sarah and Henrietta to the special line for Probationaries, visitors, and newspaper reporters. A few minutes later, a van with a loudspeaker announced to latecomers that the lines had been closed; anyone not already in line who wished to attend the second White Robe ceremony should return at 3:00 P.M.

It was an orderly scene. The mounted policemen rode up and down the five separate lines, reassuring the Browns, Greens, Reds, Blues, and the laity that there was room for all. A group of men and women in blue robes were moving through the crowd selling ceremonial programs. There would be no collection at the services today; instead one could make a gift by purchasing a program for $25.

"Get four, Harry," the woman in front of Henrietta whispered to her husband. "I can resell them at $50 or $100 each. Everybody wants one."

"Four, please," said Harry to the program seller.

Henrietta and Sarah each bought one. They were handsome but simple white and gold souvenirs, eight by ten inches, with eight printed pages. Everyone seemed to be buying one either through a desire to contribute or to possess a permanent record of the White Robe ceremony. Henrietta made a rapid calculation: eight thousand people times three ceremonies (1:00 P.M., 4:00 P.M., and 7:00 P.M.) equaled $600,000.

The contents were brief. On page 1 there were exactly fifteen words:

Harmonetics Temple, New York City
The Third Sunday of October, 1982

Page 2 was equally simple:

In Memoriam

The Six Members of the White Robes
Who Have Passed On to Eternal Peace

Pearce Roberts   Michael O'Toole
Armand Stephenson   Leonidas Koutros
Katherine Gray   Jennifer Holiday

There was a full-page picture of Dr. Josiah Minden on the next page. It had been taken at the Harmonetics Temple during a sermon. The picture showed the full figure. He looked young, vigorous, and inspirational.

"God, he's handsome," Sarah whispered to Henrietta. "Do you think it would be utter madness if I signed up for a seminar with him?"

"I might too," Henrietta whispered back. "I'll talk to Elliott and I'll let you know next week."

Pages 4, 5, 6, and 7 listed the current twenty-four members of the White Robes. There was a head shot of each, then the name, and a short identification.

Page 4

Allen, Crandall
President, Allen Communications

Ames, Andy
Actor

Crane, Harper
President, Harper Crane Advertising

Dazzio, Roger
President, Amalgamated Metal Workers

Page 5

Fronzhold, Heinrich, M.D.
Director, Harmonetics Hospital

Johnson, Stacy
President, Federated Union of Textile Workers

Kent, Byron
President, Kentwood Mining Corp.

Kohl, Anton, M.D.
Neurosurgeon

298

Edgebrook, Margaret
Chairman, Board of Trustees,
Harmonetics University

Koutros, Marcella
Philanthropist

Emley, Robert
Governor of New Jersey

La Mause, Lila
Actress

Page 6

Little, H. Bracewell
Supreme Court Justice
United States of America

Page 7

Spriggs, Robert T.
U.S. Senator, New York

McDonald, Francis X. (Ph.D.)
Religious teacher

Stuart, Henley
Judge, N.Y. Supreme Court

Matthews, Minnie
Philanthropist

Tandy, Frederick
President, Conoil, Inc.

Mulhern, Sean
President, International
Truckers' Union

Tibbett, J. N.
Attorney

Rawlins, Edgar
U.S. Senator, California

Trotter, Clarence
Professor of Government
Harvard University

Rockwell, Marshall, III
President, Rockwell Stores

Zindler, Reginald (Ph.D.)
Author

The last page was entitled "Happiness." A picture of a nursery. A tot in a playpen, another going down a slide. A couple of three-year-olds sitting in front of a stack of blocks. In the foreground, center, a woman in her late seventies wearing a Harmonetics robe. She was holding an infant and kissing the top of the baby's head. Henrietta looked at the smile on the woman's face and thought the caption was justified.

"This is delicious," said Sarah after she had thumbed through her program. "I know nine of the White Gowns personally and," she whispered conspiratorially, "I've slept with two of them."

Henrietta laughed. "Which two?"

"Robbie Spriggs, of course, and Harper Crane. That was years ago. Harper was indefatigable, day or night, drunk or sober. He was ten years younger than I and quite adorable. He didn't have a dime, poor dear. He was twenty-five and had just been hired by Byron Kent at an absolute pittance."

"He's come a long way in thirty years," commented Henrietta.

"He made a good solid marriage," said Sarah. "His wife, Poppy, is a Rockwell. Poppy's cousin Rose married Judge Henley Stuart. Rose has no clothes sense and no money but she's tons of fun. Henley is a terrible bore. Can you believe Henley's a White Robe? So is Marshall Rockwell. It's quite a nice list of people."

Sarah flipped through her program. "Look at page 2," she said. "The only one I haven't heard of is Michael O'Toole. Who on earth could he be? Pearce Roberts was a good friend of my brother. His mother was an Edgebrook, and Pearce was utterly divine. He was President of the Wild Birds Society for years and years."

Henrietta half-listened as Sarah plunged into the genealogy and marital history of the social White Robes. "Fred Tandy's new wife, Bitsy, is only twenty-three. Have you seen her? She's got absolutely marvelous cheekbones and a sensational figure. Fred must be at least fifty-eight. No one sees Coco Tandy any more. She was desolated when Fred asked her for the divorce. I hear Poppy lent her her villa in Nice. Poor Coco, but she brought it on herself. The more Fred played around, the more Coco ate. I hear she got up to 250 pounds. Last year she bought all those incredibly delicate Venetian chairs at the Princesse de Sévigny auction, and she couldn't sit on any of them.

"We saw Bracewell and Emily Little in Palm Beach. Emily brought him there to get some sun—he's been so sick, you know. Naturally Morna Campbell came with them; she and Emily are inseparable. Everyone knows about them except Bracewell. It's been going on for at least four years.

"Oh, Henrietta, if you could have seen Harper Crane when he was twenty-five. He was absolutely smashing. All the women adored him and he adored all of them, although he was quite selective. He said there was something special about rich, social women—their hair, their perfume, the way they carried themselves. He was quite right, you know. He had a mad affair with Coco when she was twenty-nine and a size 6, but I think his big passion was Alicia Koutros. Leonidas wouldn't hear of it: his daughter was going to marry into one of the Greek shipping firms or never marry at all."

Henrietta had tuned out her friend. She knew Poor Coco, she had heard about Bitsy, she had been at a luncheon with Emily and Morna, and she had met various members of the Rockwell family. She also had had a brief affair with Harper Crane; it was the one romance in her life she had regretted. The only point in common that Harper and I shared, she thought, was for a short moment when we were both in love with Harper. He could never pass a mirror without glancing in it and what he saw there always pleased him. He had dedicated his life to making love to size 6 women who smelled of French fragrances, but the big passion of his life was not Alicia Koutros; it was Harper Crane.

They had reached the Temple doors. The lines were still orderly but the noise level increased as they entered the inner doors. The organist was playing a Bach toccata and fugue with the fury of a deaf Calliope. The intricate arrangement of reed sounds throbbed through the organ pipes, which extended the full four stories of the hall. The organist stomped on the pedals, pulled out the stops, and played the Bach composition with abandon. Sarah's voice was mercifully drowned by the sounds of oboe, trumpet, and bassoon emanating from the pipes. She and Henrietta found seats in one of the last rows, close to the far wall.

The lights began to dim. The organist's fingers once more touched the keyboard but this time it was a well-tempered clavichord. The 8,000 devotees, subdued by the softer music, were silent or spoke only in whispers. So many of my friends, thought Henrietta, are active members of the Harmonetics Society. They need to feel useful and beautiful and young, they adore rituals and ceremony, they want to be loved by everyone (including those they would never have over for dinner) and they desire promotions and recognition in the form of dignified robes. What's so wrong with that, she asked herself. Nothing at all, unless the founder-leader of the group is a rogue. Good God, she wondered, how many cults have leaders who walk on cloven hooves.

The organ music softly ended. Through the loudspeaker system came the smooth voice of the announcer:

"Fellow members of the Harmonetics Society . . . Dr. Josiah Minden!"

Spotlights shone at the rear of the hall. The beams were focused on a door in the far wall. Everyone rose. The door, six feet from Sarah and Henrietta, opened. For once Sarah could not complain about her seats. Standing almost close enough to touch was Josiah Minden himself. He was wearing a flowing white robe, the hood pulled up to make a cowl. His eyes flicked over those nearest to him. He looked like an angel of God, kind, strong, and infinitely powerful. Sarah gave a small gasp and extended a trembling hand toward her friend. Henrietta, too, felt the dynamic appeal of this bearded leader whose dark eyes had, for a brief second, looked directly into hers. Slowly he walked toward the center aisle, and from there with measured step he moved toward the podium far in the distance.

"Crandall Allen . . ." said the voice in the loudspeaker.

The czar of the communications world stood in the doorway nearest Sarah and Henrietta. The shaggy eyebrows, enormous nose, and flabby jowls of this fierce defender of free enterprise were lent a dignity by the simplicity of the white robe and the hood that covered his massive dome. He walked with the same measured step as Josiah Minden, following his path at a distance of thirty feet.

"Andy Ames . . ."

The comedian stepped into the hall, pausing at the doorway. His button eyes were solemn and the animated mouth was in repose. He looked tender and gentle, not at all a comic figure. The white garment endowed him with an aura of sadness. The small figure looked touching and ennobled as he made his way toward the center aisle.

"Harper Crane . . ."

The man who stood six feet from Henrietta had the pampered look of the shaved, oiled, massaged, and well-fed successful American entrepreneur. Henrietta thought she smelled the faint odor of a masculine cologne. The heavy, soft face with its extra folds of skin had the pious expression of a medieval prelate. He rings false, thought Henrietta, but perhaps it's because I know him so well.

"Roger Dazzio . . ."

One by one the elite members of the Harmonetics Society

stepped through the doorway and into the Temple. Fierce Roger Dazzio, born in Appalachia, frame undernourished, lungs black with coal dust, arms and shoulders strong from a world where brawn determined one's position in the ranks. Frail Margaret Edgebrook with her long, beaked, patrician English nose, just as undernourished but from choice rather than necessity, her mind a clutter of accumulated names from the world of grand opera, the Ballet Russe, the symphony, and the museum. Governor Robert Emley, who had acquired his smile while running for president of the high school student body and who had recently smiled his way through a New Jersey landslide election. Here they were, from glowering Dr. Fronzhold to folksy Minnie Matthews, small Byron Kent to towering Senator Spriggs, arrogant Marshall Rockwell to egalitarian Sean Mulhern.

The last white-robed figure climbed the six stairs to the dais. The members of the White Gowns stood by their chairs, facing the endless rows of hushed, respectful fellow members of the Society. Josiah Minden advanced to the center front. The great moment had arrived.

"Please open the doors of the Temple," said Dr. Minden. His voice was low but it thundered through the hall.

The fifteen-foot doors were opened. Ever so slowly a figure entered, an infinitesimal figure to those in the front rows.

"Who is it?" "An actor?" "The Governor?" "Does anyone know who it is?"

"My God!" said Sarah. "It's Franklin Parson, Mary Hamble's son-in-law."

Excerpt from Presentation Ceremony by Dr. Josiah Minden
at the Harmonetics Temple, New York City
October 18, 1982

No member of the Harmonetics Society is better than any other member. The novitiate who has just received his Blue Robe is as valuable and as precious to all as the older member who wears the Brown Robe. The color of the gown denotes service; each Presentation is a recognition of contributions to the aims of the group.

The members of the White Robes are small in number. They are selected on the basis of their ability to guide and lead as well as on their probity, integrity, and dedication. Our newest disciple is a man who stands at the top of his profession, an exemplar of familial devotion, a leader whose morality and way of life can serve as a model to all of us.

Franklin Robert Parson is a gifted architect but, far more, he is a man of sensitivity, a humanitarian, and an idealist. It is with the greatest of pleasure that I present him with the White Robe and welcome him as an associate in the echelon of our most honored members.

Jade was finishing the last of her hospital tasks on Sunday. Nurse Ellen Dixon had been a trial: she did not need Jade to wheel the medication cart, Jade was not to change the bedding or bathe any of the patients, and the only way Jade could make herself useful was by sweeping the Nurses' Lounge, washing her hands, brewing coffee, washing her hands, and scrubbing bedpans.

Jade had reached the hospital at 7:15 A.M. Nurse Dixon had already filled the hypodermics and arranged the potions and pills in their paper cups. She would administer them by herself, she informed Jade. Promptly at 8:00 A.M.

Would Nurse Dixon like some help? No!

Could Jade sweep the patients' rooms? No!

Should Jade answer the phone? Well-l-l, that would be all right if she didn't screw up the messages.

Hey, Ellen, can I make you a fresh pot of coffee? Well-l-l, yes, thank you.

Ellen Dixon just missed being pretty. Her features were regular but her hair was overcoiffed, her eyebrows over-plucked, and her face too mobile. She moved her mouth and eyebrows continuously to express disgust, pleasure, amusement, anger, or interest. After saying "Well-l-l," she would raise her eyebrows and twist her lips upward to indicate "doubt."

Nurse Dixon finished her coffee at 7:47. She disappeared into the bathroom at 7:50. Jade rushed into the Medication Room at 7:51, carrying the coffeepot. She measured one-third part coffee to two-thirds part water in a fresh thimble cup for Mary Hamble. She switched pills for both Mary Hamble and Steven Clay. Then she took out a new hypodermic for Dr. Clay and put the old one in her purse. She emerged from the Medication Room at 7:54 and returned the coffeepot to the Nurses' Lounge. She sat by the telephone at the Nurses' Station and stared down the hall. Four minutes later Nurse Dixon, walking briskly, exited from the bathroom and went straight to the Medication Room. At 7:59 Ellen Dixon pushed her cart into Room 1.

Nurse Dixon and the orderlies handled all the requirements of the patients until noon. At 12:00 on the dot, one of the orderlies brought Ellen Dixon a ham on rye and a Coke.

"May I join you?" asked Jade, pulling a small package of peanut butter crackers out of her purse.

"Sure," said Ellen. "Pull up a chair."

Nurse Dixon sprawled back in her chair and relaxed. "I'm taking ten minutes off. If anyone dies between now and 12:10, that's their problem."

"You're fantastic," said Jade.

"What do you mean?"

"You're organized. I hate it when people can't keep to a schedule."

"Damn right," said Ellen.

"The patients get their breakfast at 7:00, medication at 8:00, and lunch at 11:00."

"Then dinner at 5:00 and medication at 5:45," Nurse Dixon added. "Everyone's bedded down and asleep by 6:30. I leave at 7:00 P.M."

"That hardly leaves you any time for fun."

"Oh, I have some fun," said Nurse Dixon obliquely.

"I know this great guy named Arnie," said Jade. "He's a sports nut. We go to the basketball games and the hockey games and the fights . . ."

Jade stopped. Ellen Dixon wasn't listening; her eyes were staring blankly and her mind was elsewhere.

"Do you go with anyone special?" asked Jade.

"What? Oh, yes I do."

"Is he attractive?"

"Very. He's a Greek god." Nurse Dixon's mind had returned from its trip.

"What does he look like?"

"Well-l-l, he has curly, dark-brown hair and a beautiful wide mouth. He's always sitting in the sun so his skin is a lovely bronze. The skin is perfect, all over his body. He hasn't got a blemish. It's incredible."

"What color are his eyes?"

"They're a greenish-gray. Little flecks of green. They're like the marbles we used to play with when we were children. He's fastidious. I love clean men, and he's the cleanest I've ever seen. His toenails are as immaculate as his fingernails. I get sick when I see long, untended toenails. His are perfect, just the right length. No bunions or calluses. He's good-looking in clothes but he's like a Greek god in the buff."

Ellen Dixon proceeded to describe his fingers, his neck muscles, and his shoulder blades. She had reached his chest when Jade looked at her watch.

"Excuse me, Ellen, but it's 12:10."

"Oh, thank you for reminding me. Good heavens, I lost all track of time."

"Tell me more about him later, will you? He sounds divine!"

"I will, Jade." Nurse Dixon got up.

"What should I do now, Ellen?"

"Well-l-l, here's our order sheet. Call Hospital Supplies and tell them we need this stuff today. Then you can give the Nurses' Lounge a good cleaning."

"Good. I will," said Jade cheerfully.

After Nurse Dixon disappeared, Jade called Jerry.

"You have to phone her exactly at 3:45," said Jade. "I'm going to need two minutes only, maybe only a minute and a half. Can you arrange a disturbance on the line so she can't hear? You've got to keep her occupied while I fix the medications . . . Yes, I'm fine, Jerry . . . Don't worry, everything is sailing along . . . You, too, Jerry."

Jade put the orders through Hospital Supplies and then began on the Nurses' Lounge. She vacuumed, polished, and scrubbed. The room was reasonably neat before; when she finished it was spotless.

At 3:45, when the phone rang, Jade was mopping the hall.

She was three feet from the Medication Room, just behind the Nurses' Station.

"Hello? Operator, I can't hear you. Hello, hello?" said Nurse Dixon.

Jade slipped into the room. She was back in the hall in less than ninety seconds.

"Operator, I've already hung up twice and you've called me back twice," said Ellen irately. "Tell your party to try the call later." She slammed down the phone. It rang again four seconds later.

"You want me to handle it?" asked Jade.

"Well-l-l, okay, go ahead."

"Hello?" said Jade, picking up the phone.

"Honey, are you okay?" asked Jerry.

"Operator, I can't hear you. Whom do you wish to speak to?"

"Call me when you get home tonight," said Jerry.

"There's nobody by that name here," said Jade. "Try the Reception Desk." She hung up.

"Who did they want?" asked Ellen.

"Somebody named Steven Clay."

"Never heard of him," said Ellen indifferently.

At 5:00 P.M. the dinner trays arrived.

"Can I help?" asked Jade.

"No, you might make a mistake. Just listen for the phone."

At 5:45 Nurse Dixon started the evening medication. Jade guarded the phone. At 7:00 P.M. the night nurse arrived and Nurse Dixon got ready to leave.

"If you give me ten minutes, I'll come with you," Jade said to her.

"Sorry, I can't wait," said Ellen. "I've got a date."

"Have a good time and I'll see you tomorrow," said Jade.

"Okay, and thanks for helping, Jade. You're a peach."

As soon as Nurse Dixon left, Jade boldly walked into Room 1. The night nurse either didn't care or didn't know the difference. Jade looked at the sleeping patient, waited a minute, and went into Room 2. The night nurse was busily reading the evening paper. Jade skipped a few rooms until she got to 16.

"Dr. Clay!" she said.

He opened both eyes.

"How are you feeling?" Jade asked.

"Afraid. When the nurse came in with the hypodermic, I thought it might be the real thing."

"Your eye looks better. Do you have a bad heart, Dr. Clay?"

"No, my heart's fine."

"Have you ever had any kind of a seizure?"

"No."

"By the way, I saw a picture of you when you were in medical school. Your nose looked much nicer then. So did your eye."

"So you know I'm Steven Clay?"

"Yes. Did your associate, Dr. Waterhouse, ever practice at the Harmonetics Hospital?"

"No. Neither did I."

"Then how did you have your run-in with Dr. Fronzhold?"

"The same way as Dr. Jean de Moraille. God knows where he is now."

"What happened?"

"He was my mentor at Lenox Hill. A hell of a doctor when he was young. He had joined the Harmonetics Society because he supported their attitude toward older people. He had a few patients at Lenox Hill when he was still on the staff. He also had some patients, not many, at the Harmonetics Hospital."

"Did he like the hospital?"

"At first he did. Then he had a major fight with the hospital administration. He'd brought in a patient for varicose veins. Suddenly he was told he was off the case and another doctor was named the attending physician."

"Can a hospital do that?"

Clay shook his head. "They did. They claimed the patient had developed complications and needed a specialist."

"Is that why Dr. Jean de Moraille had the fight with Dr. Fronzhold?"

"No. The patient's son-in-law also told Jean he was off the case. Jean's battle with Fronzhold was over something far more serious—the death of Jennifer Holiday."

"What happened?"

"Jean found out his name was signed to Mrs. Holiday's death certificate. He hadn't seen her in a year. He was furious. I walked into his office when he was on the phone with Fronzhold." Clay paused for breath.

"Then what did he do?"

"I don't know. I never saw him again. A few days later I dropped by his office. I was told he had decided to retire. He was moving out west."

"Did you believe he had retired?"

"Yes, for a few days. No one had his address. They said he was traveling. He'd send a permanent address later."

"What made you suspicious? Was it the phony death certificate?"

"Yes. I decided to phone Fronzhold."

"Why didn't you go to the police or the AMA?"

"Doctors don't do that kind of thing to doctors. I thought there might be a reasonable explanation. Fronzhold was very cordial on the phone. A simple misunderstanding, he said. He asked me to come see him."

"And you went. Didn't you tell anyone you were going or what your suspicions were?"

"I told my associate, Dr. Waterhouse. He's probably dead now."

"He's very much alive. He's affiliated with the Harmonetics Hospital."

"He's WHAT?"

"Your car was smashed and burned the night you disappeared. Waterhouse identified your body. He said you had a bad heart."

Steven Clay's face was distorted with rage. He picked up his arm and clenched his huge fist as though he were getting ready to smash it into the face of the enemy.

"God in heaven," he croaked, "my best friend put me here."

Clay tossed on his hospital bed, punching the air futilely. He looked like a madman, the killer that Fronzhold had described.

"He consigned me to hell," he rasped.

"You've got a few friends, Steven," Jade said.

Steven dropped his arm. The rage ebbed as he stared into Jade's big, sad eyes. He was still breathing hard and the fist was clenched.

"You went to see Fronzhold?" asked Jade.

"Yes." Steven's voice was calmer, almost normal. "He offered me a cup of tea. Then he talked to me about the Harmonetics Hospital, the great facilities, the marvelous progress. He said he wanted doctors like me on the staff. He mentioned the great men involved in the Harmonetics movement. He said he would be happy to sponsor me. I asked him about the death certificate. A simple mistake, he said. How could the wrong name be signed, I asked. Some one had signed Jean de Moraille's name. I wanted to know who had signed it and, I added, what had happened to Jean."

"And then?"

"I don't remember anything clearly. I can't remember if Fronzhold answered my questions. I woke up hours or maybe days later. The nurses kept me drugged; my vocal chords were paralyzed. I would see Fronzhold come into the room. I tried to shout, and no sound came out. I lived in terror and hatred. I wished myself dead."

"Steven, I've got to go. I'll remember. We'll take care of Dr. Waterhouse, you and I."

Jade bent down and kissed him.

The night nurse was still reading her newspaper. Jade walked down the hall to Mary Hamble's room, poking open several doors on her way.

"Mrs. Hamble, it's Jade."

"Oh, my dear, I'm so glad you're here."

"Did you do what I suggested?"

"Yes. I started after the night nurse came on duty."

"She didn't come in your room?"

"No. She never does."

"How many times did you get up?"

"Six. At first I could only stand. I got so tired. The second time I walked to the end of the bed and back."

"How about the sixth time?"

"I made it to the door. Then I walked around the room."

"I knew you could do it. Don't forget to practice again tonight."

"I will, dear. Thank you so much."

Jade walked up the corridor to the Nurses' Station.

"It's 7:15," she announced. "I think I'll go home."

The nurse looked up from her newspaper. "Everyone resting peacefully?" she asked.

"Yes, it's been a very quiet day," said Jade.

"The Tomorrow Man"
Excerpt from a book by Harper Crane,
President, Harper Crane Advertising

The Tomorrow Man is the corporate chief, the college president, the foundation director, the U.S. Senator, and the Supreme Court Justice of the 1990s. Today he is filled only with ambition and hope. But he is observant, conscientious, and dedicated. He is a good listener and a selective culler of facts and theories. He will reach the pinnacle of his field because he not only has the basic educational skills and practical training; he also has the ability to "sell" himself in a tough buyer's market.

The Tomorrow Man could be Joe Brown, Bill Smith, John Jones—or you. He is a student of life. He looks for the qualities that make for success and he incorporates them in his personality and character. This is his portrait:

He is a hard worker. He puts in far more than the required number of hours at his office, and often he brings his work home with him. He is both meticulous and imaginative. He is not capable of shoddy work nor will he neglect any phase of his obligations.

He neither jumps to premature conclusions nor does he drag his feet in the decision-making process.

He is neither argumentative nor disputatious. If his immediate superior makes a decision that, on the surface, seems arbitrary or unwise, he thinks about the positive aspects of the decision before expressing any negative comments.

He is not a show-off. He does not lord it over his staff nor does he dress more expensively, dine more extravagantly, or buy bigger cars than his superiors.

He has a happy attitude. He never groans at the work load, complains about his salary or status, or beefs about the conditions at the office. No one hears him gripe about management.

He is neither a hippy nor a radical. He believes in democratic government and he knows the United States offers more justice and freedom than any other country in the world. He is proud to be an American.

He seeks to enlarge his circle of acquaintances but he is discriminate. He does not deliberately socialize downward nor does he push to develop friendships with those on a higher social level. Ordinarily his upward mobility will come through business, social and athletic clubs, and through such philosophical groups as the Harmonetics Society. Here he will have social and intellectual exchanges with achievers in many fields— bankers, attorneys, corporate officers, judges, architects, publishers, authors, and statesmen.

He has a solid, happy home and a good marriage but his wife is not his slave. She has both a mind and a life of her own. Although her family and her home come first, she enjoys people and she often takes an active part in school projects, club activities, and civic affairs. She is interested in current events, the arts, and her husband's career. She does not espouse causes or political movements without careful consideration of the effect on her family. Her career is just as important as her husband's: she has the responsibility for the everyday organization of the household and the continual supervision of the health and education of the children.

Seldom does a man reach the top of his profession without the complete support of his wife. She may have a career if she chooses but it should not be her primary goal: she does not try to rival her husband in earnings and honors, nor should her business associates become more important than husband or children. She can participate in sports and be active in the tennis or country club. She too can join such sociophilosophical organizations as the Harmonetics Society where she will meet other like-minded people.

Missy Tompkins had been staying with Caroline Ryder ever since the two ladies had paid a call on Betty McLaughlin. Bill

Harding had arranged for their continuous protection. As a result a Rappaport Agency guard was stationed downstairs and another was on duty in the foyer by Caroline Ryder's front door. He was seated in a leather chair, eating a piece of cake and drinking some coffee that his two new friends had made for him. He had been on the New York City Police Force for twenty years and, during his tours of duty, he had had many a fine free meal. None compared with the cuisine of Mrs. Ryder.

The doorbell rang.

The guard stood up, put his hand on his holster, and cautiously opened the door.

"I'm Dr. Jon Mahaffey," said the tall, sandy-haired man with the small black satchel.

"Identification?"

Mahaffey produced his driver's license.

"How do you do, Dr. Mahaffey," said Caroline. "Bill Harding told us you were coming. This is my friend Missy Tompkins and this nice young man is Patrick O'Malley of the Rappaport Agency."

Mahaffey stared. Caroline looked a good sixty-eight or seventy and her friend Missy, so wizened and wrinkled, seemed at least eighty-five. The "nice young man" was probably fifty.

"Er, how do you do?" said Mahaffey, shaking their hands.

"How much of the stuff did you bring?" asked Missy.

"What's that?" Mahaffey asked.

"Is there enough for thirty cookies or sixty cookies or what?"

"Well, I, uh, maybe we better sit down and go over the situation," said Mahaffey.

They entered the living room. Caroline politely ushered the visitor to a faded peach silk love seat. Underneath were two petit-point footstools. Mahaffey sat down, facing the fake fireplace with the flickering glass embers.

"We plan to make the cookies tonight," said Caroline. "We'll carry them with us to the hospital tomorrow. Bill Harding said they should be strong enough to knock out the nurses for a good four hours."

"Yes," agreed Mahaffey nervously, "but one has to be extremely cautious with the quantity of drugs used. If you put in too little it could be highly dangerous for all of us, and if you use too much you could kill the nurses."

"That's why I asked you how much you brought. Enough for thirty cookies or sixty cookies?" asked Missy.

"Perhaps I could save you some trouble. My wife could bake the cookies and insert the required dosage. I'll then have the cookies delivered to you early tomorrow morning."

"He thinks we're a couple of dopes," said Missy to Caroline. Mahaffey's face reddened.

"I might be so senile I'd put in a cup of poison instead of a teaspoon. Maybe our brains would get so addled we'd put in a teaspoon of flour instead of a cup," Missy said, her eyes dancing like an old witch.

"He's right, Missy. I might put in the eggshells and throw out the eggs," retorted Caroline haughtily.

"We might turn on the stove and set fire to ourselves," Missy added gleefully.

"Or we'll forget what we did and eat all the cookies ourselves," said Caroline disdainfully.

Jon Mahaffey stood up. He put his hand in his pocket, pulled out a small bottle, and placed it on the coffee table near Caroline.

"Ladies, I apologize. I've made a fool of myself. There's enough here for thirty cookies."

Caroline's hauteur disappeared. "Thank you, Jon," she said.

"What do we do," said Missy, "if one nurse eats one cookie only and another one gorges herself?"

"That's a problem," said Jon. "Let's hope everyone has at least two. Don't let anyone eat more than four or five."

"If one of the nurses is on a diet, we're dead," said Missy. "Have you got something we could slip in their coffee?"

"I believe I do," said Jon. He opened his black satchel and took out a green bottle. "Two drops per cup. It's tasteless. That's for the noncookie eaters or those who only eat one."

"Thank you, Jon," said Caroline sweetly. "And now may I offer you something to drink?"

"How about a Scotch?" asked Missy.

"I will if you will," Jon replied. "May I make the drinks?"

"Certainly," said Missy. "I take mine on the rocks with a twist."

At 9:00 P.M. a 1980 Impala belonging to Bill Harding pulled into the garage at East 89th Street.

"We're only going to be an hour," said Jerry Marconi to the attendant.

"Don't you see the sign 'Full'? Can't you guys even read?" The attendant, looking up from his hard porn novel, was exasperated.

"I thought I might double-park in the back. I'll leave the keys in the car and we'll probably be back in thirty minutes," said Jerry, extending a $10 bill.

"Okay," said the attendant sullenly, pocketing the money. "Be sure you leave the keys."

"I'll wait for you here," said Jade, getting out of the car.

The attendant watched Jerry manipulate the car along the crowded garage lane.

"How much does it cost to park here by the month?" Jade asked the attendant.

"We ain't got no room. We're full."

"We're thinking of moving into the building. Would it be long before a space becomes available?"

The attendant's eyes stopped following Jerry. He stared at Jade. She was wearing her green elastic jump suit that hid the bruises on her neck and arms. She moved toward the garage entrance and looked out toward the street. The attendant examined her butt and her legs.

"When would you move in?" he asked.

Jade turned around. "The first of next month. My name's Spacey Nussbaum and I'm a professional bike rider."

"Oh, yeah? You Jewish?"

"Yup."

"I'm Jewish too. I might get you a space by the first. It's $125 a month, you park your own car."

"That sounds okay. What's your name?"

"Morris Katz. The tenants call me Morrie. I never heard of no Jewish lady bike riders."

"My mother doesn't like it. She wants me to go back to school and become a teacher."

"Education is very important," said Morris.

"I'm a high-school dropout," said Jade.

"Mrs. Nussbaum, I'm going to give you some advice."

"Please call me Spacey."

"Spacey, go back to school and finish. I got two sons, they're both in college."

"What are they going to do when they get out?"

"One's going on to dental school. The other's gonna be a CPA. The dentist, he goes with a nice girl, she's a nurse, a real RN."

"You live in the city, Morrie?"

"Nah, we got a nice little place in Brooklyn."

"The boys live at home?"

"The dentist does. The CPA stays with my wife's brother, a block from the college."

"I was born on the West Side, Central Park West. My parents still live there."

"Go back to school, Spacey. You'll never regret it."

Jerry walked up the ramp toward them.

"Morrie, this is my husband, Herman Nussbaum."

"Hello, Morrie," said Jerry, putting out his hand.

"You don't look Jewish," said Morris.

When they were on the street again, Jerry pulled a small piece of metal out of his pocket and showed it to Jade.

"What's that?"

"The distributor from Beth's car."

"Did you get her sticker?"

"Yup, that's what took so long." From his other pocket he pulled out a windshield sticker. It said "Iris: Marple."

Bill Harding marched down the hospital corridor.

"Where do you think you're going?" asked the stout, matronly Head Nurse sharply.

Harding did not break his stride.

"Visiting hours are over! You're to leave this hospital at once," snapped the nurse.

Harding reached Gondoler's room. He knocked on the door.

"Harold?" he said softly.

"Come in, Bill."

Harding entered, the nurse two steps behind him.

"How dare you defy the hospital rules?" she said. "I'm going to report you if you don't leave immediately."

Harding wheeled around, his hooded eyes staring at her angry face. "Are you going to give me a demerit?" he asked softly.

"The patient is not permitted to have any visitors. I will not have my corridor disturbed. You are to leave right now!"

"How are you feeling, Harold?"

"I said right now!" the nurse shouted.

"I'd feel a lot better if I were out of here," Harold replied.

"I'm going to call the hospital administrator, you . . . you . . ." the nurse sputtered.

"Suppose I pick you up tomorrow?"

"Great. I'll need a little help. I can't walk yet."

The nurse stormed out of the room.

"Tomorrow is D-Day," said Harding.

"What's the schedule?"

"Franklin Parson will be arrested at 11:00 A.M. We've alerted your friend, Nell Arden, at the *New York Times*. She'll be outside Parson's office with a photographer from 10:00 A.M. on."

"That's perfect. What about Mary Hamble?"

"The plan is to sneak her out as a Blue Robe. There's not much risk unless a nurse takes a careful look. It's unlikely, we think. The dangerous part is getting Steven Clay out. He's immobile. If the nurses see what's happening, the entire hospital will be on alert."

"Will our guys get in trouble if they're caught?"

"Yes, bad trouble. We can't get any help from the police: they can't march into the hospital without a court order. Once it goes that far, a loyal Harmonetics member in the police department or the judiciary could inform Josiah Minden or Fronzhold. That would be the end of Steven Clay."

"Doesn't Jade have any of the conversations on tape?"

"Only one with Steven. It won't help him if he has psychosurgery."

"So the plan is to drug the nurses. What if a nurse or a doctor from another floor walks into Iris?"

"Jade assures me she can handle it."

"You're not going ahead with the original Minden plan?"

"No. We're all against it, except for Jade. The worst that will happen to Minden tomorrow is a busted nose or a couple of missing teeth."

"Does Jade know her plan is canceled?"

"No. She won't find out until Mahaffey, Jerry, and Arnie get there. There won't be anything she can do about it."

"I'm sorry to say, Bill, but Minden will probably walk out of this scot free."

"I agree. There's no way to connect him with Mary Hamble or Steven Clay. Jade can't touch him on the rape. If that goon who arranged for Roger's murder says he got his instructions from Josiah, whom will the District Attorney believe—the goon or Minden? We may never find out who shot you and who drugged Martha."

"The Society will never be as influential again but it will probably survive."

"Yes, as a small sect in bad odor."

"Bill, is there any hope for Martha?"

Harding walked over to the window and looked into the night. He could see the street and building lights across the river and the big neon sign advertising Pearl-Wick Hampers.

"Mahaffey thinks there's no chance."

Harding stood with his back to Gondoler. He had a sudden, sad picture of Martha, a cigarette dangling from the corner of her mouth, ashes falling on her blouse, one hand trying to pat down her cowlicks, and the other brushing off the ashes. Martha with a smudge on her nose or a coffee stain on her purse. Martha putting an ashtray on her lap, then knocking it off accidentally. Martha on the phone taking notes, the inevitable cigarette hanging from her lips.

"There he is!" said the Head Nurse triumphantly, pointing to Harding. He turned slowly. The nurse had returned. She stood with legs apart, both hands on hips. Beside her were two strong young doctors in white jackets.

"If you don't leave this room at once, these doctors will physically assist you out," the nurse said in a firm, loud voice.

"If he leaves, I leave," said Harold, pushing himself up on his elbow.

"Oh, no you don't," replied the nurse. "You will remain here until your doctor authorizes your release."

"I'm going right now, with or without your authorization," said Harold.

"Over my dead body!" said the nurse.

"If you keep him here against his will," said Harding, "I'll have a warrant for the arrest of all three of you within the hour. The charge will be kidnapping."

The two doctors looked at each other. They turned around and walked out the door.

"Come back here!" the nurse yelled at their retreating backs.

"Go away, you bully," Harding said to her.

She stood sputtering, helpless. "Humph," she snorted. One final glare meant to wither Bill Harding, then she stalked out with the air of a victorious German general.

"That nurse is the product of her victims," said Harding. "She's allowed to tyrannize because the patients never fight back."

"I want to get out in the morning, Bill."

"You will, Harold."

(Reprinted by permission of the *New York Daily News*)
October 19, 1982

Leaders of Social World Mingle with Political Notables at Harmonetics White Robe Affair

Yesterday Franklin Robert Parson was elected to the White Robes, the highest order of the Harmonetics Society (see Section 1, page 1, for the complete story). Notables of society attended the function but, for once, we cannot report on their gowns or their jewelry. At most we can say that Bitsy Tandy's sensational figure was still in evidence despite the simple brown robe that covered her elegant dimensions. The fabulous Bitsy attended the ceremonies with lovely Emily Little (wife of Supreme Court Justice Bracewell Little) and her close friend Morna Campbell. All three ladies were seated in the first row of the Brown Robe section.

We spoke to Poppy Crane who looked simply marvelous after a summer of water-skiing on the Mediterranean. Two nights ago she attended Odile de Guermont's Autumn in Paris Ball. Husband Harper Crane was called back to New York on business, so Poppy's last-minute escort was Fernando Montes, the popular young art critic of Paris Match. Poppy and Fernando were joined at the ball by Marshall Rockwell III (Poppy's father) and Marshall's bride of four months, the heavenly Antoinette Le Blanc. Antoinette, Poppy said, is enciente and hoping for twins.

Clarissa Kent was surrounded by admirers both before and after the ceremony. She and husband Byron Kent have one of the best marriages in the city. He adores her and she is wild for him. Clarissa sat with Alicia Koutros who, we hear, is currently getting the big rush from famed neurosurgeon Dr. Anton Kohl.

The ceremony was simple and inspiring. We couldn't take our eyes off Margaret Edgebrook, one of the four women who currently hold the Harmonetics Society's highest honor, the White Robe. Mrs. Edgebrook, looking as beautiful as she did in 1925 when she was first presented to society, had flown in from Gstaad where she maintains a small chalet. She will spend the next two months in New York and Palm Beach, where she will visit the Arthur Popples. Then back to Switzerland for the winter skiing. Mrs. Edgebrook no longer skis herself but she adores the snow and the ambiance of Gstaad. Her guests in November will be Sarah and Edward Robinson. Sarah, we hear, is one of the Harmonetics Society's newest recruits. She went to the ceremony with one of our great favorites, the charming, witty Henrietta Beale.

Other well-known personalities who participated in the ceremony were popular New Jersey Governor Robert Emley, Senator Robert T. Spriggs (New York's most eligible bachelor), distinguished New York Supreme Court Judge Henley Stuart, and, last but certainly not least, Broadway's darling, Lila La Mause.

Monday
D-Day

5:30 A.M. A night nurse opened the door of Harold Gondoler's room and switched on the light.

"Are you awake?" she asked cheerfully.

"I am now," he replied.

5:30 A.M. The radio alarm went off to the sound of trumpets. It was Rimski-Korsakov's *Scheherazade*. "Shit," said Jade as she turned off the dial. "Shit," she said as she staggered out of bed. "Shit, shit," she moaned as she staggered into the kitchen to turn on the coffee. "Oh, crap," she sighed as she staggered into the bathroom to take a shower. The bruises on her body still looked ugly. One breast had turned purple. There was a terrible pain in her groin that she had not felt earlier. She closed her eyes and the scene of the attack came back vividly: the heavy breathing of Josiah as he held her throat with one hand and pummeled her breasts and stomach with the other. The crack on her cheek and the twisting of her neck. The horrible wrench as he opened her legs. The hand holding the rock, ready to smash it into her face. The shameful crawling out of the room.

Jade came out of the shower, set the radio alarm in the bedroom for 8:00 A.M. to make sure Arnie got up, then poured herself a cup of coffee. She took a couple of pills Jon Mahaffey had given her and got dressed: a turtleneck under her gray Probationary gown and her motorcycle glasses. By the door she picked up the materials she had spread out the previous evening. Baby pictures from her album for Nurse Charlene Calderwood, a *World Tennis* issue with a color story on Fort Lauderdale for Nurse Jackie Volts, and a sensational shot of a Punk Group rock artist for Nurse Ellen Dixon. Her pills and hypodermics were in her purse. She was fully prepared.

6:30 A.M. Jerry Marconi awoke with a start. Thank God it was only a nightmare. A creature, perhaps a huge black bat, was circling along the ceiling of his room. Jade was seated in a chair, reading page proofs of *National News* magazine. The bat, Jerry knew, was about to swoop down on the unsuspecting Jade. Jerry tried to warn her but the muscles in his throat were frozen. He rushed toward the hideous monster to protect Jade, but something, someone, was holding his arms. He screamed silently as the black bat, talons extended, slowly hovered over Jade.

7:00 A.M. Missy and Caroline were both feeling perky this lovely Monday morning. It was going to be a clear day, brisk enough for a fall coat and pleasant enough for a walk on Park Avenue.

"I'm going to put on a pot of tea. Would you like some?" asked Caroline.

"Fine," said Missy. "I'll join you, but hold the cookies."

7:30 A.M. Bill Harding woke up to the glorious aroma of cooked bacon. Mary Sue, who had taken care of his father during that last painful year, had pulled the curtains. The sunshine poured into the plain, large room. He stretched his arms pleasurably, in front, upward, and sideward. Once. That was his concession to calisthenics.

"Here's the morning paper," said Mary Sue.

On the front page was a picture of Franklin Parson and Josiah Minden. Parson had never been, and might never again be, so happy.

It was D-Day.

7:45 A.M. Henrietta Beale finished brushing her teeth and critically examined her skin in the mirror. This was the face that Heinrich Fronzhold planned to rejuvenate. What was it that young men and women saw in older faces that they found unbeautiful? Would that I were a television producer, thought Henrietta. My heroines would be mature, perhaps sixty to sixty-five. They would have jowls, puffy noses, cheeks reddened from the bursting of small blood corpuscles, and dozens of fine lines around the eyes and the mouth. Every line, every swollen pocket, each broken vein, would prove that my heroine had lived fully. The smile lines would indicate her humor, the red cheeks her enjoyment of alcoholic beverages, and the black lines under her eyes would be a firm indication of the hundreds of nights spent in wild lovemaking.

My heroine (I'll call her Henrietta) is lying on a couch, one arm carelessly thrown around the shoulders of her young male companion (I'll call him Bill). In her other hand is a glass of Dom Perignon. She takes a sip, then allows Bill to kiss her on her neck, her ear. He buries his head in her bosom, mad with excitement.

Enter Miss Rheingold. She is twenty-two, a size 6, and has tight skin and a thin nose. Bill raises his head and sees her. "Faugh," he exclaims in disgust. "She's too young. Where are the lines of experience and passion, the permanent red flush of booze?" He turns back to Henrietta and softly kisses her wrinkled lips.

Only in America, sighed Henrietta, have the young advertising genius, the brilliant movie producer, and the gung-ho television director decided that young is beautiful.

Three hours until my appointment with Heinrich who promises to return me to a youthful appearance I don't really want.

Jade arrived at Iris V at 7:00 A.M. There was a small crisis at the Nurses' Station. Charlene Calderwood, the boss on the floor, was berating the night nurse, who was softly crying.

"I don't care if Jackie Volts is late," said Calderwood. "You will stay here until the entire medication tray is in order. You could easily have fixed it an hour ago. I'm sick and tired of your excuses. All you do the whole night is sit on that big fat can of yours."

The night nurse wiped her tears with the back of her hand. "Yes, nurse," she said, "but Jackie gets away with murder . . ."

"For God's sake, that's enough! I'm going to inspect the patients' rooms now. If there's anything wrong you can bet I'll be straight back."

"May I assist her?" asked Jade.

"Yes, you may," Nurse Calderwood said kindly. "You did a nice job yesterday cleaning the lounge and the halls. The floors are positively gleaming."

"Thank you," said Jade modestly.

Calderwood entered Room 1 while Jade followed the night

nurse into the Medication Room.

"She's so mean!" sniveled the young night nurse. "I put in my full twelve hours. Now she wants me to do Jackie's work. Jackie's the one who's lazy, not me."

"Don't worry, honey, you'll be out of here in ten minutes. I'll put the medication cups out and I'll count out the pills," said Jade.

The night nurse started pouring the doses from three different bottles. She worked much faster than either Jackie Volts or Ellen Dixon, but she also put the wrong pills in four different cups. Jade was horrified. She checked every dose twice to make sure there were no more mistakes. When the last wrong dose was poured, the night nurse said, "Thanks," and hurried out the door. Jade corrected the prescriptions for Steven and Mary, switching hypodermics and pills.

Jackie Volts arrived at 7:15. "I'm so sorry I'm late," she said to Nurse Calderwood.

"That's all right, dear," Calderwood replied. "At least you do a good job when you're here and you're interested in the patients."

"Is the woman in Room 8 going to get better?" asked Jade.

"I'm afraid not, Jade. She'll probably be transferred to Permanent Care. There's nothing we can do for her here."

"Will she live long?"

"She might live a week or a year or ten years. The heart continues to beat but the brain is dead."

"Poor woman," said Jade. "Can I comb her hair and wash her face?" That's the least I can do for Martha, she thought.

"Of course you can. You have a good heart, Jade. That's the key to good nursing."

Henrietta Beale entered the Main Building of the Harmonetics Hospital. She had read Harold Gondoler's description of the entry hall but she was unprepared for the wild beauty and variety of plants that covered the walls and hung in tiers in the center of the room. "Tiger aloe," she said to herself. "Rabbit's-foot fern. Philodendrons."

"May I help you?" a blue-gowned woman interrupted.

"Thank you. I have an appointment with Dr. Fronzhold."

"Please follow me."

Henrietta was escorted to a glass-enclosed partition. The woman behind the partition asked her name and address. She typed it into the computer, then pressed several buttons. Henrietta heard the buzzing sound of small wheels rapidly turning. A card popped out of another machine. Henrietta had been identified and her appointment confirmed.

"You're all set," said the woman behind the partition. "Please wait just a minute and a guide will take you to Tulip I."

The guide was an elderly man in a red gown. He explained to Henrietta that Tulip I was the reception area for Rejuvenation. He escorted her through a maze of corridors, identifying each in turn by name and disease.

"This is Rose II. Hysterectomies," he said. "It's the largest ward we have. I'm taking you the long way because I want to avoid Orchid I."

"What's that?" asked Henrietta.

"Prostates. I'm superstitious."

Two corridors later they reached their destination. Henrietta was turned over to a nurse who led her into a cheery room filled with pictures of young women. She was asked to take a chair and wait. After fifteen minutes the door opened and Clarissa Kent came in.

"Henrietta!" said Clarissa happily. "I'm so glad to see you here."

"I'm also glad I made the decision," said Henrietta.

"Heinrich had promised he'd do me at noon today," Clarissa said, "but he's so busy. Poor man. He's got four rejuvenations and then he'll be assisting Anton Kohl with psychosurgery at 4:00 P.M."

"That sounds like a lot."

"That's not all. He does rounds at the hospital and he has all his administrative duties. He hardly has a chance to breathe. He'll be seeing you in forty-five minutes. Meanwhile you could be filling out this questionnaire."

"Who are all these women on the walls?" asked Henrietta.

"They're Heinrich's patients. They're all over sixty and some are in their seventies."

"I can't believe it," said Henrietta truthfully. The women looked thirty-five to forty-five.

"Isn't it marvelous?" Clarissa said. "The one over there on

the left is me. It was taken four weeks after my first treatment."

Henrietta moved closer to the photograph. It showed a glorious Clarissa looking barely thirty-five. No loose skin, no wrinkles, no puffiness.

"Incredibly beautiful," Henrietta murmured.

"Thank you. I hope to look like that again in another few weeks."

"Isn't that Margaret Edgebrook?" Henrietta asked, pointing to a portrait.

"Yes. Heinrich did her three months ago."

"She looked fabulous at the White Robe ceremony yesterday. I thought she'd had a face lift."

"You should see Margaret's body now. She's one of Heinrich's great successes. Her hands are those of a young girl."

A nurse popped her head in the door.

"Mrs. Kent, Dr. Fronzhold wants you."

"Coming. Good-bye, Henrietta. I'll see you after your interview with Heinrich."

Henrietta sat at a table and proceeded to fill out her questionnaire. The first six pages were concerned solely with health. Had her tonsils or adenoids been removed? When did she last have a vaccination? What childhood diseases had she been afflicted with? Had she ever had pneumonia, typhoid, Asian flu? Did she have any allergies to strawberries, seafood, pollen, animals? What drugs had she received? What operations? How many children? Henrietta sat pensively for a minute. Then she returned to the question on allergies. She was allergic, she wrote, to dogs, cats, horses, and all other animals, including frogs.

The last two pages concerned her own and her husband's financial status. A great deal of information was required. More, in fact, than that nasty little man from the IRS had demanded.

When the last question had been answered, Henrietta pulled a small book out of her purse and began to read. She started on page 1. She was on page 58 when Heinrich Fronzhold entered the room.

"Stand up, please," he said. "I want a good look at your face."

"Good morning, Heinrich," Henrietta replied, remaining in her chair.

"Are you going to give me problems?" he asked grimly.

Henrietta smiled but made no effort to get up.

"Ach, you women," he snorted. He pulled up a chair and sat down by Henrietta. "You insist on the amenities. All right: your party was lovely and your guests were charming."

"They found you equally simpatico."

"Henrietta, it's too early in the morning for banter. Besides, I'm twenty minutes behind schedule."

"Then what's five minutes more? Let's have a cup of coffee and get to know each other better."

He was about to say something rude but he changed his mind. Nothing he did seemed to ruffle her. He got up, walked to the door, opened it, and shouted:

"Two coffees! In the china! No plastic cups!"

"I'm pleased to be in your kingdom," said Henrietta, "or should I say harem?"

"Harem is equally appropriate."

"Your ladies are lovely. I also want one last fling even if it lasts only two or three months. Do you think that's foolish, Heinrich?"

"No, you're realistic. Most women who come here expect ten years of youth or twenty years. Rejuvenation today is short term."

"When they find it's less than they hoped for, what do they do?"

"They return here, of course, and we do our best to repair the damages. The average woman has a good ten months, possibly a year, after the first transplant. Then, with each successive operation, the transplant has a shorter effect. We don't know why."

"Are there many who don't return when the effects wear off?"

"Not many, perhaps 2 or 3 percent."

"What happens to them? Slow decay and death?"

"Yes. The aging process accelerates. We tell them the truth in advance but the paradox is they know but they reject the facts. The situation is similar to the cancer-producing hormones fed to menopausal women. It's an attempt to forestall the loss of the child-producing years at the expense of life itself. At least we're more honest than the gynecologists who will deliberately conceal the potential danger."

"What's your estimate of life expectancy after the rejuvenation: two or three years?"

"Closer to three years. The first year might be very good. The next year, maybe eighteen months, are up and down. The average woman can take four or five transplants. Each one brings full rejuvenation but the last one may not work at all or it is efficacious for too short a time."

Henrietta, for the first time, felt a positive reaction toward Heinrich. He had been straightforward. He had made no attempt to "sell" rejuvenation; in fact, he was giving all the negative aspects.

"Is this Clarissa's third transplant?" she asked.

"Her fourth. She knows the truth but she expects me to perform miracles."

The door opened. Clarissa entered, carrying a tray with two Royal Worcester cups and silver cream and sugar bowls. She held her head sideways so that the ruined cheek would be hidden from Fronzhold. Henrietta brought over a small table for the tray.

"Thanks, Clarissa," said Henrietta. "Why don't you get another cup and join us?"

Clarissa glanced nervously at Fronzhold.

"We don't want to interrupt her work," Heinrich said. "That will be all, Clarissa."

When the door had closed, Henrietta had regained her original opinion of Heinrich. He was autocratic, domineering, and cold, perhaps because his patients accepted the doctor who played the role of the superior being. She knew now why he performed four or six or even ten rejuvenation operations a day. It wasn't the $10,000 fee, although the money was certainly a factor. It wasn't because the grateful patient would leave her fortune to the Society; that was of no benefit to the individual physician. It was because Heinrich liked to play God. He bestowed youth, albeit temporarily, on those he rewarded. He experimented with human beings because the lives of individuals weren't important to him. His surgery came first, not his patients.

"Each woman is told what you are hearing," Fronzhold continued. "No false hopes are given. As a matter of fact there are some cases where the first transplant doesn't take at all."

"Has the process improved? Is it better now than it was three years ago?"

"Only slightly better. We did fewer than thirty operations three years ago. Then the program was widened to 120 the following year. This year we have done almost a thousand despite the warnings and the fatality statistics that we give. We've turned down over five thousand requests for reasons of health or lack of financial responsibility. It's expensive, as I'm sure you know."

"Yes. That doesn't bother me."

"Let me see your questionnaire."

Henrietta handed it to him. He took a quick glance at the last page, his eyes scanning the lines that read "Total Annual Income" and "Total Capital, Including Investments." Henrietta's answers were satisfactory. Then he opened the questionnaire to the middle. He skimmed rapidly, then looked up at Henrietta.

"You won't be able to have the rejuvenation," he said.

Henrietta kept all expression out of her face. "Why not?"

"Your allergies. We use frogs."

At 10:45 A.M. Franklin Parson stepped out of the elevator and walked toward the door of "Franklin Robert Parson and Associates, Architects." Two men wearing Robert Hall suits approached Mr. Parson from the far end of the corridor.

"Excuse me, sir," said one of the men. "Are you Mr. Parson?"

"Yes. What can I do for you?" Parson replied pleasantly.

"Please come with us," said the stranger, flashing a badge. "The District Attorney would like to speak to you."

There was a sudden flurry of physical activity. Nell Arden came running toward the group. At the same time the *New York Times* photographer flashed his bulb twelve feet from Parson's face. Parson lifted his right arm, lowered his head, and attempted to make his way through the two policemen. One of them stuck out his foot. Parson fell to the ground. The flashbulb went off again. One policeman took out his gun. The other policeman handcuffed Parson. Another flashbulb.

"That's enough," said one of the policemen to the photographer.

"He's right," said Nell Arden soothingly to her associate. "You've already got three great photos."

At 11:00 A.M. Caroline Ryder and Missy Tompkins were picked up by Palmer, the Rappaport Agency man. He was driving a 1950 Rolls-Royce that had been rented for the occasion. There were three blue gowns in the back of the car. One of the gowns had been shortened so that Missy would not trip on the hem. Palmer gave Missy and Caroline transmitters and asked them to keep the lines open. As soon as he knew Mary Hamble was on her way out of the hospital, he said, he would drive the car up front to pick her up.

Palmer had a great deal of respect for the intelligence of his passengers but he was concerned about the possibility of violence in Iris V. One blow delivered by a husky nurse could prove mortal to the fragile Missy. The ladies seemed not the least bit worried. They were jabbering about the most curious subjects—recipes for cookies, the possibility of offering Nurse Calderwood a cup of their homemade lemonade, and the dainty watercress sandwiches that would certainly prove irresistible to a famished Jackie Volts.

The car drove up to the emergency entrance of the Harmonetics Hospital. Palmer jumped out briskly and opened the door for the ladies.

"Thank you, Palmer," said Caroline, sweeping out of the car with the haughty manner of a grand duchess.

"Please assist me, Palmer," said Missy majestically, handing him her small wrinkled hand.

The huge blue-robed guard stared at the arrogant ladies.

"I beg your pardon," he said to Caroline, "but you don't have your badges . . ."

"Of course we don't," said Caroline. "Give us two, please. Iris V." She waved a dismissal to Palmer.

"You'll have to pick them up at Admissions."

"Nonsense!" said Caroline. "Phone Nurse Calderwood in Iris V and tell her we've arrived."

"Does she know you're coming?"

"Of course she does. Dr. Minden personally informed her."

"Your names?"

"Mrs. Dorset and Mrs. Cummings. Tell her that Dr. Minden's Blue Ladies are here."

Caroline turned her back on the guard.

"I'm perfectly furious with Charles," she said. "He kept me waiting for forty-five minutes last Thursday. I've half a mind not to use him anymore."

"I've always despised Charles," said Missy. "He gave me the most dreadful haircut fifteen years ago. I have never forgiven him."

"Whom do you use?"

"He cut my hair so short I looked like one-of-those-you-know women. Henry wouldn't speak to me when he came home that night."

"Where do you go now?"

"Maurice, of course."

"But Maurice takes anyone! Some of the most dreadful women. Where on earth do they come from? How can you bear to go in there?"

The guard listened to their conversation, shrugged, and went to the house phone. He looked up Iris V and dialed.

"Nurse Calderwood? There are two Blue Robes here . . ."

"Ah, yes, Dr. Minden said he was sending them."

"Yes, they're from Dr. Minden."

"Good, good. Send them up."

Missy and Caroline were given their badges.

Jade put a quarter in the pay phone.

"Hello?" she said. "This is Jade Boren. Is Dr. Minden there? . . . Yes, I have a message. Tell him I called . . . Jade Boren. . . . Tell him I can't leave Iris V now because there's a problem with Martha. . . . Just Martha, no last name. . . . Martha's feeling perky. Have you got that? Perky . . . I have more, but I'll try again in thirty minutes. . . . No, it's better if I phone him. . . . Thank you."

Jade hung up and returned to Iris V.

"I just spoke to Dr. Minden," she told Nurse Calderwood. "He wants to know if Mrs. Dorset and Mrs. Cummings have arrived yet."

"They're on their way up now," said Nurse Calderwood.

"Dr. Minden says they're marvelous women and he *does* want them to feel helpful on Iris V. One of them was a Red Cross volunteer in World War I."

"World War I!" echoed Nurse Calderwood.

The corridor door opened. Missy Tompkins and Caroline Ryder entered.

"Jesus Christ!" said Calderwood.

Harold Gondoler was in a makeshift bedroom on the ground floor of Bill Harding's town house. A phone was resting on the pillow by his head. The receptionist at *National News* was reporting the happenings as fast as they occurred. Harold had almost forgotten his pain.

"Franklin Parson has been booked on three counts of grand larceny. They're holding the kidnapping charge until they can get a statement from Mary Hamble. The story won't break until 4:00 P.M. Nell Arden already has it but she's not giving it to her paper until then. She says thanks a million to everyone at *National News*. . . . Here's a report from Palmer Tillingsby. Missy Tompkins and Caroline Ryder are in Iris V. Nurse Calderwood says it's quite all right if they read stories to some of the more tranquilized patients. . . . There's a call coming in from Henrietta Beale. She's coming here in twenty minutes to write her story on rejuvenation. . . . Hang on, Harold. I'll be back with you in four or five minutes."

Jerry Marconi looked at himself in the mirror. He was wearing an open white shirt. A stethoscope hung from his neck. "Madam," he said in a world-weary tone to the mirror, "please undress. I want you to remove everything. You may be Farrah Fawcett to millions but you're just another body to me."

He looked at his watch. The car would be picking him up at 1:30. Nothing could go wrong unless Fronzhold or Anton Kohl or Esme Jennings showed up. Arnie would drive the car, they would park in "Iris: Marple" and go directly to Iris V. Jade said there would be a wheelchair. No problem in wheeling Clay out, she had assured them. No need to worry about anything, she had repeated.

Of the six people directly involved in the rescues, two of them (Jon Mahaffey and himself) were nervous, one (Arnie) was terrified, and the three women—Jade, Missy, and Caroline—felt secure and confident.

He looked at his watch again: 12:15. One hour and fifteen minutes to go.

"We read the loveliest story to the patient in Room 1. She seemed so appreciative," said Caroline to Nurse Calderwood, who was sitting at her desk in the Nurses' Station. The nurse lifted her eyes to the ceiling in exasperation.

"Jade," Nurse Calderwood yelled. Jade, thirty feet away, came immediately. "Get these two women, I mean, take these two ladies to one of the tranquilized patients. I've got a million things to do. I've no time to supervise new Blue Robes."

"I hope you'll try some of our watercress sandwiches first, and a nice cup of lemonade. We've got some homemade cookies too," said Missy.

"I haven't time to eat!" Nurse Calderwood was almost shouting. "Jade!"

"Yes. I'll take care of Mrs. Cummings and Mrs. Dorset, don't worry. But they're right about one thing. Just one quick bite for energy. Mrs. Cummings, give us each a plate of sandwiches and some lemonade, please."

Mrs. Dorset had two plates in hand. Mrs. Cummings whipped open her reticule and took out the box of dainty tea finger sandwiches. Mrs. Dorset, the elderly one of the pair, had unscrewed a thermos and was pulling the cork out with her teeth.

"There!" said Missy. "Wasn't that speedy? Now we're off to Room 4 to read a story to that nice young girl."

"My God, where did they come from?" Nurse Calderwood said bitterly. "I have no time to eat this stuff. Here, throw it out." She handed the plate and cup to Jade.

"I've got one question to ask you first," Jade interrupted. She put her hand in her purse and dug out her wallet. "I've got a thirteen-month-old niece who's totally adorable. She sings and coos and she can even say a few words but she won't walk. She'll stand if her mommy holds her but when she lets go, Sissy gets down on the floor and crawls. Do you think there's something wrong with her?"

Jade extended the wallet to Nurse Calderwood. There was a picture of Jade, age thirteen months.

"She's perfectly charming," said the nurse. "Thirteen months, did you say? I have a grandson who's fourteen months. He walked when he was only nine months old. That's very early, of course. He stood at six months."

"You're joking! I never knew they could stand so young. He must be very strong."

"He is. I've got a picture of him walking. Just a minute while I find it. Ah, here it is."

"Oh, he's heavenly!" Jade sighed. "Look at those beautiful eyes!"

"He's really quite cute," said Nurse Calderwood, biting into a sandwich. "I baby-sat with him last night while his parents went to the movies. He calls me Gama."

"How long has he been speaking?"

"Well, he doesn't actually say much," said Nurse Calderwood reaching for another sandwich. "He says MaMa and DaDa and Gama."

"Does he eat everything? My niece is allergic to orange juice."

"Bobby eats everything on his plate. He's so neat too. Oh, I'm thirsty. May I have the lemonade, please, Jade?"

"Of course. Boy, I'm tired. I don't know why. I got plenty of sleep last night."

"I'm . . . tired . . . too. So very . . . tired."

Jade caught Nurse Calderwood just as she was slipping off the chair. She gently laid her on the floor by the front wall of the Nurses' Station. The glass partition started four feet off the ground. Charlene Calderwood was invisible to anyone standing outside the Nurses' Station.

Jade walked unhurriedly to Room 4. She stuck her head in the door.

"One down and two to go," she said to Missy and Caroline. "Ellen Dixon should be finishing up any minute now. One of the orderlies usually brings her a sandwich."

"Where does she eat it?" asked Caroline.

"I'll try to get her to eat with me in the Nurses' Lounge," Jade said.

"We'll be there in a few minutes."

Nurse Ellen Dixon was walking briskly toward the Nurses' Station.

"Ellen!" Jade called to her from the door of the Nurses' Lounge. "Come quick! I've got a surprise."

Ellen Dixon hesitated.

"You'll die when you see him," Jade said. "He's totally gorgeous. I bet you he's better looking than your Jason."

"I bet he isn't," Ellen said. She entered the Nurses' Lounge and looked around.

"Over here," Jade said, pointing to the wall. She had thumbtacked a color photograph of "Psycho" Punk-Eye, leader of the Psycho Punks, on the wall. Punk-Eye had long, curly green hair. His eyelids, plus a quarter-inch area under his eye, had been painted solid black. The picture was an action shot. It showed Punk-Eye expectorating. The spit had shot out of his mouth and was coming toward the camera.

"He's wild," said Ellen, fascinated. "Do you know him?"

"Not really. I've been to a couple of his concerts."

"Does he actually spit?"

"Just a little bit. On the floor and things like that. In England he spits on people. Psycho Punk-Teeth, who's a member of his group, can vomit at will but he's not nearly as cute. His teeth are painted black."

"I'd love to hear the Psycho Punks. Are they coming back to New York?"

"They're going to play two nights only the week after next. I've got tickets, fourth row. You want to go?"

"You bet your ass I want to go. How much are the tickets?"

"I got them from a friend. You and Jason will be our guests."

"Fantastic!"

Missy and Caroline entered the room.

"Hello, you must be Nurse Dixon," said Caroline. "I'm Mrs. Cummings and this is Mrs. Dorset. Dr. Minden sent us here to help."

"How nice," said Ellen, eyeing the two elderly women.

"The orderlies had a sandwich for you," continued Caroline. "We noticed it was a HAM sandwich. My goodness, what would Dr. Minden say if he knew anyone in the hospital was eating meat?"

"We threw it away," said Missy, her eyes dancing.

"You threw away my lunch?"

"Never mind, dear. We've got some lovely, healthy sandwiches. We bought the watercress in the Harmonetics Health Food Store and we squeezed fresh lemons for the lemonade. Please have one, my dear."

Ellen glared at the tray and looked furiously at the two women.

"Don't get into a fight with them, Ellen," Jade whispered as though the two older women were deaf. "Eat one and maybe they'll leave."

Ellen angrily picked up a finger sandwich and stuffed it in her mouth.

"Ugh," she said in disgust. "What I suffer in the name of the Harmonetics Society!"

"Wash it down with a little lemonade," suggested Missy.

Ellen reached for a cup and tossed down the brew. She made a face.

"I wish I had Punk-Teeth's nerve," she muttered to Jade. "Particularly if these two sweet ladies had to clean up after me."

"Try one cookie and we'll go," said Caroline, smiling sweetly.

The food was actually quite edible, Ellen thought, but she wasn't about to tell the old biddies. She bit into a cookie. Umm, chocolate chip. Very tasty. Might take home a few for Jason. He loves fresh cookies but . . . they're so . . . hard to . . . make . . . all that . . . batter . . .

"Two down and one to go," said Missy. "Shall we put her in the closet?"

"It's pretty small," said Jade doubtfully.

Caroline opened the closet door. "If we can sit her up, she'll fit quite nicely."

"Missy," said Jade, "wait outside to see nobody gets near the Nurses' Station. Caroline and I will take care of the body."

Nurse Jackie Volts was running late as was her custom. She came breezily down the hall, whistling a nontune.

"Hey, Jade," she said, spotting her friend in the corridor. "Where is everyone?"

"That's what I was going to ask you."

"What a day! I'm thirty minutes behind schedule. I've got to feed the patients, do a prep on Room 16 for psychosurgery, and then get the goddamn medication trays ready."

"Why don't you let me start on the lunches? There's a chart that shows the rooms, isn't there?"

"Yes, it's with the lunch trays. It shows which ones have to be helped and which can feed themselves. It takes forever."

"I'll be careful."

"I know you will. I'll start prepping Room 16."

"What do you have to do?"

"Not much. The head has to be shaved. Then I wheel him into the corridor. An orderly will pick him up at 3:30. He should be back in his room at 5:00 P.M. at the latest."

"By the way, Jackie, have you met the two Blue Gowns who are helping us out?"

"Not yet."

"They're in the Nurses' Lounge eating lunch. I gave them my copy of *World Tennis*. It's the issue on Fort Lauderdale. You'll go wild over the color photos of the beach and the city."

"I'll take a look at it later."

"Jackie, I'm so sorry, but I told one of them, Mrs. Dorset, that she could keep it. She has a grandchild who plays tennis. Maybe if you can catch them, you could take a look now."

"Good idea," said Jackie. "If Nurse Calderwood comes looking for me, tell her I went to the john."

"Sure, Jackie."

Nurse Volts moved happily toward the Nurses' Lounge. She entered. Two women in blue robes, one perhaps sixty-five and the other over eighty, were seated on a couch looking at *World Tennis*. On the table in front of them were a trayful of sandwiches, a pitcher of lemonade, and a dish of cookies.

"Hello. I'm Jackie Volts."

"How nice to meet you. Do have a sandwich, dear. We made them ourselves."

"I wonder if I could have a fast look at your magazine," Jackie asked hesitantly.

"You certainly can. It's all about Fort Lauderdale, Chris

Evert's hometown. We'll move over and you can read and eat at the same time."

"That's very nice of you," said Jackie. She took the proffered magazine with one hand and grabbed two sandwiches with the other.

"Umm, this tastes good," Jackie mumbled, turning pages with one hand and stuffing food in her mouth with the other.

"Please don't eat so fast," said Caroline. "It's very bad for you. That's your third sandwich!"

"They're so small I can eat 'em in one bite," said Jackie. "Hey, where are you taking that tray?"

"I promised the other nurses I'd save some for them. I'll bring them right back, I promise. Then you can have the rest."

"Okay," Jackie said cheerfully. She started to turn the pages of the magazine. What a beautiful color picture! Next page. Very pretty . . . the colors seem to be moving . . . can't make out . . . what the picture is . . . sandy beach . . .

"Three down," said Missy, "and one to leave. Let's go see Mary."

Jade sat in the Nurses' Station. She picked up the phone and carefully removed the receiver. She then inserted a small plug connected to an equally small recording device. She checked the switches and dialed Josiah Minden. He wasn't there but he was expecting her call. She was given another number to try. He came on the phone immediately.

"What's up, Jade?" he asked.

"It's Martha. She's regained consciousness."

"That's impossible!"

"I know it's impossible but it's happened. The nurses don't know yet. I wanted to speak to you first."

"What has she said?"

"She knows who she is but she doesn't yet remember what happened. She mentioned your name several times, Josiah. That's why I don't want anyone to see her."

"That's very good, Jade. What has she said?"

"She keeps repeating a story about a woman named Rhonda Mahaffey. Josiah, I'm so worried. If anyone hears that story they'll misunderstand."

"Jade, I'm coming over myself. Can you keep everyone out of Martha's room?"

"Honey, I'll kill 'em if they try to go in."

"Dearest Jade! I'll be there in forty-five minutes."

She placed another call, this time to Bill Harding.

"It's working, Bill," said Jade. "Is Rhonda out of her apartment?"

"Yes. The police are there. Jade, did you record your conversation with Minden?"

"I did but I don't think we can use it. I sound like a co-conspirator."

Mary Hamble was weeping. Caroline was drying her eyes and doing her best not to cry herself.

"Jade says you can walk, Mary," said Missy.

"Short distances. From my bed to the door and back, maybe twice."

"That's fine. We can wheel you to the end of the corridor. You'll only have to walk a few steps to the elevator. When we're downstairs, it's a very short walk to the Emergency Room exit. Our car will be waiting outside."

"It's a cinch, Mary," said Caroline.

"You could do it on one foot," Missy corroborated.

"You could walk it on your hands," Caroline added.

Mary laughed.

"We brought underthings, your shoes, and a blue gown," said Missy, unpacking her reticule.

"Oh my, oh my." Mary started to cry again.

"You and I are going out together," Missy explained. "Caroline leaves with the next shift. The only one who saw Caroline and me come in together is the guard outside the Emergency Room door. I'll walk in front and talk to him. You go straight to the car. The driver's name is Palmer and your name is Mrs. Cummings. Got it?"

"I'm receiving you," said Mary.

"We'll check with Jade while you get dressed. Roger?"

"Roger. Over and out," said Mary.

Arnie slid the Impala into the slot reserved for "Iris: Marple." The three men got out of the car and walked to the garage elevator. Each was wearing an open white shirt and carrying a small black satchel. Jerry Marconi was the guide. He had studied the chart Jade had given him and he walked confidently to the correct bank of elevators. The others followed a few steps behind.

Up to the first floor, then down one corridor, a right turn, through another door. Another bank of elevators next to the Emergency Room. Jerry pressed the "Up" button.

The elevator door opened. Two women, both wearing blue gowns, stepped out. Jerry recognized Missy. The other woman was very pale. She walked slowly, painfully. Missy was chatting rapidly about a hairdresser named Maurice.

Jerry's hands were sweating. As he got into the elevator he felt physically ill. Mary Hamble had a good forty yards to walk. He was afraid she couldn't make it.

The two men entered the building by the service entrance. They were carrying a six-foot-long package. It did not seem heavy but it was awkward to manipulate.

"Where to?" asked the service elevator man.

"Mrs. Mahaffey. Package from W & J Sloane."

"Sixteenth floor," said the elevator man.

The men rode up to the sixteenth floor silently. "It's 1608," said the elevator man, "through the service door and to your right."

They carried their package to 1608. One of them rang the doorbell. There was an intercom just above it.

"Who is it?" asked a female voice.

"Package for Mrs. Mahaffey."

"Come in," said the voice. A buzzer sounded, releasing the front door. The two men walked in. They stepped through the small foyer into a darkened living room. At the far end of the room, barely visible, a woman was seated on a couch. The two men walked toward her. When they were fifteen feet away they took out their guns and fired. The sounds were dulled by their silencers. The woman's body fell across the couch. One of the men walked over to the body and started to run when he saw it was a dummy.

The living-room lights went on. A voice magnified by a speaker ordered: "Throw down your guns or you're dead men.

You're surrounded." They looked around; they saw no one. "You have exactly three seconds," thundered the voice. One of the men tossed his gun to the floor. The other one hesitated, then dropped his gun. Six men entered the room.

"I'm arresting you," said one of the policemen, "for the attempted murder of Rhonda Mahaffey and the attempted murder of Harold Gondoler. I am warning you that anything you may say can be held against you . . ."

"How did you know?" said one of the gunmen.

"Josiah Minden told us."

"He couldn't have," said the gunman. "He's the last guy in the world who'd of told you that."

"Why?" asked the policeman.

"I want to speak to my lawyer," said the gunman.

Jerry Marconi's heart was pounding as he stepped into Iris V. He saw Jade sitting in the Nurses' Station. He forced himself to walk over to her at normal pace. She seemed her usual self, relaxed and happy.

"Come in," she said through the glass partition.

Jerry opened the door and saw the body on the floor. He was speechless.

"This is the Head Dude, Nurse Calderwood," said Jade. "We'll have to move her into the Nurses' Lounge. Will two of you give me a hand? Then I'll need some help on moving another body out of a closet. Arnie, would you like to volunteer?"

"Oh, Christ," Arnie groaned.

"They're not dead," said Jade, "just doped. Missy and Caroline fixed it."

"Let me take a look at them" said Jon Mahaffey. "First let's get this one into the other room."

Nurse Calderwood's body was gently borne into the Nurses' Lounge. She was spread on the couch. Nurse Dixon's body was then removed from the closet and placed in a chair. Dr. Mahaffey quickly examined the three nurses. Pulse and respiration were satisfactory. How long until they awakened, Jade asked. Probably by 4:00. However, if no one disturbed them, they might sleep until 6 or 7.

"Where's Steven Clay?" asked Mahaffey.

"I'll show you," said Jade.

Jon followed her to Room 16.

"Steven, you're free," said Jade. "You'll be wheeled out of here in less than an hour. Are you all right, Steven?"

"I'm all right. The nightmare is over, it's all over. I'm no longer afraid. I'm free!" The tears were running down his face. He lifted an awkwardly stiff arm to wipe them away. Then he buried his head in the pillow and sobbed.

The hypodermics, thought Jade. He had to pretend paralysis each time a nurse came in the room. He could never be sure I had switched needles. The panic and terror each time he got the shot. The relief when he knew he could still move his arms and legs.

"This is Jon Mahaffey," said Jade. "He'll help you, Steven. He's brought you some clothes."

Jade backed out of the room. She was just beginning to feel the terror that had already gripped Jerry. The nightmare was over for Steven; it was just beginning for her.

The phone rang by Harold Gondoler's bed. He picked it up and felt the twinge in his side. The pain was bearable. He listened to the voice on the phone and the pain diminished. It was Bill Harding.

"Mary Hamble's on her way home. She made it," said Bill. "We brought the cook, Gretchen, in to stay with her. Missy insists on staying there too. I also contacted your friend at the pharmacy, Ellie Sue. The bad news is Martha. The drug they gave her killed the brain. There's no hope."

Both men were silent.

"I'm awfully sorry, Bill," said Harold.

Another long pause.

"Damn fine woman," Harold said. He waited for Harding to continue.

"More news, Harold. The plan to trap Minden worked. He sent two thugs to murder Rhonda and they were caught in the act. The police are sure they're the men who gunned you down."

"So much in one day, Bill."

"The best is yet to come. The District Attorney is getting an indictment against Heinrich Fronzhold and Judge Henley Stuart."

"And Josiah Minden?"

"Still a possibility. If the two thugs who tried to kill you and Rhonda will talk, he's through."

"Are they talking?"

"Not yet, Harold."

"I'll feel better, Bill, when Jade is out of the hospital."

"So will I."

Caroline Ryder had left her beige Ultrasuede coat in the limousine. She now removed her blue gown. She was wearing a nurse's uniform. She opened her reticule and took out a pair of white stockings, white shoes, and a nurse's cap. She tossed her blue gown on the floor of the john so that it would easily be found. Then she went to the Nurses' Station and seated herself at the desk. When Dr. Minden entered, her back would be turned so that she would not see him. To see him would be equivalent to committing suicide.

The three men were in Steven Clay's room. The door was open a crack so that they would hear Josiah Minden's approach. The men had not yet told Jade that her plan had been canceled.

Jade stood in the hallway. She had been waiting for Josiah Minden for ten minutes. She heard the elevator doors open. A figure was coming toward her. It was he.

Minden looked at Caroline Ryder's back. She was absorbed in a book. Jade was standing in the middle of the corridor smiling conspiratorially.

"Come quickly," she whispered, pulling him into Room 7.

Minden looked around. The patient was an elderly man. He was comatose.

"Martha's in Room 8," Jade said. "I had to talk to you before we go in. We won't have to hurt her, will we, Josiah?"

"I think you already know the answer, Jade."

"I'm frightened. I don't think I can do it."

"My life's in your hands, Jade. You've got to help. It won't be difficult. I promise."

"All right. I've got to have a drink first. I've got the shakes. God, my mouth's so dry."

"One drink," said Josiah.

"I swiped the Scotch from the Drug Room," said Jade, taking a flask and two cups out of a paper bag. "Pour me one."

Minden poured a small drink for each of them.

"Close your eyes before we drink," said Jade softly. "I have something special I want to give you."

Minden looked at her face, guessed what it was, and closed his eyes. He felt her lips and tongue flutter against his mouth. He did not see the small pill that she dropped in his cup.

"Down the hatch," said Jade.

Minden threw his head back and drained his cup. Jade tried to do the same. She managed only half.

"One more sip," she said.

"Hurry it up, Jade."

"Yes, darling." She took two quick sips and finished her drink.

"My throat's burning," she whispered.

"Nonsense. Let's go."

"Okay. I'll check the corridor first. It's free, Josiah."

They slipped into the hallway, Jade going first. She opened the door of Room 8, walking four or five steps ahead of Josiah. She moved past the bed where Martha lay in a coma. She turned around, faced Josiah, and screamed as she had wanted to scream the night that Minden had raped her.

Josiah glared murderously at Jade. He tried to shout but the words wouldn't come out. His vocal cords were paralyzed. He lunged furiously across Martha's bed, his fist catching Jade on her left arm. He grabbed her gown, ripping the sleeve with his last remaining strength. He heard footsteps behind him. Jon Mahaffey dashed into the room, followed by Jerry and Arnie. Minden turned but he couldn't defend himself. Mahaffey's fist smashed into his face; slowly Josiah dropped to the floor.

"Did he hurt you?" Arnie asked Jade.

"I'm fine, don't worry, he didn't touch me," Jade replied breathlessly.

"He'll never play the role of the handsome devil again— unless he finds a good plastic surgeon," said Mahaffey, staring contemptuously at Minden's prone body.

"We've got to work fast," said Jade. "We've only got twenty minutes to get him ready."

"We're not going through with your plan," Jon told her.

"You've got to. You promised."

"We can't, Jade. It's equivalent to murder."

"I can't do it alone. I'm not strong enough."

"I'm sorry, Jade. He'll be punished in other ways."

"What ways?" said Jade, shaking her head sadly. "All right, you win. You better get going. I'll follow as soon as I can."

"No hard feelings, Jade?" asked Jerry.

"No hard feelings."

Arnie gave Jade a hug and kissed her cheek.

The men left Iris V in the prearranged pattern. First Arnie and Jerry, who would wait in the car. Then Caroline pushing Steven Clay in the wheelchair, and, walking a few feet behind them, Dr. Jon Mahaffey.

The rescue had been safely accomplished and Jade's plan had been scratched.

As soon as the men had left, Jade got the long dolly out of the supply room and pushed it into Room 8. She bent down to examine Josiah Minden. His nose had been broken by Jon Mahaffey's powerful fist. One eye was swollen and his lips were puffy. She opened her purse and took out a hypodermic. She stuck the needle into Josiah's arm and pushed the plunger. Then she got up and leaned against the bed, gasping for air. She waited a few minutes until her lungs and her heartbeat were again normal.

The hardest part was getting the limp body of Minden onto the dolly, not because he was heavy but because Jade didn't want to put her arms around his body. She undressed Minden, then covered his middle section with a sheet. Only the head, part of the shoulders and the toes were exposed. She took his clothes into Steven Clay's room and put them in the closet. Then she returned to Room 8 to finish the preparations. She shaved Josiah—the head, the eyebrows, and the beard. She stared at his face. There was no resemblance to the Harmonetics leader.

Minden's eyes were opening. He struggled to speak. His eyes rolled wildly.

Jade took some gauze and adhesive. She bandaged Josiah's nose. He didn't exactly look like Steven Clay, but then Steven's head had not been shaved. If Fronzhold noticed, Jade's plan would fail. That gave Minden a fighting chance, which was much more than Minden had given others.

Last of all, Jade took a tag out of her purse. She had removed it from the big toe of Steven Clay that morning. Now she tied it around the big toe of Josiah Minden. She rolled the dolly into the hall and placed it just outside Room 16. She had not spoken to Josiah once. She hoped she would never speak to him again.

Jade walked to the Nurses' Station. She dialed Lilac II and asked for Dr. Waterhouse.

"Dr. Waterhouse? This is Nurse Calderwood in Iris V. Dr. Josiah Minden was just here. He wants you to watch a psychosurgery operation to be performed today at 4:00 P.M. Dr. Anton Kohl will be operating and Dr. Heinrich Fronzhold will assist. Please phone me as soon as the operation is completed, will you? My name is Nurse Calderwood. Thank you so much, Dr. Waterhouse."

Jade walked into the Nurses' Lounge where Charlene, Ellen, and Jackie were resting peacefully. She sat on a chair and waited. It was 3:25. She listened for footsteps in the corridor. She waited quietly, patiently. At 3:45 she stuck her head out the door. The dolly with Minden on it was gone.

At 5:15 the telephone rang in the Nurses' Station. Jade gave a heavy kick to the couch on which Nurse Calderwood was lying. Charlene Calderwood groaned. Then she heard the phone. She shuffled out of the room groggily.

Jade opened her eyes. Ellen Dixon and Jackie Volts were awakening too.

"Oh, my head!" said Jackie.

"What happened?" asked Jade. "Good heavens, it's 5:15."

"The medications!" said Jackie.

"I'll help," Jade said promptly.

Nurse Calderwood returned. "A crazy call from a Dr. Waterhouse. He said I called him two hours ago."

"We must have been drugged," said Jade.

"The two old ladies!" said Ellen Dixon. "Christ, I'd better check the patients."

Nurse Calderwood stared at the half-empty tray of sandwiches. "It's impossible," she said. "It couldn't have happened. But don't any of you eat any more of these."

The nurses and Jade moved into the corridor. Ellen Dixon

began a bed check. Jade followed Jackie Volts as she walked to the dolly.

"I never prepped Room 16," said Jackie. "I wonder who the hell did. He obviously had his psychosurgery and he's awake. They keep them awake during psychosurgery," she explained to Jade.

Jade leaned over the dolly and looked at the dull eyes. She started to scream.

"Stop it, Jade," said Jackie angrily.

"It's Dr. Minden," Jade shouted. "Dr. Fronzhold operated on the wrong man. He's destroyed our Leader!"

Epilogue

Excerpts from a Speech Honoring Dr. Josiah Minden
by Dr. Francis X. McDonald, Acting Head, Harmonetics
Society,
Harmonetics Temple, New York City
November 8, 1982

*We are gathered together on this tragic morning to pray for
the complete recovery of our beloved founder, Dr. Josiah
Minden. We have been informed by members of the Harmonet-
ics Hospital staff that his physical condition has improved greatly.
Dr. Esme Jennings reports that many patients have undergone
similar brain surgery without any damaging permanent effects.
Her report is encouraging, and we hope that time will improve
Dr. Minden's condition.*

*As most of you have heard, there has been a complete
reorganization in the Harmonetics Hospital staff. We have
regretfully accepted the resignations of Dr. Heinrich Fronzhold
and Dr. Godfrey Waterhouse. Within a few weeks we expect to
announce the name of the new hospital administrator, but until
the permanent appointment is made, Dr. Esme Jennings will be
the Acting Head. There have been several other resignations
that many of us view with sadness, but in this practical world of
ours the businessman and the government official often do not
have as much time as they would like to devote to affairs of the*

mind and spirit. Although we have lost fourteen members of the White Robes in the last two weeks, this is not without some benefit: it will enable us to honor other distinguished members of our glorious Harmonetics Society.

Today Governor Ralph Emley of New Jersey was to address you. Unfortunately, an unexpected emergency has prevented him from attending, but he has sent a telegram in which he offers his sincere regrets.

I want to personally thank all of you who are attending the services at the Temple today. Your numbers may be few but your dedication is great. I hope next week you will return, and you will bring your friends and your friends' friends.

For the third consecutive day we are omitting the Presentation ceremony. I beg of you, beloved fellow members, search among your business associates, your acquaintances, and members of your family for people in need, lonely people, those who have suffered and could use a brother's helpful hand, and bring them with you to the Temple. The two or three hundred that are present today will become two or three thousand and then twenty thousand. How glorious it will be to see our Temple filled once again.

Today's collection has been designated to honor one of the great men of this century, Josiah Minden. When the envelopes are passed among you and you make your contribution, be as generous as you can in the name of this noble man. Please write your names on the back of the envelopes. Each envelope will be brought personally to Dr. Minden. He will know who has remembered him and who is praying for him on this solemn November morning.

Henrietta Beale tiptoed into the living room carrying a small silver tray. Elliott was seated at his desk, absorbed in the *New York Times*.

"I've brought you another cup of coffee, dear," she said softly.

"Ah, that's nice," said Elliott, looking up. "Put it over here."

Henrietta placed the tray on the desk. She measured a teaspoon of sugar and poured a small amount of cream into the cup. Elliott always relished the ceremony of the presentation of the tray and the careful addition of the final ingredients.

"Good, good," he said, nodding his approval. "Staffordshire, isn't it? You haven't given me this cup in several months."

"It's the Chinese Willow pattern. I thought you might enjoy it this morning."

Elliott tinkled the spoon against the delicate cup. Hardly any restaurants and only one or two clubs took the trouble to offer one's coffee properly. They slopped the beverage into a thick porcelain mug and served it with a clumsy stainless steel spoon. The sugar was offered in paper packets and the cream in an ugly, serviceable jug. Frequently the coffee had spilled over into the saucer. How much more delicious a hot beverage tasted when it was served in bone china and when it was stirred with a small carved silver utensil.

"I'm going out for a few hours," said Henrietta. "Is there anything I can get you before I leave?"

"Not a thing, thanks. I have a few appointments myself a little later. I'm out for the entire afternoon. Whom are you seeing?"

"First I'm going to Wall Street to have lunch with Arthur Popple. He just got back from Palm Beach and he's feeling absolutely marvelous. There's a codicil in my will I want to discuss with him. Then I'm meeting Mrs. Boren. She's the mother of a young friend of mine. I spoke to her on the phone this morning, and we're going to the Harmonetics Hospital together to visit a sick friend."

"Who's sick and why on earth would she be in the Harmonetics Hospital?"

"It's a man from the Harmonetics Temple. He's quite ill. My young friend knew him very well, and Mrs. Boren and I are really going just to please her."

"You shouldn't go if it's a viral infection."

"No, it's nothing contagious. He had surgery."

"Well, that's all right, then. Was it prostate by any chance?"

"No. I believe it was something far more serious."

Elliott shuddered. Poor old duffer probably had cancer. Rotten luck. Bad way to go.

"Good-bye, dear," said Henrietta, kissing Elliott on his smooth pink cheek.

"Don't go just yet. I want to read you an amusing item in the papers. It's about Byron Kent."

Henrietta sat down. She avoided glancing at her watch

because Elliott would find it offensive. She had at least ten minutes to spare before leaving for her luncheon with Arthur Popple.

"Listen to this," said Elliott, reading from the newspaper. "'Industrialist Kent Indicted. Byron Kent, president of Kentwood Mining, was indicted yesterday on three counts of bribery and five counts of perjury. The charges stem from the allegation that he tried to sway the votes of Senators Stanley Peters (R, Iowa) and Manfred Ellis (D, Texas) on the Emergency Coal Bill by promising them special privileges in the Harmonetics Society. Originally Mr. Kent had denied any such offer when he was brought before the Grand Jury. Later it was discovered that Senator Peters had taped a conversation between Mr. Kent and himself in which the order of the Brown Robe was promised in return for an affirmative vote on the Emergency Coal Bill.

"'Efforts to reach Mr. Kent at his office and home were unsuccessful. Senator Robert T. Spriggs (R, N.Y.), when asked to comment on the Kent indictment, said he would reserve any opinion until all the evidence had been presented.'"

"Poor Byron," said Henrietta, "and poor, dear Clarissa."

"It's his own fault. I'll never understand how he got involved with such a sleazy bunch as the Harmonetics Society. Robbie Spriggs is the only one in our group who was active in the Society who'll get out of it untarnished. Even you, Henrietta, with all your common sense, you were taken in by those thugs for a couple of days."

Henrietta had heard similar recriminations from Elliott on several dozen occasions during the last two weeks. She responded, as usual, by lowering her head and saying nothing.

"That McDowell toad you had at the dinner party, he was one of the Harmonetics bunch too. I'll never forget that boozeless, meatless dinner you served. Thank God you came to your senses quickly."

"Clarissa must be terribly depressed. We should have her for dinner one night to show support."

"Good heavens, Henrietta, what would we talk about? If you must see her, have her for lunch when I'm not at home."

"Yes, lunch is a better idea. I'll ask Rosalind Schulte too."

"Rosalind Schulte? Her husband was a common thief! At least what Byron did was for the good of the industry."

"Rosalind and Clarissa knew each other from the Harmonetics Society. I ran into Rosalind at Bloomingdale's yesterday. She was shopping for children's clothes. She told me the revelations about Josiah Minden and Dr. Fronzhold were so horrible that she hasn't been back to the Temple since. Do you know what she's doing instead? She's adopting two Vietnamese children. She got them last week and they're living with her now. I've never seen her look happier."

"If you're going to have Clarissa and Rosalind, you might as well ask Sarah. She fell for that Harmonetics garbage too," said Elliott, unable to resist another small jab.

"Sarah's too busy. She enrolled in Real Estate School and she's trying to do the required sixty hours in four weeks. That scarcely leaves her time to go to Elizabeth Arden or Tiffany's or Gristede's," said Henrietta with a gentle laugh.

"Why on earth is she going to Real Estate School? You think she's going to show two-bedroom apartments between Second and Third Avenue to middle-class nouveaus from Riverdale? She'll despise her clients. The only ones she'll want to show homes to are the ones who already own palaces in Nice and Phoenix and Newport."

"That's her plan," replied Henrietta. "She figures she only has to sell one client one home once a year to be prosperous. She says she already knows all the good property in Palm Beach and Southampton."

"Well," said Elliott, losing his skepticism, "it will be a lot less expensive than being a Brown Gown."

Ben was standing by his post at the doorway, legs apart, arms behind back, and eyes gazing dreamily at a rusty tug moving slowly down the East River. A taxi pulled up at the curb; Ben was thrust back into reality.

"Good morning, Mrs. Ryder," he said, opening the taxi door and extending his hand toward Caroline's elbow. "A bit nippy today," he added as he walked her to his entrance.

"One solitary cloud sailing over Manhattan," said Caroline, looking upward, "and of the seven million people working or living in the city, perhaps two dozen will see it. Don't you think we should walk with our heads in the clouds?" she asked Ben.

"Particularly on a day like this," said Ben in his most gallant tone. He didn't enjoy poetry or philosophy unless it was spoken by Mrs. Ryder, who had a great deal of class. He longed to ask her if she thought he should change his name to Bentley. It seemed more fitting for a man in his position. "Ben" was fine when he wore overalls and ran the back elevator. It was a bit common for a man who mingled with the elite of the city.

"It's nice that Mrs. Hamble is home again," said Caroline.

"That it is. You go straight to the elevator now, and I'll buzz Gretchen to tell her you're on your way."

"Thank you, Ben."

Gretchen was standing in front of the open door when Caroline Ryder got out of the elevator. Mary Hamble was waiting behind her. Caroline hugged them both.

"I think I'm going to redo the apartment," said Mary as they walked into the living room. "When Franklin first married Angela, I gave him a free hand. He tore down walls and widened doorways and he furnished it in his own taste. I never really liked it; now I hate it."

"If it reminds you of that blackguard, get rid of it," said Caroline.

It was a large airy room filled with light blues and white. The walls were covered in a blue print fabric that matched the large sofa and two of the overstuffed chairs. The heavy draperies were a rich white and blue with a multicolored blue pattern sash. A large mirror framed in three shades of blue cloth hung on one wall. On a Swedish glass table were a cluster of blue and white Sèvres figurines. The chairs around the table were Swedish contemporary, and the seats were upholstered in solid blue. The thick carpet was white.

"What will you do with the furniture?" asked Caroline.

"Gretchen and Helga can have what they want. The rest will go to the Salvation Army. I don't intend to give one stick to Angela. Does that sound dreadful for a mother to say about her daughter?"

"No. She doesn't deserve a thing. If she were my daughter and if she and her husband had conspired to drug me senseless and lock me up in a psychiatric ward, I'd have nothing to do with her again."

"I need someone to reassure me over and over. I feel totally negative about her and I don't want to see her again, but I've got a strange sense of guilt because she's my own flesh and blood."

"Don't. She's a cruel, mercenary, and unnatural daughter."

"But should I cut her out of my will? Wouldn't that be just awful?"

"It would be awful to keep her in. Missy agrees with me. So does Gretchen. She's a beast."

The doorbell rang.

"That's Missy. I wish Jade could have joined us but she's still in Florida."

Gretchen entered the room. "Mrs. Tompkins," she announced.

Missy, wearing a Hattie Carnegie dress for which she had paid $400 in 1926, was looking more fragile than ever. Enormous blue veins pulsed through her tiny hands, and the skin on her matchstick arms was as withered as crepe. She wore a three-strand choker of pearls around her wrinkled neck. The dress naughtily exposed six inches of ankle.

"God, I'm exhausted," she said. "I need a stiff drink."

"Sherry, or would you like something stronger?"

"A Bloody Mary, please," Missy replied. "I'd have a martini but I've got to be back at the office after lunch."

"What office?" Caroline asked.

"I've got a job," said Missy.

"You what?"

"I'm working for Ruder & Finn," Missy replied.

"Doing what?"

"Publicity and promotion. I get our clients interviews with the press and book them on talk shows. I do a little TV myself."

"Missy, how on earth . . ."

"I would've preferred doing investigative work for Bill Harding, but when *National News* ran the Harmonetics story and printed that big picture of us, Caroline, it blew my cover. I took a couple of issues of the magazine with me and paid calls on several companies. I'd go to the front desk and tell the receptionist I wanted to see the top man—Bill Paley, Bill Phillips, Bill Ruder, or whoever. I would give her a handwritten note, clip it to a copy of the magazine, and ask her to deliver it to the president. I usually wrote a one-liner such as 'May I have two minutes of your time?' It almost always worked."

"Then how did you sell yourself?"

"I'd say, 'If I could get in to see you, I can get in to see anyone.' Bill Phillips laughed himself sick."

"Did he offer you a job?"

"Yes. I was tempted."

"Why did you turn it down?"

"It didn't have much of a future. I've got a lot of upward mobility at Ruder & Finn."

(Reprinted by permission of the *New York Times*)
October 21, 1982

Judge Henley Stuart Arrested for Malfeasance in Office

At 4:00 P.M. yesterday Judge Henley Stuart of the New York Supreme Court was arrested on four counts of malfeasance in office and three counts of accepting a bribe. Lieutenant Michael Corrigan, who made the arrest, was accompanied by Greg Findley of the District Attorney's office. Judge Stuart is a member of the White Robes in the Harmonetics Society.

The charges are as follows: Judge Stuart, at the request of Franklin Parson, committed Mary Hamble to the Psychiatric Ward of the Harmonetics Hospital and, at the same time, he named Mr. Parson (Mrs. Hamble's son-in-law) as her conservator. Judge Stuart did not meet with Mrs. Hamble personally nor did he request any medical or psychiatric documentation before issuing the commitment and the conservatorship. Mr. Parson said in a sworn affidavit that in return for the favors, he had issued four checks in the amount of $1,000 each to the campaign fund of the judge. Additionally, Mr. Parson claims to have turned over $16,000 in cash to Judge Stuart.

Judge Stuart categorically denied all the charges. He said he was unaware that Mr. Parson or any member of his family had made a campaign contribution. He claimed never to have received any cash from Mr. Parson. As for signing the commitment and conservator papers, he stated it was merely an error in judgment, not a criminal offense. Mr. Parson, he said, had told him his mother-in-law was desperately ill. Mr. Parson was a highly respected member of the community and he, Judge Stuart, had believed him.

Judge Stuart said he was instructing his campaign manager to return the four $1,000 checks. He said the fact that the checks were deposited within two days after the signing of Mary Hamble's commitment and the awarding of the conservatorship was pure coincidence. He added that he had complete faith in the American judicial system and he was positive he would be exonerated.

Arthur Popple was a fine figure of a Wall Street lawyer. He stood a full 5'5", weighed 120 pounds, had a clear, pinkish complexion, a thick white mane, and bright blue eyes. He was seventy-six and the titular head of Blake, Chatterly. Henrietta Beale was almost two inches taller, twenty-five pounds heavier, and twelve years younger. Nevertheless, as Arthur Popple escorted her into Oscar's, he grasped her arm firmly, as though she would topple over without his physical support. Mr. Popple guided his slightly overweight luncheon companion to Oscar's back parlor where the velvet was thicker, the decor richer, and the tips more extravagant. The osso buco was identical in all the rooms.

After they were seated and had ordered, Mr. Popple addressed his companion.

"Henrietta, I'm glad you brought me the tape of your conversation with Austin McDowell. I found it most informative. But tell me, why did you tape the talk in the first place?"

"My mind doesn't work the way yours does, Arthur. I don't know anything about wills or tax laws or legal phraseology. When I talk to a lawyer or an accountant, he assumes I know about tax-deductible gifts or the latest IRS rulings. I feel a fool when I continually have to ask what this or that means. I didn't know Mr. McDowell and I didn't want to look stupid so I used the tape."

"Why did you decide to bring the tape to me?"

"I've been reading the newspapers. All those scandalous

stories about Josiah Minden and Dr. Heinrich Fronzhold. Each day when I saw the *Times* I got more uneasy. I wondered if I had done the right thing. I looked at my new will which, by the way, I had never signed, and I thought what I had done was perfectly horrid. Then I played the tape, and as I listened to it I realized Mr. McDowell had planted some of the changes in my mind. Am I right, Arthur?"

"It's very hard to make a judgment without hearing Austin's side."

"Arthur, am I right?"

"Ah, here come the oysters."

"I shall eat my oysters and I'm sure they'll be delicious, but I haven't forgotten my question, Arthur."

"How persistent you are. Of course you're right about McDowell and of course we'll have to dismiss him. He's finished with the New York Bar. But I'm right about you, Henrietta."

"What do you mean?"

Arthur Popple measured three drops of Lea & Perrins and two small dabs of horseradish, then blended them into his sauce. He speared a raw oyster with his fork, dipped it in the sauce, and ate it. He tapped his immaculate lips with his white linen napkin before answering.

"You called me in Palm Beach to talk about your will and you manipulated me into recommending Austin. He immediately called you and you set up an appointment. You took a tape recorder with you and you turned it on without Austin's knowledge. You played dumb—and he played dumber. Henrietta, if I had your brains and your acting ability, I might never have lost a case."

"Arthur, dear, you're marvelous. Your compliments are making me lightheaded."

"Never lightheaded, Henrietta. What a pity you never went to law school."

When their lunch was finished and the check paid, Arthur Popple flagged down a cab and helped Henrietta into the back seat. Then, ever the Wall Street Knight, he thanked his lady fair for her company and praised her youthful looks and charm. Finally, with an almost imperceptible bow, he closed the door of the cab and watched its occupant disappear into the stream of traffic.

Henrietta was in an excellent mood. The food had been exquisite and Arthur had been in top form. Furthermore, Austin McDowell's tenure at Blake, Chatterly was being terminated. She was looking forward with exhilaration to her afternoon appointments.

The cab swept along the West Side Drive to the 72nd Street exit. The circular turn was accomplished at fifteen-miles-an-hour faster than the safety factor. The driver negotiated the five blocks from Riverside Drive to the apartment house on Central Park and 73rd in a series of maneuvers that included constant short blasts on his horn to stimulate the car in front of him to exceed the speed limit, and repeated switching of lanes so that he could better his time per block by three seconds. Henrietta, the ideal taxicab passenger, was oblivious to potholes, jolts, sudden brakings, and sharp toots. Her mind was working out the forthcoming scenario between herself and Jade's mother, Roberta Boren. Mrs. Boren, she thought, had one trait in common with Elliott and Sarah. Elliott presumed that everyone in America, other than Communists, was for free enterprise and would like to be a member of the Union League Club. Sarah was confident that all women lived for massages, manicures, and facials, and appointments with their chiropodist, tailor, and analyst. Mrs. Boren also had implicit faith in her own beliefs. For two years everybody she knew, with the exception of Alfred Boren, had been connected in some way with the Harmonetics Society. The revelations of the venality inside the Society were shocking, but Mrs. Boren was not convinced that Josiah was personally involved. Jade had never enlightened her mother; Mrs. Boren did not know her daughter had worked on the *National News* story.

Bill Harding had scheduled a wrap-up article on the Harmonetics saga for the next issue. He wanted an accurate account of the physical and mental condition of Josiah Minden. Mrs. Boren, he suggested, could make the arrangements. She would be delighted to talk to a friend of Jade and would be only too happy to set up a hospital visit to Dr. Minden. Henrietta called Mrs. Boren, and it was just as Harding had predicted. Mrs.

Boren was ecstatic: the very social Henrietta Beale had telephoned her to ask for a favor. Furthermore, Mrs. Beale, who seemed to be a member of the International Jet Set, absolutely adored her daughter Jade. Henrietta was pleased and surprised at Mrs. Boren's cordiality. She was looking forward to meeting Jade's mother.

The taxi pulled up to the Berington.

"Please hold your flag," said Henrietta. "I'm picking up a friend and we're going on to the Harmonetics Hospital."

Mrs. Boren came downstairs as soon as she was buzzed. She and Henrietta looked each other over and each made a fast appraisal of her companion.

"Old New York family," thought Mrs. Boren. "Born rich, educated at a social private school, very clothes-conscious, and a bit superficial."

"Artistic," thought Henrietta. "The daughter of an actor or pianist, raised in a Greenwich Village atmosphere, doesn't give a damn about society or convention."

They were both wrong.

As they rode in the taxi to the Harmonetics Hospital, they conversed politely, each trying to discuss a subject the other might like. Occasionally, as the driver took a corner on two wheels to beat the light, one of the women was hurled into the bosom of the other.

"I understand the Guggenheim is having a Pre-Columbian art exhibit next week," said Henrietta.

"Is it?" replied Roberta Boren indifferently. "What are the dates of the April in Paris Ball this year?"

"I haven't the faintest. We're hoping to get tickets for the New York City Ballet season. I can never get enough of Baryshnikov."

"Is that so?"

The conversation faltered. Mrs. Boren nervously twisted her rings and her bracelets. Henrietta's face felt stiff from her determined efforts to smile.

"You two ladies visiting someone in the Harmonetics Hospital?" asked the cab driver.

"Yes, a sick friend."

"Mind if I give you some advice, ladies? It's a terrible

hospital. A couple of doctors there, they murdered one doc and they almost killed another one. If your friend ain't real sick, you oughtta get her outta there."

"I heard they were having problems."

"Lady, you oughtta listen to the radio. It's on all day long. There's this German doctor, Fronzhold his name is. He's worse than these sex crime freaks. You know what he was doing? He was transplanting sex glands of frogs into people to make them look younger. They had a bunch of pictures in the *Daily News*. It showed the victims. Boy, did they look far out! This one old broad, she'd had four transplants, and she looked one hundred, maybe older. They showed another one, you couldn't tell whether it was a man or woman. The head was completely bald and the features were swollen outta sight."

"How awful!"

"You think that's bad? I'll tell ya something worse. In our neighborhood we gotta coupla punk kids. One of them, he's always in trouble. He steals cars, he goes for joyrides, he gets arrested over and over. His mother's always crying. My wife knows the mother. Matter of fact, the mother's her second cousin. The kid don't beat up on people but he steals. It's always night jobs when no one's there. Finally he gets caught swiping the furs in a warehouse. It's his eighth or tenth offense and they throw him in the slammer, this time for maybe fifteen years. Then he gets the chance to volunteer for medical treatment. If he takes the treatment, they tell him, he'll be cured and they'll let him outta jail. He volunteers. It wasn't no medical treatment, it was surgery. That German guy, Fronzhold, he did the operation. Now his old lady never stops crying. The kid, he just sits in a chair or lies in bed all day long. He can talk but not so hot. It takes him an hour to read a comic strip. He won't steal no more but he won't work neither."

"How terrible!"

"The *Daily News*, they showed pictures of the prisoners. You know where they did the surgery? In the Harmonetics Hospital. There was a bunch of guys there waiting for this operation. The D.A. gets 'em sent back to prison. The guys are so happy they wantta chip in and give the D.A. a present. None of them wanted no operation.

"Today I hear on the radio where a bunch a the prisoners'

families are gonna sue the Harmonetics Society for a hundred million bucks. Who would want a million if you can't even read the comics? You better tell your friend to get outta that hospital fast!"

"We're here. What a fast drive," said Henrietta, spotting the hospital a block away.

"Good heavens, what's happened to the place?" said Mrs. Boren. "It used to be so beautiful."

The garden paths were littered with garbage. The plants and shrubs were dying, the victims of neglect, abuse, and vandalism. Some had broken branches, others had been picked bare of their flowers and leaves, and in many spots there were ugly holes where a beautiful plant had once been carefully nurtured. There were no volunteers in blue robes pruning, trimming, and cutting. The tennis court nets were gone and it looked as though someone had emptied the garbage cans on the courts.

On the outside hospital walls the people indigenous to the area had written messages in black paint and colored chalk to friends, relatives, and enemies, extolling or insulting various parts of their anatomy. The more artistic of their number had attempted imaginative sketches of unusual physical attributes. The slogans, rhymes, and pejorative instructions were crowded together, filling the entire outer wall space to a distance of almost six feet in height. Occasionally, at a higher level, there were large black or green or orange splashes where a vandal had thrown a can of paint.

Henrietta paid the taxicab driver who issued a final warning about removing their sick friend from the premises. Henrietta thanked him for his solicitude.

Once the two women were inside the hospital, the changes they saw were the result of omission rather than destruction. The floors had not been cleaned in several weeks and the plants had not been watered. The philodendrons, rex begonias, and tiger aloe were dead. Only the cacti looked healthy. The once immaculate Italian marble tile was stained with caked mud, old cigarette butts, and dead petals. Behind the glass enclosures at the rear was one woman only. She was wearing a nurse's uniform and she looked harassed and angry. Several phones were ringing. She picked them up in turn, answering curtly. Henrietta waited quietly until the nurse had time for her.

"Well, what do you want?" said the nurse.

"We have an appointment with Clarissa Kent in Iris V."

"You'll have to fill out these forms and show me some identification," she snapped.

The women filled in their forms, then waited to get the nurse's attention.

"Hello, Admissions. If it's an emergency, bring the patient to the side entrance. The patient must have $500 in cash or a credit card before being admitted." Click. "Hello, Admissions. Yes, any doctor may bring his patient to Harmonetics. The membership requirement has been temporarily waived." Click. "Hello, Admissions. If it's a surgical patient, the relatives must bring a $1,000 deposit." Click.

The nurse grabbed the forms from Henrietta and flung them into a basket without looking at them. She scarcely glanced at their identification cards.

"Here's a hospital map," she said, shoving a mimeographed diagram at Henrietta. "You'll have to find Iris yourselves. We're too understaffed to help individual visitors. If you get lost, try another corridor."

The nurse returned to the phones.

"You lead," said Roberta Boren to Henrietta. "I once got lost trying to find the Triborough Bridge."

The map was difficult to read but Henrietta had a good sense of direction. She and Roberta walked along the silent aisles, past open doors that led to empty rooms. Several times they saw a solitary nurse, a patient, or a doctor. Only once did they see a volunteer. Ten minutes later they were on Iris V.

"Anybody here?" called Henrietta, looking into the vacant Nurses' Station. She knocked on the door of the Nurses' Lounge, then opened it. "Anybody here?" she repeated.

The two women stood in the empty corridor.

"I think you should try the rooms," said Roberta.

Henrietta knocked on the first door, then pushed it open. The bed was empty. The second room was also vacant. Halfway down the hall a door opened and a brown-gowned figure emerged. Her face was swathed in an operating mask, revealing only the eyes and the forehead. It was Clarissa. Henrietta was filled with pity and Roberta was horrified. The folds above

Clarissa's right eye were so heavy that they fell in huge wattles, preventing the upper lid from opening. The left eye looked puffy and a thick flap of skin was pressing down against it. The forehead was a series of frightful lumps, half hidden by the thick bangs that came down to the eyebrows. The hair was obviously a wig.

"Clarissa, are you feeling all right?" Henrietta asked anxiously.

"It's bearable. I have very little time, Henrietta. Poor Heinrich. Have you heard what they did to him? They put him in prison! My God, Henrietta, that great man is sitting in a cell."

"Clarissa," said Henrietta weakly, "he's been accused of a capital offense."

"There should be different laws for men like Heinrich," said Clarissa. A frightful teardrop burst out of the corner of her left eye, hovered for a second, then fell on the surgical mask. "The laws were meant for you and me and people like Byron. Not for the geniuses. But you wanted to see Dr. Minden. I'm sorry I sound rambling but there's so little time. Please, follow me."

Clarissa led them to Room 24. She opened the door and ushered them in. She did not go in herself. A large nurse with heavy blonde hair, perhaps six feet and weighing a good 190 pounds, got up from her chair and put down her magazine. She greeted them with a warm smile.

"I'm Nurse Bonnie Alexander. You must be Mrs. Boren and Mrs. Beale. How nice of you to come." She moved toward the bedside where her patient lay silently. "We've got some visitors, dear," she said in a singsong baby talk, patting his lifeless hand. "Now why don't we give the nice ladies a big smile to show them how much better we're getting? Would you like to sit up? Here, let me help you."

She put her two strong arms around his body and lifted him into a reclining position on the tilted bed. "There, now, isn't that better?" she asked her patient.

Roberta Boren was staring at Josiah Minden, endeavoring to hide her repulsion. His hair and eyebrows were beginning to grow back except for one large bare patch on the right side of his head. The face was clean-shaven but the muscles were lax.

Only the lower lip and the eyeballs seemed capable of motion. The eyes flew back and forth, toward Henrietta, then toward Roberta Boren.

"Can he understand us?" asked Mrs. Boren.

"The doctors think he sometimes grasps what we're saying. He can't speak and, unfortunately, there's been paralysis of the limbs so there's no way for him to communicate. I believe he tries to speak to me sometimes with his eyes. See how he's looking at you, Mrs. Boren? He wants to tell you something. Here, sit next to him, take his hand, and talk to him. Don't speak too fast. If the brain is functioning, it isn't functioning at the normal rate."

"Hello, Josiah," said Mrs. Boren. "It's good to see you again. You're looking well."

The room was silent. Henrietta felt intensely uncomfortable with Mrs. Boren's greeting.

"I haven't seen you, Josiah, since the night you brought me the Brown Gown," said Roberta. "Do you remember?"

"Do go on," whispered the nurse.

"I shall never forget that night. You were wonderful. My daughter Jade was there. She met you for the first time and thought you were marvelous."

"Look at his eyes," said the nurse. "He understands! He's trying to tell you something!"

Josiah's eyes were moving frantically.

"You've got his attention," the nurse whispered. "Don't stop."

"Jade's in Florida now, getting a little sun. She phoned me last night. She says she might get a job doing promotions for Bancroft. She'd taken a bad fall when she was at the hospital as a volunteer, but she says the bruises are almost gone and she's able to wear a swimsuit again."

"Jade Boren, of course, I remember now," said the nurse. "She worked in Iris V just before I was transferred here. You know, all the nurses in the corridor were fired after they found Dr. Minden. The only one they said could stay on was Jade."

"Did they ever find out what happened?" asked Mrs. Boren.

"According to Nurse Calderwood, all three nurses and your daughter Jade were drugged by two elderly women. The two old ladies kidnapped two of the patients on the floor. Then they knocked out Dr. Minden, prepped him for surgery, and left him in the hall to be picked up by the surgical orderlies. Of course the old women must have had accomplices, undoubtedly doctors."

"Josiah," said Mrs. Boren, "can you tell us who did this terrible thing to you?"

Again the violent eye movement.

"He's exhausting himself," said the nurse. "He's got to conserve his strength. I suppose you heard he's being moved to Bellevue at the end of the week."

"No, I hadn't," said Mrs. Boren. "Why don't they leave him here? Bellevue's a charity hospital. I'm sure Dr. Minden has plenty of money to pay for the best possible care."

"The courts have tied up all his funds because of the lawsuits by the families of the prisoners. He can't stay here because the hospital is being shut down temporarily. Almost all the volunteers have left, some of the doctors and nurses were fired, and more than half of them have resigned. There aren't enough patients to keep the place going."

"The hospital went downhill so quickly," said Mrs. Boren.

"It certainly did. The day after your daughter found Dr. Minden, the volunteers began to disappear. Within a few days half the patients had left. There's hardly anyone in Iris V now. That friend of your daughter's, Beth Marple, she quit the first week. They say she got an offer from a Chicago hospital."

"Well, I guess we should be going. Thanks so much, nurse," said Mrs. Boren. "I'm sure you've been taking marvelous care of Dr. Minden."

"And of course you'll say good-bye to our patient."

Mrs. Boren turned toward Josiah. She raised her arms and extended her hands toward his face, but when her hands were six inches away she dropped them. She couldn't bear to touch him. Josiah Minden was dead; this was merely a disgusting, irrational clone.

"Good-bye," she said to the patient.

Henrietta had not spoken since they had entered the room. She did not address the patient as they left it. She was surprised at herself: she felt no pity toward the body lying on the hospital bed. Minden's condition chilled her, repelled her, but it seemed inevitable. The devil that had been Josiah Minden was effectively locked in a living coffin. He would never again be able to issue death warrants, eliminate former associates or dispatch inquisitive investigators by drugging their brains. No one, Henrietta was sure, would ever try to read the desperate messages in Minden's flashing eyes. He would remain incarcerated in his own body for the rest of his life. Henrietta felt the sentence was just.

Before the door closed behind them, Henrietta and Roberta could hear Nurse Bonnie Alexander talking to Minden.

"Time for our bath. Now be a good boy and when you're all cleaned up you can have your din-din."

(Reprinted by permission of the *New York Daily News*) November 19, 1982

Prominent N.Y. Doctor Is Murder Victim

Ex-Harmonetics Chief Still in Custody

Police Lieutenant Michael Corrigan announced yesterday that positive identification had been made of the decomposed body found in Van Cortland Park last week. The victim was Dr. Jean de Moraille, a prominent Fifth Avenue physician who had been affiliated with the Harmonetics Hospital. Identification was made by comparing the teeth and bones of the murdered man with X rays in the files of Dr. Jean de Moraille's dentist and orthopedist.

The exact cause of death could not be determined since the body was in an advanced state of decay. The neck had been broken and the skull smashed.

Within two hours after the police announcement, the District Attorney's office said that Dr. Heinrich Fronzhold was being questioned in connection with the murder of Dr. Jean de Moraille. Ten days ago Dr. Fronzhold, the former head of the Harmonetics Hospital, was charged with nine counts of aggra-

vated assault in the cases of Dr. Steven Clay and Mrs. Mary Hamble.

Dr. Fronzhold's lawyer, Austin McDowell, said no statement would be made at this time.

It was 9:00 P.M. A half-dozen rooms were lit in the *National News* building. Upstairs the Pitney Bowes and the two Elliott 300s were clattering. From some hidden office a staffer was typing erratically with two fingers. In the back room of the ground floor, Bill Harding was checking the editorial pages for the next issue with Jerry Marconi.

"I'm going to hold the Museum story for another week," said Harding. "It's too thin. That gives us two extra pages, enough to include Henrietta's recap on the Harmonetics Society. Leave her name off, and of course no mention of Jade. As Missy would say, we don't want to blow their cover."

"You want to use the picture of Minden lying in the hospital bed?"

"No. Too gruesome. I might change my mind so put it in the pile of possibles. What else have we got?"

"Here's the stack. Heinrich Fronzhold and Lieutenant Corrigan in front of the 7th Precinct, Byron Kent's arrest, Judge Henley Stuart being helped into a police car, Dr. Godfrey Waterhouse being escorted into the Criminal Courts Building, and Franklin Parson after the preliminary hearing. On the more pleasant side, Mary Hamble going for a walk on the East River Drive, Harold Gondoler sunning in Central Park, and Missy on the phone at Ruder & Finn. Then we've got some panoramic scenes: the litter in the gardens at the Harmonetics Hospital, the rows of empty seats at the Temple services this morning, students at Columbia University taking down the Harmonetics signs at Butler Library, the President of Josiah Minden College meeting with the Governor of Mississippi to discuss a new charter and a new name for the school. Here's one unusual picture: some of the residents at the Harmonetics retreat near Conroe, Texas, still wearing their gowns. They say they're going to keep them: they're comfortable, they're drip-dry, and they protect them from the sun. You can just make out the new sign. It says 'Carefree Retreat.'"

"Have you checked on the report that the Sheraton chain wants to take over the Harmonetics hotels and hostels?"

"They lost out to a Japanese syndicate. A Saudi-Arabian prince has put in a bid for the Harmonetics Sanatorium in Phoenix."

"How about the Brooklyn Temple?" asked Harding.

"If nobody wants it, the Mayor would like to turn it into a welfare hotel. There's a rumor that Dr. Samuel Moorback, the founder of the Psychoenergetics movement, would like to make it the headquarters for his group. He's got a pretty big following. He's picked up thousands of disillusioned Harmonetics members."

"Do we have the staff report on what is happening to the typical Harmonetics believer?"

"It's almost finished. Of the 700 people interviewed in New York, we got over 650 completed forms. Wait a minute. I have the figures here. Of the 662 members who responded, only 13 say they are still attending Harmonetics services; 9 are now under the care of psychiatrists, 23 have turned to est, 83 are Born-Again Christians, 61 have joined Dr. Moon, 194 are attending church more often, 7 have tried Primal Scream, 32 are into some form of water therapy, and 116 have experienced a Psychoenergetic phenomenon; 314 say they have not been able to recapture the happiness they once experienced in Harmonetics. Interestingly, none of those who experimented with Psychoenergetics are in this group of 314. They say the Psychoenergetic surge is the greatest experience they have encountered."

"What about the correlation figures?"

"They're as overwhelming as you predicted. Of the 662 interviewed, 619 believe in the influence of the planets on our destinies, and all 619 have at some time or other consulted astrological charts. All but two of the 662 believe in the existence of God; 596 believe in some form of life after death."

"Any suicides?"

"None that we know of but there were a few cases of serious depression. Over six hundred said they were deeply disillusioned when the stories broke. Almost all of them mentioned Josiah Minden's involvement in the attempted murder of Harold and Rhonda and in the killing of Roger Silberstein."

"What a curious phenomenon it has been," said Harding. "Harmonetics captured the fancy of hundreds of thousands of people. More than two million believers earned the right to wear the Blue Robe, and in less than a week the membership fell to under 20,000. I guess there hasn't been a similar phenomenon on a major scale since the Nazi party. They both provided the same two requirements that so many people need."

"What's that, Bill?"

"The answers, Jerry, and a strong leader."

Jade Boren had spent the last three weeks bumming around the Florida beaches, playing some tennis and reading. Whatever she did, wherever she was, her thoughts kept returning to Minden. Over and over she relived the evening in his apartment, the dialogue as he took her through his rooms, and the violence of his attack in the nympharium. She remembered the terrible moment when she saw Martha's empty face in Esme Jennings' office. She heard Harding's voice on the phone again as he told her Harold had been shot and Roger was dead. She was riding in Minden's private elevator or seeing his private chapel or staring at the tapestry on the refectory wall. He was always there, terrorizing her, laughing at her panic, relishing her helplessness.

Jade stayed in Florida although she knew the idleness and boredom gave her too much time to brood. It seemed better to hang around Fort Lauderdale than to go back to the grind of *National News*. But she was lying to herself and she knew it: she wanted to go back to work. The real reason she was staying in Florida was the fear that the Minden incident had killed off an entire emotional area. She still cared for Arnie, but she had doubts about herself. If she went back to New York and spent the night with Arnie, she would find out for certain. She would rather stay in Florida and remain in doubt.

Jerry Marconi had phoned several times. He was a sweet little puppy who desperately wanted to please her. He offered to go to her apartment once a week to water her plants. Jade told him it wasn't necessary. John, the doorman in the building, was taking care of it. Jerry said it would be no problem to pick up her mail each day and forward it. Jade answered lethargically. She wasn't expecting anything but bills and charity solicitations. Everything could wait. Jerry asked when she was coming back to New York. Pretty soon, said Jade. She would let him know.

At the end of the third week Bill Harding telephoned. He told Jade he had come across some interesting information on Matthew Brewer, the lawyer who was defending confessed rapist-murderer Monte Devlin. Matthew Brewer had been out of law school for five years. He was a junior member of Pepper, Dimbly, Leonard. Pepper, Dimbly, Leonard was a rather large law firm with a reputation for accomplishing the impossible. In an earlier case, an ex-convict who was caught standing over the body of the victim with a smoking gun in his hand was eventually acquitted by a jury of twelve men and women. An ambitious young lawyer from Pepper, Dimbly, Leonard had raised enough doubts in the minds of the jurors to prevent conviction: the accused had been framed by the wife of the victim or by the arresting officer or by a combination of the two. Lawyers with Pepper, Dimbly, Leonard were known for their vivid imaginations: the screams from the rape victim were fake, the bloody wounds on her head and body were self-inflicted, and the accused was in reality a fine, upstanding citizen who was happily married and had never even looked at another woman.

Now Matthew Brewer was defense attorney for Monte Devlin. Brewer was a tennis buff. He was thirty years old, slightly athletic, and a physical fitness freak. He was considered brilliant by his colleagues at Pepper, Dimbly, Leonard. If his future were unimpeded, said Harding, he could conceivably become the best known criminal lawyer in the country. Would Jade be interested in writing an article about Matthew Brewer, L.L.D.?

Jade felt her adrenalin flowing. When was the Monte Devlin trial due to start? Where did Matthew Brewer hang out? Was anyone else assigned to the story? When did Harding want her back in New York? Tomorrow?

"I'll catch a plane tonight, Bill," Jade said briskly. "Is it possible to get Jerry to leave a folder on Matthew Brewer in my apartment? I'll read it when I get in and I'll be ready for

Matthew by 9:00 A.M. tomorrow. How am I feeling? Just super, Bill. Absolutely first rate."

As soon as Jade hung up she began to hum. "De-de-dee-de," she sang as she opened the small icebox in the kitchenette and pulled out a beer. "De-DEE-de-de-DEE," she trilled as she dialed Eastern Airlines. "Dum-de-dum-dum," she murmured as she opened bureau drawers and began to pack. "La-la-la-la," she lilted as she wrote a note to Bob and Doris Painter to thank them for lending her their apartment.

She stopped singing and went over to the telephone. She stared at the phone, trying to make up her mind. She went to the refrigerator, got herself another beer, and returned to the phone. She hesitated, picked up the receiver, and dialed, giving the operator her credit card number.

"Hello, Arnie . . . Yes, I'm fine. How are you? . . . I'm coming home tonight . . . The 6:30 flight, Eastern Airlines . . . I miss you too, baby . . . Arnie, I love you . . . It is not mush. I love you . . . See you tonight."

She hung up and began to hum again. "Arn-ie, Arn-ie, Arn-ie," she crooned.

The plane landed at Kennedy five minutes early. As Jade deplaned she saw Arnie waiting behind a column, off to one side, as though he were angry with himself for meeting his girl. Jade rushed over to him and threw her arms around his neck.

"I can't believe you fought the traffic to meet me," she said.

"Meet you? I didn't come to meet you. I'm waiting for someone else," he said, trying to disentangle her arms.

"I didn't eat on the plane. I'm starved, Arnie."

"I think I got an apple in the car."

"Where are we going for dinner, Arnie?"

"Dinner? You got enough money to pay for your dinner? I'm not springing for any more meals for you, you dumb broad."

"Arnie, it's so good to see you. Let's get my bags and go."

"I hope you don't think I'm going to carry your bags. I've got to watch out for my arm. It's very sensitive."

"Arnie, do you love me?"

"Shit, are you going to get on that subject again? All you ever talk about is love and women's tennis. My two least favorite subjects."

Jade put her arm through Arnie's. He pretended to fight her, mumbling under his breath about "aggressive broads." She was glad she'd come home. The thrill of seeing Arnie was still there. She liked hanging on to his arm. His skin had a sweet fragrance and his breath seemed faintly perfumed. She felt the old longing to make love. Memories of Josiah Minden would soon fade. Minden! She hadn't thought about Josiah since Bill Harding's phone call.

They drove into the city for dinner. They went to Nicola's on East 84th and dawdled over their wine, Arnie talking nonstop.

"You get one course only," said Arnie when the waiter came over. "You want the soup or the pasta? Take your choice. Maybe you'd just like a small salad. My friend isn't hungry," he explained to the waiter.

"I'll start with the moule, then the veal piccata, a little broccoli and mushrooms, the salad . . ."

"Don't forget to give her the check," Arnie told the waiter.

As they ate, Arnie talked a stream of nonsense. Jade's cheeks were flushed and her eyes sparkled. Her hand kept dropping onto Arnie's leg. Several times she bent toward him to whisper in his ear and nibble on his lobe.

"Christ, let's get out of here," said Arnie while they were in the middle of the entrée.

"I'm still eating."

"Stupid broad," said Arnie, kicking the base of the table.

"Birdbrain," Jade replied as she cut her veal.

An hour later they arrived at Jade's apartment. Arnie was carrying a corsage box, which Jade tried to wrest from him.

"Arnie, you didn't buy me a gardenia?" she asked.

He didn't answer.

"Are you taking me to the Senior Prom?" Jade persisted.

"Don't bug me," said Arnie. "I'm putting the box in the bedroom. I'll give it to you later."

"You're so weird, I don't know why I let you hang around," said Jade as Arnie took the box into the next room. He was a dear fellow but he had such hang-ups, particularly verbal ones. Since he couldn't say the affectionate words, he did absurd things such as buying her carnations or gardenias.

Five minutes later their love games began. Jade started by putting her arms around Arnie. They worked their way from the couch to the living-room floor to the wall and into the bedroom, leaving a trail of clothes in their wake. As Jade lay on the bed in the semidarkness, she felt possessed by her desire for her lover, her crazy, passionate, endearing Arnie. What was he doing now?

Jade opened her eyes. She was lying on the sheets, ready to become one with her lover, but he was fiddling with the bedside lamp. What the hell was he doing? He was opening the corsage box, taking out the flowers. He was putting them on the night table. Jade looked at them, then turned toward Arnie in horror.

Arnie was dumbstruck. He had brought her the most expensive orchids he could find. He had asked the florist for the rarest, most beautiful corsage, and he had been told the yellow orchids with the large purple veins on the petals (veins that looked as though they were bleeding) were the loveliest. They had just been flown in from South America. They grew in the Amazon where they attained a much larger size and a heavier petal than the more delicate Hawaiian orchid. Arnie had been sure that Jade would like them.

Jade lay on the sheets bathed in sweat. Her eyes slowly moved from the terrible flowers to her naked lover, who was sitting on the bed staring at her. The flowers, those sickly orchids that Josiah carefully nurtured in his hothouse, those hideous petals, the overpowering scent of the jungle, that madman in his aerie, feeding his monstrous plants . . .

Arnie, his eyes reflecting Jade's pain, gently stroked her arm. He bent over her limp body and softly kissed her lips.

"Do you want me to throw out the stupid flowers?" Arnie asked.

Jade twisted her hard, suntanned body toward her lover. She raised a hand toward his shoulder and pulled him toward her.

"Pin the flowers in my hair," she said softly. "Then let's make wild love."

It was the night that Jade began to forget Josiah Minden.